Curse
of
the
Shadow
Beasts

Curse
of
the
Shadow
Beasts

by
Christine Morgan

Pittsburgh, PA

ISBN 1-56315-188-X

Trade Fiction
© Copyright 1998 Christine Morgan
All rights reserved
First Printing—1998
Library of Congress #98-85369

Request for information should be addressed to:

SterlingHouse Publisher
The Sterling Building
440 Friday Road
Department T-101
Pittsburgh, PA 15209

Cover design & Typesetting: Drawing Board Studios

Printed in the United States of America

For Matt Keating,
who once said I never did him any favors.

Foreword
by Steve Jackson

I should start by cautioning the reader that I am going to discuss roleplaying games. If you have never enjoyed such a game, as player or observer, I apologize for the lack of context. If you are one of those who still believes that roleplaying is strictly a juvenile pastime, be warned: you are about to be exposed to a favorable opinion about the effect of such games on the course of literature.

Roleplaying is simply another type of make-believe. A group of players take on fictional personae—usually 'characters" which they, themselves, have invented—and share in an adventure moderated by a Game Master. The details of the adventure are created by the players as they go along, and even the final outcome is usually not certain.

Roleplaying is not limited to the fantasy genre. Horror, science fiction, "film noir," Gothic, Western any body of literature or imagination can support a roleplaying adventure. But it was with fantasy that roleplaying began, and its roots remain firmest there.

Roleplaying games provide a new lens, a more human lens, through which we can view the conventions of classic fantasy. The book that you are about to read uses those classic conventions, but its approach is different because of the nature of the roleplaying experience. Different, and very readable.

High fantasy, more often than not, concerns itself mostly with the working out of the plot and the hero-quest of the protagonist. The supporting cast is too often relegated to the role of spear-carriers. Their job is to exhibit a few interesting personality quirks, expound on the history of their peoples, and then, often as not, to die picturesquely.

Consider *The Lord of the Rings*. Tolkien may have set the pattern for much of modern fantasy, but he was also following older patterns. His treatment of subsidiary characters is, in the end, perfunctory. Legolas and Gimli are little more than cutouts, emblems of the rivalry between their races. Tolkien permits them mutual respect and eventually friendship, but even this is meant more as symbolism than as character development!

Roleplaying teaches us differently. A roleplaying adventure is not about one or two mythic heroes by its very nature, it is about a group, their strengths complementing each other. Each is given life by a different player; each has the opportunity for full character development and for interactions with all the others.

Inspired by fiction, roleplaying games inevitably have given life to new fiction. This has taken several forms, beginning with straight retelling of roleplaying adventures. In recent years, though, the richly detailed worlds created by and for roleplayers have been recognized as fertile ground for original fiction. The *Dragonlance* books released by TSR, based on a background first created for their *Dungeons & Dragons,* have actually achieved best-seller status.

And roleplaying-inspired fiction, or at least the best of it, follows the pattern of the game. It's not about a single mythic hero. It's about a band of comrades, often thrown together by circumstances, who meet a problem and do their best to deal with it. And in that, though it may be "fantasy," it resonates more truly with the world we live in. It's about *people.*

This is such a book. Christine Morgan is writing about *people* here. They're not mythic heroes, doomed by destiny. They may live in a fantasy world, but they work, age, scheme, love. . . and, very often, foul up royally . . . just as we do. You won't want to put this book down.

"Game fiction," once barely acknowledged as literature, is beginning to come of age.

—Steve Jackson
Austin, Texas, July 1997

Special thanks to:
Bree, Doug, Eileen, Jess, Max, Tim, Matt, Mike, the Humboldt State
University Fantasy Gamer's Guild, and the staff of Steve Jackson Games.
GURPS references used by permission of Steve Jackson.

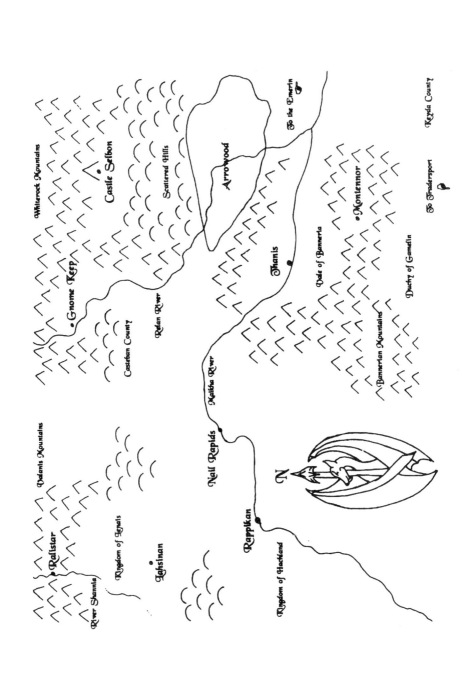

Part One: The Castle

It has been said that the world is a strange place. This is not true. The world is a very strange place.

The Book of Yor,
a Collection of Observations by Talus Yor,
Archmage of Thanis.

Arien Mirida wasn't thinking as he turned the corner. This mistake, which would change his life in unimaginable ways, at first seemed but a simple error.

He walked for several paces before realizing it and turning his attention from his book to his surroundings. "Oh, dear," he said in a low voice.

He turned to leave, but already two of the rough-clad men had moved to block his way.

"Pardon . . . I do not want any trouble," he said.

"Want it or not, you've got it," one replied. He was the shortest of the lot, but his mouth had the cruellest twist.

Arien drew himself straight, hoping that his height would overcome the apparent fragility of his form. He let one hand rest lightly on the satchel slung at his side. "Please, sir, let me pass."

"Whoo, aren't we the fancy sort," chuckled the man. "Look here, chaps, we've caught ourselves an elflord."

"Elf!" growled the largest of them, whose yellow skin and brutish features marked him as orckin. He lunged to seize Arien painfully by the shoulder.

He tried to pull away, but was no match for the other's strength. His effort only made the orckin grab him with both hands, lift him, and slam him against a stone wall.

"Hold, Jornic. Don't break him yet," the first man said, coming closer. His cold eyes darted over Arien as he struggled for breath. "Nice clothes," he sneered. "Linen and velvet don't come cheap."

"I assure you," Arien gasped when he could speak, "that I have no desire to become embroiled in a conflict."

The orckin, Jornic, pulled Arien away from the wall and slammed him back again, forcing him to drop his book. "I'll kill him! Fancy-talking elves, all the same!"

"Hold, I said," the short man commanded.

"Jornic cares not for your sort," said an older man with a scar scrawled across his face. He idly flipped and caught a knife with easy skill. "They done in his family."

The remaining two, as they moved in to get a better look at their captive, were revealed in the dim light to be little more than children. Sprawled behind them was a man, an earlier victim, badly beaten.

"If it is money that you seek, you are welcome to it," Arien said, willing himself not to swoon from the pain in his back and shoulders. "I haven't much, but it is yours." He groped for his belt pouch and suddenly found himself looking at the tip of a bloodstained knife.

"Don't move, point-ears," snarled the short man. "Else you'll be trying to find your head down in the trash."

Arien froze, all too aware of his physical shortcomings. His childhood training at arms had never seemed longer ago than it did at this moment.

"He's lying, Rolle," the man with the scar said. "All elves are near rich as dragons."

"Aye," chimed in one of the younger ones, grinning greedily. "Sure as sunset, he's got gold, maybe even gems!"

Jornic slid Arien up the wall until his feet dangled well off the garbage-strewn alley floor. "His blood's enough for me."

"How about it, elf? Any gold?" the one called Rolle asked. He tore away the belt pouch and backed off a step. Moonlight gleamed on the small silver coins that he poured into his hand. He counted it, then angrily thrust his hand in Arien's face. "Where's the rest of it?"

"That is all that I have," Arien said. "I swear it."

"Lies. He takes us for fools," said the one with the scar.

"Search him," Rolle commanded. "We'll make a good profit tonight, see if we don't. Scarface, see what's in the bag. You and you, quit standing around like washerwomen at the gossip fence and get rid of that one." He jerked his head at the beaten man.

Arien clutched his precious satchel, its contents of more value to him than any amount of wealth. Concern for his own safety melted away like frost on a windowpane, letting him see clearly.

"Touch it not!" he said sharply as Scarface reached out.

His jaw exploded with pain. His head snapped back and hit the wall as Jornic's fist drew back for a second blow.

Purely by reflex, he kicked out. His soft doeskin boots connected with the solid mass of Jornic's stomach, having only the effect of making the orckin laugh harshly.

Scarface set the point of his knife to the tip of Arien's ear. "Move an inch and I cut it off," he hissed.

Arien froze, already imagining the blade slicing into that most sensitive flesh. How had this brute known the best way to instantly quell the struggles of an elf?

"I grow weary of this!" Rolle jerked the satchel from Arien and opened it, by his expression expecting some great treasure.

"No," Arien breathed, but the ruffians paid his feeble protest no mind. He focused his thoughts on his only possible hope, trying to put the threat of the knife from his mind.

"Books," Rolle said in the tone of a man who had just discovered a dead mouse in his porridge. "Worthless paper and ink? Bah!" He threw them to the ground and trod with his filth-caked boots upon the white leather covers.

Arien closed his eyes to that near-blasphemous sight. Anger, unfamiliar as most emotions but oddly welcome, seethed in him. Anger, yes, cold as the biting frost. He could give them frost in return—

No. Their deaths were not his to dole out. Let them instead sleep. Sleep.

He opened his eyes and looked at Rolle, and something in that even gaze made the short man pause warily.

"*Dhalas Noran,*" Arien whispered. Spoken in the ancient language of the elven Archmages, the words carried the essence of power. A simple gesture of his slim fingers directed its flow as the mystic energy rushed out of him.

For a moment, nothing happened. Then Jornic's wide, ugly face split in a massive yawn. He slumped to the ground. Arien dropped, landing with a jolt that sent twinges through his ankles and made his teeth click together.

Scarface collapsed, pillowing himself in a pile of garbage. The younger thugs, too far to be caught in the spell's effect, cried out in confusion.

Rolle, whose will was proved stronger than his wit, merely blinked drowsily before shaking his head and glaring at Arien. "Wizard," he spat, as if the word tasted foul.

"Indeed I am a wizard, and would suggest that you take this opportunity to depart." He gathered another spell to mind, pausing as he heard a sound from above. Stealthy, but purposeful. A footstep, perhaps? A sixth ruffian, as yet unseen?

A rock flew from the hand of one of the youths. It struck Arien on the forehead, driving him to his knees. The spell he had summoned was lost, the energy wasted as the pain broke his concentration.

"I got him!" the boy cried, dashing forward.

Arien wiped his own blood from his face, and looked up to see Rolle advancing with a sword. "I know how to kill wizards."

No time to cast a spell, no time, not with his concentration shattered like a crystal goblet fallen on a stone floor. He pulled a tiny dagger from his boot and drew what he suspected would be his final breath.

A shadow dropped from above as Rolle struck. Moonlight ran like liquid along the blade of the saber that parried his blow. Steel rang loudly in the close confines of the alley.

Arien fell back, unable to believe that he was still alive. He wiped more blood from his eyes and stared at the sight that met them.

His defender was a young woman! Barely past girlhood, slim and lithe, clad in close-fitting garments of grey and midnight blue.

"Greetings, Rolle," she said with a slight grin.

"Cat," Rolle said grimly, still holding his sword in a fighting stance. "Can't you see I'm working, you cursed wench?"

Her grin widened, becoming something deadly and feral.

"One-Eye's had enough of you acting against the Guild. You're dismissed." She shifted the sword to her left hand, handling it as confidently as with her right. Rolle hesitated.

"Get her, Rolle!" called the boy who'd thrown the rock.

"Get her, do!" chimed in the other, leering. "Save a piece for me, aye? She looks like a fun tumble!"

Arien shuddered at what the youth was suggesting. Every time he thought he had seen the worst of the humans, they managed to surprise him again.

"I've had my fill of One-Eye and his rules," Rolle snapped. "He and Stryker think they run this city."

"Dead or running, Rolle," she said impatiently. "Your choice."

"We'll see about that!" He brought his sword around, slashing at her legs.

Arien gasped, expecting to see her fall, but she parried deftly. She moved like a dancer, he saw, never stumbling over the books and other objects littering the alley.

"I guess you choose dead." She shrugged. "All the same to me."

"Easier said than done, whelp!" Rolle shot back. He swung at her again.

Their swords clashed repeatedly, making the walls ring with the echoes. It soon became clear that Rolle was badly outmatched.

As Cat whirled to avoid a sword stroke, her dark curls flew about her head. There beneath them, Arien saw something that spellbound him with shock. She was not human! Her ears . . . tapering to a point . . . not human, not elven, but having an element of both!

"Elfkin?" Arien breathed in horror. An elfkin, alive, grown to maturity? It could not be!

The fight was over with stunning swiftness. Rolle swung in a lethal arc at his rival's neck. Cat ducked under it and thrust her blade hilt-deep in his chest. The point emerged from Rolle's back. He sank to the ground, the sword still stuck through him.

Cat placed a booted foot on Rolle's chest, pushed him back, and pulled her blade free. "Easier said than done, true," she commented, looking down at the body. "But not much easier."

The two young thugs stood staring at her in disbelief. She whirled to face them. The alley, so loud only seconds before, was now nearly silent.

"Don't throw your lives away," she advised the youths.

One of them fisted a dagger in each hand and dropped into a fighting crouch. "That was just luck," he muttered, as if to reassure himself. "No crossling is going to beat me."

Arien felt a bone-deep chill sweep over him at the words. Elfkin. Not a rumor, not a secret or a scandal, but standing before him in proof undeniable.

The second youth, showing a wisdom that had perhaps come upon him too late in life, ran to wake Scarface.

Cat waited. Her foe came toward her, moving slowly, until he suddenly lunged with both knives. She spun with uncanny speed, knocking one of the blades away. The other dug into her side. Instead of crying out, she kicked his knee. He howled.

Scarface grunted and came fully awake. Instantly assessing the situation, he raised the knife he'd used to threaten Arien, and held it in a throwing position.

"Beware!" Arien cried as the knife flew.

She heard him and sprang to one side. The knife plunged into her shoulder. Had she not moved, it would have found her throat. Again, she did not voice her pain, though Arien saw her eyes widen. She dropped her sword.

The youth lunged but misstepped and collided with her, making both fall. Cat came up on top, driving her knee into his groin. Again, he howled.

Scarface pried Rolle's sword from his dead grasp.

Arien saw Cat grit her teeth and yank Scarface's knife from her shoulder. Blades flashed, his slicing her brow, hers sinking into his stomach.

Anger filled him again. Whatever she might be, whatever foul deeds had spawned her mixed race, she had come to his aid and he could not sit and let her fight alone.

Scarface reached her as she rolled to hands and knees. She raised her head to look at him, blood trickling down her face like tears. The sword rose.

"Niamis!" Arien cried, extending his hands with thumbs touching and fingers splayed. His cold fury had gotten the better of him. This time, he would give them ice.

An icy wind issued from his fingers and swirled around Scarface. In the blink of an eye, the man's skin had gone stiff and blue-white. Icicles hung from his arms. His mouth was a gaping ice-cave. He tottered and fell, and broke apart on the cobblestones.

The last remaining ruffian stared for a long horrified moment, then fled.

Arien found himself on his knees again, fighting nausea at the realization that he had killed a man, killed him in a most grotesque manner.

"Are you all right?"

He painfully turned his head and saw her. The elfkin. She was sitting with her back against a wall, holding one hand to the wound on her shoulder.

He tried to nod, though he was anything but all right. The motion sent waves of pain through his aching head. He let his head fall forward, his long hair hanging in his face, and groaned. "Upon consideration, perhaps I am less than well," he choked out.

"Consider yourself fortunate. They meant to kill you."

"Yes." He sat back, and looked full upon her, well-revealed in the moonlight. "You are . . . elfkin?"

"Fear not, I'll not offend your elven sensibilities with my foulness any further." The bitterness in her voice, so much for one so young, stunned him as she rose to leave.

"Wait. Please." He coughed. "How do you come to be here? I thought . . ."

"That all my kind were drowned at birth?" Her eyes fixed him. They, at least, were purely elven, large and deep, the color of finest sapphires. "I've heard the tales."

He winced, knowing the truth of her words. Drowned at birth, yes, those few abominations born when humans happened upon elfmaids and forced their will upon them. Drowned at birth, not only to spare the mother's honor but because none thought they would live to maturity, that even if they somehow did, their dearth of magic and misshapen features would make death preferable.

Until now, he had unquestioningly believed. He recalled how his schoolmates used to frighten one another with stories of such monsters. How he too, had once taken part in the telling of such. Now, so many decades later, he felt sudden shame.

"I owe you my life," he said. "My spells of healing are not as strong as the god-given powers of the priests, but can mend some of your hurts."

She glanced down at herself, grimacing in pain as she did so. "I'll be fine. Just a few scratches."

"Let me help you, as you helped me," he said gently.

"Why waste your magics and sully your elven hands?" she threw at him. "I know how your kind see me!"

"My kind." He startled himself by laughing with bitterness that mirrored hers. "They're not overly keen on exiles, either. In that, we are alike, you and I. I'll keep my silence if you keep yours!"

At her nod, he concentrated, feeling the warm energies of the healing magics fill his hands. He reached out, faltered in momentary disblief that he was about to touch an elfkin, then laid his hand on her shoulder. *"Salahin Roas,"* he murmured.

Her eyes closed. The tension fled her face as the spell took away the pain. He was suddenly struck by her beauty. But no, it could not be! She was elfkin, supposed to be monstrous, bestial! How could he think such a thing?

Beneath his fingers, the gash on her forehead faded to a pale line. Her skin was an unusual tone, not so fair as the elves, more golden than most humans. The feel of it was quite soft, quite pleasant.

She opened her eyes, and he swiftly took his lingering hand away. "My thanks," she said, adding, "You should take care of your wounds, too. You're a complete mess."

He realized that his face was smeared with blood, and his jaw swollen from Jornic's fist. But his pains were forgotten when his gaze fell upon his precious books. He uttered a low cry and began gathering them, brushing grime from the covers.

Cat helped him, handing him three volumes. As he tucked them back in the satchel, she turned her attention to the ruffians and stunned him anew by pocketing their valuables.

Nightsiders! Of course! She had mentioned them, that band of thieves. She was one of them.

As he contemplated this, she reached Jornic. She drew a knife and made to slit the orckin's throat.

"No!" He scrambled to reach her. "What are you doing? He sleeps! Helpless, harmless, asleep!"

"Mercy for an orckin? Healing for me? What manner of elf are you? They were ready to kill you without a second thought. They'd do the same thing again. Look there."

She pointed to the man Arien had noticed earlier, the prior victim of Rolle and his gang. The man still had not moved, and Arien now saw that he never would.

He touched Cat's arm. "My spell will hold him for hours. There has been enough blood. If this makes of me a poor excuse for an elf, I accept it gladly. Please."

She gave him a long look, then sheathed her knife. "All right, he lives. And speaking of poor elves, here. This is yours." She tossed him his own pouch, and smiled at his surprised expression. "Did you think I was going to keep it? If that's all you have, you need it more than I do. I'd offer you some of their coin, but I doubt you'd take it."

"That is so." He caught himself returning her smile. "You are an unusual young lady."

She shrugged. "Blame it on my father." She cocked her head, her posture changing to one of alertness, and it seemed most fitting in that moment that she bore the name of Cat, for it fit her better than any other name he might devise. "City Guard's coming."

Arien listened. Footsteps, jingling chainmail. The commotion had not gone unnoticed.

"Can't let them catch me here," Cat said. She quickly picked up her weapons.

"There is no other way out," he said, gesturing at the blind alley.

"You may be a scholar, but you've a lot to learn." She ran at the wall, and before his amazed eyes, climbed it as easily as a cat going up a tree. In moments, she was on the roof. "Farewell."

And then she was gone, her passage as silent as that of a cloud across the sky. Bare seconds later a group of the Thanian City Guard rounded the corner and stopped, gaping at the scene.

"By the Black Moon!" one of them swore, looking from Arien to the bodies and back to Arien again. "What happened here?"

Arien shook his head. "I will tell you, sir," he said. "But I doubt that you will believe me."

*   *   *

Arien closed the book and put his head in his hands.

It was over.

Living among humans, he'd observed their tendency to set unattainable goals for themselves, goals that they could never hope to accomplish in a mere fifty or sixty years. They were hampered by the closeness of old age and death, scampering about like squirrels with but a few desperate days to gather nuts before the snows came. Was it any wonder that his long-lived people found them so foreign?

Even for an elf, who might devote ten years to a courtship and forty to an apprenticeship, eighty-seven years was a long time to spend on a single project.

He had read every book in the Great Library of Thanis.

Every one. The arrival of new volumes had not kept pace with his reading, this had been the last.

He glanced around the tiny room. Being one of the Librarians, wearing the sash and carrying the quill, suited him. It was a life of quiet obscurity, which would let him pursue his goal uninterrupted.

Now he had come to the end of that path, and he was at a loss. He'd read and studied, in hopes of finding the answer to the question that haunted him. Now he found that he was no closer than he'd been when he'd begun.

"No," he told himself softly. "That is not entirely true. You do have some clues. You are merely powerless to follow them."

He sighed. It would take a man of daring and action to undertake such a quest as now faced him. He was not such a man.

Through his narrow window, he could see the people of Thanis going about their early evening business. Summer had finally come, bringing festivals and merchants from far lands. The streets were filled with music, haggling, arguments, laughter, and the other threads that made up the vibrant tapestry of human society.

A pair of lovers paused near the Library gate to embrace, and Arien watched them with a wistful yearning he'd thought long forgotten.

His fingers, resting upon the stone casement, seemed instead to feel soft golden skin.

He drew back his hands as if burned. How long until the memory passed from his mind? How long would he be troubled by these thoughts? Companionship was not for him, least of all that of an elfkin! Such an absurd and horrifying thought would make his parents rest uneasy in their rosecloth bindings! And dishonor the perfect memory of—

No! He closed and locked that mental door.

Solitude. Isolation. An exile not just of the body from the homeland, but of the spirit from the world. That was better suited to him. So it had been, for almost a century. Why now, was it suddenly dissatisfying? With his goal completed, the books read, he was at loose ends.

The people below called out to each other, joyous, alive, vibrant. Just to sit quietly among them, perhaps allowing himself a single glass of wine, yes, what a simple pleasure that would be! He need not join them, need not speak, but to watch from the edge of their merry circle would be enough.

*   *   *

He walked through the streets of Thanis as if for the first time. Its wonders were fresh and new to him, never heeded before, but now a source of amazement. The eight Rings, stepping up like tiers, were laid out with a precision that bespoke the skilled minds of the dwarves of Montennor.

Indeed, Arien knew from his reading that the mountain folk had designed the city. Their crafters built the high walls separating one ring from another, the lifts which raised heavy loads to the upper rings, the majestic bridge stretching from the Fourth Ring to the fortress of Tabash.

The view from any of the Ring Walls was breathtaking. Arien paused as he had never done before to admire the sight of the wide Maikha River and the towering majesty of the Bannerian Mountains surrounding the city. To the west, he knew, lay the sprawling kingdom of Hachland. To the east—his chest tightened at the thought—his own homeland, the wooded Emerin.

The view of the city itself was nothing to be scorned, either. From any point, even in the lowly Eighth Ring, it was possible to look up to the First Ring, where the Tower of the Archmage Talus Yor glimmered like a unicorn's horn above the functional bulk of the Highlord's castle.

For the first time, he was curious about those men. Forty years ago, they had come to Thanis, saved it from civil war. All of that turmoil had swirled around Arien like a maelstrom, leaving him untouched, unaware, uncaring how these humans sought to settle their differences. Not even the arrival of the Four Heroes and the subsequent restoration of the city had been enough to lift his eyes from the books.

He paused now to peer up at the Tower of the Archmage. Magical talent, as common to the elvenfolk as breath and life, was a rare occurrence among humans. Yet the man called Talus Yor was said to have powers to rival the great elven Magelords of old.

Duncan Farleigh, a warrior of renown, had become Thanis' Highlord, ruling over the Vale of Banneria with the power of a king. Arien only knew of him because the loss of the Highlady to sudden tragedy had struck a chord in his own soul. He felt a certain kinship with the Highlord on that account.

Now, as he stood and mused over those days, he remembered that the third of the Four Heroes had been a priest of mighty Galatine, and the fourth had been a one-eyed thief.

A one-eyed thief, perhaps even the selfsame One-Eye who commanded the Nightsiders, and thus Arien's thoughts were brought smartly back to the elfkin girl, Cat.

"Leave my mind, little thief," he murmured. "We shall not meet again."

Every morning and evening, he passed the Inn of the Golden Lion on his way between the Library and his rooming house. Tonight, he stopped and opened the door.

Noise, light, and scents washed over him in a pleasing conglomeration. Hot bread, music, fireglow, dark ale, laughter, colored glass lanterns.

Along one wall of the large common room was a raised stage, where a tall man in an elaborate costume of star-sewn robes performed minor magics for the audience, assisted by a young woman in revealing garb.

It was loud, crowded. So many people, so many humans. Overwhelming. Too much for one accustomed only to the quiet and solitude of the Great Library.

Arien hesitated, reconsidering, and then he saw her. His hand slipped from the handle, letting the door swing closed behind him.

*   *   *

"Here you go, Cat," Osnard said, placing a steaming plate in front of her.

She smiled up at the portly innkeeper. "Smells wonderful, as always!"

He lowered himself onto a stool and mopped his brow with his apron. "We've not been seeing you so much lately. Tell me, Cat. Was it those elves?"

Cat averted her eyes. "I was tired of making you lose money. If only you'd let me pay you for it—"

He flapped his hands at her. "Go on, what would your mother say if she heard you talking like that? She'd give you a right scolding, that she would. Never took no nonsense from the likes of them, that was our Miralina. She'd have marched right up to them, told them off—if anyone ever tells you your temper comes from your da, I'm sitting right here saying you get a full measure from your mum as well!—and then like as not taken hold of your da and given him a kiss for all the world to see!"

She smiled sadly. "I wish I could remember her. All I have is images, and what you and Da told me. I miss him so, Osnard, that I don't know what I'll do! It's been two years already, and every day seems like another eternity!"

"Now, stop it." He ruffled her dark curls. "He'll be back, if I know Tahm Sabledrake! One night, mark me, that door will open and he'll come strutting in just like he used to, with your mum on one arm and a bag of jewels under the other. What little I've lost because of stiff-necked elves that walk out will be more than made up for when he returns. Now, you sit right here and eat your supper, and I'll bring you a special treat."

"Thank you, Osnard." He left, and she tried to nibble at her bread, but found she'd lost her appetite. She moved it around on her plate and finally shoved it away with a sigh.

"Cat, darling!" a sultry voice hailed her.

Cat looked up and stifled a groan. Sybil had arrived, and like always, she knew how to make an impression. Cat knew that everyone wondered how two such different women had become friends. Sometimes, she wondered herself.

Sybil was tall, with a figure lush and voluptuous enough to stagger the mind of the most imaginative poet. She showed nearly all of it in the shockingly revealing garb of a priestess of Talopea.

The servants of the Goddess of a Thousand Pleasures didn't believe in modesty. Two rectangles of silk were laced together down the sides with gold cord, forming a strapless, sleeveless garment that stopped halfway down the thighs. Sybil's thick blond hair was piled high in an elaborate design of coils and braids. Part of pleasure was finery, so Sybil was also well-adorned with gold and rubies.

In all ways, she and Cat were unalike as could be, yet, somehow, they were the closest of friends.

"So," Sybil purred as she sank languidly into a chair. "How's my sweet Cat-burglar tonight?"

"I am the wind," Cat replied, quoting a favorite saying of One-Eye's that had nearly become the motto of the Nightsiders. She laid a folded cloth packet on the table. "This is for you, from the Nightsiders with thanks. We got to the emeralds just before the Ferrets arrived."

"What about Lord Taron?" Sybil asked, unfolding the cloth and squealing in delight at the six square-cut emeralds nestled therein. "Oh, Cat! These are stunning! I must gift one to Talopea. She does so love pretty things, and she has been so very kind to me lately. Should I have them made into a necklace, do you think? No, a circlet for my hair!"

Cat smiled at Sybil's happiness. "The Ferrets are not very pleased, and Lord Taron should have a task explaining to them how their emeralds slipped through his fingers. He's a dangerous man. We've been trying to get at him for years. One-Eye appreciates your help."

"I'll help anytime, especially if I can help that tall one with the smoldering brown eyes. And such a chest! Here I'd been thinking that all thieves had to be little and wiry, like you. What was his name again?"

"Do you mean Stryker?" Cat asked dubiously. "I think he has brown eyes."

"And that adorable crooked smile." Sybil licked her full lips. "He has the most kissable mouth I've seen in months."

"Stryker?" Cat repeated. "Kissable?"

"Oh, Cat," Sybil sighed. "What are we going to do with you? This Stryker's a fine, virile male, and it's time you started noticing. You have a lovely body and a sensuous spirit. It goes against the will of Talopea to deny it."

"Sensuous? Me?" Her face flamed brighter and she swiftly downed her wine. "I do not!"

"You do so." Sybil gripped her wrist. "You can't ignore it. Since you're not interested in other women, to my everlasting disappointment and complete lack of comprehension, you have to at least find a man!"

"Look," Cat said, pulling her arm away. "Gustav's going to do the ring trick." She stared intently at the magician on stage.

"Cat," she chided.

"I love the ring trick."

Sybil threw her hands in the air. "All right, I give up." She signaled one of Osnard's barmaids. "Red wine, please. Red as the High Priestess' lips. And dessert, something sweet and decadent."

Cat heaved a huge sigh of relief and found the energy to attack her supper after all. As she savored the rich roast lamb, she let her practiced thief's gaze roam the crowd. Not that she'd do anything to upset Osnard, of course. Just habit.

She glimpsed a figure that seemed familiar, a tall, slender man in a grey cloak. Before she could get a better look, Sybil tapped her on the arm.

"How's your shoulder? Mending well? That was a nasty wound!"

"Hmm? Oh, it's good as new. Thank you."

"You should thank Talopea, not me. Her power comes through me. It was foolish of you, attacking a gang of robbers by yourself."

"I won, didn't I?"

"But you take too many chances. Are you going to get yourself killed before you've truly learned to live? Talopea's powers almost couldn't heal you. I've told you over and over that Her gifts work much better on someone who—"

"Sybil!" Cat warned. "I'm fine. My father always said—"

Sybil threw her hands in the air again. "Not another Tahm Sabledrake story!"

"He just said he named me Cat so I'd have nine lives."

"And how many have you used already?" Sybil scolded.

Cat tossed her head and laughed. "Oh, I'd guess about five."

Sybil's wine and dessert arrived. She gazed rapturously at it. "Someday, when I find a man who can cook like this, I might just marry him."

"You? Get married?" Cat scoffed.

"Oh," Sybil said, picking up her spoon. She spoke with a diffidence that was so unlike her usual flamboyant tones that Cat instantly took notice. "I have something I've been meaning to tell you, but it's unpleasant news. Must I?"

"What is it?"

"Well . . . do you know of Castle Selbon?"

"Of course," Cat said. "It's north of the Scattered Hills. That's what brought my father to Thanis, he and his friends, lured by legends of the treasures of the Archmage Selbon."

Someone was approaching the table. Cat glanced up, expecting it to be Osnard with the treat he'd promised, but instead of Osnard's round, jovial face, she beheld a sight that made her jaw drop.

It was the man in the grey cloak. His hood was pushed back, revealing the elven ears peeking through satin-smooth silver hair that fell to past his shoulders. His fair skin and handsome features proclaimed him an elflord of noble blood.

"Cat? Cat, what are you—Sweet Talopea!" Sybil stared. "Who is that?"

"I don't . . ." Cat whispered. Then it came to her. "No, I do! Sybil, that's him! The wizard from the alley!"

"He's delicious," Sybil sighed. "You didn't tell me he looked like that! Why, I daresay the High Priestess herself would all but fall at his feet!"

"I didn't notice," she said, feeling a complete fool.

He stopped beside their table and bowed politely. "Forgive me, ladies. I might be mistaken, but had I correctly heard you mention Castle Selbon?" His voice was rich as cream, the sort of voice Cat would never tire of hearing.

Her throat seemed frozen. She sat looking mutely up at him. The memory of his touch, warm with healing power, made her blush.

Sybil glanced amusedly at her, then took over. "You did hear correctly, stranger. I am Sybil Narrin, of the Temple of Talopea. My shy friend is Cat Sabledrake. Do sit down."

"I am Arien Mirida, Junior Librarian." He took the seat Sybil indicated, the one beside Cat. As he turned to her, she felt her heart flutter wildly. "I believe we have already met, though no formal introductions were made."

She finally found her voice. "I hope you didn't have any trouble with the Guard."

His smile widened. "They were most unwilling to believe my tale, but what choice had they? I am in your debt. I had not my wits about me to thank you properly when we parted, so I do so now. Thank you." His silver-grey gaze held her captive.

She merely nodded like a moonstruck calf until Sybil's foot kicked her sharply under the table.

"Oh!" She floundered helpless for a moment, then gathered her composure. "You're welcome. Glad I could help." She hushed herself before she started babbling in complete idiocy.

"So," Sybil said, propping an elbow on the table and taking a deep breath. Ruby silk strained in protest as her figure threatened to overflow her garment. "What's your interest in a ruined castle?"

Arien raised a polite eyebrow, and looked back at Cat. "I am conversant with the castle's history."

"What can you tell us about it?" Cat asked.

Before he could answer, Osnard bustled up to the table. "Here we are," he declared proudly, setting it in front of Cat. "I whipped the cream myself, and the berries are fresh." He saw Arien then, and his eyes bulged. He shot Cat a quick startled glance.

She could practically hear his thoughts. An elfkin and an elf? Such a thing hadn't happened since her mother disappeared!

She mimicked his expression to show she was just as confused as he was, then had to hastily defend her treat from Sybil. "You haven't even finished your cake yet!" Cat said, swatting the priestess' hand away.

"I believe in taking my time." Sybil winked at Arien. "Good things are so much better the longer they last, don't you agree?"

"You were telling us about the castle," Cat said to him quickly, giving Sybil a desperate warning glare.

"Ah, yes." He sat back, steepling his fingers in front of him. His hands were exceptionally well-shaped, the hands of an artist or musician. "The Archmage Selbon, who was also generally believed to be one of the founders of the science of alchemy, once served a mighty king. He either betrayed the kingdom or failed in its defense at a crucial point during a war. Selbon fled the vanquished kingdom with a fortune in gold. He constructed a mountain fortress to isolate himself from the world and devoted himself to darker magics. Nearby villagers told of the hideous beasts that dug out the mountain, making chambers and tunnels. It is said that Selbon himself used his powers over the earth magics to shape the front of the mountain into a sinister skull-face to deter trespassers."

"It doesn't work," Sybil said. "I just met a priest who was up there."

"You did?" Cat asked, eyes widening.

"That's part of what I was going to tell you," she admitted. "But it can wait until Arien finishes his story." She batted her long lashes at the elf.

He cleared his throat. "The castle's reputation for evil continued to grow. There were tales of fiendish experiments and sacrifices, of workers vanishing from the fields, of maidens and infants stolen from their homes, of the living dead. As for Selbon himself, some said he became a vampire, extending his own life by draining the lives of the young. Others claimed he had sworn a pact with Haarkon, God of the Dead."

Sybil shivered and touched her gold pendant. It was a holy artifact of her church, similar to the black disk carried by the Knights of Blackmoon or the many-rayed sun worn by priests of Helia. Cat herself had no such object to ward off the name of the evil god, and admired Arien's boldness in saying it aloud.

"When I was a boy," he continued, "the daughter of the Baron of Keyda was stolen away by Selbon's henchmen on the eve of her wedding. The baron's armies marched upon the castle at once, despite the winter's chill."

"You're not talking about the Battle of Red Snow Field, are you?" Sybil asked. "That was at least a hundred years ago."

"A hundred and twenty-three, to be precise." he said mildly.

"But you don't look that old," she pressed.

He merely smiled.

"I heard about that battle," Cat spoke up. "The armies were attacked by their own fallen, raised as undead to aid the enemy. Didn't Selbon respond to their demands by sending the baron his daughter's severed hand?"

Sybil wailed in disgust. "What a hideous tale!"

Arien nodded. "Correct. By the time the battle was over, it was said that even Selbon had perished and only the walking dead remained to guard the castle and its vast treasures. The size of which, I'm sure, has become greatly exaggerated over the years."

"Only if men do the telling," Sybil murmured into her wine. "They often exaggerate the size of things."

Cat grimaced. "Still, there must be some truth to it."

"Which is why foolish fortune-hunters keep going up there and getting killed," Sybil pointed out.

"Tales of treasure interest me little," Arien said. "However, the Archmage possessed a rare book, which I would greatly wish to find." He spoke slowly, carefully, as if he was trying not to reveal too much. A wry grin twisted his mouth. "In fact, I had thought of going there myself. If I but had the courage."

"Cat?" Sybil said in a low voice completely unlike her usual throaty tones. "That brings us back to what I wanted to tell you. I met a priest, Hedron, of the Nahle Dalia, like me. He's a traveler from Hachland, and was with some companions who sought their fortune by adventure, hoping to be like the Four Heroes."

Cat smiled. "My father and his friends hoped to be like them too, but their deeds never went as planned!"

"Hedron and his friends decided to seek Selbon's treasure," Sybil went on. "They were captured by orcs before even getting through the gates. I can't bear the thought of one of Talopea's own locked in a crude iron cage, fed by orcs and sleeping on straw. Thank Talopea they managed to escape!"

"I fail to understand." Cat said, puzzled. "What has it to do with me?"

Sybil reached over and took her hand. "Cat, dear, while they were locked up, they overheard the orcs complaining about having more prisoners to feed. They said that taking care of the elf in the dungeons was enough work already."

Cat's hand shook as she reached for her glass, only to discover it empty. "By the powers, Sybil," she breathed. "Do you know what this could mean?"

"That's why I was afraid to tell you. Cat, promise me you won't do anything foolish!"

"I seem to be misunderstanding part of the conversation," Arien commented. "What meaning has this for you, Cat?"

"The elf in the dungeons . . . it may be my mother," Cat said. "I have to go up there."

"Cat, no!" Sybil cried. "Just think of that horrible place, with its ugly glowing-eyed skull head, acrawl with orcs and the walking dead! Why do you think I didn't want to tell you? You'll be killed!"

"That's a risk I must take." She winked impishly at Sybil. "Come with me?"

The priestess drew back. "Me? Cat, don't be a fool! Listen to yourself. The two of us going to that horrible place, when Hedron and his friends were lucky to escape with their lives? They had swordsmen with them. Big, muscular warriors." Sybil spread her hands and looked down at herself. "This body was not made for crawling around in crumbling ruins. This body was made for cushions, a lover or three, and a pot of scented oil."

Cat winced at Sybil's words but pressed on. "If it's warriors we need, Alphonse would go."

"Alphonse!" Sybil's face puckered in disgust. "He's as horrendous as any of the monsters we'd find up there! This plan of yours goes steadily from bad to worse!"

"He is not horrendous!" Cat flared. "He's my friend!"

"Cat, he's orckin," Sybil complained.

Cat went deathly still. "He has as much human blood as I do," she said in a biting whisper. "And is the most loyal person I've ever known!"

Arien laid his cool hand over hers, which had clenched into a fist of useless anger. "I pray you, be patient with Sybil. She is speaking not with her heart, but with misguided beliefs."

His touch, unexpected and startling, sent tingles up her arm. It, even more than his words, quelled her temper.

Sybil sighed. "I'm sorry, my dear little Cat. I'll go with you, and if Alphonse must come along, so be it. As long as he doesn't sing," she added decisively. "Our ears were made to listen to more pleasant things. The gentle fall of rain, a lover's whisper, fine music. Not orcish war ballads."

"I'll speak with him about it," Cat promised.

Slowly, almost reluctantly, Arien pulled his arm away. "When do we depart?"

"We?" Sybil blurted, sitting up rapidly. "You, as well?"

"I must," he said firmly. "It may be my only opportunity to find the book I seek. I am not unskilled with magic, though I have had little practice."

"Well," Sybil cooed. "This is sounding better and better." She let her eyes roam over what she could see of him. "I was afraid I'd have to miss my nightly devotions."

Arien said nothing and looked at the stage. Cat did the same, seeing that Gustav was gone and a troupe of gnomish jugglers was getting ready to perform. Each was about half the height of humans, with a shock of thick brown hair that stood up like the pelt of a hedgehog. Their faces were wrinkled, from merriment more than age, and nut-brown in hue. Their hands, large in proportion to their small, stocky bodies, were well able to handle the brightly colored balls.

"I wonder where Greyquin is?" she mused, reminded of another gnome by the sight of the jugglers. "He'd join us, and come in handy, too."

"The last I'd heard, he was off on some treasure hunt," Sybil said. "Claimed he'd found a secret map to the tomb of a minotaur warlord, and was going to make his fortune. Greyquin the Short and his might war-dog, Bear."

"A fortune. Wouldn't that be wonderful?" Cat laughed. "Maybe we'll be the ones to find the Archmage's lost treasures. We'd be set for life."

"As if you'd quit your thieving ways," Sybil sniffed. "That's about as likely as me retiring from the Temple. You'll be climbing over rooftops and dodging the City Guard forever, no matter if you had a pile of diamonds."

"Not necessarily," Cat protested, though in her heart she knew that she loved her work more for the thrill than for the coin. "But since we speak of money, we'll need supplies. Rope, horses, travel food."

Sybil made a face. "Travel food? You mean those salted strips of meat and hard bread? Oh, Cat, say it isn't so. You know I can't go long without a good meal at a fancy inn."

"This isn't a vacation, Sybil. It's not like we're riding out to Lake Jeline for a boating holiday."

"That sounds like more fun," she muttered.

"It isn't supposed to be fun!" Cat said, exasperated. "If there's a chance I might find my mother, I'll take on a whole army of orcs with my bare hands."

"From the way that you handled those ruffians, I would surmise that it would bode ill for the orcs," Arien said, smiling.

"I was lucky," she admitted. "That knife would have killed me if you hadn't warned me." She rubbed her shoulder, then remembered his touch, and felt suddenly shy.

"Had they overpowered you, I would have lost not only my coin but my life as well. It is not every man who can admit to being rescued by a fair lady, but I do so, and gladly." He gazed at her, holding her spellbound.

"My, how late it's getting," Sybil said, getting quickly to her feet. "No, no, don't get up," she added as Arien started to rise. "I'm sure there's still a lot of planning to do, and Cat could tell you I've no head for that sort of thing at all."

Cat threw Sybil a desperate and imploring look, which she pretended not to see. The thought of being left alone with Arien was at once exciting and alarming.

"Alas, it is late," Arien said, glancing at the large hour-candle that Osnard kept by the bar. "If I am to be absent from the Library for this journey, there is much I should attend to beforehand."

"I'm sure you can worry about that tomorrow," Sybil persisted. "It's only a job."

"It has been my job for ninety years," he said. "I do enjoy my work, and, as Cat can doubtless affirm, I need the money."

She laughed. "Was that really all you had?"

He nodded ruefully. "Sadly, it was."

"So you could use some gold as much as the rest of us."

"Gold is incidental to me," he said. "*What is a man without knowledge but a child in a dark room? I seek that which will light the way.*"

Sybil looked completely puzzled by the quotation, but Cat recognized it instantly. "Elwyndas Maevannen, *Nightfall in the Emerin.*"

"You know the classics?" he asked, stunned.

"My mother loved them. Da bought her a complete set one Wintersfest."

"Well, Cat," Sybil tried again. "Why don't you take Arien over to your room and show him the books? I'm sure he'd be interested."

"Sybil!" she hissed.

"Shall we plan to meet here again, two days from now?" he asked. "That should give us all adequate time to prepare."

"So be it," Cat said. "I'll talk to Alphonse tomorrow."

Arien bowed to them both. "I bid you farewell, then, ladies." With a faint smile, he turned to Cat. "*Fallia tomis eriam teilek.*"

She gasped at the words, spoken in the fluid, musical language of the elves. It took her a moment to search her memory and find the correct reply. "*Salan reia fos lepia,*" she said.

He raised an eyebrow, pleased and impressed. With a final nod, he turned and made his way through the crowded tables. She watched him go, biting her lip, her hand pressed to the base of her throat.

As the door closed behind him, Sybil whirled on Cat. "You like him," she announced. "I can see it shining in your pretty blue eyes."

"Sybil!" she protested. "I said no such thing!"

"Oh, Cat, for pity's sake. There's no reason to be ashamed. He was barely able to take his eyes off you, and what was that he said at the end? From the look on your face, it was a devastating compliment."

"No! It's but a traditional elven farewell. All he said was that the hours would seem endless until we met again."

"My, my. And what did you say? Please tell me that it was something suitable. *Drink from my lips, for you will find no wine sweeter.* Something like that."

Cat choked. "Certainly not! All I said was may the skies see you safely home."

"Cat, how boring. Now, admit it. You like him."

"I just never met an elf that would talk to me before," she said. "Except to insult me, that is."

"Cat."

"Sybil!"

Sybil continued to stand there, hands on her generous hips, staring at Cat. Cat looked at the harper who had replaced the gnomish jugglers. She looked at Osnard blowing the froth from a mug of ale. She looked at a young couple arguing in the corner. She looked everywhere but at Sybil, hoping she would give up and go away. When she refused to budge, Cat finally raised her eyes to see her smug smile.

"Well, mayhap a little," she admitted.

Sybil whooped in joy. "At last, the light has dawned! With Talopea's help--"

"I don't want Talopea's help!" Cat cried, alarmed. "Sybil, please! It isn't like *that!*"

"Cat, you don't even know what *that* is all about," Sybil snorted. "But I do, and I can help. Don't worry. We'll get the two of you together."

Cat buried her face in her hands. "Oh, gods," she moaned. "Please don't do anything. Please don't embarrass me."

Sybil patted her shoulder. "Trust me."

*   *   *

3

It has been said that he who lives by the sword shall die by the sword. Of all the fighting men I've ever known, none would want it any other way.

The Book of Yor.

The inner courtyard of the massive Temple of Steel was bustling with activity as Cat Sabledrake entered. Men of all ages and descriptions practiced different forms of combat with weapons and bare hands.

She realized she was the object of much attention. Looking around, she saw that she was the only female in sight. Unlike the chaste Knights of Blackmoon, Steel's faithful eyed her with lusty appreciation.

Timidly, feeling quite out of place, she crept up to a tall man in robes, who wore the symbol of Steel on a chain around his neck. The pendant was in the shape of a miniature broadsword, perfect in every detail. It was said that a priest of Steel could call upon the power of the sword and the pendant would grow into a full-sized weapon.

"Excuse me," she said.

He turned and looked down at her from his imposing height. His dark eyes flicked over her, then he grinned broadly.

"Well, hello little lady," he said. "Looking for someone?"

She nodded. "Alphonse Bugbedead."

He stepped back and looked her over again, more seriously. "*You* seek Brother Alphonse? Who'd have thought that the big lug would have himself such a pretty lady?"

She closed her eyes, thought about explaining, and decided it would just be easier to let the tall priest think what he wanted.

"Alphonse is over there, wrestling with Gornak." He jerked his head toward a crowd of men, all cheering and shouting.

"Thank you," she said swiftly, darting away before he could say anything more.

She made her way to the edge of the crowd. A thick wooden flagpole was nearby, the top fluttering with banners. She climbed up it to a point where she could see over the heads of the crowd, and there was Alphonse.

Alphonse Bugbedead stood almost half again Cat's own height, weighed more than three hundred pounds, and was as solidly built as a border baron's keep. He was far from handsome, with a large nose, deepset eyes, and a prominent jaw dominated by the tusks that protruded over his upper lip.

Some said that his father had really been an ogre, but Cat knew that he was the son of an orc chieftain and very proud of it.

A powerfully-muscled dwarf with a plaited rust-colored beard currently had a grip on one of Alphonse's arms. As Cat watched, the orckin swung his other arm around. Cat herself would have been sent flying, but the dwarf only staggered a step.

"Come on," Gornak invited, spitting on the ground.

Alphonse dove at him, and the two of them hit the ground so hard that Cat felt the pole shake. She clung tighter as the two combatants rolled across a padded leather mat.

Cat noticed another robed man, his hair also cut in a peculiar style, standing in the midst of a group of young boys. They were all watching the fight intently and listening to the man's comments.

It ended when Alphonse squeezed Gornak's knee until something popped, leaving the dwarf writhing and swearing on the mat. The crowd cheered and began to disperse, some paying off bets, others arguing over techniques.

Gornak finally got up and raised one fist in an insulting gesture. "Next time, I'll break your stinking neck," he sneered.

Alphonse grabbed the upthrust fist in his left hand and bent the wrist back. He leaned down, lowering his battered nose to within inches of Gornak's sweaty face. "You can try, mushroom-breath," he growled.

Cat slid down the post. "Alphonse!" she called.

He straightened up, not letting go of Gornak. Gornak cursed, stretching up on his tip-toes and clawing at Alphonse's big fingers with his free hand.

"Cat!" Alphonse bellowed gleefully.

His welcoming grin turned into a grimace of pain as Gornak seized his littlest finger and bent it brutally backward. Cat faltered, hearing a sound like a chicken bone cracked between a dog's teeth.

"*Dzgok!*" Alphonse swore in his father's language. "You broke it!"

"Get your sweetheart to kiss it better," Gornak suggested with a mocking leer.

Alphonse roared, seized him by the beard and hauled him off the ground. "Mind your manners," he snarled. "I'll hollow you out and use you for a backpack, see if I don't." He hurled the dwarf away.

Gornak landed hard in the dust, grunting as the wind was knocked out of him. He shot a deadly glare at Alphonse and limped toward one of the long, low stone buildings that surrounded the courtyard.

"Defending my honor again?" Cat asked lightly.

Alphonse stood staring after the dwarf, his wounded hand held away from his side. "I hate that dwarf. Comes from some clan called the Orcslayers. Orcslayers!"

"You should see somebody about that," Cat said, examining his finger, already swollen and purple. "Doesn't it hurt?"

"Hurts like fire." He gripped it and waggled it back and forth.

Cat made a face and turned away. "Alphonse!"

"It's broken, all right. Want to walk over to the infirmary with me?"

They walked through the courtyard, toward a large stone building with the symbol of the healers painted on the door.

"You must like it here," Cat said, glancing around at the racks of weapons shining in the sun, hearing the steady *twang-thunk!* from the crossbow range, and smelling leather and oiled metal. "I'm surprised you'd join a temple, though."

"Steel's not that much different from Teruzan," he said, naming the only god of the orcs. "Same teachings. Battle, glory, a good quick death. What I like most is that nobody cares where you're from or who you are, as long as you're a good fighter."

She followed him into the spacious room, taking in the rows of cots, many of which were filled with battered, groaning men. "What happened to them?"

"Just standard training," he shrugged. A young man in priestly robes, the white band of a healer around his upper arm, approached and Alphonse held out his mangled hand like an offering. "Think you can mend it, Brother?"

"If Steel is willing," the priest replied. He glanced curiously at Cat.

"My sister," Alphonse explained, sitting down.

"Alphonse, quit that." She turned to the shocked priest. "We're just friends, not kin."

He looked relieved, then surprised Cat by, instead of bowing his head in prayer for the power of healing, turned and started rummaging through a cupboard. He came up with a small glass bottle, full of a bruise-colored fluid.

"What's that?" she asked curiously.

"An elixir of healing," the young priest explained. Seeing her confused look, he added, "We servants of Steel do not have powers of healing. We must rely on other methods, medicine, and alchemy." He dabbed a length of clean cloth with the fluid and wrapped it around Alphonse's finger, then gave the orckin the rest to drink.

"How is it?" Cat asked.

He smacked his lips. "Not bad. Tastes like blackberries."

"Go easy on that shield hand for a few days," the priest cautioned. "It's yet weak."

"Good thing it wasn't this one." Alphonse flexed his right hand, making muscles pop out all the way up his arm. "I can still wield Emily." Emily was the affectionate name he'd given his five-headed flail.

"Speaking of which," Cat interrupted, "that's why I'm here. How do you feel about traveling?"

"Not to Arrowood again." Alphonse rolled his eyes as he got up and started for the door. "Jessa doesn't like me, and there's nothing to see but a bunch of trees and harmless little animals."

"That was what I was thinking," Cat said, following him back into the courtyard. "North into Arrowood, and beyond. Do you remember my mother?"

"Of course not. I don't even remember mine."

"But you've heard me talk about her."

"And how she vanished when you were barely more than a babe, and how your father went off two years ago to look for her and never came back," he finished.

She took a deep breath. "I think I know where she is. I think she's a prisoner in the dungeons of Castle Selbon."

"That haunted ruin up north?" His eyes lit up, making him appear absurdly boyish. "Full of wild orcs and walking dead? I'll get Emily, and we can be on the road by noon."

"Slow down, big fellow. Not so fast. We're not leaving until tomorrow."

He looked down at himself. "That's probably best. I need a bath. Cleaner you are, the fewer bugs you get. And I hate bugs. That's why they call me Bugbedead." He paused, and his eyes narrowed so much they almost vanished into his craggy skin. "Wait a minute. Who else is going?" Before she could answer, a huge expression of dismay dawned on his face. "Not Sybil!"

She looked helplessly at him.

He heaved a sigh that nearly blew her over. "Does she know I'm going?"

"She says she doesn't mind as long as you don't sing."

He muttered something in the language of the orcs. From the grumbling tone she was sure it wasn't complimentary, even though all orc-speak sounded like swear words.

"I heard that," she said.

"Maybe, but you don't know what it means." He shook his head. "You, me, and Sybil. Pure madness, Cat. Pure madness."

"There is someone else going," she said slowly. "An elven wizard."

"An elf? Since when, elfkin scum, would an elf go anywhere with you?"

"I don't know," she confessed. "He's not like anyone I've ever met. He's . . . well, he's . . ."

"Never mind," Alphonse said, watching her with a peculiar, unreadable expression. "Think I understand. I'll see you tomorrow."

*   *   *

Arien approached the tavern cautiously, listening to the sounds of a fight in progress. He winced at each heavy thump of a body hitting the floor and each crash of splintering furniture. At last, all was quiet. He went to the door.

The sign above the door had no lettering on it. Instead, the placard bore a picture of a sinister red dragon with a cloth bound over its eyes. The Blind Dragon. According to Librarian Apprentice Pellander, the best place in town to hire a swordsman.

Arien took a deep breath. Wiser thoughts were driven from his mind by the promise of Selbon's grimoire and the image of Cat's pair of sapphire blue elven eyes, alight at the prospect of adventure.

He cautiously opened the door and peered into the gloomy interior. No Golden Lion, this!

Three of the four hanging lanterns were broken, one of them still swinging and dripping oil onto the scuffed wooden floor. What few pieces of furniture that yet stood looked to do so only by some quirk of the gods. A bedraggled wench carried mugs to a table, stepping over two groaning men. The customers were tough-looking men with sharp eyes and ready swords.

It was, in other words, exactly the sort of place he was looking for.

He shuddered. His life had changed drastically indeed, that he should find himself in such a place again. He was reminded of a time when taverns such as this had been familiar to him and forcibly put such memories from his mind.

"Pick them up, you lazy louts!" the wench rasped at some of the men, gesturing to the obvious losers of the recent brawl. "Was you all born stupid? Throw them out!"

The losers, still groaning in protest, were picked up and unceremoniously pitched out the door to the laughter of the rest.

Suspicious looks came Arien's way. Then one of the men slammed down his mug and swaggered over to him.

"You must be lost," he said. He was a burly, red-bearded fellow wearing a hardened leather vest. Not unhandsome, but a scar at the corner of his mouth twisted it into a perpetual sneer.

"This is the Blind Dragon, is it not?" Arien inquired politely.

"That it is, but you're no hired sword. My grandmother looks meaner."

"Ah." Arien steepled his fingers before him. He felt a brief urge to give up this crusade and go back to the safety of the Library. He could face a lifetime of solitude, could continue to bear the great burden that had led him to this.

Then the image of night-blue eyes framed by a tumble of dark curls rose again unbidden in his mind, and he knew he couldn't let her go alone. Go she would, questing for her mother. A mother she knew, and cared for. He had to go along, if for no other reason than to meet this elfwoman who had permitted her crossling child to live, against all custom.

"And if I am not a sword for hire, good sir, why ever would I be here?"

The man looked puzzled, then grinned. "I'd say you must be wanting to hire. The name's Rayke. Buy me a drink and we'll talk it over."

Much time and many mugs later, Rayke nodded. "Sounds good, but you haven't answered the most important question yet. What's the pay?"

Arien did some quick calculations and felt his purse. "Two hundred silver marks, plus, of course, a share in any found wealth."

"Two hundred?" He stifled a belch. "Not a lot to risk your life for."

"True. I risk mine for even less, for I seek only a single book that, even should I find it, it would doubtless lead me into greater peril." A gruesome image flashed through his mind. He saw again the hideous beasts loping in a circle around—he banished the thought.

Rayke was watching him uneasily, and Arien realized that some of his thoughts must have shown on his face. He felt cold, pale.

"You're a strange one, friend Arien. My gut is telling me to stay out of whatever black trouble you've gotten yourself into, but my head's knowing that I'll go mad unless I find out what's going on. Two hundred and a share of anything we find, huh? I think I can work for that."

"I trust that you are an honorable man?" Arien asked.

Rayke laughed. "You want an honorable man, go to the Knights of Blackmoon. You want a good sword that stays bought, I'm he."

*   *   *

Bostitch sharpened his horns on a rock. It was an even, repetitive motion that soothed him. He enjoyed the sound of horn grating against stone, the rough but shivery feel of it in his head.

He dimly remembered a place where there had been others like him around. Other bulls and cows, and calves frolicking in the long grass.

His long, massive face twisted into a frown. They didn't like him there anyway. They made fun of him and called him names. Was it his fault he hadn't grown as big as the other bulls? He'd made up for it by being meaner and stronger, and that had only made them madder.

He lifted his head and tried to look at his horns. They must be good and sharp by now. No matter how he turned, they remained just at the edge of his sight.

He touched the tip of one and found it sharp enough to poke through his tough, leathery skin. If it would poke through his, it would poke through anybody's.

Standing, he stretched. He straightened the wide bronze-studded belt that held his sword, and adjusted his loincloth. Looking down, he saw that his hooves were dirty. He bent to dust them off, and noticed something odd next to him. It was a big pile of straps and wooden planks, all hooked together in some sort of shape. He picked it up and messed with it.

"Leave it alone, you big ox," a voice said.

Bostitch dropped the thing, thinking that the voice had come from it. He drew his sword and was about to stab it when he heard the voice again.

"It's only me, fool."

He turned and saw the little man sitting on the ground, wrapped in blood-colored cloth. One of his puny legs was stretched out, bent like an old branch. The little man had a stick with a blood-colored rock on the end, and when he hit Bostitch with it, it hurt worse than getting smashed with an ogre's club.

All that blood-color. Made Bostitch want to kill something. But not the little man!

The little man gave him food, and good drink that tasted like old barley and made his head feel funny, and shiny trinkets to play with. If anything tried to eat the little man, Bostitch was supposed to pull its head off.

"Start the fire," the little man said.

He wrapped his mouth around the word. "Fie-urh." He could understand the little man much better than he could say the little man's words, though he was still confused most of the time. The little man talked so fast.

"Oh, in Haarkon's name, just get the wood. I'm tired. I must rest." The little man picked up the badstick and made like he would hit Bostitch, so Bostitch hurried to pick up pieces of wood.

Fie-urh. The hot thing that made food smell better, and made everything warm. It ate wood. Bostitch had tried to eat wood once. Not good at all. He liked feeding it to the fie-urh, though. But he had to be careful. The fie-urh would eat him too if he put his hand too close. It was like a big mean dog that bit.

He picked up wood. Some was on trees, but trees didn't like to let go of wood the way they liked to let go of fruit. Wood that was on the ground was better. Wood in the river didn't work at all. The river made the wood wet, and the fie-urh didn't like it that way.

"That's enough," snapped the little man. "We only need a campfire. We're not roasting a dragon."

"Dragon?" Bostitch echoed, looking for the telltale shape of a dragon against the sky as he reached for his sword. He knew all the little man's things-to-kill words, even if he didn't know what they all looked like. Dragon, though, he knew. He'd seen one before, when he was just a calf, and all the bulls ran out to chase it with swords and axes.

"No dragons." The little man hitched himself closer to some rocks he'd had Bostitch put in a circle. He didn't move very fast, dragging his crooked leg like it was dead but still hooked on. "Put the wood in here."

He obeyed, making sure to stack it the way the fie-urh liked. The fie-urh wouldn't come to eat the wood unless it was stacked right. When the wood was ready, he started watching eagerly, hoping to see the fie-urh come this time. He hadn't yet, but he was still hopeful. It had to come from someplace.

He heard the little man saying the blood-color words, the words that made the coarse hairs of Bostitch's hide bristle.

Thin tendrils of smoke rose from the wood, followed by tiny tongues of flame. Bostitch sighed in disappointment. He still hadn't seen the fie-urh come. It had sneaked up to the wood when he was looking the wrong way. It was here, and he sank down to stare at it. It was so pretty, all orange-yellow.

Watching the fie-urh eat made him hungry. He rummaged through the thing of leather and wood, forgetting that he'd wanted to kill it before, and found a big chunk of meat wrapped in leaves. He poked a stick through the meat and held it in the fie-urh. Somehow, the fie-urh didn't eat it but made it crispy and black on the outside. His mouth watered from the smell. He put it on a piece of bread and munched, glancing over at the little man out of the corner of his eye as he did so.

The little man never ate. He was holding a bottle made of shiny metal. Whatever was in the bottle was all the little man ever drank, besides water. Bostitch could smell it even over the smoke and the scent of his own dinner, and it made his nose crinkle. It smelled like dead things under a log.

"We're almost there," the little man said. "Soon, Selbon's secrets shall be mine!"

"Fight soon?" Bostitch asked eagerly.

"Probably. The castle is supposedly guarded by orcs."

"Orcs, pah!" Bostitch said, spitting in the fie-urh and making it sizzle. He'd fought orcs before. He could kill as many orcs as he had fingers without even breathing hard. "Dragon?"

"Haarkon, I hope not. That's the last thing we need."

"Huh?"

"Sleep! Go to sleep!"

He hastily stuffed the rest of his dinner in his mouth and stretched out, pillowing his horned head on the leather and wood thing. It wasn't very soft, but it was better than the rocks. Moments later, he was asleep.

*   *   *

It is the elven way to shape the woodlands to suit their desires. It is the human way to shape themselves to the ways of the woods.

The Book of Yor.

She sighted down the arrow, blowing a strand of russet hair out of her thin face. The rabbit continued nibbling on the clover at the foot of the tree, not knowing that its time was at hand.

"Jessa!" a voice called.

Startled, she released the arrow. It missed, scaring the rabbit into a series of panicky bounds that carried it out of her sight. Her hawk, Kiah, screeched scoldingly. Jessa reached for another arrow, although she knew the cheery voice and the accompanying joyful bark.

As they came into view, she lowered her bow with a resigned sigh.

A dog bounded up to her. It was almost as big as a small pony, covered with shaggy black and brown fur. A saddle was strapped to its back, and clinging to the saddle as the dog raced toward her was a small figure with a huge grin.

"Greyquin, you spoiled my shot," she said.

"What?" He jumped off the dog's back. Standing, he only came up to just above her waist. His skin was as dark as her own, but his eyes were much brighter and his face was made to smile. He pulled off the bronze helmet that fastened under his chin and shook out his grayish hair, running his fingers though his salt-and-pepper beard.

"I said, you spoiled my shot," she repeated.

He held out his arms. "Is that all? No hug? Aren't you glad to see me? It's been a year, at least."

"That rabbit was as good as in the cookpot until you and Bear came along," she said sternly.

"Well," he said, glancing at the dog. "What do you think about that, Bear? We ruined Jessa's dinner. We'll have to repay her somehow."

The incongruously cheery wardog woofed, wagging his tail. He jumped up on Jessa, nearly knocking the breath out of her. Kiah screamed indignantly and launched herself skyward. Jessa tried to push Bear down and only got licked in the face for her efforts.

"Bear's missed you," Greyquin said. "So have I, but I won't lick your face. I will, though, share my supplies. It's the least I can do, since I chased off your rabbit."

"So you're staying to supper?" She brushed at the muddy pawprints on her tunic and gave Bear a stern look. The huge wardog hung his head and tried to look ashamed, though his tail twitched in suppressed wags.

"If you don't object. How have you been? You look . . . " he studied her, " . . . the same."

She nodded curtly, knowing that she looked fifteen years older than her true age of twenty. "What about your quest?" she asked. "The last time I saw Cat, she said you were looking for the burial mound of a minotaur warlord."

He rolled his eyes. "Burial mound! A bunch of bones, two bent copper marks, and an axe that couldn't cut butter." He handed her a sack. "Here you go. Early hazelnuts, some good smoked Keydan mutton, bread, and even a little pot of honey. Does that make up for one scrawny rabbit?"

She nodded again and whistled for Kiah. "My cabin's not far. You can stay a while, if you want."

"The offer is appreciated and accepted." He bobbed a comical bow and whistled for Bear.

He chattered constantly on the way back to the cabin, telling her about his travels in foreign lands. Jessa only listened with half an ear until Kiah gave a sudden warning cry.

"Shh!" Jessa hissed at Greyquin. "Something's wrong. Stay here. I'll go on ahead."

"I'm as quiet as you are," he argued.

She gave him a long look. "Not in the woods."

He opened his mouth to protest, then realized that she was right. He held Bear steady while she slipped silently ahead.

She could hear several horses, at least five, one much bigger than the rest. She held an arrow loose in her hand. If they were her father's men, they would die. *She* would die, rather than submit again.

Voices, speaking too low for her to make out words. An unfamiliar male voice asked a question, and was answered by another male voice, this one bearing an elven accent. She crept closer, staying down, until the voices became clearer.

"I guess she's not home," a woman said.

Jessa relaxed, her caution giving way to recognition and curiosity. Replacing her arrow in the quiver, she stood straight and walked out of the undergrowth.

"Hello, Cat," she said.

*   *   *

"Ooohhh, mazdek arnis falgran tordorra," Alphonse sang, strumming on his lute as he swayed in the saddle. His voice was both loud enough and off-key enough, Cat noticed, to send birds and small animals scurrying from their path. *"Dorgas tumika vovo rudanas. Oh-oh-oh-ai! Shuvda olemp—"*

"In Talopea's name, shut up!" Sybil snapped, bouncing a hazelnut off his broad back.

Rayke leaned over and patted her leg comfortingly. He whispered something which Cat, riding behind the pair, was glad she couldn't hear.

The pleasure-seeking Talopean had actually surprised everyone, even Cat and Alphonse, when she'd turned up in a sculpted suit of gleaming, form-fitting armor, carrying a sword. Of course, Sybil also took every opportunity to complain about the weight and discomfort, but boasted that all of her faith were trained to defend their pleasure-rich bodies. This came as news to Cat, who had never, in all their years of acquaintance, seen Sybil so much as swat a fly.

Jessa ranged ahead on foot, watchful and alert. Cat was glad she'd been able to persuade the dour huntress to join them, for none knew the woods as well as Jessa. Greyquin, on Bear, roamed back and forth among the horses. Upon hearing of their proposed journey, it would have taken dwarf-forged chains to keep the gnome from coming along.

Alphonse lifted his fingers from the lute. The last strangled notes drifted off into the forest. Cat swore she saw leaves wilt. He glanced over his shoulder at Sybil, smiled wickedly, and struck the lute again. His voice, surprisingly deep and clear when he wasn't singing in orcish, rose over the music.

This time, his song of choice was a popular riverdock bawdy ballad, and both Rayke and Greyquin joined in lustily on the chorus.

Even Sybil joined in the laughter. Jessa looked back, frowning. Cat groaned and buried her face in her hands.

"I do hope a stealthy approach is not required," Arien commented as Alphonse plunged into the next verse, with Rayke and Greyquin singing along.

Cat peeked at him. He was riding beside her, a book propped open on the saddle, and appeared completely unaffected by the noise and the content of the song. His riding cape of white leather lined with pearl-grey silk was thrown over one shoulder. The reins were draped indifferently across his lap and he seemed to be guiding his horse by thought alone.

"I've heard quieter barfights," she replied.

"As have I." He turned a page. A strand of silver hair fell across his face, and Cat found herself foolishly tempted to reach over and brush it aside.

"When have you been in a barfight?" she asked skeptically.

He glanced sidelong at her. "I have my secrets. At the very least, I did witness the end of one at the Blind Dragon when I hired yon singing mercenary."

"The Blind Dragon's hardly a place for the likes of you."

"You speak of it with familiarity," he replied. "Why should I not know of it?"

"Well, you're a gentleman. I'm not much of a lady."

"What is a lady?" he said, in the tone that let her know he was quoting some written work. In the short time they'd been traveling together, she could already recognize what she'd come to think of as his quoting voice, as well as his teaching voice. "Fair of face and sunshine hair, these make a lady not. Silken gown and scent of rose, these make a lady not."

His eyes grew distant, as if he was no longer seeing the trail through Arrowood, but another place altogether. His voice softened. "For many a lass may be fair, and any may don the finest of silks. Nay, 'tis gentle spirit and loving heart that makes a lady, and ever a lady shall she be."

"That's beautiful," Cat breathed. "Who wrote it? Elwyndas?"

He smiled sadly. "Flatterer. It is neither that old, nor crafted by so gifted a poet."

"You mean you wrote it?" she asked, awed.

"I did." He sighed. "But it was long ago. Please, let us not speak of it."

A hundred questions filled her, but she rode on in silence. Ahead of them, Sybil was teaching the others a Talopean ditty, while Jessa stalked along pretending she didn't know any of them.

Cat slipped one foot free of the stirrup and rested it on the saddle so she could prop her chin on her knee in her favorite thinking pose. She was still trying to come to terms with the notion that she was the leader of this misfit group. It seemed all wrong to her. She was a thief, a footpad, a cutpurse. No noble leader, no Duncan Farleigh, she!

Jessa appeared beside her, making her jump.

"I thought you were up ahead," she said, startled and a bit chagrined that Jessa had been able to sneak up on her.

"I was. I saw something."

"What?" She knew from experience that Jessa was not one to volunteer information.

"Signs," Jessa said, scowling. It was an expression that seemed at home on her long, narrow face. Cat could count on the fingers of one hand the times she'd seen Jessa smile. "I think we'd better make camp."

"Why?" Arien inquired. "There are still a few hours until dusk."

Jessa gave him a cold look, and it occurred to Cat that the huntress spoke as little to any of the others as possible, except for Greyquin. "There have been galorim here," she said grudgingly. "I saw the signs. It's not safe to be in their territory, especially at night."

"What are galorim?" Cat asked.

It was Arien who answered her, even as Jessa was starting to reply. "Galorim are evil creatures that dwell in old sections of the forest. They are also called wood hags or black druids."

"That's right," Jessa said, her scowl deepening. "Some wood spirits have powers of growth and blossoming, but galorim only bring decay. They also like to kill living creatures, especially humans."

"I'll take your word for it," Cat said. "You know the woods. But why should we stop if these things have been around here? Shouldn't we keep going?"

"This is the edge of their territory. I don't know how far it goes, so we should start through it with a whole day ahead of us."

"Fine with me." Cat raised her voice. "Let's make camp. We'll stay here tonight."

As they started setting up camp, Cat realized that not only were they all looking to her for orders, but she was giving them. Which was not at all right!

*   *   *

"This is the Arrowood," Arien said, touching a spot on the map.

Cat sat beside him on the large rock and leaned over his arm to study the page. Behind them, they could hear Alphonse and Greyquin arguing good-naturedly.

"It bears the name for two reasons," he continued. "First, as you can see, it vaguely resembles an arrowhead, pointing to Hachland and the Great Western Sea. Secondly, it is peopled by hunters and bandits, all of whom are quite good with bows and crossbows."

Cat nodded. He admired the line of her neck and jaw and the way her dark hair, still damp from her evening's wash, curled around her delicate ears. He wondered if her ears were as sensitive as those of elven women, how she might respond to the light touch of a—ye gods, what was he thinking? Livana preserve him!

"These are the Scattered Hills, then?" she asked, tapping the map.

"Yes. And these are the mountains. They are called the Whiterocks, for they are snow-clad even in the summer."

"May I?"

He gave her the book, open to the map. He'd been refreshing himself on history and geography of the Northlands as they rode. Now, as Cat studied the map intently, he looked around the campsite.

Alphonse and Greyquin were in the midst of their usual disagreement about the best way to build a fire. Jessa was nearby, her hair tied back in a horsetail as she efficiently skinned the pair of rabbits her ready bow had brought down. Her hawk waited patiently on a branch until she tossed a few pieces of meat to it.

Rayke and Sybil were gone, as he expected. A relief, indeed. The priestess, with her abundant charms and knowing eyes, unnerved him far more than the prospect of encountering bloodthirsty galorim. She was so human, so round-eared and full-breasted, utterly unappealing.

Quite unlike Cat.

"Then this must be Mount Yrej," she was saying, her slim finger resting on an inverted 'v' that was larger than the others. "Is there truly a giant skull, carved from the mountain?"

"So all the sources seem to indicate," he said, leaning closer. He saw that the laces of her tunic were slightly loose, just enough to hint at a glimpse of gentle curves beyond. He hastily looked away, chastising himself.

"The library and the dungeons," Cat mused. "We need to find them both. How will you know which book is the one you seek?"

He uttered a short laugh. "If the Archmage's library is as vast as tales would tell, I may have to devote another eighty-seven years to the task."

Her eyes sparkled as she smiled at him. "I can read, too," she said. "If you'd tell me what you're looking for, I could help."

"Dear girl," he said without thinking, "if I were to tell you, you might just leave me to fight my way to the castle alone."

"We wouldn't," she said firmly. "We're all in this together."

He patted her hand. "Would that I could tell someone. It might make my burden easier to bear. Yet I find that I value your company too much to let honesty cause you to cast me out."

"Arien, I'd never do that," she breathed. Her eyes were so deep, so blue. Her small hand turned beneath his and clasped it. "You're the first elf to be kind to me, except my own mother. What could you tell me that would be so horrible I'd forget that?"

He looked down at their hands. Her gaze followed, and color came to her cheeks. Her golden skin turned a dusky rose, he saw, not the sunrise pink of a fair-skinned elfmaid.

The thought made him close his eyes in pain as he remembered a fair-skinned elfmaid whose blushes had been as soft and delicate as a flower. He slowly pulled his hand away from Cat's.

"What could I tell you?" he echoed. "Cat, if only you knew."

"Tell me," she urged.

He shook his head. "I cannot. Perhaps someday, but not tonight."

*   *   *

"My arrows won't be much good against something that can do this." Jessa stood over the fly-covered corpses, her bow at her side. "I recognize the harness. It was one of my father's horses, but I don't know who the rider was."

The dead horse, its belly torn open, lay in a patch of bright, cheerful sunshine. The rider was scattered along the sides of the trail. Their own horses whinnied and sidestepped, tossing their heads.

"They can't be long dead," Greyquin said. "The scavengers will be at them soon."

Jessa shook her head. "Not this. Nothing will touch galorim leavings."

"Why?" Cat asked. She tried not to look.

"Can't you smell it?" Jessa asked.

"I can smell it from here," Alphonse said from his position down the trail. His crossbow looked like a toy in his big hands as he scanned the wavering shadows for movement. "Stinks like Greyquin's cooking."

"Hey!" Greyquin cried.

"The stench of galorim is all over them," Jessa said. "Every animal in the woods will know. They won't come near this place. Look at our horses. They smell it too."

"I don't blame them," Cat said. "Come on. Let's ride. I don't like this."

"Aye, captain." Greyquin saluted sharply, drawing laughter from Sybil and Rayke.

"Why the dismayed expression?" Arien asked as they rode on, following Jessa's lead to put quick yet quiet distance behind them.

"I'm the last person that ought to be in command. I'm the youngest of all of us. You're the smartest and highest born. How come you're not leading?"

"Do you think they would follow me? I knew none of them until we began this journey. You are a friend of all. And though you may be young, you have not wasted your years. You have lived more than I, though I am many times your elder."

"But you, you're an elf, and I'm—"

"If you wait for me to condemn you for your mixed blood, you shall wait until even I am old. There is one thing that puzzles, me, however. If it would not offend, I would ask—" he broke off, eyes widening in alarm as he looked past her.

Cat grabbed for the hilt of her sword, seeing a shadow besides her own fall across the path.

"*Nias!*" Arien said harshly, snapping his empty hand at her in a throwing motion. She gasped as a sharp icicle flew from his fingertips, right past her head. It was followed by a hard crack and a horrid squeal, the sound of a rusty nail being yanked out of a warped board.

Cat whipped around in the saddle and came face to face with the ugliest creature she had ever seen. It was taller than a man, with gnarled, knotted skin covered in rotted bark and moss. Its bulbous eyes were yellow marsh-fire. Just below a splinter-ringed gap of a mouth was Arien's icicle, embedded in the thick hide.

Other creatures, identical to the one facing Cat, swarmed out of the trees. Cat heard swords being drawn and the screams of the horses. Bear was barking wildly. Arien's mount reared, its hooves narrowly missing Cat's head.

She drew her sword, letting go of the reins. As she did so, her own horse bolted forward. The treelike creature snatched her from the saddle and knocked the slim saber from her hand.

She could smell it now, and knew why the animals had panicked. It reeked of decay. Its breath was hot and foul.

Cat kicked. Her foot found something as unyielding as a treetrunk. Coarse wooden claws scraped her sides as she twisted. It bit at her and she squirmed away from the splintery maw.

The teeth came at her again and she threw her arm in front of her face. They closed on her wrist, but the thick leather of her riding glove prevented them from drawing blood. With her other hand, she pulled a knife from her belt and thrust as hard as she could. The blade struck and stuck fast.

It released her wrist and chomped at her again. She balled her fist and punched it in the mouth, wincing. Wooden teeth flew, but the galorim had them to spare and closed its jaws around her wrist again.

Cat pulled up her legs, braced her feet against the galorim's trunk, and shoved backwards. She burst free of its grasp, tearing her fist out of its mouth and showering herself with broken teeth. She wrenched herself around in midair and landed on hands and knees.

She saw her sword and dove for it as the galorim came after her. She rolled into a crouch, the sword held in front of her. As it lunged, she swung with all her strength. The impact jarred her from head to foot and the blade wedged firmly. The galorim squealed again. Blood or sap spurted from the cut. She pulled at the sword, trying to free it though her arms were still numb from the blow.

The galorim's yellow eyes flickered with rage. It clawed at her. She sprang back. The claws shredded her tunic and scrawled deep scratches on her side.

Forgetting the sword, she quickly bent and came up with the two daggers that she kept in her boots. Reversing them, one in each hand, she leaped at the creature. It caught her in midair, surprised by the unexpected move. Her momentum toppled them both to the mossy forest floor. She knew her weight wouldn't be enough to hold it down, but she only intended to be there for an instant. Rising on her knees, she stabbed down with both daggers, into the galorim's eyes.

It screamed. Its body bucked hard enough to send her sailing off it. She landed beside its thrashing form. As its branchlike hands groped at the hilts, buried deep in the ruined mess of its yellow eyes, Cat grabbed her sword and wrenched it loose. Her side afire with pain, she chopped at the galorim. One of its long arms slammed the side of her head, knocking her into a tree. Her sword flew from her hand again. Her breath came in ragged gasps.

"Die, blast you!" she swore at the thrashing galorim.

It started crawling toward her voice. She stepped back and almost fell over a dead branch. Picking it up, she ran at the creature and hit it solidly. It slumped to the ground, scrabbling at the dirt with twiglike fingers that still had shreds of her tunic caught in them.

She bludgeoned it repeatedly, until it was no longer moving, then gave it one more blow just to be sure. Finally, she dropped the branch. Her pulse was racing, echoing in her ears like dwarven war-drums.

She stood over it, panting.

Sybil appeared between the trees, her armor streaked with sticky sap. Her helm was gone and leaves were stuck in her disarrayed hair. "There you are," Sybil said, relieved.

"Is everyone all right?" Cat asked, finally catching her breath. She bent and recovered her sword.

"Greyquin's leg is wounded. Alphonse and Rayke are fine, only scratched up a bit."

"Jessa? Arien?" She followed Sybil back to where the rest were gathered in a group.

"I'm fine," Jessa said.

"And luckily Arien had the sense to stay out of the fight," Sybil added. "It would be a shame to see anything happen to that pretty face."

"It was more due to my horse than any action of my own," Arien said ruefully as he brushed wood chips and leaves from Cat's hair. "In its fright, the poor thing carried me well beyond the battle before throwing me into a bush. A goldberry bush, might I add." He looked down at the stains on his tunic and shook his head.

"Ooh, Cat, those scratches!" Sybil said. "I don't want you getting that black sap in them. Arien, would you be a dear and take Cat over to the creek, get her tidied up?"

"I'll do it," Jessa interrupted sharply before either Cat or Arien could speak.

"I can get myself cleaned up," Cat said quickly, shooting Sybil a stern glare. The priestess only pretended innocence, rather poorly. "Let's hurry, though. There might be more galorim about."

*   *   *

Cat woke as the eastern sky was beginning to lighten. Her sleep had been restless, filled with anxious dreams in which her friends suffered because of one of her mistakes. Why, oh why had they ever chosen her to lead them?

She sat up in her bedroll and looked around.

Sybil and Rayke were curled close to each other, Rayke's arm draped possessively over Sybil's waist. Greyquin and Bear were closest to the fire. Cat smiled to see that Bear seemed to have claimed most of the blankets, leaving Greyquin shivering on bare ground. She gently draped her cloak over the gnome. Jessa was farthest away, with Kiah perched on a branch over her sleeping form.

Alphonse was leaning against a tree, taking his turn on watch. He was running Emily's chains through his hands and humming to himself.

Arien, awake, sat by the fire with a book open in his lap. "Good morning," he said softly as she approached. "You have risen early this day."

A pot of tea was steaming over the fire, and she helped herself to a cup of it before sitting near him. "I couldn't sleep. I've never led anyone before. I worked with my father, and I've worked with other Nightsiders, but someone else was always in command. Suppose I can't manage it?"

He patted her arm. "I trust you. We all do. You will not fail us."

"But what if I do? What if something goes wrong?"

"Worry not about what might be. Follow your instincts. You are the binding fiber that holds us together. Do you think that any of these folk could travel together without you?"

"If you trust me so, why are you keeping secrets?" she asked.

"Secrets?" His eyebrows went up.

"You're as full of secrets as a merchant's purse is of silver."

His laugh was low, and seemed forced. "Secrets, you speak of. Yes, I have secrets. I am nearly a century and a half in years, and there are many things I might never tell another soul. There are things I have done that would surprise you, seeing me as I am now."

"But what are you looking for up there? My guess is that it is a spell, or some piece of magic. Something that nobody else knows." She drew up her knees and wrapped her arms around her lower legs.

"Dear Cat, I cannot speak of it. Not yet. Could we not talk of something else? I never did get to finish my question yesterday. Would you tell me of your parents?"

"My parents? Why?"

"Forgive me if I offend, but I am most curious. From what you have previously said, I assume that you knew both of them."

"Of course. Didn't you know your parents?"

A shadow of ancient pain flickered across his features and was gone. "They died when I was quite young. I was taken in by a neighboring household."

"I'm sorry."

"It was very long ago." He shivered and picked up a stick to stir the fire into renewed life, though Cat suspected that the cold that chilled him came from within.

"I don't remember my mother very well," she said sadly. "She disappeared when I was little."

"She was elven?"

Cat nodded. "And beautiful, according to everyone who knew her. I don't know where she came from, nor met any of her kin."

"How did she . . . " he faltered. "How did she come to . . . have a child?"

She looked down, flustered. "The usual way, I'd think. That's what married people do."

"They were wed?" He sounded incredulous.

"Of course." She suddenly understood, and her eyes widened. "No! My father may have been a rogue and a scoundrel, but he would never—"

He raised both hands in a pacifying gesture. "Once again, the stories I heard as a child are proved wrong. Tell me of your father. He sounds like a most unusual man."

She smiled. "That is putting it kindly. Now, *he* was a thief! He loved wild daring adventures. It was his stories that made Greyquin decide to hang up his carpenter's apron and go out to seek his fortune. He taught me to fight and steal, always intending that I would follow in his boot tracks."

"Surely that is not the only occupation available to you," Arien said, frowning. "You are a clever, talented young woman. There must be other ways you can support yourself."

She shrugged. "It's what I know. My only other hobby is woodcarving, and I haven't the patience to sit in a stall on market day trying to sell them. I'm good at what I do. Among the best, One-Eye tells me, and he's not one for giving false praise."

"I suppose that there is no one to blame but your father, for he is the one who taught you his trade."

"He's been blamed for worse deeds," she agreed, relieved that he sounded more resigned than disapproving. "He loved excitement. He used to travel with an elf, a dwarf, and an orc. A troupe of misfits not unlike our own! Father said the elf, Donnell, was haughty and aloof—"

"He must have been from the Emerin," Arien observed wryly.

Cat giggled. "Possibly. The two of them argued like a miller and a tax collector. They stopped in Thanis, at the Golden Lion, and Donnell fancied Miralina, my mother. She worked there, you see. Da said he started flirting with her too, just to tie Donnell's ears in a knot. Osnard says that Donnell, angered, put a magic powder in Da's drink, thinking it would smite him with love for Zimka, the orc. Instead, he first set eyes on my mother, and proposed on the spot."

"And she agreed?" Arien asked curiously. He had closed the book and now set it on the ground beside him. "Most elfmaids would have been horrified at the very prospect."

"She agreed. So Da remained in Thanis while the others went on to Castle Selbon without him." She sobered. "They never did return. He often spoke of going to look for them, but he didn't want to leave Mother. A few years later, I was born."

She exhaled sadly. "Then Mother vanished, and he had to take care of me. When I was old enough to look out for myself, he went to try and find her. I've heard nothing since."

"Why is it ever so with love? Why does it end so terribly?" He jabbed at the fire.

"It hasn't ended. If they were dead, I'd know. I'm sure I would. They're alive. Maybe trapped, maybe hurt, maybe enspelled, but alive. I know it. And I'll find them."

"I admire your optimism, young Cat. And I envy your parents, for although they were together but a few short years, they had happiness. And produced a fine child who combines the best of both, no matter what the elves might say."

*   *   *

5

Many believe that evil cannot create, only destroy. It would be better to say that evil cannot create good.

The Book of Yor.

Bostitch plodded tirelessly along.

Stuffed into the strange contraption of leather and wood that the minotaur wore over his huge shoulders, Solarrin stared ahead.

He normally dozed while Bostitch walked. Today he was unable to sleep. It was partly the sun, which burned fiercely bright and hot, and it was partly Bostitch's unsteady gait as he made his way through the Scattered Hills.

Solarrin shifted, trying to ease his bad leg into a more comfortable position. It was shorter than the other, and dragged when he walked. Not that he walked. He lurched along, supporting his considerable weight with the help of a black staff, which was inlaid with golden runes of sinister design and topped with a red crystal that seemed to pulse with the beat of an alien heart.

The only drawback about traveling with Bostitch was his mindless stupidity. He was only able to follow simple commands, spoken slowly and loudly. He even thought the insults Solarrin heaped upon him were compliments and pet names.

He tugged at the collar of his robes. Velvet was much too hot for wearing in the summer, but he refused to wear any less. The robes hid his physical defects better than any other style of garment. He removed his hood and mopped his head. His white hair was receding, exposing skin that was mottled with brownish spots. As if to compensate for the baldness, he was favored with a long, lush beard. It was completely white except for a dramatic streak of black down the middle. His eyebrows were thick and bushy, stark white, meeting over his oversized hook of a nose and casting his tiny black eyes into perpetual shadow.

Bostitch paused long enough to unhook the waterskin from his belt and drank deeply. He followed it with a rumbling belch, then continued along.

Thirsty himself, Solarrin dug in one of the many pouches and compartments sewn into the sides of the leather backpack that also served him as a carrying platform. He came up with his silver flask, removed the cork, and sniffed.

He was running out of the elixir. It would soon be time to make more, if he could find fresh mandrake and hemlock. He took two quick swigs, the foul taste of death and decay flooding his mouth. He shuddered and exhaled, as always half-expecting to see a putrid green cloud emerge from his mouth. The elixir, horrible as it was, deadly poison to a normal person, was the only thing that could sustain him.

A hideous wail split the air, making Solarrin nearly spill the precious fluid. Bostitch's head came up so quickly that his right horn almost jabbed Solarrin in the eye.

"What was that?" Solarrin demanded.

Bostitch volunteered one of the few words he knew. "Monster?"

Solarrin looked around. The Scattered Hills truly deserved their name. The landscape was dotted with mammoth boulders, uneven hills, and ratty scrub brush. In places, the ground was cracked open. It was as if Kelvennor, the creator-god, had tired of his work while crafting this part of the earth and simply dumped the hills out of the Bag of Worlds, letting them lay as they fell.

Bostitch, though dumb as a stump, had keen warrior's instincts. He drew his sword and stood, tense, waiting. Solarrin grabbed his staff. The length of wood was far more than a walking stick and more than part of his image as an evil wizard.

The source of the screech sprang onto the path. It was a mountain troll, large and rugged, its muddy brown eyes sweeping hungrily over the minotaur.

Bostitch wasted no time. He roared a challenge, shrugged out of the shoulder straps, and charged at the troll.

Solarrin swore in surprise as he and the backpack crashed to the rocky ground in a tangle of limbs and leather straps. His own staff whacked him on the head.

He watched from his awkward position as Bostitch and the troll met in combat. Violence had always intrigued Solarrin, though he much preferred watching it to participating.

Bostitch swung his sword with savage delight, leaving vicious slashes across the troll's mottled-grey chest and arms. The troll fell back, raking his claws at Bostitch's eyes but only succeeding in carving shallow lines on the minotaur's forehead.

A second troll darted from behind a rock and seized the bundle of leather. Solarrin cursed again as he felt himself being hauled off the path. Behind him, Bostitch bellowed in a berserk rage.

Solarrin struggled to get out of the backpack. His bad leg was snagged on a strap. He clipped himself in the jaw with the staff, but finally managed to wiggle free. He lay gasping on the rocky ground as the second troll continued on its way. He was tempted to let it go, but all of their money and supplies were stored in the compartments.

"Hoi! Eater of children!" he called.

He had no use for the elves and their pretty spell words and gestures. The magic he used was older, different. The effects were much the same, but Solarrin wrestled with different forces every time he cast a spell, touching the ancient powers of the very primal universe itself.

A ball of fire bloomed between his hands. The troll, hearing his call, stopped and turned. Its eyes widened at the sight of fire, the one thing trolls feared.

Solarrin hurled the fireball. It struck the troll and exploded in a great gout of flame. The troll flew end over end, pawing desperately at itself and rolling in the dirt. When it lay still, Solarrin looked toward Bostitch.

The first troll was battered into a shapeless mass. Bostitch, his face frozen in a fierce snarl, held it by the arms and slammed it repeatedly against the ground. A third troll climbed onto a rock and leapt down onto the minotaur's back.

Bostitch flung the first troll to the side, where it smashed into a boulder and lay still. He grabbed at the one on his back, but the troll bit his groping hand. Roaring, he raced in a circle, then stopped abruptly and flipped the troll forward over his horns. It miraculously landed on its feet and scrambled away.

Seeing his prey escaping, Bostitch lowered his head and charged. His horns caught the troll square in the back and impaled it. He jerked his head, and the troll flew off, landing with a bone-jarring crash.

Solarrin limped toward Bostitch, grimacing as his bad leg thudded against the hard ground. He was within a few yards of the minotaur when he happened to glance down and saw his shadow outlined on the rocky ground. And looming over his rotund shape was another shadow, that of a large creature with gangling arms.

He spun, but his clumsiness betrayed him. He fell heavily. The troll leaped toward him.

Before it landed, it was snagged out of midair by Bostitch's big hands. Solarrin, wheezing, pushed everything else aside and summoned another spell of fire. Troll blood pattered down on him. The creature shrieked as thunder as Bostitch tore its arms off.

Another fireball grew between Solarrin's hands. He hurled it directly upward, at the struggling, suspended troll over him. This time, instead of exploding, it sheathed the troll in a coating of fire.

Bostitch, startled out of his fury by the burst of flame that covered the troll, let go of it and jumped back. The burning troll narrowly missed landing on Solarrin. It rolled and thrashed just as the other one had done, and in the end collapsed into a smoldering pile.

The stench of charred flesh hung thick and greasy in the air. It stung Solarrin's weak lungs and rasped in his throat. His spellcasting and exertion had left him weary.

"Little man?" Bostitch asked, bending down to peer at him. "Hurts?"

Solarrin staggered to his feet. His staff was lying down the path, a short way that would have been nothing to a healthy being. To him, however, it looked like miles. He braced himself against Bostitch's meaty leg. He could feel the minotaur's strength and vitality pulsing through the large veins in his thigh. Bostitch was barely even winded by the fight, while he, Solarrin, was close to losing consciousness. He felt the minotaur's life force, and it angered him. Why should this great dunce of an ox be blessed with such good health while Solarrin, the greatest mind of all time, was frail and crippled?

His teeth ground together in anger, and he whispered words of another spell, one sacred to Haarkon, god of the dead. Risky, especially in his fragile state. His fingers curled. His yellow, cracked nails scratched through the short brown hairs that covered Bostitch's hide. He felt the minotaur's life force, and called it to himself.

Bostitch's breathing became suddenly more labored, and his pulse quickened. Solarrin's uneven breaths smoothed out. His frantically racing heart slowed to a more normal rhythm. The energies that had been depleted by his spellcasting were suddenly restored, leaving him as fresh and relaxed as if he'd had several hours of rest. Bostitch's wide shoulders sagged as he yawned cavernously.

"Rest, good servant," he said magnanimously. "Soon we will reach the castle. All the secrets of life and death! All the powers of the darkest worlds. Once they are mine, nothing shall stop me from taking my rightful place. As Archmage!"

Bostitch, already sound asleep, didn't reply.

*   *   *

"So these are the Scattered Hills," Sybil said, looking around in disgust. "Ugly."

"Be quiet for once in your life," Jessa snapped. "Nobody asked for your approval."

Cat gave them both a warning look.

"My eye can see a bit farther," Arien commented. "I believe I can make out the Whiterock Mountains. They appear most harsh and unwelcoming."

"No shade," Sybil groused. "Do you have any idea what the sun will do to my skin? Fair, creamy skin is all the fashion now."

"Be still with your vanity!" Jessa said.

"I'd rather be vain that look like a strip of dried leather!"

Cat waved her arms in the air. "That's enough! If you must argue, let it wait!"

"Well, if she wasn't so jealous—" Sybil huffed.

"Jealous!" Jessa flared. "Of a preening slut like you?"

"Old maid!"

"Roundheels strumpet!"

"*Durak!*" Arien cried, clapping his hands overhead. The clear sky suddenly burst with the sound of thunder.

Sybil screamed, though it was lost in the rumbling roar that rolled back and forth across the hills. The horses reared and squealed. Greyquin, who had been standing beside Bear, jumped nearly half his own height off the ground.

Cat put her hands over her ears and turned to look up at Arien. He alone among them was placid, sitting astride his horse and gazing at Sybil and Jessa with calmness tinged with contempt.

Kiah spiraled dizzily downward and landed unsteadily on Jessa's arm. Rayke and Alphonse shook their heads. All of them looked at the slender elfmage as their hearing slowly began to return.

"Now then," he said evenly. "Sybil, Jessa, did you not heed Cat? If you cannot put aside your differences, perhaps one or both of you must leave us. That grieves me, for I know that both of your skills are muchly valuable and needed."

"I'm not leaving," Jessa said sullenly. "You'd never make it back through the forest without me."

"Well, I'm not leaving either," announced Sybil. "Talopea's healing powers might be needed."

"Then you both need to follow orders," Alphonse growled.

Jessa gave Sybil one last hostile glare, and started choosing a path through the hills. She moved surely, Kiah riding the air above her. Cat nudged her horse forward until she rode near Jessa.

"I wish you two could get along better," she said.

"It's no use." Jessa shifted her bow to her other hand and took a drink from the waterskin slung at her belt. She offered it to Cat.

"She's really not that bad," Cat said. "She's embarrassing sometimes, but—"

"She's mad. And she's dangerous. I'd bet my last arrow she's been telling you all about men and how wonderful they are. Don't listen to her, Cat. She's got less sense than a hatter. I don't know what herbs they throw in the fire at the Talopea temple, but there's nothing pleasant about what happens with men. It's the most awful, terrible thing you can imagine."

Cat stared, surprised. She didn't think she'd ever heard Jessa talk so much, and certainly not about this topic. "But—"

"Even the ones who seem kind are really all the same." She scowled back over her shoulder at the others. "Even him." She jerked her chin toward Arien.

"Arien?"

"Just like all the rest."

"No, not him."

"Yes, him. Just because he's got a handsome face and a soft voice doesn't make him any different from the rest of them. Greedy, ruthless bastards, all of them. They only want one thing from a woman. That's why I came along. I knew if I didn't, something terrible would happen to you. But don't worry. I know how to deal with them. As long as I'm here, you're safe. Won't be the first time I've killed men." She stalked ahead, and Cat let her horse fall back until she was even with Bear and Greyquin.

"What are you thinking, Cat?" he asked cheerfully. "You look like someone trying to unravel the riddles of the universe."

"I was just talking to Jessa," she said slowly. "She was talking about men."

His eyes widened. "Men? Jessa? That's a surprise. Why?"

"She says she's worried about me, and that if she wasn't here, I'd be in danger. But that's silly. I'm not in any danger. Not from among the seven of us, that is."

"Ah," he said, his little face growing solemn as he tugged thoughtfully on his salt-and-pepper beard. "Well, she doesn't trust many people. It probably has something to do with Arien."

"What do you mean? She hardly knows him. He's a friend."

Greyquin grinned. "Is he, now? How good a friend, little Cat?"

"Desist, I hear enough of that from Sybil! And don't call me little, I'm taller than you at least! I but do not understand why she and Sybil say such different things! Who speaks true?"

"Oh, mice." Greyquin's breath whooshed out, and he took another deep one. "I don't think that's for me to explain. Most people, most normal people, aren't like them. If I were in your boots, I'd listen to my own good sense."

"Thank you, Greyquin." She glanced back at Arien. "If only I knew what it was telling me!"

*   *   *

"Here's where we camp tonight," Jessa said.

Cat dismounted and walked slowly around the site, stripping off her gloves. "Are you sure it's safe? We won't be able to see dangers coming at us."

Several tall, jagged standing stones formed a crude ring, encircling a patch of land with a larger, monolithic stone in the center. The setting sun cast rust-colored light across the landscape. The hollows darkened into purple shadow. Stunted trees marched along a dry creekbed, their bare branches starkly outlined against the sky.

"It's fine." Jessa dropped her backpack. "The person on watch will sit up there." She pointed an arrow at the big rock. "The ground's loose. We'll hear anything that approaches."

"Yes," Arien said, swinging out of his saddle, "and the stones will shield us from the worst of the wind, and provide a blocking for our firelight. It makes for a natural fortress."

"Right," Jessa admitted grudgingly.

"If something does come, we'll be cornered like merchants in an alley," Cat fretted.

"I suppose that is an area with which you have some experience," Arien said teasingly.

She archly ignored him. "Are you sure this is a natural fortress? It seems too convenient to be natural. Besides, there are stairs."

"Stairs?" Arien moved to join her.

"See?" She motioned. "You can barely see them, but here they are. Stairs. We can't be the first people to find this place." She climbed them swiftly and easily, and gasped. "I can see the mountains! Even Mount Yrej!" She folded her legs and sat, hugging her knees. "The wind must be coming from the north. It's cold."

Arien followed her, not as surely, but still with grace. The wind threw back his hood and the dying sunlight turned his hair to silver-edged flame.

"Stairs," he chuckled. "Hardly handholds to me, but to one such as yourself who scaled a sheer stone wall before my very eyes, they might count as stairs. If ever I become of such skill to earn the rank of Archmage, and choose to build myself a mountain stronghold," he added, gazing keenly toward the horizon, "remind me to choose some other design. That is undeniably ghastly."

Though she could have sat all night watching him, Cat made herself turn her sight back to the mountains.

One loomed taller than all the others. Dark and immense, it would have been imposing even without the leering skull carved into its base. The face of the skull looked to be at least a hundred feet high, still dwarfed by the rising peaks above it. The eyes of the skull glowed, twin flickers of red in the dusky gloom. Crumbling stone walls, towers, and ruined buildings surrounded it.

Arien sighed and leaned back, bracing his weight on his elbows as he looked up at the sky. The first stars were beginning to appear. The sight of them seemed to sadden him.

"Arien," Cat said softly, "What is it?"

"One hundred years ago today," he whispered, then blinked and looked at her, shaken out of his strange mood. "Cat. Forgive me. I was lost in thought. My mind does sometimes wander. What did you say?"

"I asked what was wrong. What happened a hundred years ago?"

"Something unspeakable." He shivered, and she longed to put her arms around him but didn't quite dare. "Cat, we must find that book."

"I could be a better help if I knew all the truth."

He shook his head, sitting up and taking one of her hands in both of his. He turned it over, tracing some design in her palm. It was her turn to shiver as his touch thrilled through her.

"I wish I could tell you," he said. "I honestly do. But I dare not. Not yet. The day will come when I must tell you all of it, whereupon you will turn from me in horror. Forgive me my selfishness, for I would delay that sad day as long as possible."

"I told you before, it doesn't matter how horrible it is. Arien, I want to help." She clasped his hands firmly. "You're my friend."

"Dinner's ready," Jessa said coldly from right behind them. She had climbed the monolith so silently that neither of them had noticed her until she spoke.

"Um . . . thank you," Cat said, quickly releasing Arien's hands.

"I am not hungry," Arien said. "I shall remain here and stand the first watch."

As Cat ate, she kept looking at Arien seated high above them. For a moment, he had been about to unburden his soul, but that moment had passed. She hoped there would come another.

*   *   *

"Wyverns!" Alphonse called.

Cat wheeled her horse around, rising in the stirrups. Beside her, she saw Arien doing the same, looking skyward.

Five of the dragonlike creatures flew toward them. Their wings, though they appeared to be nothing more than thin tissue stretched over fragile bone, beat the air powerfully. Whip-like tails lashed behind them.

Jessa drew back her bow. Cat's horse bucked under her, nearly throwing her. As she fought the panicked beast for control, she heard Greyquin trying to calm Bear and Rayke and Alphonse yelling advice to each other.

"They're attacking!" Sybil cried, brandishing her sword as the five creatures dove with wings swept back and talons outstretched.

Jessa's arrow flew straight and true. It caught the leading wyvern in the breast. The wyvern roared in pain and collided with the nearest of its fellows. That one responded with a vicious bite, and the two were suddenly locked in combat, biting and clawing at each other.

The rest swerved around them and continued their dive. Cat drew her own sword, all too aware that those talons were big enough to pierce her body clear through.

"*Durak!*" Arien said, clapping his hands.

Thunder shattered the sky. The force of the sound sent wyverns tumbling through the air. Two of them dropped like stones and lay motionless. The last caught itself moments before impact and flapped its wings frantically, swirling up dust into Cat's eyes.

The two that had fallen were struggling to rise. Sybil followed Rayke and Alphonse in a charge. Jessa's bow sang again and her arrow tore through a wing, leaving a ragged hole.

That beast plummeted and landed near Cat. Still blinking dust from her eyes, she leaped from the saddle and raced toward it.

Its head shot out, amazingly fast and limber on the long neck, and its jaws snapped together inches from Cat's face. She clubbed its snout aside with her left hand and brought the sword around in her right. The blade chopped into the wyvern's neck.

The wyvern shrieked. It reared back on its stubby legs and swiftly enfolded Cat in its wings. Its head darted down and bit, catching a mouthful of her cloak but nothing more. She slashed through the wing membrane. It gave way like brittle old cloth and she ducked out under the wing bone. Behind the beast now, she scrambled onto its back.

Though its wing was shredded, the wyvern gave a mighty lurch into the air. Cat grabbed one of the short spines that ridged its neck. She clung to it, wild with excitement as her crippled steed sailed unsteadily a few feet above the ground.

The long neck bent with serpentine grace and she was suddenly confronted with the head, craned around to bite. She jammed her sword in its mouth, then, as it withdrew, hacked at its wing joint.

It plunged down. Cat jumped off, scrambling to safety. The wyvern sailed on a bit further and then piled gracelessly into the ground and lay still.

"That was quite a ride!" Greyquin called, galloping up to her on Bear. "And quite a battle! We feast tonight!"

"Feast? On that?" She wrinkled her nose. "Are they any good?"

"There's only one way to find out. I hear they serve dragon meat at the Lord's Retreat, imported all the way from the coast of Hachland. This can't be that much different!"

"The kitchens at the Lord's Retreat don't have you working in them," she pointed out. "Remember the oatmeal?"

"I wish everyone would leave off about that," he muttered. "That was three years ago!"

Doubtful, she left him to his makeshift butchery and rejoined the others. Rayke had suffered a nasty bite, but Sybil was tending it in Talopea's own unique way, causing Cat to avert her eyes.

"Wyverns do not attack in packs," Arien was saying as she joined him and Alphonse by one of the fallen beasts. "They are well-documented as solitary hunters."

"So explain five," Alphonse challenged.

"They have signs of spells upon them. Controlled. Guardians of the castle. Selbon's work, I should think. We'll find it not undefended, this I knew, but I had not expected creatures so fearsome as this. It shall prove more perilous than we had anticipated." He ran his fingers through his long hair and shook his head. "An Archmage, even one believed to be dead, is not to be trifled with. Would that we could reconsider. Yet I, for one, must go."

"And I for two," Cat said. "If there's a chance at all that my mother is in there, I have to go."

"If you're going, I'm going," Alphonse stated.

"Death to go, death not to," Arien said in a low voice. "Better to perish in the attempt than in the weakness."

Alphonse looked warily at him, then over to Cat. He raised a bristly eyebrow.

"What do you mean, death?" she asked.

"If I fail, if I cannot find that which I seek, there will be no other choice. I cannot go on living the way that I have been. If Selbon's library does not hold the answer that not even the Great Library of Thanis could provide, then my quest is hopeless. Without hope, there is no life."

"I think you'd better tell us just what it is that you're looking for," Alphonse said.

He looked at them, and there was such anguish in his eyes that Cat felt her heart constrict. Even Alphonse was affected.

Arien took a deep breath. "Generations ago, a curse of unspeakable horror was placed upon my family, by elven Archmages of old. I am the last of my line. Either I find a way to end the curse, or it dies with me. Were I not a coward, I should have ended it and myself long ago."

Cat felt his arm tense, and she knew he was expecting her to pull away in fear. She did not take her hand away. Instead, despite Alphonse's presence, she lay her other hand along his cheek and turned his head so that he could no longer look away from her.

"We'll help you," she promised.

Alphonse cleared his throat uncomfortably. "Right. We'll help." He awkwardly clapped Arien on the back, then hastily walked away.

"Why do you do this?" Arien asked. "Why do you endanger yourselves to help a stranger?"

"You're not a stranger, Arien," she said. "You're a friend. I don't have many, so I'm not going to let go of one without a fight."

*   *   *

The obvious way is rarely the right way.

The Book of Yor.

"Are we ever going to get there?" Sybil moaned, rising from her bedroll. Her hair was artfully mussed, and the thin linen undertunic she slept in had slid just far enough down one shoulder to barely cover her bosom. She stretched, turning in a provocative display, and pouted at the lack of reaction.

Arien hid a smile. Rayke, who out of all of them was the one most likely to enjoy her show, was still sprawled under his blanket, sound asleep.

Cat, on the other hand, occupied far too much of his attention. She sat on a rock, one leg drawn up, head turned to the side as she combed her glossy curls.

He was deeply troubled by his growing awareness of her. What had begun as a faintly repulsed fascination, seeing an elfkin in the flesh, had altered in the course of their journey. He had at some point quit thinking of her as elfkin, but as woman. Young, enticing, even desirable. It went against everything he had been taught to believe.

He dared not let these stirrings develop into a true attraction. If that happened, her mixed blood would be the least of her worries.

"We should reach the mountain today," Jessa said. She was already up and dressed, gnawing on a hunk of cold roast wyvern, which had despite their misgivings had turned out surprisingly good.

"Thank Talopea," Sybil sighed. She nudged Rayke with her toe. "Wake up, you lazy good-for-nothing."

"He must have been good for something last night," Alphonse said, squatting beside Greyquin. "Woke me right up. Come on, shorty, let me show you how to get a fire going."

"You?" Greyquin snorted. "You couldn't start a fire in a hayloft after a seven-year drought."

"Oh? Just watch me." He leaned over the coals and blew. Ashes swirled up in a cloud, and he extinguished the tiny flicker of flame Greyquin had managed to produce.

"Impressive," Greyquin said dryly.

Cat laughed. "You two. The way you're going, we'll need a dragon to get that fire started."

Rayke yawned, sitting up. "What's the big deal about a fire anyway? Let's just wolf down some bread and get riding."

"In a hurry to die?" Alphonse inquired.

"Just ready for some excitement," Rayke said, grinning.

"If you're in the mood for excitement . . ." Sybil trailed off, licking her lips. "I'll race you to the creek."

Rayke leapt up, abruptly wide awake. Sybil squealed girlishly and dashed off with him in pursuit.

Jessa, looking ill, tossed her chunk of meat to Bear. "Now it'll take us forever to get started," she complained.

"In that case," Cat decided, "we might as well have a fire and a hot breakfast. Arien, if you please?"

"Fire is not my best area," he warned. "Better am I at magics of chill and ice. Still, the spell should be simple." He added some wood, then nonchalantly flicked his fingers at it. "*Flammes.*"

At once, flames blazed cheerily in the ring of rocks. Greyquin and Alphonse exchanged a sour look. "Why hasn't he been doing this every time?" Greyquin grumped. "Well, it's your task now, Arien!"

Eventually, to the tune of Jessa's mutterings and grumblings, they were on their way. Mount Yrej loomed ever larger, and summer was lost in the chill winds sweeping down from the snowcapped peaks. They began to pass the decayed remnants of siege engines, the crumbling ruins of old battlements and towers, and broken lengths of wall covered with dry black vines.

At Jessa's insistence, they left the horses in a sheltered grassy nook where a small spring bubbled from a cracked rock. "We can't take them inside," she explained. "They'll be fine here. Food and water, but they can't be seen from the outside."

"If there's anybody to see them," Sybil said, looking across the desolate landscape.

Here and there, pieces of ancient armor had been exposed by wind. Arien thought again of the rumors he'd heard as a boy. These were the sole remains of the soldiers who had fought, fallen, and risen to fight again at Red Snow Field.

Leaving the horses, though Greyquin insisted on bringing Bear, they proceeded on foot. They were all more alert now, watchful. Jessa kept an arrow to the string. Alphonse kept his crossbow at hand and his eyes on the sky.

"Stop," Jessa hissed, flinging up a hand. She motioned for them all to stay back, and cautiously approached a beaten path through the overgrown grass. She bent and scanned the ground. "Tracks. Most look like boots, the kind with metal nails on the bottom."

"Probably orcish," Alphonse said. "That's what my clan wore. Not quiet, but useful for stepping on an enemy's foot."

"So that's the secret of the mighty orc warriors," Greyquin chuckled. "They stomp on your foot, and while you're hopping around and swearing, they slice your guts open."

"Want me to show you how well it works?" Alphonse growled, lifting his own boot.

"Not now," Cat intervened. "Lead on, Jessa."

Jessa nodded and waved for Kiah. The rest of them followed, and as they reached a breach in the wall, they got their first close view of Castle Selbon.

Arien paused, staring. He'd heard the tales, of course, but he was still taken aback by the sight. It was far bigger than he'd imagined. The skull face that made up the front of the castle towered ominously. The stone jaws of the skull gaped wide, revealing a rusted portcullis with bars as thick as a strong man's arm. Above, the twin eye sockets glowed with reddish light.

"Livana," he said, invoking the name of the elven goddess of magic and making a small sign of protection. "He was mad indeed to build such a thing."

Sybil shuddered. "Cat, do you really think this is a good idea?"

"It's a bit late for second thoughts now," she said.

"Look." Jessa motioned to the ground. "The other tracks. These are from something hoofed, but not a horse. The pattern's wrong. Minotaur, possibly."

"Minotaur!" Alphonse bared his teeth. "I've always wanted to try my strength against one of them."

"Yeah," chimed in Greyquin. "It's probably the only chance you'd have to fight something as big and dumb as yourself."

"What else?" Arien asked, seeing from Jessa's tight, frustrated expression that she yet had more to say.

"It stopped here," she continued, shooting him a look that suggested she didn't know whether to be grateful or annoyed. "And set something down. From there, I see two sets of tracks."

"Another minotaur?" Rayke asked, gripping his sword.

She shook her head. "Smaller. Much smaller. Maybe even a gnome."

Greyquin cocked his head eagerly. "Gnome?"

"But crippled," Jessa said. "See, how the one leg drags? The tracks lead over there, toward that round tower."

"We'd better look," Rayke said uneasily. "Don't want them coming up behind us. I've seen minotaurs fight in the sand arenas in Tradersport."

"I'll go," Greyquin volunteered brightly. "Maybe that gnome needs help."

"I hardly think so," a strange voice said, causing them all to whirl in alarm.

Arien's first impulse was to smile. The speaker was an aged gnome in robes of deep maroon. With his black-streaked beard, staff, and sinister expression, he looked like nothing more than a caricature of an evil wizard. The only flaw was that such mages were usually shown as tall and cadaverous, while the gnome was round as an egg. One look at the gnome's glittering black eyes quelled any urges to smile. Such urges faded even further when the minotaur stepped from behind a broken segment of wall. The creature was not as tall as Alphonse, but broader and thick with muscle.

Cat boldly moved forward. "Who are you?" she said, her hand resting on the hilt of her sword in a way that was almost casual but not lost on the two strangers.

The gnome drew himself up to his full height. Though Cat was not tall, he nevertheless failed to come higher than her chest.

"I am Solarrin," he announced. "Archmage of the Universe!"

As he uttered the ludicrous title, his voice broke into a fit of coughing that left him wheezing and leaning on his staff for support. When he caught his breath, he glared at Cat as if she was responsible for his plight. "Who are you, you slip of a crossling girl?"

Cat tensed. Alphonse rumbled deep in his chest and started forward, but she regained her composure and held him back with a gesture. "Cat Sabledrake, of Thanis."

"And the rest of this mismatched band of ruffians? Grave-robbers come to plunder the hidden wealth of Selbon's tomb?" He sneered, sweeping them all with a disdainful look. "You won't last until dawn."

"Solarrin," Greyquin said thoughtfully. "I'm from Gnome Keep too. I've heard of you."

"Yes! I am that selfsame Solarrin of whom you have no doubt heard countless tales of power and might! I am Solarrin, greatest of mages, come to seek the lost knowledge of one of my many, lesser, predecessors." He indicated the minotaur. "Oh, and this miserable wretch is Bostitch."

"You are a student of necromancy?" Arien asked, trying to hide the instinctive distaste he felt.

"A master of necromancy!" he corrected sharply. "Does that offend your tender sensibilities elf? Do you, like all of your airy, starry-eyed brethren, shrink from the vast powers of death? Have you a name, if it is of interest to me?"

"Arien Mirida," he replied. "Junior Librarian of the Great Library of Thanis."

"Junior Librarian?" Solarrin sniffed. "This is hardly the place one would expect to find the likes of you. What is your mission? Do you plan to write some dull historical text on this desolate place, that will lay moldering in the archives, unread and unwanted? Better you should chronicle your meeting with me, for in years to come real history shall be made! Yes elf, you are most privileged to be here! I will permit you to interview me at a later time."

"I am not a chronicler," Arien said. "My business here is research."

Solarrin snorted and turned his attention to Sybil. "A Talopean," he sneered. "A strange place to find one of your lusty order. Come you to convert the legions of orcs?"

"No! You speak offense to the ears of my goddess!"

"Quiet!" Cat ordered. She looked down at Solarrin. "Are you trying to make enemies of everyone, or is it just a knack?"

"Enemies?" He chortled, then coughed again. "The likes of you are beneath my notice.

I have no intention of wasting my energies on any of you, unless you propose to foolishly throw your lives away by attacking me."

"We can take care of ourselves," Cat said. "What are you doing here?"

"I have come to claim as mine the legacies of Selbon. Secrets of necromancy he held and guarded jealously will be mine, as they should be. What of yourselves? You have the look of mercenaries with no regard for anything but putting gold in your purses."

"Now, just a moment," Rayke began, sounding offended.

Cat waved him back as well. "Our business is none of yours. Unless you plan to try and stop us."

"Certainly not. I plan to join you."

"What?" Jessa snapped, echoed by the rest.

"Join us?" Cat repeated, frowning. "Why?"

"Yes, why?" said Greyquin. "If you're as skilled as you say, you don't need our help."

"I never claimed to need your help," Solarrin said witheringly. "It is you who need mine. You would not pass the gates without the help of a wizard."

"We have a wizard," Cat said.

"I thank you for your kindness, my dear," Arien said, "but I confess my powers are not unlimited."

Solarrin snorted. "A dabbler. Elves haven't a serious bone in their overly tall bodies. *I* control the elements, the powers of life and death. If you stand a chance of venturing within the castle, you need me."

"Cat, don't listen to him," Sybil pleaded.

"I'd rather have him with us than against us," Greyquin said.

"Oh, in Haarkon's name," Solarrin said, eliciting a round of shudders and gestures of protection to various gods. "With you or against you? Has everyone in Gnome Keep become so thick-headed that they see the world either one way or the other? I have no interest in killing you. Though it would be a simple task, it would accomplish nothing. You are insignificant in the fate of the world. Your deaths would mean as little as your lives already do."

"I don't want to listen to that all the while," Alphonse grumbled.

"It is you most of all who would benefit from Bostitch's presence," Solarrin said. "His strength, combined with yours, could topple mountains. The two of you, I doubt not, could force that portcullis."

The orkin and the minotaur looked at each other, sizing each other up. Bostitch appeared to have ignored most of the conversation, watching the others with muddled alertness.

"What do you think?" Cat asked Alphonse, quietly enough that only Arien overheard.

"I think I could take him. I wouldn't know until I'd seen him fight."

"No, big fellow, that's not what I meant. Do you think we should let them come with us?"

He shrugged. "I don't care for the looks of that fat gnome. He puts me in mind of a bloated spider, all full of poison and ready to bite."

Arien leaned closer. "However," he said softly, "if he is even half as skilled as he seems to think he is, he could be a valuable addition to our endeavor."

"Why don't the rest of you go whisper with your friends?" Solarrin loudly said to the other four. "I'll be over here, waiting for your momentous decision. Bah, you'd think the future of all life was hanging in the balance." He hobbled to a large rock and leaned on it. Bostitch moved to stand behind him, still keeping an eye on Alphonse.

"He'll slow us down," Jessa said. "I've seen snails creep along a log faster than he moves."

"Cat, you can't possibly be considering taking him along," Sybil said. She pulled off her gauntlet and felt Cat's forehead. "It's too much sun, isn't it? Come on, we'll sit you in the shade and get you a nice cool drink, and this madness will pass."

"Sybil, I'm fine." Cat batted her hand away. "Rayke, Greyquin, what do you think?"

Rayke grinned. "I wasn't hired to think, sweetheart. Whatever Arien decides, I'll go along with. I'm one of those mercenaries with no regard for anything but gold, like Solarrin said. If it matters though, he reminds me of Lord Marl. I wouldn't trust him with a bent copper mark."

"You know Lord Marl?" Cat asked, making a face as she said the detested name of one of Thanis' worst. "How?"

"He hires a lot of swords. Never worked for him myself, but I've heard a lot. Nobody stays long, because he's such a foul wart of a man."

"For once, I have to agree with Sybil," Jessa said reluctantly. "A necromancer! Dead things should stay that way."

"Wait a minute," interrupted Greyquin. "Solarrin's a necromancer. Selbon was a necromancer. There might be things in there that we don't know anything about. Walking dead, left over from the battle. He could help us."

"It would not surprise me if there were still *dira'rhun*," Arien said. "They last forever, unless destroyed. I have no power over them."

"Greyquin, you said you knew of Solarrin. What have you heard?" Cat asked.

"Magic is rare among my people. Solarrin's the only wizard in ten generations, and the only gnome ever to study necromancy. Some said he killed people on purpose so he could raise them as walking dead. Or that he drank blood, or consorted with demons. Whether he's truly of Archmage rank, I have no idea."

"We don't need him," Sybil persisted. "I can beseech Talopea's holy light to turn away the walking dead."

"Sorry, Sybil, but I think it's worth a try." Cat went to Solarrin. "Welcome, I suppose."

"You've made the right decision," Solarrin said.

*   *   *

"We're strong enough," Alphonse claimed. "Bostitch and I, we could pull the whole place down stone by stone."

"Greyquin could do that, given enough time," Jessa pointed out. "You're talking about trying to force that portcullis. They'd hear it from here to Thanis."

Cat walked away from the discussion, getting a good look at the face of the castle.

They'd had no trouble picking their way through the ruined walls to the very jaws themselves. The stone teeth, slabs the size of vault doors, reared out of the earth and framed the mouth leading to the heavy iron gate. After a quick examination, they'd retreated to a secluded corner to discuss possibilities.

She ran her hands along the curved wall that made up the lowest part of the skull. It was rough, worn by years of wind, and pitted in places. She guessed that the bigger pits were the result of catapult fire from the siege engines during the battle.

"Incredible, is it not?" Arien asked, coming up alongside her.

"How did they do it? Look, there aren't any mortar lines. No cut stones. They must have carved it right out of the mountain's own rock."

"Or shaped it."

"Shaped it?"

"Mages with a talent for working with the earth can cause stone to flow like warm wax, shaping it as they desire. When the spell is finished, the rock hardens again, but holds whatever form it was given."

"It's held up fairly well, though." She craned her head back, peering up. Overhead, the glow from the eye sockets was steady.

"The glow is most likely the result of another spell," Arien said. "I could not tell you without examining it."

"How far back do you think the sockets go?"

"Again, I could not say. I assume that they are some manner of viewing station, situated well above the height of the outer walls as they are."

"I wonder . . ." She unhooked her sword and handed it to him. "I'm going to see if I can climb it."

"What?" He drew back, looking alarmed. "Cat, you cannot be serious. You will surely fall."

"If the eyes are a way in, we could all climb up and not have to worry about the gate at all."

He laughed, a warm silvery sound. "My dear, even if you can scale this rock, I know the rest of us cannot."

"I could lower a rope. It's slanted enough. I'm sure it would work." The more she thought about it, the more convinced she was. "If I took everything out of my pack except a rope and something to affix it with, I could carry it up with me."

"Are you certain about this?"

She nodded, picking up her backpack and rummaging through it. "If there's nothing up there, we'll figure out another way to get in."

"Cat, can you help me?" Alphonse asked, coming over to them. "Somebody needs to talk to Jessa. We've come all this way, and now she doesn't think we should go in. I keep telling her that most orcs sleep during the day."

"Don't worry, big fellow. We might not have to worry about the gate. See how much rope everyone has, would you? We'll need enough to reach all the way down from that eye, so the rest of you can climb up."

"You want to climb that? Maybe Sybil's right," he said. "You have been in the sun too much. If you spend your whole life in dark alleys, the way you do, it's no surprise the sun addles you."

She swatted his arm. "I'm not addled. I'm just trying to find a way around a problem. This is worth a look, at least."

"I'll humor you," he grumbled. He gathered rope and tied the lengths together with sturdy orc-knots, known the Northlands over for securely binding captives.

"Don't do this, Cat," Sybil said. "If the orcs are sleeping, we can sneak in the front way."

"Let her try," Solarrin said, unexpectedly supportive. "If I had built this, which I obviously did not since it is so primitive, I would have located my living quarters high, away from the reeking rabble of my forces and the screams of the prisoners."

Cat took off her gloves and tucked them through her belt. She slung the rope-filled pack over her shoulders and shifted, trying to adjust the weight. "It's heavier than I thought," she admitted. "But not too bad."

"Good luck," Arien said. He looked worried, but did not try to change her mind. Instead, he touched her forehead in an elven gesture of well-wishing. "Livana watch over you."

The climb was not as difficult as she had feared. Nicks and depressions, not visible from beneath, provided handholds and footholds. The weight of the pack was awkward but not crippling. She had long ago learned that the secret of climbing was to look neither up nor down, concentrating instead on nothing more than the next hold. To the others, gathered in an anxious knot below her, she knew it must look deceptively simple.

The red light blazed more brightly as she got closer. She paused for a brief rest, bracing her legs against the stone to take the weight off her aching arms, and a sudden shriek split the air.

Something darted at her. A flurry of dark feathers filled her vision. A talon dug into her cheek, just missing her eye. She flung out a hand to ward off her attacker. It collided with her. She teetered on the edge of balance, but the extra weight of the pack settled the matter. She lost her grip.

Cat did not scream. The instant she felt herself begin to fall, she kicked both feet against the stone as hard as she could, pushing herself outward into open air.

As she plummeted, her body turning like the creature she'd been named for, she saw the black feathery thing diving at her again, talons outstretched.

*   *   *

Cat was falling.

The huge bird, the size of a swan but black as tar, swooped toward her.

Sybil screamed. Alphonse, closest to her, clapped a hand over her mouth before more than a squeak emerged.

Arien reacted faster than he would have believed possible. He raised his hand, palm cupped in a catching motion. *"Shalis!"* he cried.

At the same moment, Jessa's bow sang. Feathers puffed in a cloud from the black bird as the arrow pierced its breast.

Cat, already twisting in midair, was seized by the force of his spell. Her descent slowed until she was floating gently downward at half her former speed.

Kiah screeched in triumph and attacked the dying black bird.

Cat drifted down like a snowflake. Her look of childlike wonder made Arien laugh aloud. He moved to meet her, catching her.

"It is not often that I have young women falling into my arms," he said, smiling.

"Arien! Your magic? That was wonderful!"

"Sometimes even a cat may need a bit of help landing on her feet." He set her down, but did not immediately let go of her.

Such a joy, to hold her in his arms! He was surprised again by how small she was. The top of her head barely reached his chin. It gave her an illusion of vulnerability. She looked up at him, so shy and trusting, so lovely. How deep her eyes were! How blue, as the night sky!

He slowly raised his hand and touched her dark hair where it curled around her face. His fingertips brushed her skin. Her grip on his shoulder softened into a caress.

He started to incline his head toward her, realizing that he was going to kiss her and knowing that it was wrong, but no more able to stop himself than he could stop the seasons from turning.

"Cat! Sweet Talopea, you scared me half to death!" Sybil burst between them, pushing Arien aside and flinging her arms around the girl. "Are you hurt?"

"N-no," Cat stammered. "Just a scratch."

Sybil examined the claw mark. "It's not too bad, but I'd better heal it just the same. You don't want a scar on your pretty face. Those claws could be filthy. We can't take any chances."

"Her whole life seems to consist of taking chances," Arien said, barely hearing the words as they passed his lips. He backed away, glancing quickly around to see if any of the others had noticed his lapse. Only Alphonse seemed to be watching him coldly.

Arien turned away and began studying the cliff as if he'd never seen stone before. What he'd nearly done was unforgivable. Dangerous. Deadly. If he did not watch himself more closely, if he did not control his impulses, Cat could come to wish the fall had killed her. It would have been far quicker and cleaner than the fate which would otherwise await her.

*   *   *

"He likes you," Sybil murmured, running her fingers over Cat's healed scratch.

"Stop it," Cat hissed, glancing over at Arien. He was a fair distance away, but she knew his ears were keen. She was still trembling from his touch, affected more by that than she'd been by the fall.

Jessa came over with the bird, holding it up. Her arrow stuck all the way through it. Kiah perched proudly on her shoulder. "I've never seen anything like this before," she said.

Sybil ignored her. "He does," she insisted. "I saw the way he was looking at you. Why have you wasted so much time? Two bedrolls are warmer than one."

"It's nothing like that," she protested, feeling her face flame. "He just caught me."

"And he didn't want to let you go. Poor Cat. I had to do something, or else he would have kissed you right in front of everyone. I know how embarrassed you would have been. Believe me, it was the hardest thing I've ever done, having to separate you like that!"

"Leave her alone," Jessa said. "Do you have to corrupt other people and ruin their lives the way you've ruined yours?"

"Corrupt?" Sybil said angrily. "I am only trying to encourage Cat to release her sensual spirit. Arien would be perfect for her. You're misjudging him."

"They're all the same! I'm judging him exactly right. If I wasn't here, he'd do whatever he wanted with Cat, and you'd stand there and cheer him on."

"No more!" Cat said, standing between them. "Gods, please, no more!"

Jessa gave her a desperate, hurt look. She flung the bird to the ground and stormed off.

Sybil watched her go, then turned to Cat. "Cat, darling, I want you to listen to me," she began with uncharacteristic seriousness.

"Another time," Cat said wearily. "For now, let it rest. Let it rest. I've got a wall to climb."

*   *   *

"I object to this," Solarrin said. "He will shed. That is what dogs do. And he will shed in my transportation."

Bostitch's backpack now held a very unhappy wardog. Bear was too well-trained to bark or howl, but he whined and tried to lick their hands as they secured the straps that would keep him from falling out.

"Dog hair makes me sneeze," Solarrin complained.

"It's all right, Bear," Greyquin said soothingly. "Not much longer. All right, he's ready."

Cat's second climb had gone much better. The rope was now secured, dangling from the socket to the ground, and time was of the essence because Alphonse heard orc-drums sounding from the gates.

And now the gnomes were giving them trouble. Greyquin, for not being willing to leave Bear below, and Solarrin, for objecting to Cat's solution.

"Here we go." She tugged thrice on the rope and it began to rise, drawn from above by Alphonse and Rayke.

Bear whined again. Only his head, tail, and one paw poked out. The awkward bundle twisted as it rose, bumping against the stone a few times. Arien waited, watching intently, ready with his sorcery should the rope give way.

Greyquin chewed his thumbnail nervously. Finally, Bear was high enough and hands reached out to pull him in. Rayke tossed the bundle back down.

Cat turned to Solarrin, giving him her sweetest smile. "It's your turn," she said.

"Have you lost what little sense the gods saw fit to give you?"

Greyquin held the backpack open. "In you go."

Even Bostitch seemed amused as Solarrin laboriously settled himself in, grumbling under his breath. He held up something.

"Dog hair," he announced.

Cat tightened the straps. "Not much longer," she said, using the same tones Greyquin had used to comfort Bear.

"This is horribly undignified. I am the Archmage of the Universe, not a heap of undone wash!"

"Can you scale the cliff?" Cat asked, trying to keep a straight face although Arien's eyes were twinkling most amusedly at her.

"My mental and magical powers are without equal!" he snapped.

"Yes, but can you scale the cliff?" She tugged three times.

"Someday," he muttered darkly as the bundle began to rise, "you shall all regret treating me with such flippancy."

*　　*　　*

Golems are far preferable than the walking dead in matters of loyalty and ability, and most of all, cleanliness.

The Book of Yor.

"Cold light," marveled Cat, turning the pale, radiant coin back and forth.

"A simple spell, really," Arien said, flattered by her awe. "The coins will glow for a few days. We will need neither torch nor candle. Should you need darkness, conceal it within a pouch."

She tossed it in the air, snapped her other fist around it, walked it across her knuckles, and abruptly made it disappear.

"Such tricks are difficult with that coin," Arien said. He took her hand, glowing with captive light, and gently unfolded her fingers. "Yet you are skilled."

Greyquin, whose senses were sharpest, led the way with a second enspelled coin in hand.

"The dungeons would probably be down," Cat whispered. "We need to find some stairs, or a shaft, or something."

"But Selbon's study will be up here," Solarrin said from his perch atop Bostitch's shoulders. "We must find that first. Why are you interested in the dungeons anyway? Planning to get caught and want to pick out a good cell in advance?"

"My mother may be here somewhere," Cat said.

"Haarkon's bony hand," Solarrin swore. "You're here on some barking mad rescue mission? For that, you risk all of your lives?"

"Ssh!" Greyquin motioned for them to stop. "We've found a door, and it is locked."

"Locked!" Arien repeated in dismay. "We've come so far for nothing?"

"Oh, please!" Cat laughed, worming past Rayke. "Allow me."

"Ah, yes," Arien said. "I'd forgotten your . . . profession."

"I can bash it down," Alphonse volunteered, flexing his large fists eagerly.

"Let's at least try to be quiet, you thundering ogre," Sybil said crossly.

Cat paid them no mind but withdrew a small leather packet from her boot. Within were several small tools and skeleton keys. She gripped the glowing coin in her teeth and went to work. Moments later, she stood with a satisfied "There!" as the door opened.

The air was dry and musty, but the room was free of dust. Expecting gloomy dungeon, she was surprised to see that it was a sitting room, with long velvet-covered benches along the walls and a rug on the floor. Another door was in the opposite wall, flanked by two pedestals holding decorative suits of golden armor.

"As predicted," Solarrin said smugly, ducking as Bostitch came through the doorway, "the living areas."

Arien started to agree, when he noticed strange green light growing in the room. One of the empty suits of armor turned its helm toward him. The light, green and eerie, beamed from the helm's eyeslits.

"Beware!" he called.

Cat gasped and drew her sword. The golden suit of armor stepped down from its pedestal and raised a sword of its own. The second, armed with a crescent-shaped axe, followed the first.

"Clan Bloodfist!" Alphonse roared, unhooking Emily from his belt.

The axe-wielder closed on Cat. She leaped back and the curved blade passed through the space where her waist had been. She slashed at it. Her sword rang loudly on its breastplate, scratching the metal but not penetrating.

Alphonse whirled Emily overhead and launched a terrific blow that made the empty suit of armor clang like a bell. It staggered, five deep dents showing where the flail had landed.

The one in front of Cat paused. The light pouring from its helm grew brighter. It was too cool and soothing to come from anything harmful. She gazed into it. She could almost hear music. If she just held still and listened, she could hear it much better.

Someone gave her a sudden shove. She dropped to one knee, and looked up to see Rayke's sword deflect the axe.

"Look lively, sweetheart!" he yelled, bringing his blade around. It sheared through the breastplate, leaving a jagged rent through which poured more of the unholy light.

"Beware the light!" Cat called, holding her hand in front of her face. "It's sorcery!"

Rayke halted, her warning come too late.

As the suit of armor advanced on him, Sybil's wild swing chopped the gauntlet from its weapon arm, then drove her sword into the opening of its visor. Cat was stunned at the skill with which the pleasure-seeking priestess dealt her blows.

Green light flared, filling the room. Sybil cried out in pain. The suit toppled with her sword still jutting from its head.

Bostitch froze, cocking his head as he stared into a visor. An expression of utter peace and happiness settled onto his wide face.

"No, fool!" Solarrin yelled, covering his own eyes. He thumped Bostitch on the head.

Alphonse swung Emily again and the helm was torn completely off. Green light spouted up and vanished. Metal rained down as the armor fell apart at his feet. He immediately kicked at it, scattering the pieces. Those stunned by the light shook their heads as if awakening from a long sleep.

"Sybil, are you all right?" Cat asked.

The priestess turned. "My arm feels numb," she said, "and look at my sword!"

The blade was shot with strange greenish cracks. She tapped it lightly against the floor and it broke into several jagged chunks, leaving her with only the hilt. She stripped off her glove. Her skin was pale, with a faint greenish tinge.

"It doesn't hurt," she continued. "But it's not at all pleasant. What were those things?"

"They were magical creations," Arien said. "Golems."

"What about you, Alphonse?" Cat turned.

He shrugged. "Nicked me once," he said, showing her a shallow cut on his leg. "Nothing to worry about. I'll bandage it later."

"Now," Cat said. "We can't have you bleeding all over the place."

"Pretty take," Bostitch said to Sybil, holding out the sword he had recovered from amid the shattered wreckage of one of the suits of armor. "Pretty for pretty."

"Well, Sybil," grinned Greyquin. "I think he likes you."

"It's beautiful! Look at these gems! It must be worth a fortune." Sybil sheathed her new sword. "Thank you, Bostitch," she cooed, making the minotaur fidget and scuff his feet.

"Are we going to stand around here all day or are we going to go?" Jessa demanded.

"We're going," Cat said. "We've got to find a way down." She waited as Alphonse tied a bandage around his leg.

"Everything's quiet out there," Greyquin announced after pressing his ear to the door. He opened the door a crack, then wider. They all stared in surprise.

The ceiling of the enormous hall arched high above their heads. It was inlaid with murals and decorative carvings. Several arched doorways lined the walls. The hall was illuminated by five crystal chandeliers, all aglow with magical light. A narrow line of blue carpet stretched the length of the hall, ending at a tall set of double doors at the end.

"Marble," Sybil breathed. "Crystal. What about the ruins? What about the orcs and hauntings?"

"So many doors," Cat said. "Which one leads to a way down?"

"We could separate and try them all," Greyquin suggested.

"A typically bad idea," Solarrin said. "Suppose that each door conceals an army of the undead? Although I can control an unlimited number of them, some of you might be inept enough to get killed."

"Aren't you charming!" Sybil said.

"I don't like this," Alphonse grumbled. "There are too many ways for them to come at us."

Cat opened a door at random. On the other side was a tiny cubicle, with bare walls and a threadbare rug on the floor. Cobwebs festooned the corners. The surface of the desk was deep in dust. "Empty."

"Let me try," Greyquin said. He went to the middle of the hall and began turning in a slow circle. As he did, he began chanting softly in the sing-song language of the gnomish people and pointing at each door.

Solarrin listened closely, then rolled his eyes. "You must be mad," he chortled.

"That one," Greyquin said, starting toward a door on the other side of the hall.

"Why that one?" Jessa asked.

Cat was glad somebody had asked. She adored Greyquin, who could cheer her up no matter how foul her mood, but she had to admit he could be odd at times. This looked to be one of those times.

"Why not?" he said, grinning abashedly.

"What were you doing? The singing and pointing?" Sybil put her hands on her hips and looked sternly down at him. "Is your helm on too tight?"

"It's my ancient family divination spell," he said defiantly, sticking his chin out.

Solarrin snorted. "You call *Dragon, Ogre, Giant Bat* a divination spell?"

"What?" Alphonse snarled. "What the blazes is that?"

"It is," Solarrin said, his voice dripping scorn, "a child's rhyme for choosing something. In rough translation, it would go something like this:

> *Dragon, Ogre, Giant Bat*
> *My old granny wears a hat*
> *How many flowers on the hat?*
> *One, two, three, four, I'll take that.*"

Everyone stared at Greyquin. "That is your ancient family divination spell?" Jessa finally asked. Kiah made a short noise of indignation, as if the hawk, too, had understood.

"Well, does anybody have a better idea?" Without waiting for a reply, he strode to the door. He looked around at them all with the expression of a man on his way to the gallows. "If this doesn't work, you're going to pick me up by the heels and bounce my head against the floor, aren't you?"

"Just open the door," Rayke muttered.

He did.

"Livana Silvermoon," breathed Arien.

"Great Haarkon," Solarrin said in the same reverent tone, which couldn't have pleased either the elven moon goddess or the stern lord of the dead.

The library.

It was two stories tall and open in the center, with a walkway around the second level reached by a spiral stair. The walls were completely lined with bookshelves. The spacious floor was covered with a dark rug. Ornate brass lanterns glowed without fire. The chairs were carved cherrywood with embroidered cushions. Near the fireplace was a huge marble-topped desk and a dark leather chair with brass dragon's head armrests. The desk was stacked with books. At the bottom of the spiral stair was a rack stuffed with rolls of parchment. Near it was a large round object in a wooden stand.

"My friends," Arien said, crossing the threshold as if entering a temple, "we have found the true treasury of this place."

Solarrin nudged Bostitch to follow. "Look at them all! Just look at them! So much power fills this room! I can feel it!"

Jessa closed the door behind them and they began to examine the books. Alphonse could read a little, something that Cat herself had taught him. He quickly found something that made him chuckle, and sat in a fancy chair that looked too weak to support his bulk. He began muttering to himself, running his thick finger along the pages as he read.

Cat chose to examine the round object beneath the stairs and found it to be a map like none she'd ever seen before, a map painted on the surface of a ball.

"Da, you were right," she whispered, spinning the fascinating thing.

Her father had always insisted that there was much more to the wide world than anyone suspected. This round map was proof of it. She looked at all the different areas of land, and the oceans between them.

After a bit of a search, she found the Southern Plains, supposedly so vast but looking so very small. To the northeast of the Plains she found a patch of green that had to be the fabled Emerin. A tiny region of mountains was all that represented the Bannerians. To the west of the mountains was Hachland, and above that was another patch of green labeled Lenais.

"Lenais," she murmured questioningly. It sounded familiar, but she could not figure out why. She doubted it was a place her father had ever mentioned.

On some other pieces of land were places with names she could barely pronounce. Tiz'ak'kan. Perrifaul. Caenokria. Zembdaran.

"Aha!" Solarrin cried out. He was clutching a book to his chest. A feverish, unpleasant gleam lit his black eyes and his teeth were bared in something between a smile and a snarl. As the others turned toward him, he backed toward Bostitch. "Stay away! This, no eyes shall read save mine!"

"What is it?" Arien inquired.

"A spellbook, fool! The spellbook! It is what I have been searching for all of my life. You could not possibly understand!"

Cat saw sorrow pass over Arien's face. "Wouldn't I?" he said quietly.

Solarrin ignored him, laughing as his stubby fingers flipped through the pages. The book was bound in leather the color of blood, dark as Solarrin's robes. "Now is the time," he gloated. "With Selbon's secrets and my own, the world will bow to me! Kings will be my slaves!"

"Oh, please, Steel, strike me deaf," Alphonse said, rolling his eyes. "Better yet, strike him mute!"

"Your scorn ill masks your fear. I do not yet plan to leave you, although I have found what I sought. You may yet be of use to me in discovering the other secrets of this place."

"Imagine our relief," Sybil said.

"Is it wise to let him have that?" Cat whispered to Arien.

"No, but less wise to try and force the matter now. Until we have safely left this place, best to indulge him. He is powerful."

"Is he?" she said. "We haven't yet actually seen him do anything."

He paused, then nodded. "Quite true, my clever girl!"

"Well," she said briskly, gesturing around. "What of you? Have you found what you seek?"

"Alas, how could I? It would take days merely to identify them all. There are many works here that are unknown, or considered lost! Look on this!" He held up a creamy scroll tied with a violet ribbon. "This is a spell to call a familiar. Rare indeed, and valuable."

"Are you going to try it?" she asked, catching his excitement even though she didn't fully understand what he meant by a familiar.

"Why not?" He mused aloud, turning it over in his hands. "A familiar. A lifelong companion."

She started to say something daring, but caught herself in time. "I've never seen so many books! How does it compare to your Library?"

He absently tucked the scroll into his satchel. "The Library in Thanis would leap at the chance to add any of these to its shelves."

"Too bad we couldn't take them all," she said. "Make a pile of coin!"

He nodded wistfully. "Indeed. But I will settle for choosing a few that I could not bear to leave behind, and hope that I will stumble across the one that I need."

"Can we keep some?" Alphonse asked. "Can we really?"

"Of course," she said. "Why? What did you find? Orcish legends?"

"Orcs don't write. They pass stories from one generation to the next out loud. Maybe when I get too old to fight, I'll start writing them down. Not that anybody who could read them would want to."

"Well, what is the book, then?" Cat asked. He held it out to her and she read the title aloud. "*The Anatomy of the Humanoid Races: A Physician's Guide.* Why?"

He grinned and flipped it open. "Drawings. In colored ink."

"Ooh!" Sybil exclaimed in delight.

*   *   *

"This is madness and greed," Jessa complained. "You'll never get all of those out of here."

They ignored her. The two of them, different in appearance but similar underneath, kept adding books to the pile that was growing in the center of the room. Arrogant, single-minded males! Sybil was no better, insisting on reading aloud from a book of disgusting Hachlanian poetry once she'd learned to her dismay that Alphonse's book was nothing more than depictions of innards.

Even Greyquin was wasting his time looking at books. She could feel the immense weight of the mountain pressing down on her. She could taste the air, unbreathed by human lungs for more than a century, flat and stale and old.

"These are worth a fortune," Solarrin said, directing Bostitch to stack still more onto the pile. The fat gnome was sitting on a stack of books, his robes around him like a spreading bloodstain.

"Who would have believed it?" Arien marveled. "The entire *Mysterion.* What a treasure!"

"What is it?" Cat asked.

"Never you mind," Solarrin said quickly, rapping Arien's arm with his staff as he appeared about to speak. "It hardly concerns you."

"She was merely interested," Arien said. Jessa saw the grateful smile Cat flashed at him, and her frown deepened.

"Jessa's right, though," Cat said. "We can't carry them all."

"Sadly, you are right." Arien gazed at the pile and sighed. "It is a dream come true, yet like all dreams, that which we most desire is forever out of reach."

"Can I keep this one?" Greyquin asked. "It's a cookbook."

"You? Cook?" Cat chuckled. "I remember your oatmeal. We could have laid cobblestones with that stuff."

"Alphonse ate it, didn't he?"

He smiled broadly. "Just like my grandma used to make. Needed a bit more gravel, though."

"There wasn't any gravel in it!" Greyquin protested.

"Oh," said Alphonse. "Then you'd better take the cookbook and learn a few things."

"In the meanwhile," Cat said, "why don't you come over here and have a look at these shelves. Tell me if you see what I think I see."

After examining the section of shelves that so interested Cat, Greyquin nodded. "It looks to me like a catch for a hidden opening."

"How do you know?" Rayke asked, scratching his beard as he looked at the shelf. "I don't see anything."

"Live as a carpenter for fifteen years," Greyquin suggested with a grin. "Gave me quite the knack with things like this."

"What might it conceal?" Arien wondered aloud.

"Selbon's secret workroom," Alphonse guessed. "Oh, look at this. Did you know the bowel can be upwards of twenty feet long? Next time I gut somebody, I'll have to string it out and see for myself."

"Alphonse, stop it!" Sybil wailed.

"I'd rather hear that than those filthy poems," Jessa said, standing as Greyquin prepared to open the secret panel.

"This should do it," he said, reaching behind the books.

A section of the bookshelf rotated on an unseen axis, revealing a dark room beyond. Enough light reached in to allow them to see tables cluttered with glass vials and other strange items. A peculiar smell drifted out.

Greyquin took a cautious step forward. He peered into the room.

A gleaming metal hand shot from the darkness and grabbed his shoulder. He yelped, arms waving in surprise as he was pulled out of sight. Bear began barking fiercely.

"Greyquin!" Alphonse roared. He dropped his book and thundered through the opening, nearly trampling Bear, who was also charging to the gnome's rescue.

"Light!" Cat yelled, tossing her glowing coin into the room. It reflected off a large metal figure before Alphonse's huge shadow blocked it out.

Metal against metal echoed through the peaceful library. Bear's barks ended in a startled yelp. Cat drew her sword and sprang through. Rayke and Sybil collided with each other, and both were knocked into the room by Bostitch as he ran into them from behind.

Jessa moved forward. The first thing she saw was Alphonse, staggering and bleeding from the corners of his mouth. Greyquin was little better off. She took one look at their foes and understood why.

There were six of them. Six perfectly identical men who looked as if they had been dipped in molten gold. It coated their skin, bald heads, and sculpted muscles. One was lying by the wall, legs moving slowly. She noticed that the side of its head was caved in, but no blood leaked out.

"What are they?" Cat gasped.

"More golems," Arien said. "Made of bronze."

Jessa looked at her bow. She doubted her arrows would harm the metal beings. Neither would the long knife she carried, which was used primarily for dressing game.

"Golems, you say?" Solarrin wheezed, limping up to the opening. "Let me through."

Sybil and Rayke stood back-to-back, barely able to hold off the determined attack of the bronze men. Greyquin jabbed at the one facing Sybil. Behind him, Bear lay crumpled under a long table, having fallen in defense of his master. Greyquin's jaw was set in a grim line of worry and revenge.

Bostitch had a golem pinned on the floor. His fists bled as he pummeled it. Alphonse had another trapped in a corner. The last one had seen the group gathered by the door, and started toward them.

Jessa let an arrow fly. As she'd feared, it shattered on contact, leaving only a small dent.

"Fast, nicely made. Strong, too," Solarrin observed as Rayke's shield split in two under a blow from a metal fist.

"Yes, very professionally crafted," Arien agreed hastily, backing up. "Admire them later. How can we stop them?"

"You're remarkably hasty for an elf, but fear not. They are no match for my magic," Solarrin said pompously.

"Now would be a good time to show us!" Cat cried in alarm.

The golem lunged at her, swinging. She sprang to the side, crashed into Arien, and both of them tumbled to the ground. The golem loomed over them.

Cat, lying on the elf, twisted and raised her sword as the golem reached down. Her sword rebounded off its arm. Jessa hurled her knife. It, too, bounced uselessly away and nearly skewered Bostitch.

Solarrin uttered some harsh, guttural words and slammed the end of his staff on the floor. The golem disappeared.

"What?!" Cat said, staring at the space where it had been.

"Teleportation!" Arien choked. Cat had evidently knocked the wind out of him.

"No," Solarrin sneered. "A secret of the earth magics. That metal monster is trapped in the earth, far below us. It is locked in a small chamber, sealed in solid rock, and cannot escape unless I will it so. Just a minor example of my power."

Cat got to her feet. "So you *do* have powers! Can you use it on the other ones?"

"And waste my energies? The warriors seem to have them under control."

Jessa saw that he was right. Rayke and Sybil, with some help from Greyquin, had managed to cripple two. Bostitch was briskly twisting one's head around. Alphonse had hammered another into a bent lump.

The one against the wall was still moving. Greyquin lurched over to it, looking strangely like Solarrin as he limped. His ankle was badly turned, but he didn't let that stop him from delivering a solid kick to the thing.

"That's for Bear," he growled, the expression of anger unfamiliar on his perpetually cheery face. He kicked it again. "So's that."

Bear, hearing his name, wobbled unsteadily to a sitting position. Blood matted the side of his head. He panted, his tongue hanging out. Greyquin went to the dog and hugged him.

Cat helped Arien up. Jessa noticed the way the elf was watching Cat. She didn't like it. She'd seen that sort of look before. If he so much as laid a finger on her, Jessa vowed she'd have an arrow through his heart before he could draw another breath.

"Is it broken?" Rayke asked as Sybil examined his shield arm. His shield lay in pieces amid the tangle of bronze limbs.

"No, thank Talopea," Sybil sighed. She closed her eyes and her body swayed as she prayed to her sluttish goddess. Jessa looked away.

Arien knelt beside Greyquin, who was still hugging and consoling Bear. "Greyquin. You are hurt. I have some small healing ability. Allow me to attend you."

"I was so worried about Bear that I hardly felt it."

"Now that you know he is well, I suspect you will begin to become aware of the pain," Arien said. "Let me help."

Greyquin sighed in relief as Arien cast a spell of healing upon him. "But what about Bear? Can you heal him?"

"I do not know. I have never used my spells on an animal before. However, I will attempt it."

He repeated the words and gesture, this time cradling Bear's head. To Jessa's surprise, Bear seemed to improve. He licked Arien's hand, his tail thumping on the ground. Jessa reluctantly admitted to herself that perhaps the wizard had his uses.

"Alphonse? Are you all right?" Cat asked.

"Might have cracked a couple of ribs," he said. "Where's my book? I want to see what'll get poked if there's any broken ends moving around in there."

"Alphonse, eew!" Sybil said. Her face was flushed from her lusty communion with her depraved goddess.

"I don't see you offering to heal me," he leered. "Don't you have to tumble someone first?"

"It helps, but it's not necessary." Sybil swept her gaze over him and wrinkled her nose. "Thankfully."

"Can you heal him anyway?" Rayke asked, experimentally moving his arm. It seemed fully healed. "If there are any more of those things, we'll need him whole."

"Oh, I suppose." She approached the orckin reluctantly, surprising Jessa again. She would never have expected to see Sybil unwilling to use her powers on any male of any species.

"Alphonse was correct," Arien said, looking around. "This must be the Archmage's workroom."

*   *   *

8

Alchemy is hardly what we might call an exact science, but it does have spectacular results.

The Book of Yor.

"I don't know where to look first," Cat said, awed.

A pentagram was scrawled on one side of the room, the lines faded to ghosts. The shelves held jars of unidentifiable things floating in thick fluid. A grinning skull had a candle half-melted over its bony crown. An hourglass, three feet tall and full of blood-red sand, stood on a smaller table. There was a crystal ball in a golden stand shaped like a coiled serpent.

"Quite nice," Solarrin commented enviously, gazing greedily around.

"Look at this!" cried Sybil, carefully picking up a figurine of a nude woman that had been carved from a single large ruby.

The worktable was scuffed, stained, and scorched. The top of it was littered with scraps of parchment. A book lay open on the desk. Arien picked it up and glanced through it. "Behold," he said. "This would appear to be some sort of journal."

"Selbon's journal? Let me see that!" Solarrin limped to Arien as fast as his short legs would take him.

"I've got a question," Greyquin said. Cat noticed that the normally curious gnome's hands were clasped behind his back.

"Yes?" Arien asked, casually turning and holding the book out of Solarrin's reach. Cat hid a smile, seeing Solarrin's jaw clench in frustration.

"Isn't it just a wee bit dangerous to just go poking about a sorcerer's workroom? Who knows what might be enspelled, or cursed? And that," he added, pointing to a table full of strange equipment and glass vessels, "that's alchemy, isn't it? And alchemy, unless I miss my guess, explodes."

"Explodes?" Rayke echoed in alarm

Everyone stopped, and began gingerly setting things back down exactly where they'd gotten them.

"An excellent point," Arien said. "Let us use all due discretion."

"Oh!" Sybil sniffed in disappointment as she put down the ruby. "Surely you wise wizards can tell us what is safe."

"Perhaps his journal might." Still holding it above Solarrin's head, Arien began turning pages. "Wait, here, this last entry is of some interest." He read from it aloud. Though the words were chilling, Cat still thrilled at the sound of his smooth voice.

"I have discovered a problem with the Deathshade powder. When the smoke is inhaled, it has the desired effect. However, I have learned the hard way that the unburned powder cannot, must not be mixed with liquid. This warns against accidental ingestion, as my test subjects have suffered a resulting painful death.

"I know not how or why, but the wet powder becomes as a living thing, not unlike the amoeba creatures found in deep caverns. It is quick, incredibly so, and voracious. It flows from one victim to the next with amorphous ease, as I have learned.

"The pain matters not. I am beyond pain. However, I do regret the loss of my arm. I need it not for my spells, but my penmanship suffers. The oh-so-powerful, oh-so-sanctimonious priests will not aid me, and my own spells of healing cannot repair an injury of this nature. I

consider myself fortunate that the one arm was all that was lost. I kept my wits about me and was able to return the creature to its dormant, powdery form.

"This has great potential as a weapon; I must ponder it further."

"Don't touch anything!" Cat ordered sharply. Greyquin looked vindicated.

"It ate his arm?" Sybil said, aghast.

"A moment." Arien turned some more pages, toward the front of the book. "Perhaps I can find a description of this powder, that we might avoid it."

"Or find it," muttered Solarrin.

"After numerous attempts," read Arien, *"I am unable to produce the powder in a more innocuous form. I would prefer it white and fine-grained, but it seems this coarse black dust is the best that I can do at this time."*

"Black dust?" Alphonse asked.

"Like that, maybe?" Greyquin pointed to a sealed glass jar, half-full of gritty black powder, careful to stay well away from it.

"Possibly very much like that," Solarrin said. "Shall we douse it with water and find out?"

"Let's not," Sybil said, inching away from the table. "Leave it be!"

"Nonsense. I intend to take it and study it."

"Are you out of your tiny little mind?" Alphonse ground his tusks against his lip. "I agree with Sybil. Leave it alone."

"Yuh," Bostitch unexpectedly chimed in. "Black dirt. Bad."

"This superstitious fear is unwarranted. Selbon was clearly careless. I shall be wiser. This is far too great a discovery to leave behind."

"It's far too big a risk to the rest of us," Cat said. "What if it gets broken? What if you fall in a pond?"

"What if you all suddenly became less cowardly and foolish? But let us not concern ourselves with the unlikely. Once I am in control of it, it will be worth a fortune to the right people."

"Oh, the right people! Lord Marl, for instance?" Cat scoffed. "He would love to get ahold of something like that. I don't want to make my fortune at Thanis' expense."

"A peculiar sentiment from a thief," Solarrin flung at her. "You already earn your living at Thanis' expense."

"That's different! I want nothing to do with that powder."

"Very well. I shall take it, and I alone. The risk shall be mine, as shall the reward. You lot may have your burden of morals, but morals do not fill an empty purse." He took the jar, and they all backed away from him. He motioned impatiently to Bostitch. "Here. Put this in the pack and mind you it's well padded."

"No." Bostitch slowly shook his huge head.

"What? Did I hear that correctly? Put it in the pack, you worthless beast!"

Bostitch crossed his arms and shook his head again.

Solarrin turned to Arien. "Well, my fellow wizard and the only glimmer of awareness in this entire blighted group, what say you? Do you not know what this could mean to the science of magic, not to mention our own personal careers?"

"I know full well what it could mean. Death, darkness, and despair. It is just one more way for people to cause each other pain. I stand in agreement with the rest. Leave it behind."

Sighing heavily, Solarrin set the jar back on the table. "I grow so weary of dealing with such ignorance," he grumbled, heading over to the table of alchemical equipment. "Are you meek mice going to forbid me from taking these elixirs? I normally disdain alchemy, but since these are already finished . . ."

"What's all this about alchemy, anyway?" Rayke asked. "Isn't that supposed to turn things to gold?"

"Simpleton," Solarrin began, but Arien's smooth voice overrode him.

"Alchemy is not precisely magic," he said. "It also is quite new, being all but unknown only a mere two centuries ago. It is even now exceedingly uncommon among the elvenfolk. Selbon was one of the first mages to practice it. Most find it a dangerous science, for, as Greyquin noted, it tends to have somewhat flamboyant results, particularly when errors occur."

"This one looks just like that elixir the priest used to mend your finger," Cat said to Alphonse. "I know an alchemist in Thanis, but I've never dared try one of his potions. Those little bottles cost a fortune."

"Elixirs tend to be expensive due to the cost of the materials that must go into them, and the risk to the alchemist." Arien raised a vial to the light and examined the silvery liquid that swirled around inside. "Still, these completed ones are safe enough, provided we do not sample or spill them. And, as Cat observed, they are most valuable."

"What about the ruby?" Sybil urged. "Is it safe? I would so dearly love to have it!"

"A moment." Arien made some gestures and murmured quietly, then shrugged. "It carries no enchantment that I can detect."

As Sybil eagerly tucked the ruby into her belt pouch, Cat noticed Greyquin behind a tapestry that ran the length of one wall. The tapestry, though smoky and stained with residue from alchemical spills, still clearly depicted a chilling scene of a moonlit graveyard.

"What kind of weaver would do something like that?" she wondered aloud.

"I am certain," said Solarrin, "that Selbon was able to pay or enslave as many craftsmen as he wanted."

"There's a door back here," Greyquin announced, his voice muffled by the thick cloth. "It smells damp, and has a cold draft. It might lead down."

"So let's see," Alphonse said, yanking down the tapestry. It tore, and Solarrin winced.

"Must you destroy everything you touch?" he snapped. "We'll be lucky if you don't bring the whole mountain crashing down on our heads."

Greyquin cautiously opened the door, standing well back from it in remembrance of what had happened last time. He held a glowing coin aloft.

"I see stairs!"

"The dungeons!" Cat exclaimed. "You're right. It smells foul."

"What do you expect from a dungeon?" Solarrin said acidly. "Fresh flowers in all the cells every morning? It's not an inn, for Haarkon's sake!"

Cat started down the stairs, sword in hand. The staircase curved down. The walls were streaked with wetness, and greenish moss grew in the cracks. She heard the others following her. The steps were slick and treacherous.

"There are possibly springs or other water sources," Arien said, close behind her. "Such would account for the dampness."

Bear whined unhappily. Tendrils of stringy fungus dangled from the low, sloped ceiling. The smell made Cat think of the alleys in the lowest Rings of Thanis, where beggars lived in rude hovels cobbled together from the cast-off trash of others.

Alphonse growled and suddenly slapped the wall. His gauntlet scraped loudly against the stone. Cat whirled in surprise. Her foot slipped, and she would have tumbled all the way down the stairs had Arien not caught her by the arm.

"Bug," he explained, holding up his hand to show the flattened remains of a large centipede.

At the bottom of the stairs, Cat found a single door. The wood was warped from years of exposure to the damp. Large spongy mushrooms lined the floor, breaking open like blisters under their boots.

The door handle was so thickly clotted with rust that it was barely recognizable. A plump spider crawled leisurely over it. Cat used the tip of her sword to knock it away, and tugged on the handle.

She was expecting it to be warped shut, so she pulled hard. When it gave way with sickening ease, she stumbled back into Arien. He steadied her again.

A draft of cold, dank air floated out, a drifting vaporous trail of whitish-green mist that hugged the floor. Their lights threw little illumination into the cavernous room beyond.

Swallowing hard, Cat stepped forward and raised her light. The pale gleam showed her a vast hall, the dripping walls lined with stone tombs. The very stone looked soft and crumbling.

"A crypt," she whispered.

Solarrin urged Bostitch forward. "Let me see," he commanded.

Cat gladly stepped back. She could already see far more than she wanted. In the center of the room was a raised circular stone slab. Set atop it was a large block of whitish stone in the shape of a flat-topped skull.

"An altar to Haarkon," Solarrin murmured, touching his forehead in a gesture of respect. He nudged the unhappy minotaur further into the room. "Take me over there. I want a better look."

"That is an evil altar!" Sybil hissed, horrified. "Stay away from it!"

"It holds no fear for me," he sneered. "Haarkon does not threaten one of his own."

Sybil clutched her pendant and began to pray softly. "Blessed Talopea, Desired One, keep us safe in the face of this evil . . ."

"I think I see another door on the far side," Greyquin said, peering into the crypt.

"You mean we have to go through there?" Jessa stroked Kiah's head, trying to soothe the hawk and conceal her own nervousness.

"The rest of you can stay," Cat said, stepping over the threshold. "But I have to go."

"Not alone." Alphonse immediately moved to her side.

The low mist swirled around their ankles. Cat walked slowly, testing the ground ahead of her with her toe before setting her weight upon it, mindful of pits or other hazards. Ahead of her, Bostitch had plodded to the altar and helped Solarrin out of the backpack.

"This is an unhealthy find," Arien said from a few feet away.

Cat turned and saw him looking at something on the floor. As the breeze from the open door stirred the mist, she saw wide black lines inlaid in the floor. None of the mushrooms grew on the lines, and the streams and puddles did not cross them. They seemed to form a many-cornered design. At each outer corner was a black candle.

"A pentagram?" she guessed. "No, there are too many lines."

"Alas, no. This is an octagram, eight-sided. It is a device of the god of the dead, for use in summoning the most fearsome of evil creatures, by the intervention of one of the darker gods."

"Now, creatures of Haarkon," Solarrin called. "Rise! Rise and attend me! Rise, and bow to your new master!"

Arien whirled. "Solarrin, no!"

"He's waking the dead!" Alphonse grabbed Emily. "Steel protect us!"

The lids of the crypts were sliding aside. Hands reached out, groping, covered with moss and dangling with blind worms. Rotted corpses rose slowly from their resting places and tottered unsteadily toward Solarrin.

Greyquin grabbed Solarrin's arm. "Stop it! Send them back!"

Solarrin cuffed Greyquin aside with his staff. "They obey me, as you should have the sense to do! Bostitch, move him."

Bostitch picked Greyquin up by the scruff of the neck and held him with his feet kicking the air.

"I will send them back!" Sybil cried. She marched toward the nearest one, holding her Talopean symbol in one hand and her sword in the other. Her voice rang true and sure as she called upon her goddess. "In Talopea's name, back to your graves, you displeasing wretches!"

The corpse paused. The tatters of a soldier's uniform hung from his shoulders. Patches of hair clung to his scalp. His sunken eyes stared in different directions.

"Yes! Back, I command you!" Sybil advanced on it.

"Get out," Solarrin snarled. "You will ruin everything, you empty-headed trollop!"

"Bostitch, put me down!" Greyquin squirmed.

Several skeletal figures came out of the shadows. They wore breastplates of hardened leather with leather straps hanging from the bottom. Each held a spear and small round shield, and their eyeless skulls turned back and forth as they surveyed their prey.

"Just like bowling for ninepins!" Alphonse charged, hefting Emily.

"There are many of them," Arien said, his voice calm. "Can we make it to the far door?"

Greyquin twisted in Bostitch's grip and managed to grab his thumb. He bent it back. Bostitch let go and Greyquin dropped. He struck the raised edge of the stone slab and vanished into the low mist.

Emily sang through the fetid air and struck a walking skeleton hard enough to send bones flying in all directions.

"Niralnia!" Arien said, holding his palms a few inches apart and gazing intently at the area between them. A glimmer of blue-white appeared, growing rapidly into a solid ball of ice the size of a man's head.

"No! No!" Solarrin, enraged, hopped up and down beside the altar like a toad on a hot stone. "Don't attack them, you idiots!"

Sybil was holding some at bay, but they seemed to be growing bolder. Rayke was at her side in an instant and launched a fierce swing that sheared through one, then yelled in pain as a spear bit into his side.

Arien drew back his arm and hurled his ball of ice at the nearest skeleton. It fell apart in a rain of bones, ice shards, and cold water.

"Arien!" Cat called. Another was coming up on him from behind. She was faster than it, and reached it just as it was about to stab him in the back with a wickedly pointed shard of bone. She slashed her sword across the backs of its legs.

Sybil and Rayke were surrounded by a ring of undead. Her pendant no longer seemed to affect them, only their weaving blades now keeping them at bay.

Alphonse was steadily beating back the ranks of skeletons. Jessa, prudently near the door, was shooting as fast as she could draw her bow, but her arrows did little to slow the loathsome hoard. Wounded, they did not feel the pain but kept mindlessly fighting.

"You'll ruin everything!" Solarrin yelled. Some of the creatures he'd called were now moving toward him with deadly intent.

Bostitch moved between Solarrin and the advancing dead. He swung his huge sword so hard that he chopped one cleanly in half and the blade went most of the way through the one next to it.

Cat tried to reach Sybil, but found her way blocked. She grimaced and hacked until the corpses fell, and even then they kept sluggishly stirring. No clean kills, these, just a ceaseless slaughter of rotting flesh.

She put her back to the wall as yet more corpses closed in on her. They were moving more swiftly now, becoming more animated. Cat shifted, felt a loose stone press in beneath her back, and the wall slid away behind her.

She stumbled backward into another chamber. A small bony hand closed over her ankle.

It was a child. A dead child with bulging eyes, sunken cheeks, and lank blond hair falling over its thin shoulders. It clutched pathetically at Cat's leg. Others, some barely more than babies, crawled toward her, wailing hungrily.

Cat pulled her leg free and raised her light. Its dim glow revealed a larger form, the moldering corpse of a woman in once-fine robes with a high collar that fanned out behind what was left of her head.

The child grabbed Cat again. She sliced at it. Her blade sheared easily through its fragile bones, though the fingers were left clamped around her leg.

The dead woman held out her arms. One of her hands was missing, only a splintered stump jutting out of the moss-covered sleeve. Her shriveled mouth moved. Strange words slurred forth on a foul rush of air.

Cat suddenly felt as if things were crawling over her. She struggled with the sudden urge to flee, to run for her life.

"Cat, beware!" Arien called from what seemed a tremendous distance. "She is *lichma'rhun*! An undead mage!"

The woman lurched forward, fast despite years of decay. Her cold, dead hand seized Cat's left arm. The light coin dropped, lost amid the strewn body parts.

She tried to jerk away, but this corpse was much stronger than the child. The woman pulled her closer, until Cat could see bugs creeping through her lank hair. The bloodless lips moved again. More words, a gurgling rattle, issued forth.

The tomb was gone.

A shaggy beast leapt at her, its dark fur silvered by moonlight. Its razor claws flashed. Foam dripped from its jaws. It bore her to the ground and she felt its hot breath on her face as it burrowed under her chin and sank its teeth into her throat.

Cat shrieked. The vision vanished as suddenly as it had come, leaving her shaking uncontrollably. She slammed the hilt of her sword against the dead woman's head. Her glove shredded and her wrist burned as she pulled her arm free.

One of the children, a little boy, hit her in the side with the knobby end of a bone. She jumped back, unsteady on the litter of bones, and fell. The children were on her, greedy, hungry fingers digging at her arms and legs.

One of them dropped onto her chest and crushed the breath from her. Tiny teeth sank into her bleeding wrist. It crouched there, ready to feed.

A ball of ice struck the child-thing and knocked it away. Cold water showered over Cat. She flailed at the others, scrambling to her knees.

The woman was in front of her, pointing at her and chanting something. Cat dove to the side, expecting a gout of fire or other magical attack. Instead, she was struck by a burst of raw terror. The entire crypt seemed alive, a shifting mass of crawling, clattering dead things.

She had to get out. Had to get away!

Her heel caved in the pallid little face of a child-thing chewing at her boot. Cat fled through the darkness, screaming uncontrollably. All around her, she could see the dead things stirring and moving, pulling their mangled bodies together to come after her.

She collided with one at full speed, almost running it through with her sword. It grabbed her, trying to crush her, and pulled her to the ground. Its mouth was near her ear, trying to bite into her exposed flesh.

*   *   *

"Cat!" Arien said urgently, holding her tightly as she struggled with him. "Cat, stop. I mean you no harm."

She looked up at him, and for a moment he was afraid that, lost in the grip of the spell, she would not recognize him. "Arien?" she whispered.

"Yes," he said. Her struggles stopped and she huddled against him, trembling so much that he swore his own bones shook from it. "It is a spell of fear. Let it pass. Let it go. She will not hurt you or frighten you again. I promise you that. Do you hear me? I will not let her hurt you."

She nodded. Her shuddering eased a bit. He stroked her hair, holding her close. He could feel her heart, beating as fast as a rabbit's.

Around them, the battle continued to rage. He saw Solarrin, backed into the shadows by a creatures that no longer sought to obey him despite his frantic orders. Bostitch fought to reach him, but his way was blocked by still more of the walking dead. How many of them were there, Arien wondered. How many uneasy corpses in this vast room, just waiting for the evil of a Solarrin to come along and renew their black energies?

Alphonse stood over Rayke as Sybil tried to heal him, but even from this distance Arien could see all was not going well. Sybil could not achieve her healing trance with the hoards of undead crowding around them and crying out for their blood. Alphonse would not be able to hold them off forever. Of Greyquin and Jessa, he could see no sign.

"Our friends need help, Cat. They need us. We must go to them."

She shivered again, still caught up in the spell of the *lichma'rhun*. As long as the creature was alive, Cat would be held in terror's icy grip. There was only one was to end the spell.

He looked up. The undead sorceress was slowly coming toward him.

"Cat." He tipped her face up so that he could see her beautiful blue eyes. "Stay here. You will be safe. Stay here, and do not fear." Then, before he could stop himself, he pressed a soft kiss to her forehead.

He reluctantly let go of her and stood, facing the *lichma'rhun*. He knew no spells of necromancy, no words of power to send this semblance of a woman back to her tomb. Nevertheless, he moved to meet her.

The woman smiled hideously and stretched out her hand. Behind her, the children capered eagerly.

He calmly reached out and clasped the corpse's hand. Even as her lips started to move, he spoke in a firm, clear voice.

"*Fesednia,*" he said, feeling the power of the spell flow from his head and heart down his arm and through their linked hands.

The dead woman shrieked. She tried to pull away, but Arien held fast although her strength pulled him with her as she retreated. Her skin dried, crumbling like old parchment under his fingers. The flesh beneath the skin withered. Her face cracked and peeled. Her eyes shriveled and fell in. Like a leaf in the last days of fall, she twisted and curled in upon herself until only a brittle husk remained.

The children swarmed at him. Weakened by his spellcasting, he could not evade them. His feet turned on skulls hidden in the mist and he went to one knee. They fell upon him.

Cat snared one by the hair and yanked it back so that its teeth snapped on empty air. She drove her sword through its torso. No longer fearful, her mouth set in a grim line, she methodically cut down the rest.

"In Haarkon's name, I command you!" Solarrin bellowed. Arien could barely see him, standing by the altar. His upthrust hand was engulfed in a ball of energy that pulsed green light like an alien heart. He brought it down sharply, striking the altar. The stone skull split in two.

The undead all stopped where they were. One was about to run a spear through Jessa, but it was frozen with the point not six inches from her chest. The room was plunged into sudden silence.

"What in the . . . ?" Alphonse said, staring at the motionless undead soldier that was brandishing a sword at him.

"Quickly," Solarrin panted. "It will not hold them long."

"What happened?" Cat asked.

"A paralysis spell," Arien said. "I suggest we take his advice and depart."

"Hurry!" Sybil helped Rayke to his feet. He leaned heavily against her, one arm dangling limp.

Bear came out of the shadows, dragging an unconscious Greyquin by the collar. Jessa, with a last glance at the spear that had been about to end her life, ran to the dog and draped Greyquin over his back.

Rayke collapsed. "No!" Sybil screamed. Alphonse shoved her aside and scooped him up.

Cat looked across the room at the other door. Arien, practically able to read her thoughts, shook his head. "There is no time. We will find another way, or come back when we are better prepared."

The door slammed shut behind them, cutting them off from the deep crypt. Cutting them off from the way down.

"Mother," Cat whispered, anguished.

*   *   *

Sybil threw herself into a chair. "I must rest. Talopea's kindness is unlimited, but I'm only Her vessel, and I'm at the end of my strength. I need sleep, and food."

"Rest is perhaps not an unwise idea," Arien agreed. "Though I, for one, doubt I could eat after that."

Greyquin nodded. "By my way of thinking, it must be well past dark by now. Maybe we should sleep here a while."

"Sleep here?" Alphonse looked doubtful. "What about the orcs?"

"The doors are locked," Greyquin said. "We can take turns on watch, like always."

Alphonse unbuckled his breastplate. "Fine. Wake me if there's trouble." He stretched out on the rug, pillowed his head on his shield, and was asleep almost at once.

Cat roamed around the library, exhausted but not sleepy, watching as the others made themselves comfortable. She still shivered occasionally form the memory of her terror.

"You should rest," Arien said gently.

She shook her head. "We'll never pass that chamber, Arien. Never find the dungeons."

"Do not give up hope, dear girl. Hope is all that we have." He took her hands and squeezed them firmly.

"I don't know if I can go back in there. I've never been so afraid. That woman . . . that dead woman . . ."

"She is gone." He drew her against him and put his arms around her. "My spell ended her semblance of life. Do not be ashamed of your fear. You were the victim of her sorcery."

"Thank you," she breathed, resting her head against his chest.

"There is no need for thanks. You would have found your own way past the fear soon enough, so brave and spirited as you are. It would take more than a mere spell to stop you for long."

"Arien, I . . ." she raised her head, looking up at him. Had she thought his eyes were cool mirrors? No, they were warm and velvety.

He began to lean toward her. She caught her breath, sure he was about to kiss her. But at the last moment, he started, and released her, stepping back. Flustered, not knowing what she had done wrong, Cat randomly plucked a book from the shelf and began flipping through it without even seeing the pages. Arien tugged on his sleeves, straightening them, seeming nearly as uncertain as she felt.

She wanted to say something but had no idea what to say.

A moment passed, taking an eternity. Then Arien happened to glance at the book in her hands, and the blood drained from his face.

"What's the matter?" she asked, alarmed.

"Might I perchance see that book?" His voice wavered and he stared at it as if he was afraid it would vanish before his eyes.

She gave it to him. "Of course."

He held it gingerly, studied the cover. There were letters, golden runes on the dark brown cover, that Cat could not read. Unbelieving, he turned to the beginning. "Oh, Cat," he breathed. "You are a marvel! You've found it! By purest chance, you've found it!"

"That's it? That's the book you've been looking for?"

"It may be!" He clasped it to his chest, his gaze faraway and fever-bright. "Livana Silvermoon, could it be? Am I finally to be free of this horrid burden? Cat, Cat, if this contains what I hope and pray that it does, I shall be forever in your debt."

*   *   *

"Shall I try my spell again?" Greyquin asked brightly.

A good night's rest and some dinner, even if it was traveling food, had done wonders for his spirits. He felt ready to take on an army of orcs. Bear, padding friskily beside him, felt the same. Everyone looked better, though Rayke was still weak from his wounds.

"There is still a matter to settle," Solarrin said. "It concerns yesterday's events."

"Damn right there's something to settle," Rayke said. "You almost got us killed, dung-pile!"

"You blame me?" Solarrin was incredulous. "What about her?" He jabbed his staff at Sybil. "I had everything under control until she came along and ruined my spell! Those creatures would have bowed down to me! They would have led us anywhere I wished! They would have delivered Selbon's fortunes over into my hands!"

"They tried to kill us!" Jessa cried.

"They would not have attacked had you left them alone!"

"They wouldn't have even gotten up if *you'd* left them alone!" Rayke shot back.

"That's enough!" Cat strode to the middle of the angry circle that was growing around Solarrin, hands on her hips. "We have enough trouble without fighting among ourselves. We got out alive. That's the important thing. It doesn't matter whose fault it was."

"His!" Sybil pointed at Solarrin.

"Hers!" He pointed right back.

"Let us not act like children," Arien said mildly. He, too, had awakened with renewed hopes, his soul lifted by the discovery of the book.

"Children!" bristled Solarrin. "You call me a child?"

"Aged as you are, I believe that I am still your elder. And I did not call you a child. I merely did say that you were acting like one. Which, in fact, you are."

"Greyquin, do your rhyme," Alphonse said, exasperated. "Let's find a way down so we can rescue Cat's mother, ransack the treasuries, and get home. I need a mug of ale."

"Go ahead," Solarrin said. "I will let this quarrel pass. You still need me, and will need me more before you see daylight again. I look forward to that inevitable time with extreme delight."

Cat motioned to Greyquin, and he unlocked the library door and proceeded out into the vast hall. The magical lights were still aglow. He went to the middle of the hall and started his chant, skipping the doors they'd already tried. He ended with his finger pointing at one directly opposite the one they'd originally entered.

"That one," he said, starting toward it.

The immense double doors at the end of the hall swung open even as Greyquin pointed.

A bored-looking group of orcs filed in, all wearing identical drab uniforms. They were followed by a yellow-skinned man, orckin by the look of him, in elaborately embroidered robes.

"Uh-oh," Greyquin muttered.

The orcs saw them, and suddenly weren't bored anymore.

The glory of battle comes only in remembrance.

The Book of Yor.

"Run or fight?" Greyquin demanded as the orcs reeled in surprise.

Cat hesitated in an agony of indecision.

"Run!" cried Sybil. "There are too many!"

"Take them alive!" the robed orcin yelled, spurring the soldiers into action.

"Fight!" Alphonse growled eagerly. Bostitch bobbed his head enthusiastically.

"Fight," Arien agreed heavily. "If we flee, they will follow."

"Surrender may be the way to the dungeons you were hoping for," Solarrin pointed out.

"We fight," Cat decided, drawing her sword.

The orcs charged down the hall, boots clattering against the marble floor. Some, carrying crossbows, ducked behind columns to shield themselves while they loosed their missiles. Jessa immediately did the same, reaching for an arrow. In her haste, she dropped her quiver and spilled all of her few remaining arrows on the floor. Cursing, she knelt and grabbed for them.

"Bloodfists!" Alphonse bellowed, running toward the approaching orcs.

"Skullcrushers!" some orcs yelled, while others cried, "Deathblows!"

"Here we go again," Rayke muttered, but he followed right behind Bostitch with sword in hand.

"*Firalel*," Arien whispered, closing his eyes and passing his hands in a circle in front of his face. He stepped to the center of the hall, making no attempt to hide himself.

"Wizard!" the robed orcin gasped. He looked wildly around at the crossbowmen. "The elf! He's a mage! Shoot him!"

"Arien, get down!" Cat cried, running toward him. She was too far away to get there in time, too far to knock him out of the way, even too far to throw herself in the path of the bolts though she would have done so without hesitation.

Six orcs popped out from behind columns and fired in unison. In her mind's eye, Cat saw the bolts strike Arien, saw him fall. "No!" she screamed, as if she could stop the deadly hail by sheer force of will.

They sped toward him. He stood calmly, watching them come, watching them as every one of them somehow missed him by mere inches.

Cat skidded to a halt, nearly running into him and impaling him with her drawn sword. "Get down!" she cried. "You'll not be so lucky again!"

"My magic protects me," he said with just a touch of pride. "Stand back, my dear. You are not shielded as I am."

Another bolt passed between them. She spared a final moment to stare at him, then dashed for cover. She ran from one column to the next, realizing that the crossbowmen were following the orcin's orders and concentrating on Arien, freeing her friends for face-to-face combat.

The orcin brought his wrists together, clanging a pair of copper-hued bracers. Sparks danced around him. Another wizard! Sorcery against sorcery! Would Arien's magic prove the stronger?

A bolt of lightning crackled through the air. It streaked past Arien, missing by the barest of margins, and left a large black mark on the far wall.

Arien retaliated, hurling a ball of ice. It sailed between Bostitch and Alphonse, toward the orckin mage. He, evidently not shielded, was knocked off his feet by the impact.

An orc ducked away from Rayke's swing and hid behind the same column that concealed Cat. His lip curled, revealing tusks that were larger and more gnarled than Alphonse's. He stabbed at her leg.

Bright pain sizzled through her. Gritting her teeth, she slashed at him. He parried the blow, returning one of his own. Cat drew her knife in her other hand and attacked with both.

The knife pierced his chest, not a mortal wound but a painful one. Enraged, he swung at her again and missed, striking the column and losing his grip. Cat plunged her sword into his gut.

Another orc in front of her spun and dropped, the feathered end of an arrow under his chin. Cat jumped over bodies and threw herself to the floor as another bolt of lightning split the air.

She risked a look, and saw that Arien was still standing, unhurt. But neither his luck nor his spell would last forever. She limped toward the orckin, intent on him, so that she didn't have a chance to escape as she was grabbed from behind.

The orc was huge, almost as tall as Alphonse. He wore a heavy steel breastplate. His helm was too small, so his meaty face and jowls bulged out from under the cheek guards. His hot breath was like wind off the docks on a bad day, and he leered at her with a grotesque lust that gave new strength to her struggles.

He caught her wrist, bending it until she dropped her sword. She drove the knife at his face and the point scraped along the side of his helm. He butted his head against hers. As she sagged in his grip, fighting unconsciousness, he slung her over his shoulder like a bag of grain.

The orc began shoving a path through the battle, clutching his prize. He suddenly bent double, uttering a bleat of pain. Cat tumbled from his shoulder and scrambled away, breathing a silent thank-you to Jessa as she saw the arrow jutting from his leg.

An orc body, the chest caved in, fell across her path. She crawled over it and nearly got stepped on by Alphonse.

"Cat? What are you doing down there?" He reached down and hauled her to her feet.

"Thanks, big fellow," she gasped.

Alphonse stood in a the midst of a heap of motionless or groaning orcs. He was bleeding from a few small wounds, but the pain did not slow him at all. The eddies of orcs parted briefly, allowing her brief glimpses of her friends. Sybil was wounded, Rayke defending her. Bear, all his friskiness gone, stood astride a screaming orc, his jaws dripping. She could not see either wizard, and fear seized her heart. Where was Arien?

"Go help Rayke," she said to Alphonse. He nodded and kicked a wounded orc aside as he made his way toward Rayke and Sybil.

Cat heard movement behind her. She spun and saw the orc who had captured her. He threw down the bloody arrow that he'd pulled from his leg, and came at her.

She felt very defenseless with only the knife. She backed away and tripped over a body, and though she did not fall, the orc saw his opportunity and lunged.

The orc's blade impaled her just above the belt. White-hot agony flared through her. A cry burst from her throat as the orc yanked the sword out.

She clamped her hands over the wound, feeling her own warm blood. The orc loomed over her, grinning triumphantly as she fell to her knees.

A tremendous scream of fury, loud as a dragon's roar, sounded right behind Cat. It was followed by the whistle of air through chains as Emily passed over her and wrapped around the orc's head. The spiked iron balls cracked his helm and skull like eggshells.

Cat slumped slowly to the floor, seeing Alphonse standing over her. He was as tall as a giant, his face a mask of rage. The last thing she heard before darkness swept over her was him calling frantically for Sybil.

*　　*　　*

"No, Livana, please, no," Arien prayed, taking Cat's limp hand in his own as Alphonse laid her carefully on the carpet. There was so much blood, far too much.

"She lives, thank Talopea," Sybil said, nearly as pale as Cat as she pulled off her helm and gloves. "Oh, my poor Cat!"

"Wail later," Jessa said sternly. "Or save her, and wail not at all."

Sybil nodded. She herself was suffering from several wounds, but she ignored them all as she pressed her hands to Cat's stomach and began to murmur softly.

Jessa grimaced and turned away. Seeing some orcs still moving amid the carnage, she motioned to Rayke and Alphonse. "We've work to do, warriors!"

"Will she be all right?" Arien asked softly. For so many years, he had kept himself from showing any depth of feeling, but now he knew fear and anguish enough to make up for all of those years. He rubbed Cat's icy hand in both of his, trying to warm it, willing his own life into her still form.

Sybil didn't immediately answer. Her eyes were closed, her lips parted. She sighed as if in pleasure. Beneath her touch, the horrible wound drew together. Arien saw that her own injuries were mending even as she healed Cat. At last, Sybil's eyelids fluttered.

"She needs to rest," she said huskily, exhaling in relief. "She's lost much blood, and Talopea cannot always help people like Cat."

Arien felt unfamiliar anger rise in him. "Why? Because she is born of mixed blood, even the gods withhold their gifts?" He was surprised at the extremity of his anger, and the coldness of his tone.

Sybil blinked in surprise. "That isn't what I meant at all!"

"Then what do you mean when you refer to people like Cat?"

She smiled at him. "How can I put this so as not to offend you? People who . . . have not yet learned to appreciate Talopea's other gifts. People like Cat."

"Ah," he said, uncomfortable under her smoldering hazel gaze. "I see." He looked down at Cat. She seemed now to be sleeping. Her color was better, her dark lashes sooty against her golden skin. He could see her pulse beating in her graceful throat. It was slow, but it was there. She would live.

"You know, Arien," Sybil purred, touching his hand. "Maybe you could . . . help her."

He met her eyes, giving her the coldest look he could, knowing it was cold indeed. "There are others in need of healing. Should you not see to that?"

She stared at him, open-mouthed. "Well," she said after a long moment had dragged by. "I suppose I should."

He nodded curtly, then, as she headed for the others, returned his anxious gaze to Cat. She moaned softly, stirred and opened her vividly blue eyes. Arien wanted to crush her to him, so overjoyed that she was alive!

"Arien? What happened?" She tried to sit up and fell back weakly. "Oh. The orc. I remember now." Alarm flashed over her face. "Is everyone all right?"

"Worry for yourself a bit, my dear. You suffered the worst by far." He slipped an arm under her and helped her sit, leaning her against him so that she could behold the aftermath of the battle. "Your company did well."

"The orckin mage?"

"Not a mage, no. There is no magic in the orcish race. His power came from enchanted bracers." He hesitated. "He is dead. I slew him." Grim pride filled him, then shamed him. There was no glory in killing, none at all. Yet on some base level, he had taken vicious delight in seeing his foe fall.

Cat frowned, and at first he feared she would denounce him as a murderer. But instead, she pointed. "What *is* Solarrin doing?"

*   *   *

"In neat categories," Solarrin ordered, wheezing as he moved. "Those that are too chopped-up to move, pile over here. The rest, lay out neatly."

Four orcs, all curiously blank-eyed, moved to follow his instructions. They were the only survivors, and Solarrin had been able to forestall Jessa's vengeful blade with some words of sorcery that had bound them to his will.

"Why go to all the trouble of sorting them?" Greyquin asked, tightening a bandage around Bear's leg and patting him consolingly.

"I have uses for them," Solarrin said.

"What use is a dead orc? What use is a live one, for that matter?" Then it came to him, and his stomach, already upset by the stink of blood and orc bodies, churned rapidly. "You don't mean you're going to raise them!"

"Precisely. Many of these will make strong and durable undead warriors."

"But won't they rot away, like the ones down below?"

"Those had been animate for decades," Solarrin pointed out. "And even when the flesh has gone soft and dropped completely from their bones, they shall still be capable servants."

As the enspelled orcs lifted the body of the orckin mage, whose chest had been caved in by iceball pummelling, a gem fell from his robes and rolled to a stop against Greyquin's boot. It was a small opal, polished into a smooth ball, the colors swirling and glittering over its surface. He bent to pick it up but Solarrin, for all his girth and lameness, was quicker.

"Hmm, interesting," Solarrin muttered as he rolled it between thumb and forefinger. "This explains much."

"It's just a gem," Greyquin shrugged. "Cat's gotten better on a night of cutting purses. Here she comes. You know, she probably won't let you make undead out of those."

Solarrin scowled. "Do you think that I follow the orders of a crossling who hasn't even the sense to stay out of the way of a sword?"

"Go ahead and ask her, then," Greyquin challenged.

Solarrin coolly ignored him, continuing to study the gem as Cat and Arien approached.

"You've got prisoners," Cat said. "I want to talk to them."

"Orcs are not known for their witty conversation," Solarrin said. He turned to Arien. "Observe. What do you make of this?"

"*Ilgilean,*" Arien said. "A powerstone."

"What are you talking about?" Cat asked. "It's just an opal. I've seen better after a night of cutting purses."

"Told you so!" Greyquin grinned at Solarrin.

"It is a magical gem," Arien explained. "You see, the energy that a mage uses to cast spells comes from his own life force. Rest is required to replenish those internal energies. Too much spellcasting in too short a time will deplete his life force and begin to cause him physical injury."

"Powerful mages, with study and practice can draw energy from the *aether*," Solarrin added with an air of smug superiority. "That is the invisible, intangible energy of the world itself and all the living and non-living things in it."

"A powerstone, *ilgilean*, in the elven," Arien went on, "absorbs *aether* and stores it. A mage may draw upon its energies instead of his own, allowing him to cast more spells without needing to rest."

"The elves prefer opal," Solarrin said. "I have one of my own, given me by one who instructed me before I far outmatched him in skill." He showed his yellow teeth in an evil smile. "A bloodstone, of course."

"Are they worth much?" Cat asked.

"They expensive and difficult to make." Arien smiled, much less evilly than Solarrin. "On my salary, I could not afford one."

"Keep it, then," Cat deftly plucked it from Solarrin's grasp and passed it to Arien.

"My orc found it," Solarrin pointed out crossly.

"You said you've already got one," she said. "And I'm surprised that a mage as skilled as you claim to be would even need one."

"Are you well enough to be moving around, crossling? You gushed like a punctured wineskin."

"I want to question these orcs. Arien says you must have them enspelled, so tell them to answer me truthfully."

"Fine, fine," Solarrin groused. "But not here. We could be discovered at any time."

"How about that way?" Greyquin suggested, pointing at the door he'd picked before the orcs appeared. That was less than an hour ago, but it seemed like forever. "It'll stink like orc, though, if we're taking those four with us."

"Well, at least it won't stink of dead orc," Sybil said, approaching in time to hear him.

"You will have to get used to it," Solarrin declared, gesturing grandly to the bodies. "I will soon have an undead army of my own, small though it may be."

"No! Not more of that disgusting sorcery!" Sybil stumbled back into the protective circle of Rayke's arms. "How can you even think of such a thing?"

"Solarrin," Cat said wearily, "I don't want to argue with you, but couldn't you do that later? The dungeons, first, if you don't mind?"

"Oh, very well. I shall wait." He produced a small silver flask from inside his robes and drank from it, shuddering as he swallowed. "They're going nowhere."

"Sweet Talopea," Sybil breathed as Greyquin opened his chosen door. "What a luxurious bedchamber!"

The walls were polished walnut, dark and glossy as Cat's hair. The floor was covered with a rug of black, red and gold. Opposite the door was a white marble fireplace under a painting of a red-robed man calling lightning from the sky. In the middle of the room was a huge four-poster bed with dark red curtains tied back at the sides and furs heaped atop it. Two doors flanked the fireplace, both closed.

"Think you that necromancers live like ghouls?" Solarrin gave Sybil a sour look. "Dwelling in dank tombs and sleeping in coffins when we're not gnawing the bones of the righteous?"

"We should make sure we're safe before we start questioning orcs," Greyquin said. "I'd feel better knowing what's behind those doors."

Beyond the first, he found a small round room with a domed ceiling, painted to resemble the night sky. In the center of the floor was a smooth disk of white marble.

"What's that?" Greyquin wondered aloud.

"*Ralan,*" Arien murmured, making a diamond of his index fingers and thumbs and looking through it at the circle. To his eyes, the circle shimmered with spectral light. "Hmm, it is enchanted. Given a few hours, I might fathom its powers."

"Do," Cat said. "We'll rest here while I question the orcs. This circle could be dangerous, or it could be helpful."

"Thus it is with magic," Arien commented. "Like any tool, its morality is defined by how it is used."

*   *   *

"Answer her questions," Solarrin said casually, reclining in a rich leather chair by the fireplace with his feet propped up. Cat saw that the foot on his bad leg was a misshapen lump, though whether natural or the result of an accident she was unable to guess.

"Where are the dungeons?" she asked.

The orcs pointed toward the floor.

Alphonse snorted. "This ugly lot is even stupider than my clan back home. Let me try." He leaned close to one, baring his tusks. "*Pok dizdek, dompa? Dompa?*"

The orc rattled off a long string of grunts and glottal syllables. Alphonse nodded and urged him to continue.

"*Bosta eyani ton? Eyani?*" He pointed at Arien, who was sitting on the padded lid of an ornate chest and fastidiously wiping blood from his sleeves.

Cat realized that it was her blood, and looked down at herself. The front of her tunic was soaked with blood. It felt cold and clammy against her healed skin.

"*Eyani?*" repeated the orc, glaring at Arien. "*Eyani, yah. Okoh.*"

Alphonse turned to Cat. "He says there is an elf in the dungeons. One elf."

She bit her lip and clasped her hands anxiously, forgetting about her stained tunic. "Can we get there? Is she alive?"

"*Bruda sif?*" Alphonse asked.

The orc shrugged.

"He doesn't know. But he told me how to get there." Alphonse frowned. "It won't be easy. We'd have to go through the halls where the orcs live."

"How many are there?" Rayke asked.

"*Dusta orc? Kenst? Babin?*"

"*Babin,*" the orc said. "*Tibo klan.*"

"He says there are more than a hundred," Alphonse translated grimly. "Three clans."

"A hundred orcs," Jessa mused, running her fingers over her two remaining arrows.

The thoughtful silence was broken by Greyquin's delighted whoop from the next room, which had proved empty save a desk, a portrait of a mirthless old woman, and a chest. He and Rayke had set to forcing the top open when they could find no lock for Cat to pick

"Anybody think to bring a sack?" he called cheerily. A moment later came the sound of hands scooping through coins.

Cat glanced that way, seeing that the chest was brimming with gold and silver coins. But her mind was more concerned with three clans of orcs, and how she could slip away from her friends to make the dangerous trip alone. There was no way such a large group could pass undetected, and since Arien had fulfilled his quest, the only mission remaining was hers alone.

"Does not the sight of all this wealth tempt your criminal instincts?" Arien asked

"No. It but lays there. Where's the challenge?"

"The challenge?" he laughed. "Need I remind you that you were nearly dead not an hour ago? How much more challenge do you require?"

"I'm not here for a reward," she said seriously.

He took her hand and led her into the room. "Fill your pockets, dear Cat. Gather yourself a fortune, so that you need never steal again."

Cat smiled. "Only if you do likewise, poor Librarian!"

She soon had her backpack heavy with gold, although she doubted that it would stop her from being a thief. As the rest were still happily stuffing their pouches and exclaiming over all the things they planned to buy, Cat studied the portrait.

The woman wore an old-fashioned high-collared black dress, relieved only by a bit of stiff lace and a cameo pin. Her hair was iron-grey, pined back in a tight bun. Her eyes were cold little chips of ice. Cat wondered amusedly if she was Selbon's mother.

There was something unusual about the painting, Cat decided. She looked closely at the edges of the frame and nodded to herself. The painting hid a compartment.

Cat reached up and ran skilled fingers along the frame. She found the tiny catch and pressed it.

The woman in the painting stared directly at Cat. Her mouth opened. "Thief! Thief!" the picture cried.

The woman's cold eyes flashed. The white light filled the world.

*   *   *

True friends are more valuable than dragon-gold.

The Book of Yor.

"There must be something we can do," Arien said. "We cannot leave her like this."

Treasure forgotten, they stood around the statue.

Cat's hands were raised in a warding-off gesture. Her head was turned to the side, eyes tightly closed, shock and pain etched clearly on her features. Every line of her body, her clothes, weapons, and all, had been captured in perfect detail. Frozen in smooth marble. No sculptor had ever crafted such a flawless piece of work.

Bostitch held Solarrin up so that he could inspect the painting. "A spell, of course. Just waiting for some meddlesome fool to come along. Let it be if you value your fleshly state."

"There's a compartment behind it," Greyquin said. "Cat must have been trying to open it."

Alphonse looked at Arien. "You're a wizard. Do something."

"I cannot," he said, touching the cool marble waves of Cat's hair. "This sorcery is beyond my simple skill."

"Not beyond mine," Solarrin said. "I could transform her to flesh with a nod."

"Well, don't just stand there," growled Alphonse. "Get on with it."

"In a moment." He lurched to the center of their loose circle and placed a possessive hand on the statue, his black eyes glittering.

"And what is your price?" Arien asked angrily, resisting the urge to slap Solarrin's hand away.

"I will not change her back until you have all admitted my superiority."

"Why, you little—" Alphonse reached for Solarrin's neck.

Arien gently pushed down his hands. "Alphonse, we must think of Cat."

"He's right, Alphonse," Sybil said. "Let me handle this." She crouched to look Solarrin in the eye and gave him her most winsome look, which had been known to stop a ten-man brawl. "We really are helpless without you. Please, please, please, give us our Cat back."

Solarrin preened, stroking his beard. "And what about the rest of you?"

"We agree with Sybil," Jessa said grudgingly.

"Not good enough. Say it! Each of you, say it!"

"Solarrin, please," Arien said. "This is not necessary. You have proven your power. Are you so uncertain of it yourself that you need us to confirm it for you?"

He reddened. "Nonsense! I only want to be sure that you appreciate how lucky you are to be blessed with my presence."

"Oh, we do," Alphonse muttered. Greyquin nudged him sharply.

"Help her," Arien said softly. "Show us that you are merciful as well as powerful."

"I will!" Solarrin declared. He closed his eyes, furrowed his brow in concentration, and whispered chilling words of magic. He tapped the statue with his staff.

The marble softened. Cat took a breath, let it out in a sigh, and collapsed. Arien caught her, lowering her to the ground. Again, she was in his arms, and again, for all the wrong reasons.

The others crowded around him, but looking past and between them he saw something that made him uneasy. Solarrin, pale with exhaustion, gripped Bostitch's leg as if for support. Arien saw the gnome's lips move. Bostitch sagged in sudden weariness, while Solarrin himself straightened and looked around with renewed vigor.

"The painting—!" Cat gasped, jerking upright.

"It's all right, Cat," Sybil said. "Solarrin turned you back."

"Turned me what?" she asked warily.

"You had been turned to stone," Arien said, reluctantly releasing her. "The portrait is enchanted. How do you feel?"

She rubbed her arms and legs. "Well, I'd rather not go through that again."

"Why did you do it in the first place?" Solarrin sneered. "You should know what curiosity does to cats."

"But there's a hinge, a compartment. I was trying to open it."

"You could have warned us," Greyquin said. He stuck his tongue out at the woman in the picture.

Cat got unsteadily to her feet. "But now I'm more curious than ever. There must be something of value, if it's protected by such a spell."

"Oh, no," Arien said. "A challenge is one thing, but please, dear Cat, leave it be. I do not want to see you made stone again."

"No, she's right. Someone went to a lot of trouble to keep that compartment closed." Greyquin joined her by the wall. "Alphonse, come here."

"Why me?"

"Because you're the biggest. I want you to lift me up so I can get a better look."

"If you're going to tinker with that again, I'm going to wait in the other room," Sybil declared.

"That's a good idea," Greyquin said. "Jessa, would you take Bear? Maybe the rest of you should go with her. "

"And let you have all the fun?" Cat laughed, completely recovered from her experience.

Arien envied her resilience. Twice in one morning, she had nearly been lost to them forever, yet she remained vivid and fresh and so full of life that it made his heart ache. "I will stay," he said. "If I cannot stop you, I can at least try to help. Failing that, I will share your fate."

"I, too, will stay," Solarrin announced in tones that hinted he expected them to all fall down weeping in gratitude. Bostitch stood behind him.

"You're going to get me killed, shorty," Alphonse grumbled, lifting Greyquin. He grunted. "What have you been eating, bricks?"

"No, just his own oatmeal," Cat teased.

Greyquin ignored their teasing and drew a knife. "Farewell, old witch," he said to the woman.

"No!" Solarrin cried, lurching forward.

Too late. Greyquin stabbed the knife through the canvas.

Arien pulled Cat against him and turned her face away from the painting. "Don't look!" He shielded his own eyes.

A flash of light and force knocked them all back. Alphonse dropped Greyquin on Solarrin, tripped over them both, and fell against Bostitch. The two massive warriors collided with the wall hard enough to make the room shake. At the end of it, only Cat and Arien remained standing.

Cat raised her head and looked around. "What happened?"

"Ask Greyquin," Alphonse grunted, rubbing his elbow. "It was his brilliant idea."

"But it worked," Greyquin said, crawling off Solarrin, who lay on his back helpless as an upended turtle. "The magic is gone."

"The whole painting is gone," Alphonse said.

"You have ruined a perfectly good spell," Solarrin complained, struggling to roll onto his side. "Not to mention nearly getting us all killed. Do you think you can just go about willy-nilly, destroying enchantments whenever you feel like it? If you really want to meet Haarkon face to face, come here and hold still."

Cat stepped over Solarrin and peered into the open space revealed behind the shreds of the canvas. "Oh!" she gasped.

"What is it?" Greyquin jumped up and down. "Mice and rats, I can't see!"

Cat reached in and came out with a thick gold bar. "A five thousand mark bar!" she said.

"Five thousand marks?" Rayke said from the doorway. He turned to Arien. "I want a raise."

"I promised you a share of any profits," he reminded him.

Cat pulled out more bars. "Five, six, seven! Thirty-five thousand marks!" She handed them to Greyquin, who held them as if they were eggs. "And a bag, and a box." She took out the bag and shook it.

"Gems," Greyquin said happily. "Want to bet?"

"No bet," she said, cupping a hand and tipping the bag into it. Jewels of all colors poured into her palm, trickled through her fingers, and bounced on the floor.

"Excitable children," Solarrin muttered as the others exclaimed in delight, but his disdain did not keep him from snatching up a dusky black gem.

"Arien, look." Cat turned to him. He held his own hands beneath hers and she let the stones spill into them.

He picked out a gem, oval-shaped and glittering with small facets. It was a midnight sapphire, so blue it was almost black. He closed Cat's fingers around it. "For you, Cat, because you are as precious."

She held it tightly, staring up at him. The jewel paled in comparison with her dazzling eyes.

"What's in the box?" Greyquin asked eagerly, tugging on her cloak, distracting her.

Arien turned away, hastily returned to the other room where his only company was Solarrin's spellbound orcs. "*Ista vai ella?*" he whispered in elven. "What am I doing? I did not think that I would be . . . that she would be . . . ah, I cannot even keep my own thoughts clear!"

He dropped into a chair and buried his head in his hands, his thoughts dark and troubled.

*   *   *

"The Lord's Retreat," Sybil said firmly, rattling her pouch. "Dragon steaks in honeyed sauce, lemon cream pie . . ."

"Sybil, stop!" Greyquin groaned. "You're making me hungry."

She giggled and threw herself backward across the bed. "Oh, if my father could see this! He told me I was ruining my life by joining the Temple. Said I wouldn't have two marks to rub together."

"What did you tell him?" Rayke asked.

"That it wasn't marks I was interested in rubbing," she said, and shrieked laughter.

"She's gold-giddy," Alphonse said, chewing his lip in concentration. His battered breastplate rested across his knees as he tried without much success to repair a jagged hole.

Bostitch sat like the world's largest child, gleefully sorting gems. Jessa sharpened her knife in long, methodic strokes. Though she had initially seemed as happy with the find as the rest of them, she had now returned to her dour demeanor. Only the banded green malachite pin on her cloak proved that she had even been a part of the excitement.

Solarrin appeared in the doorway, looking tired but incredibly self-satisfied. Arien was behind him, calm as ever.

"We have divined the secret of the disk," Solarrin intoned, then coughed until he could barely stand. Gasping, he gestured to Arien. "Perhaps you should tell them."

Arien nodded. He paused, seeming to gather his thoughts, until all attention was focused on him. Then, in what Cat had come to recognize as his instructor's tone, he began explaining to them what teleportation was and how it worked.

*   *   *

Excerpt from *An Apprentice's Handbook of Magical Theories*, by Talus Yor, Archmage of Thanis:

Certain magics involve affecting the position of objects by force of will. Beginning students may find themselves limited to small inanimate items, *apporting* or moving them slowly without physical contact. Eventual refinements can lead to the manipulation of catches, knots, and similar fastenings. A mage might then gain control over his own person, *levitating* or even mastering *flight*.

It is the nature of inanimate objects to resist movement with their weight. A feather is easier to move than an iron bar, whether done by hand or mind. Living things also resist movement that is not within their control, so while a wizard may attempt to *levitate* another, it will be far more difficult with an unwilling subject.

Most of these spells cause simple movement visible to the eye. There is, however, a rare and complex spell with the power to move objects from one place to another instantly, without crossing the space in between. This is called *teleportation*, among the most difficult of all sorceries to master.

Legends are filled with tales of *teleportation*, including magical portals, enchanted items, mages that have attempted to travel to one of the moons, and many others. It is important to remember that these are legends, and while they may have a basis in truth, should be examined with a critical mind.

*   *   *

"Another one?" Arien moaned as Sybil struggled through the door.

"It's antique," Sybil said defensively, running her hand along the edge of the table she was carrying. "Look at the gold inlay!"

They had already decided that the disk would provide the best escape if they were forced to leave the castle hastily. "One step ahead of the City Guard," was how Cat had put it. In the meanwhile, however, it could be used to send other things to their chosen destination. Which, since only a wizard could use the disk and Solarrin had never visited Thanis, meant the task fell to Arien.

Arien sighed. "I've already sent six piles of books, in addition to the chest of coin. My room is quite small, you know. I shall have nowhere to sleep."

"You could always stay with a friend," she suggested, shifting her shoulders in a gesture of temptation. "There's always room at the Temple."

He paused and looked dubiously at her, untempted. "I think not."

"Well, how about Cat? She's got a nice place. Cozy, quiet. I'm sure she would—"

"If you do not step off the disk, Sybil, I shall be forced to transport you as well," he said coldly.

Sybil huffed, searched for a retort, found none, and flounced out of the chamber. Arien shook his head and went back to work. By the time he was finished wrestling with the necessary magics, he was so weary he could barely walk to the door.

His weariness left him in a flash as he heard what Cat was saying.

"—back to Thanis. I'll stay behind and sneak past the orcs alone."

Immediate outcry greeted her. Alphonse's voice cut through the babble as he rose to his full impressive height and stood over Cat with his fists on his hips. "No," he declared.

"Blast it, Alphonse—" she began.

"I'm not leaving you to face the orcs alone. The rest can go. I'm staying."

"I'm not leaving either!" Sybil said. Rayke and Greyquin nodded.

"I myself feel no particular urge to accompany you," Solarrin said, "but I will do so if for no other reason than to observe your inevitable failure."

"What makes you think we'll fail?" Jessa demanded.

"How many arrows do you have?" he shot back.

"Two," she admitted.

"Two," he said, rolling the word around his mouth as if savoring it. "Two arrows. How many orcs can you kill with two arrows?"

"Two," she said firmly, her eyes flashing as if daring him to say anything.

"Leaving a hundred less two." Solarrin chuckled darkly, not intimidated.

"There has to be another way down there," Rayke said. "Selbon wouldn't want to wade through orcs every time he went to gloat over his prisoners. Those evil wizards don't like dealing with the hired help."

"And how do you, oh lord of wisdom, know so much about evil wizards?" Solarrin sneered.

"I've been watching you," Rayke shot back.

"Now, wait," Cat said as Solarrin began to bluster. "Rayke could be right! One of those doors might lead to another way down. I wouldn't have to confront the orcs."

"I am afraid we must contest your decision, Cat," Arien said. "You cannot lead us by sending us away while you go on alone. There are such things as loyalty and friendship to consider."

"Arien, it's too risky!" Her eyes were sapphire flame, her jaw set in determination. "I'm not going to lead you to your deaths. You're going back to Thanis."

"How is that possible if I refuse to activate the teleport disk?"

"I'm trying to save your lives!" she said desperately, but he knew he'd won.

"We accept the risks," Arien said. "Now, lead us."

She heaved a sigh, shaking her head. "Greyquin, find us a way down."

Greyquin snapped a salute and hurried into the hall with Bear padding at his heels. This time his finger stopped while pointing at a door at the far end of the hall. The door, tucked between two pillars, was small and somehow shy, as if it didn't want to be noticed.

"That one," Greyquin said. "The way down. I'm sure of it."

They stopped in front of the small door, which both Bostitch and Alphonse regarded skeptically.

"We'll have to crawl," Alphonse said. The top of the frame was lower than his chest.

"Set me down," Solarrin ordered, tapping Bostitch between the horns.

"Good thing for you it's short instead of narrow," Jessa said.

Solarrin scowled at her. "I grow weary of you, woman. The presence of death surrounds you like a cloud, and you still mock me. We shall see who laughs when Haarkon's bony hand rips your soul away."

"I'm not afraid of you," she spat. "From what I've seen, you're nothing but talk."

"Oh? Look upon them, then!" He spun unsteadily on his bad leg and pointed at the enspelled orcs standing in a silent row behind him. "See how they obey me? It is my power that has done this, power that a mere mortal like you could never begin to comprehend!"

In his anger, he slammed the butt of his staff down for emphasis, but it hit the orc's foot instead of the marble floor.

"Aiee!" the orc howled. Before any of them could react, he had seized the staff from Solarrin. With a savage cry, he brought it down over the wizard's head. There was a hollow thunk, and Solarrin collapsed.

"His spell!" Arien said. "He broke it by striking the orc!"

The moment Solarrin fell, the remaining three orcs started as if suddenly awakened. The one with the staff swung wildly at Jessa, but missed as she ducked. He flung it aside and raced for the double doors at the end of the hall.

"Jessa!" Cat called urgently.

The huntress set an arrow to the string. Greyquin jumped onto Bear and charged after the fleeing orc, who was loudly crying, "*Zhagaz! Zhagaz!*"

"Alarm," Alphonse translated grimly, joining Bostitch to swiftly subdue the three other orcs. "We're caught."

The fourth orc reached for the handle. At that moment, Jessa's arrow flew. It hit his outstretched hand, nailing it to a door. He shrieked but tugged the point free of the wood. With the shaft still jutting from his hand, he jerked one of the doors open and stumbled through. Greyquin and Bear were right behind him.

Cat ran after, ignoring the others as they yelled at her to come back. She was almost to the door when Bear came charging back through, a wild-eyed Greyquin clinging frantically to the saddle.

"Cat, run!" he yelled.

The doors flew wide. Orcs thundered into the hall, bristling with weapons. Cat's boots skidded on the marble as she tried to stop, turn, and start running in the opposite direction all in the same heartbeat of time.

"To the disk!" she called to Arien. "Our only chance!"

An orc leapt at her but was caught in Bear's powerful jaws. His teeth sheared through flesh and bone, shook the orc like a rag, and dropped him. More orcs were gaining on her rapidly.

"Grab on!" Greyquin held out a hand.

"Bear can't carry us both!"

"He can try!"

There was no more time to argue. She let him haul her onto the dog's back. They were both light, and Bear was strong, but he slowed under their combined weight.

Ahead, she could see the others reacting all wrong. Instead of escaping to the disk, and to Thanis as they should be, they were holding back, waiting for her and Greyquin. Then, to make matters worse, Alphonse and Rayke decided to charge.

"For Steel and for Bloodfists!" Alphonse cried.

Bostitch swept Solarrin up as if he weighed no more than a child. His nostrils flared as the conflicting urges to protect his master and attack the orcs raged in him.

Cat leaped from Bear's back. "Go! Everyone! There are too many of them!"

"They'll follow," Jessa said, calmly watching the fight and looking for the right target.

"No, the disk! Arien—"

Arien suddenly stumbled, and Cat's heart stopped. She leaped to steady him, terrified that he'd been shot, but then felt herself unbalanced. It was as if the ground was moving beneath her feet.

She looked down and caught her breath. The ground *was* moving beneath her feet, rippling like water. It lapped up, licking at her boots. Her feet sank into it. Only her hold on Arien's arm kept either of them from falling. There was nowhere to go. The marble was like tar, like wax, flowing smoothly over their legs.

Alphonse crashed to his knees and was immediately engulfed to the hips in living stone. The orc nearest him was about to drive a broad-tipped spear into his chest when a powerful voice rang out.

"Hold, we command!"

The orcs lowered their weapons. The stone stopped flowing and solidified around them. Cat jabbed it with her sword, to no avail. Only Greyquin, still astride Bear, was unaffected. He jumped down and ran to Cat, over the frozen waves of stone.

A drum pounded with a stately rhythm. The orcs marched to a smoother patch of floor and lined up in two rows, facing each other with an aisle between them. They stood straight, shoulders back, and snapped their heels together. Those with spears began thumping them on the floor in time with the drums.

"Ghamban's teeth!" Alphonse swore. "Not even the fiercest chief commands that kind of obedience." He pulled at his trapped feet, muscles bulging, but the stone would not give way.

"We're going to die," Sybil sobbed, struggling uselessly. "I can't move!"

"Solarrin!" Arien said in a low, urgent voice. "Now would be an excellent time to show your vast skill!"

Solarrin blinked at him groggily, rubbing the purple bump that had risen on his forehead. He was half-buried in stone, stuck where Bostitch had dropped him when the minotaur had lost his balance. Bostitch lay nearby, one of his horns trapped so that he could barely move his head.

"That orc really shook the apples from his tree," Greyquin said. "Cat, what can I do?"

"Save yourself, Greyquin. You can't help us."

"I won't leave everyone stuck here!"

"See if you can aid Solarrin," Arien suggested, the only one of them to remain calm. "Sybil's powers cannot help him, but perhaps that healing elixir Cat espied might."

"But you said not to meddle with those!" Greyquin said.

"Under the circumstances," Arien said, turning his gaze to the doors, "I think we can risk the attempt."

Cat looked, and felt her hopes sink all the way down to her boots.

A tall and forbidding man entered the room, resplendent in robes of deep green edged with gold. The robes trailed behind him for several feet, and the collar rose into a stiffened fan that framed his head. His skin was wrinkled, withered, and dry. Wisps of fine white hair clung to his scalp and cheeks. He moved slowly, but with grandeur. In one hand, he held a smooth black staff tipped with a polished egg-shaped piece of amber. His other arm had been fashioned from solid silver.

"Welcome," he said in the same rich, commanding voice that had ordered the orcs to stop. "It has been long since we have had guests. We are Selbon. The Archmage Yrej Selbon."

*   *   *

Death is a period of transition, of contemplation and serenity between this world and the next. It can also be quite an inconvenience.

The Book of Yor.

"But you're dead!" Sybil gasped.

Selbon chuckled. "Death is a matter of perspective. And we perceive," he continued darkly as he looked around the room at the stacks of dead orcs, "that you have dealt a good deal of it. Can you withstand as well as you give? We think we shall find out."

"Not if you go first!" Jessa moved with fluid speed, raising the bow she'd held out of sight behind her body and firing in a blur of motion.

"No!" Arien cried as her last arrow sped straight and true. "He'll be shielded!"

Selbon stood perfectly still, smiling, as the arrow flew at him. Just before it would have pierced flesh, it seemed to reverse its flight mid-air. Not losing speed, it arced directly back the way it had come. The sound as it struck home was the only sound in the room.

Jessa looked down at the feathered shaft embedded in her chest. She wrapped a hand around it, lowering the bow. Her lips moved, but no words emerged as she sank slowly to the floor.

"Jessa!" Cat's voice cracked with the force of her cry. The name echoed off the vaulted ceiling and smooth walls, to return mocking her in a string of fading echoes.

Kiah dove from a hidden perch high among the columns. Talons outstretched, the hawk was a blur of brown as it went for Selbon.

The Archmage made a simple gesture. Power crackled through the air. Kiah's flight became a plunge, and the lifeless bird landed next to Sybil.

"Save your grief," Arien counseled Cat. "Let it cloud not your wits, else we will all surely join her."

Cat nodded, blinked away stinging tears. She glimpsed Greyquin, out of Selbon's line of sight, rummaging through Bostitch's pack.

"Now we can have a proper talk," Selbon said. "Have you sated your greed upon our gold?"

"We didn't come for gold," Cat said. She could not look at Jessa. Arien was right, she would have to be strong to save her friends.

Selbon looked at her. One eye was yellow and filmy, the other a brilliant green. "Elfkin. Intriguing. If it is not our gold you have come for, why does it fill your purses? Why do our gems glitter on your fingers? What, pray tell, have you come for, if not for gold?"

"We've come for the elf you hold in your dungeons." She saw Greyquin raise the elixir, and Arien's approving nod.

"Him? What would you want with him, even if he yet lives?"

"Him?" Cat's heart sank clear to her boots. "Not a woman?"

His laughter bubbled forth. "We have better uses for women than to keep them in dungeons." He approached Sybil and trailed a silver finger along her cheek and down her neck.

Sybil twisted away, but she could not move far.

"Leave her alone!" Rayke shouted.

"Are you the next to die?" Selbon asked him. "You have the gall to be rude to us? To deny us the simple pleasure of a woman's company?" He turned back to Sybil. "Ah, pretty pastry, it has been long since we have enjoyed a living woman."

She moaned in horror and shrank back. Cat, holding Arien's arm for balance, wiggled one foot free of her boot, leaving the boot standing empty in the stone. The other foot was squeezed tighter, and she winced as she tried to work it loose. Greyquin dumped the elixir down Solarrin's throat and he promptly went into a choking fit.

"So," Selbon said, seeing loathing and disgust in Sybil's face, "Our sweet one recoils from us. You will learn better, we promise. But that will come later. We first have some other matters to settle." He glanced curiously toward Solarrin, who was coughing and sputtering but now very much awake.

"That we do!" Cat cried, freeing her other foot and raising her sword. "Your death, necromancer!"

"Cat, no!" Arien gasped.

The watching orcs dared not break ranks, but she was aware of many crossbows swinging to track her advance. Still, she kept her head high, mentally urging Solarrin to hurry. It would be just like him, she thought, to wait until after she'd confronted the necromancer to make his move.

"Tasty crossling child, we have no wish to kill you," Selbon said. "Such a waste that would be!"

Solarrin spread his hands flat, palms down, and muttered harsh words. The stone encasing him flowed smoothly away.

"Our spell! Impossible!" Selbon's mismatched eyes bulged.

"Hardly," Solarrin sneered, back to his usual arrogant self. "Is this the best you can do?" He made the merest contemptuous nod, and the rest of the floor melted back to its normal shape.

"Very impressive." Selbon regained his composure. "You and we must have much in common. Much to discuss."

"I'm sure we do," Solarrin agreed, stroking his beard. "What did you have in mind?"

"You fat weasel!" Sybil cried. "I knew you'd betray us!"

"We are in need of a new apprentice," Selbon offered.

"Apprentice?" Solarrin said slowly.

"That's done it," Arien murmured to Cat. "Prepare to flee!"

"Apprentice?" Solarrin repeated. His voice rose to a bellow. "I am Solarrin! Archmage of the Universe! I am no one's *apprentice*!" He grabbed Selbon's arm. "*Harak!*"

Selbon hissed in pain, writhing in Solarrin's grip. "You dare to use the Touch of Death upon us? Fool, we will see the maggots feast upon you!"

"Now" Cat cried. "Run!"

"Stop them!" Selbon ordered. "We want them alive!"

"*Kininia!*" Arien called, making a gesture as of flicking water from his fingers. Cat felt a rush of cold air pass her. The floor in front of the orcs was suddenly covered with a thin sheet of ice. Their charge turned into a comedy of slips, trips, and falls.

The ice field separated Solarrin from them, but he was locked in a deadly exchange of spells with Selbon and barely glanced their way. Bostitch roared a battle cry, but his attempt to join his master ended ingloriously when his feet shot out from under him.

The nearest orcs had scrambled to secure footing, so Rayke doubled back. "Go on! I'll hold them!"

Alphonse, with Jessa's body in his arms, shouldered open the door to the bedchamber. Greyquin urged the others through.

"Take them home!" Cat said to Arien.

"Wait!" he caught her arm. "What about you?"

"I'll not leave them behind, not even Solarrin!" Before he could protest, before Sybil could do more than open her mouth in horror, she raced from the room.

Bostitch was a huge island in the midst of an angry sea. Several orcs were already sprawled on the floor, but more stood between him and the duelling wizards.

"Escape while you can, crossling!" Solarrin cried above the din of battle. "Take that oaf of a minotaur with you"

"No leave little man!" Bostitch roared.

"Yes, leave little man!" Solarrin yelled. He dealt Selbon a blow with his staff, which briefly enveloped the taller mage in a burst of black energy that exposed the bones beneath his withered flesh.

An orc came at Cat, but Rayke got to him first and beat him back onto the ice. The orc landed heavily on his face. Rayke plunged his sword into the orc's back.

Selbon used his amber-tipped staff to sweep Solarrin's good leg out from under him. At the moment of contact, there was a flash of unlight that left Cat blinking. Solarrin, flailing for balance, went grey. Selbon sprang on him and they both fell.

Bostitch roared again, seized the two nearest orcs, and slammed their heads together. He hurled the limp bodies at two other orcs and pressed forward. "Little man!"

Rayke, much braver than Cat would have ever been, slapped Bostitch. The minotaur turned and looked down at him, eyes bulging and bloodshot. "You heard him!" Rayke hollered. "He told you to go! Don't disobey, or you know what happens!"

Cat cried out in sudden pain as an orc slashed her leg. Two quick thrusts of her sword finished him, but she landed beside him as her leg refused to support her.

"But little man—!" Bostitch protested.

The duel was over, and it was down to old-fashioned brawling for the mages. Neither was terribly suited for it, but they pummelled and punched and bit and kicked with ferocity enough to make up for their lack of skill. Selbon's silver fingers locked around Solarrin's neck and squeezed.

"He gave you an order!" Rayke grabbed Cat and thrust her at Bostitch like she was a sack of vegetables. "Take the girl and run! I'll hold them off!"

"Rayke, no—!" Cat began, then lost her breath as Bostitch flung her over his shoulder.

He raised his sword in a salute. The orcs closed around him. Beyond them, she saw Selbon crouched over Solarrin, feasting on him like a jackal.

"Bostitch, wait," she gasped weakly.

"Bostitch, this way!"

"Oh, no!" Cat looked toward the voice, seeing from her jostled upside-down vantage Greyquin standing in the doorway, beckoning. "I told you to go!"

"Not without you!"

He scrambled out of the way just in time to avoid being trampled. The bedchamber passed in a blur, and then Cat saw the others, standing on the marble circle. Bostitch almost plowed through them like ninepins.

"Cat! You're hurt!" Arien said, looking as if he himself had taken the wound.

"Where's Rayke?" Sybil cried shrilly.

"Little man say go. Red-fur-face man say go too. So go!" Bostitch stomped his foot. "Go now!"

"Rayke's still back there!" Cat struggled, but in Bostitch's grip she might as well have been wrapped in dwarf-forged chains.

Hobnailed boots on clattered on marble. "They're right on us!" Alphonse put himself between the rest of them and the doorway, though he was burdened by Jessa's body.

Sybil, sobbing hysterically, started for the edge of the disk, but Greyquin caught her by the cloak. As if from very far away, Cat heard Arien's voice, cool and soft, speaking words of magic.

The world turned inside out. The only sight was a white blurriness, the only sound the frantic beating of her own heart. She could no longer feel Bostitch holding her, or her own desperate grip on her sword. Then, in a rush, sensation returned.

With a curse, a bark, and a series of thumps, Greyquin and Bear and a stack of books fell all over each other. Sybil knocked over her own cherished antique table. Alphonse rapped his head on a low beam. And Bostitch, in his surprise, nearly dropped Cat on the floor.

Arien collapsed weakly into a chair. His face was ashen with fatigue.

"We're home," he breathed. "Thanis."

"We made it!" Greyquin whooped in joy, but cut the sound off mid-whoop as he looked around at the rest of them, and they all realized just how high a price they'd paid for their freedom.

*   *   *

Part Two: The Curse

Wealth hath its privileges.

The Book of Yor.

Cat paused in the shadows, pulling her fur-trimmed capelet tight around her, though it was not the night breeze that made her shiver. The summer night was warm. It was fear that coiled its icy tendrils around her.

Ahead of her, lit by many brilliant lanterns, was a place to her even more daunting than the crypts of Castle Selbon. A place no elfkin should dare venture.

The Lord's Retreat.

Thanis' finest and most fabulous inn.

Taking a deep breath, she stepped into the fall of rainbow lights. An approaching carriage sent her back into hiding, especially when two elflords and their ladies emerged.

This was a mistake. She did not belong here. Her place in relation to the nobles of Thanis was lurking behind them in the dark, stealing what she could by guile, never being seen and certainly never speaking. She could never pass herself off as a lady of quality, no matter how costly her dress.

Still, her friends would be expecting her. This was to be their celebratory dinner, and also a feast to honor the passing of their valiant friends Rayke and Jessa. Even, mayhap, to lift a glass in Solarrin's name. The prospect of such a grand meal had been one of the few things to bring a smile to Sybil's lips in the week since they'd returned from the castle. Cat couldn't bear to see Sybil continue in her melancholy, couldn't bear to continue in it herself.

Emboldened by those thoughts, she stepped into the light again. Then once more sprang back, this time in a panic as she recognized Lord Taron, he of the emeralds, entering the inn.

She berated herself for being a fool. Lord Taron wouldn't know who had robbed his home, had never seen her, wouldn't know her.

Lord Taron and his wife disappeared through the doors, and once again, the night belonged to Cat. She steeled herself to step forward again.

A hand closed on her arm, another clapped over her mouth, she was yanked back just as she left she shadows for a third time.

"You flit back and forth into the light like a moth to flame," a man whispered into her ear.

She twisted in her captors' grasp and brought herself face to face with a black-haired elf. Her eyes widened as she recognized him.

"You spoke true, uncle," a second elf said, staring at Cat in repulsed shock. "She is of mixed blood!"

"Cat, was it not? A fitting name for an animal. I see that you remember Tanneivan. Do you remember also how I was driven from the Nightsiders because of you? When that aged fool One-Eye admitted you into the ranks, who spoke against him? Only I, Tanneivan! And for my pains, dismissed!"

"Will you slay her now, uncle?"

"Patience, Tiercel," Tanneivan began, but Cat wasn't about to let him finish. She sank her teeth into his hand and drove her dainty slipper-clad foot into his belly. Freed, she whirled to run but was hampered by her long skirt.

Tiercel blocked her path with a drawn sword. "Clever beast. You should never have been allowed to live, but we shall remedy that now!"

"This kill is mine!" Tanneivan declared angrily. "Stay your hand, nephew."

Cat cursed her gown and its makers, who hadn't foreseen the necessity of adding a swordbelt. She whipped her capelet from her shoulders and ensnared Tiercel's blade, yanking it from his grasp. His surprise lasted long enough for her to dart past him, but Tanneivan seized her by the hair before she had taken three steps toward freedom.

She hissed in pain but knew that if she quit struggling, she would be dead in an instant. She reached back instead, finding mostly by luck the hilt of Tanneivan's dagger. In a flash, it was in her hand, and then she buried the point in his arm.

Several strands of her hair came loose as Tanneivan yanked his arm away, but Cat barely noticed. She leapt at him, seeking his eyes with the dagger and missing by a fraction, scrawling a bloody line across his cheek and brow.

Tiercel lunged at her as his uncle cried out. She socked the hilt of the dagger against his temple and dropped him like a stone.

The sound of a blade leaving a sheath made her spin. Tanneivan leveled his sword at her, glowering through his bloody face. "Enough of this!"

Cat wedged the toe of her slipper beneath Tiercel's sword and flipped it up, into her waiting hand. Elf and elfkin eyed each other for a moment, in which he seemed to savor his inevitable victory and she only hoped that she would give him a fight to remember.

The exchange began. Even had she been dressed for this sort of thing, Cat knew he still would have been the more skillful, by far. Only her innate speed and a goodly portion of luck let her turn his blows aside, never getting an opening to attack. He backed her deeper into the shadows, where his dark garb let him blend in while her silver-blue gown glimmered like starlight.

He swung low and she leapt, sparing her legs a vicious strike. As she landed, her feet tangled in the hem of her gown and she fell onto her back. Tanneivan stood over her and set the point of his blade beneath her chin.

"Now," he said in smug satisfaction.

"Nias!"

An icicle skimmed his ear, missing by a hair's breadth. Tanneivan whirled.

"The next one shan't miss," Arien said calmly.

Tanneivan's mouth worked. "You . . . you defend this . . . thing? Look on her, brother elf! She is abomination! Turn your magic instead to cleanse her foulness from the earth!" When Arien's gaze didn't waver, Tanneivan's lip curled. "Who are you, that so disgraces your people?"

"Go now and you'll be spared." He poised his hand to throw. Cat moved to Arien's side, holding the sword.

Tanneivan stared at them in utter loathing, then bent to sling his nephew's arm over his shoulders. They melted into the shadows and were gone.

"We must stop meeting like this," Arien said gravely.

"Now we're even." She retrieved her cape and discarded the sword. "Thank you. He meant to kill me."

"You know him?"

"Tanneivan. He was a Nightsider, but left in outrage when One-Eye welcomed me. I thought he had quit Thanis. I never expected to see him again. A good thing you happened along!"

"I had come looking for you. Sybil feared that you might have second thoughts. I heard the sound of steel and chose to investigate. But now, we had best go, before they return."

He took her arm and led her into the light, and they both paused, staring at each other.

In their travels, he had always preferred garments of light colors. White, pale grey, light blue. Now, though, he was clad all in black velvet, a cape thrown over one shoulder. His silver hair was crowned by an onyx circlet.

For the first time, Cat truly noticed the pleasing litheness of his form, and wondered not what it would be like to kiss him but what it would be like to do more, to do the things Sybil spoke of. In that moment, such things seemed neither confusing nor frightening.

"Cat, Cat," he said, consuming her with his silver-grey gaze. "You are as lovely as the night."

She didn't trust herself to speak. He seemed about to say more, then shook his head and passed a hand over his eyes as if waking himself from some dream.

"Let us put this misfortune behind us. Come, our friends are waiting."

She let him lead her across the cobblestoned street to the inn. When they passed through the doors, the steward blanched in shock but quickly recovered.

"Milord," he bowed politely. "You've found your missing companion, I take it?"

"Indeed." Arien inclined his head, his manner exactly that of a high noble.

Cat heard a shocked intake of breath and her heart sank when she saw one of the elven couples she'd noticed earlier, standing aghast on the sweeping marble staircase that led to the second floor ballroom. Arien spared them an aloof glance, then smiled down at Cat.

"Shall we really give them a fright?" he murmured, eyes twinkling.

Did he mean to kiss her? She'd yearned for it, but never dared hope it would be true, certainly never in such a place as this!

He leaned toward her, but instead of a kiss he pushed back her curls and traced his fingertip along the taper of her ear. Tingles shot through her. Never had she thought her ears were so sensitive.

The elf woman on the stairs swooned, making her escort rush to catch her. Cat felt a little like swooning herself, though for different reasons altogether.

"I pray you, Cat, forgive that liberty," Arien said, a trifle unsteadily.

She nodded, puzzled. "Of course." All he'd done was touch her ear . . . but if it was such an innocent gesture, why did she feel as she did?

He tucked her hand into the crook of his elbow and led her into the smallest of the inn's four dining rooms. This, the Garden Room, indeed overlooked the lush rose gardens. There was a cleared space amid the tables for those who wished to dance without going upstairs to one of the elaborate ballrooms. Minstrels played harp, flute, and mandolin.

Sybil waved excitedly as they approached. Her blond hair was piled high under a tiara that sparkled with emeralds. Familiar emeralds. Cat briefly closed her eyes and prayed to any gods that might be listening to have Lord Taron be taking his meal in another dining room tonight.

Greyquin was neat and dapper in dark brown and rust-colored velvet. His salt-and-pepper beard was closely trimmed for the occasion. A cap with a jaunty feather was slung on the back of his chair.

"Cat, darling, you look simply delicious!" Sybil gushed. "Doesn't she, Arien?"

"Quite," he said, drawing out a chair for her as she sat. "As do you."

"Do you really think so?" Sybil preened and turned, showing off her clinging misty green gown and abundant figure to great advantage. ""How very kind of you to say!"

"Greyquin, I think that's the first time I've ever seen you without that motheaten jerkin," Cat said teasingly.

"I think it's the first time I've ever seen you in a dress," he teased back. "I only wish Bear could be here."

"I don't think they would have let him in," Sybil said. "Speaking of which, is Alphonse coming?"

"Sybil!" Cat said sharply.

"I'm only in jest, Cat. Believe it or not, I've come to be rather fond of the big lug. So, he's not joining us?"

Cat shook her head. "I asked him when we took Jessa home to Arrowood. He knew how he'd be welcomed here, which is to say not at all. Besides, he's intending to join the Order of Steel, and the priests require a period of fasting."

"I have already selected a wine," Arien said as the bottle arrived at their table. "Never did I think to find it here. It comes from the far eastern regions of the Emerin."

The wine was bluish-black, dark, rich, and mysterious. It was smooth and cool in the mouth, but swiftly warmed from within. It was also quite potent, much more so than other wines, so that by the time their food arrived, they were all in a fine mood. Cat felt light, euphoric. Even Arien seemed to relax, fingers tapping to the melody.

"This has long been one of my favorite songs," he commented. "I heard it first at an inn in Keyda, on my way to Thanis. It was the first time I had heard music that was not elven."

"Why not ask one of these lovely ladies to dance?" asked Greyquin.

"Oh, I don't feel like it right now," Sybil said quickly, nudging Cat under the table.

"Would you care to dance, Cat?" Arien said. He stood and held out his hand.

"I never learned," she admitted, ashamed.

"Too busy learning knives and lockpicks," Greyquin said cheerfully. Then, "Ouch!" as Sybil poked him in the ribs.

"That matters not." Arien pulled her to her feet. "All you must do is follow my lead. You are possessed of more grace than any other lady here. Dance with me, Cat."

She couldn't refuse. Holding her right hand, slipping his other arm around her waist, he whirled her expertly into the dance pattern. With slight signals, he guided her movements.

Soon, her initial awkwardness fell away and she could scarcely feel the floor beneath her feet. All she was aware of was the music, and Arien. He spun her away from him, her skirt swirling about her legs, then pulled her close.

She was breathless, lost, swaying in the music like a tree in the wind. It was as if she'd been dancing all her life, and she never wanted it to stop.

But of course it had to end. The song finished to the scattered applause of the diners. Arien reluctantly released Cat and bowed. She curtseyed in response, barely aware of what she was doing. Her mind and heart were still lost in the dance. He led her back to the table, where Sybil and Greyquin were beaming happily.

"There, you see," Arien was saying, "you dance beautifully." Did he seem shaken, or was it her imagination? She wanted to believe that it was true, wanted to believe that he, too, felt what she was feeling.

"It was wonderful," she whispered.

"It certainly was," Sybil said. "That was enchanting, and I've seen many good dancers." She wagged an accusing finger at Arien. "You're no librarian."

"I am indeed a Librarian."

"You don't dance like one."

"I used to dance quite frequently. Long ago. In my youth, in the Emerin." A shadow of sadness crossed his face. "So very long ago."

*   *   *

"You're correct, Sybil," Greyquin said, setting down his napkin. "Dragon meat is much better than wyvern, especially wyvern that we cooked ourselves."

"Isn't it, though?" She licked her lips dreamily, using a bit of soft bread to soak up the last of the delicious sauce. "But then, it was you that did the cooking . . ."

"Will you never leave me be about my cooking!" he cried, grinning. "Aside from the oatmeal, I do a fair job!"

"I can't believe this came from a dragon," Cat said, nibbling at another bit.

What Arien could not believe was Cat. When first he'd seen her by moonlight, he'd barely recognized her. Who would have thought that the delightful, childlike Cat could transform into such a vision? She had been attractive enough in tunic and boots, but this!

The gown clung to her slender form like water. He longed to run his hands over the fabric, feeling its coolness over the warm curves beneath. The starlight blue color made her golden skin glow. He had known she would be beautiful, but he hadn't suspected how the sight of her would steal the very breath from his lungs.

He sipped his wine, smiling as he half-listened to Greyquin's amusing chatter. He had told himself that he would drink one glass and one glass only.

But that had been before he'd done the unimaginable thing of defending an elfkin against one of true elvenblood. He needed another glass, although it would be the worst possible thing he could do. The more he drank, the more tenuous his grip on his control would become.

Though he hated it, he was helpless to keep his mind from wandering. Back in time. Back, back, a full century. Beyond the days when he'd known all too well what wine could do to a man. Back to the Emerin, and the life he'd lost forever.

Cat touched his hand. He started, realizing that he'd been lost in thought for several minutes. Sybil was gone, out on the dance floor in the arms of a young soldier who wore the stunned expression of a man unable to believe his good fortune. Greyquin was nowhere to be seen.

"Are you all right?" she asked. "You seemed a hundred miles away."

"A hundred years, more likely," he said, covering her hand with his own. He would tell her, he decided. He would tell her everything. Now, tonight, before it was too late. Before her life was in danger. "Cat—"

"Do you see him?" She did not point, but he followed her eyes and saw a grossly obese man leaving the dining room.

He nodded.

"Lord Marl." She uttered the name as if it was a filthy oath.

Marl glanced around with an overdone air of nonchalance, then proceeded to the garden doors. Arien had heard him mentioned before, by Rayke and Cat and Apprentice Pellander. The man's reputation was unsavory at best.

"I'm sure he's plotting something," Cat said. She made as if to rise.

"You're not planning to follow him, are you? Dear gods, Cat! Is it safe?"

She smiled. "Not if I'm caught. But I won't be caught."

He held her hand more tightly. "Cat, why?"

"Because it's what I do," she said simply.

He watched her go until she was out of sight. Then, slowly but relentlessly, his gaze turned to the bottle of wine.

*   *   *

Overheard conversations and intercepted letters are the most interesting.
The Book of Yor.

"You have pulled me away from a fine meal, Marl. What do you want?"

"I've a business opportunity to discuss with you, Taron. I've also done you the favor of getting you away from that lotus-drugged shrew you married. Still, if you're in such a hurry to get back . . ."

"I've told you before that I've no interest in doing business with you."

"Yes, but this time you do."

"What do you mean?"

"Walk with me, and I'll tell you."

The two lords moved down the path. Cat crept after them, keeping to the shadows, moving as silently as she knew how, though she was more hindered than usual. Her lovely gown was as unsuited for this sort of thing as it was to combat.

Lord Taron was tall and striking, with greying hair and a spade-shaped beard. His dark blue doublet was of the finest cloth and cut, encrusted with gold and gems that winked in the moonlight.

Lord Marl, on the other hand, was a fat, slovenly excuse for a man. His pavilion-sized red tunic was stained. He had a cap of thinning, oily brown hair and a wispy moustache with bits of food trapped in it.

"I'll be blunt, Taron. You've more wealth than anyone knows, even your wife. You could buy this place," he waved a many-ringed hand at the inn, "without depleting much of your coffers."

"And what are my fortunes to you?" Taron's hand came to rest casually, on the hilt of his knife. It was a smooth, neat gesture that Cat admired.

"My friend, you wound me."

"If you force my hand, I shall do so literally. Do not call me friend. Of the few who hold that title, none of them are you, loathsome toad."

"Hear me out. We are both men of culture and wisdom. We have no need for cold steel between us." Marl spoke hastily, nervously.

"Very well. Speak. But know that I listen with a skeptical ear." Taron crossed his arms and leaned against a tree.

Marl glanced furtively around. Cat made herself one with the willow, glad for the deep shadows.

"A plan is in its infancy," he hissed. "A plan to deliver Thanis into my hands within the next decade. I am prepared to be generous to my allies."

Taron arched an eyebrow and said nothing.

"You have money to spare and," Marl continued. "I have the means to use it well. I offer you a partnership. Would you like to rule Thanis?"

"Only one head can wear the crown, Marl. If I rule Thanis, what do you do?"

"You misunderstand me. I intend for the Highlord to keep his crown. You and I, we could rule the Highlord."

"What nonsense is this?" Taron shook his head scornfully. "You've gone daft. No one rules the Highlord, save perhaps Talus Yor. Is he a part of your scheme as well?"

"Shh!" Marl went pale. "Speak not the names of wizards, for they shall hear you."

"Rubbish. A child's tale."

"Your mockery offends me, Taron. Enough! Are you with me or not?"

"And what would you want of me?"

"Simply your aid, your . . . shall we say, financial support for this endeavor?"

"You have not told me what this endeavor is."

"I have! A plan to deliver the control of the city to us!"

"I will not risk my fortune on whim and fancy."

Marl laughed greasily. "Are you not a gambling man? What of the time when you wagered your daughter's hand in marriage on a spin of the wheel?"

"I won," Taron said simply.

"And you would win this time." Marl's face lit up with fevered excitement. "The richest city in the Northlands, the plumpest fruit of all, resting in your hand."

"I think not, Marl. Look elsewhere for your pigeon."

Marl's eyes narrowed, almost vanishing in the piggy folds of his face. "So you're against me," he said, so quietly that Cat had to strain to hear.

"I am not with you," Taron replied.

"It is the same thing. Within ten years, the city will be mine. And if you breathe a word of this to anyone, it will prove your downfall."

"Now, will you threaten?" Taron dropped his hand to his knife again. "You will find me more than a match for you!"

"Ah, but what of your family? Your daughter, your nephews? What of them? What would your ladywife do if she learned of the girl you keep in a private house? There are more lives to consider than yours, my friend."

Taron's knife flashed in the moonlight. He held the point in front of Marl's bulbous nose. "If so much as a whisper of danger touches my family, I will slice open that bag of bile you call a body!"

Marl squeaked and stumbled back. Cat swiftly ducked behind a row of rosebushes.

"I'll remember this, Taron. Just you wait. No man draws steel on Lord Marl without dire consequence!" With that, he fled as fast as his girth would allow, crushing flowers and trampling bushes as he went.

Cat hardly dared breathe.

Lord Taron watched Marl go, then sheathed his knife. He took a deep breath and walked toward the rosebushes. Cat made herself as small as she could. Taron paused by the bush. She tensed in expectation of discovery. He plucked a rose from it and walked back up the path to the inn.

She finally dared breathe again and stood, brushing petals from her skirt.

.

*   *   *

"Why won't you tell me?" Sybil purred. Her shoulders were moving in time with the music, her torso swaying voluptuously.

"Why are you so insistent?" Arien asked, sounding very exasperated.

"Talopea teaches us that if we want something, we should keep trying until we get it." She licked her lips. "There are many things I want. To begin with, I want to know the truth."

Cat stopped in her tracks, then ducked behind a pillar before either of them could see her. It was turning into her night for overheard conversations.

"I've already revealed that I was born and raised in a noble house," he said.

"That's where you learned to dance," Sybil said. "They taught you well."

"Thank you," he said absently.

"Why, just watching you, I almost thought you had feelings for Cat," Sybil continued blithely.

"I was taught to dance with each lady as if she was the only lady worth dancing with," Arien said. "It is a matter of politeness."

"I don't think Cat knows that. That dance just swept her away. I could see it in her dazzled eyes. Believe me, Arien, I know what that look means."

"You misjudge the situation, Sybil." Arien aligned his silverware neatly, his movements clipped and precise.

"Don't you like her?"

"I am quite fond of Cat, as you well know. She is a dear friend."

"That isn't what I mean, Arien. Don't you think she's pretty? Don't you desire her?"

Cat smothered a groan and pressed her burning face to the pillar.

Arien folded his hands. "Always it comes to that," he said. "It impresses me that your faith is so devout."

"Oh, Arien," laughed Sybil. "Just take her to bed. You're a man, she's a woman. What more do you need?"

Arien sat quietly for a moment, seeming to arrange his thoughts. He raised his head and smiled at Sybil in a way that made Cat's heart flutter. She thought that if he ever smiled at her that way, she would simply faint.

"Dear woman," he said in a low tone, "The elven way would never permit me to do such a thing. We are a race of artists, musicians, and wizards. In all things, we require patience and skill. A woman, like a musical instrument, responds best to the gentle touch of an artisan."

"Oh," Sybil breathed. Her face was flushed, her bosom rising and falling rapidly. "Come back to the temple tonight!"

Arien's intense manner dissolved in a short burst of bitter laughter. He shook his head ruefully. "I fear you would be more than I could withstand."

Sybil fanned herself and took a sip of wine. "That might be so. Besides, I could never do that to poor Cat. Especially after that dance." She made a purring sound and caressed her own arms. "Mmm, that dance."

"Sybil, say no more."

"I'm just so happy to see her finally falling in lo--"

"No!" Arien's expression changed from puzzlement to stark fear. He looked like a man suddenly doused in icewater. "Do not say it, Sybil! Do not even think it!" He stood, hands fisted in the tablecloth, tipping his wine.

Sybil caught the glass before it could spill and set it carefully on the table, looking at him as if he was crazed. "Sweet Talopea, what's the matter with you?"

He stared grimly into space. "Oh, gods, what a fool I've been. Telling myself it was not so . . . it must not be so!"

"Arien!" Sybil tapped his arm warningly. Other diners were looking at them and whispering among themselves.

He seized Sybil's wrists. "Sybil, listen to me. By all you hold holy, *never* speak of these things again." His eyes blazed. "She is as a sister to me. A sister and a dear friend only. That is what must be!" With a tremendous, visible effort, he brought himself back under control and released Sybil.

Red marks braceleted her wrists from the terrible strength of his grip. She rubbed them, looking at him warily. He drained the glass he had come so close to spilling, tossed his cape over his shoulder, and managed a bow.

"Forgive me," he said. "I would explain, if I could, but you would not understand."

Cat huddled back into her hiding place as Arien passed within a few feet of her. He should have seen her, but his eyes were very far away.

Though she knew it was wrong, once more she could not resist, and followed him into the gardens, quiet as a wraith and about as pale.

*   *   *

How could he have been such a fool? How had he not seen this coming? He only prayed that it was not too late.

He should have ended it a hundred years ago. Fool! A man who prided himself on intelligence, he was in truth a blind fool. He should have known it was not over, would never be over. Why hadn't he seen what was happening to Cat? To him? Why hadn't he been able to resist?

His wandering feet carried him to a clearing in the garden. It was graced by a fountain, white marble that glimmered in the moonlight, haloed by silver spray. The centerpiece of the fountain was a rearing unicorn, spouting water from its horn. Around the rim of the basin was a series of unicorn images, carved into the stone. The sight of it struck to his heart as cleanly as a well-aimed arrow. It was not the same, but so similar, so much like the other fountain . . . the fountain back home . . .

He fell to his knees in the grass. A terrible pain and grief swept over him, as sharp now as it had been a century before. He raised his anguished face to the sky.

"Livana," he prayed, voice breaking, "Fair Silvermoon, do not let this happen again. I am sorry. So sorry. Let it be over."

The sound of the fountain was fairy music, soft and beautiful.

"So many lies," he said to the moon. "I have always sought to be truthful, yet the lies must build upon one another. Now I even conceal the truth from myself. I thought I was strong enough. I thought I could keep my vow. I have failed." He sighed, a sigh that shook his entire body.

"Would that I had the courage to do what I should have done all those years ago! I would be free, if not of my guilt, at least of the curse, the dread!"

He lowered his head into his hands. Memories he had forced into locked rooms strained at their confining doors. Memories of sunlight-golden hair, eyes as green as new leaves, screams as sharp as shattered glass . . .

Gazing up at the silver orb again, he sighed heavily. "I am so weary of being alone. But what of Cat? She is so young, so innocent. What will become of her?"

He knew the answer to that question all too well. He had seen it before. No matter how hard he might wish to forget, the memories filled his dreams and haunted his waking thoughts.

From nearby windows, he could hear bright music and laughter. The sounds of happiness drove like daggers deep into his heart.

"Alinora," he breathed, almost silent in the rising breeze. It was the first time he had let himself say her name in over eighty years. Oh, if he could do it over, knowing what he now knew, she would not die. He would have gladly given his life to spare hers.

He could not let it happen again. If that meant dying, then so be it. At least it would be an end to the pain.

*   *   *

Arien swore violently.

It was so uncharacteristic of him that Cat rocked back on her heels in time to see him do another unthinkable thing. He hurled a book across the room.

The book. The object of his quest.

"Hundreds of ways to do it!" he said, shaking his fists at the ceiling. "A mere handful of ways for it to be undone!"

He started to kick his chair, then changed his mind and dropped into it, resting his elbows on the desk and his head in his hands.

"There has to be a way," he muttered.

She held absolutely still. Finally, the silence became too overpowering and she had to speak.

"Arien?" she asked hesitantly.

He whipped around and saw her kneeling amid the last of the Castle Selbon treasures, where she had been collecting items to have the Nightsiders sell.

"Oh! Cat. I am sorry. You are so quiet that I forgot you were here."

"I've never seen you throw a book before," she said.

"I never have," he admitted. "Such an outburst is unlike me. It is only that I had pinned all my hopes on that book." He slumped, his head thrown back, hands clenched in his hair. "I was so certain that would be the one!"

"Are you never to tell me what this is all about?" she asked without much hope.

He sat up and glanced from her to the book. In a heavy, weary voice, he said, "I do owe you an explanation. As I recall, I did promise in Selbon's library to explain all to you once I had finished the book. Now, although it did not give me the answer I sought, I must keep my word. Perhaps then you will understand why I must be the way I am."

She sat at his feet, since all the other chairs were piled with books. Now, finally, there would be some real answers instead of the wild speculations that had been running through her head.

"It began over a hundred years ago," he said, "though the real beginnings were much farther back than that, back in the mists of ancient history. I do not understand all of it, but I will tell you what I can."

Someone knocked on the door.

"I knew it," Cat moaned. "I'll never find out."

"Who is it?" Arien called, sounding irritated.

There was a pause, followed by a deep rumbling voice. "Bostitch."

"Bostitch?" echoed Cat.

Since their rapid return from Castle Selbon, they'd barely seen the minotaur. He'd taken only a bag of coins and left, still terribly upset about the loss of his "little man".

Arien opened the door and let him in. Cat noticed that there was something different about him, but she couldn't precisely say what it was. Maybe that he didn't look as dull as usual.

"Want books," Bostitch said.

"I beg your pardon?" Arien replied.

"Little man's books. Big magic."

"You want Solarrin's share of the books?"

"That is what I said, fool---" He broke off and coughed. "Yuh. Books."

Cat stared, a horrible suspicion growing in her mind. Arien glanced at her, eyebrows raised, and she knew that he felt it too.

This wasn't Bostitch.

It couldn't be. His entire posture had changed. He filled the room imposingly. Bostitch had always been an intimidating sight by virtue of his size and strength, but an air of menace clung to him now that had never been there before.

"Is that you, Solarrin?" she asked, knowing even as she spoke that she was right.

Bostitch glared at her. "Little man dead," he said firmly.

"Livana save us all," Arien said, awed. "It is Solarrin."

"But how?" Cat asked, slowly getting to her feet.

"It is the result of a spell commonly known by necromancers," Arien explained, carefully watching his uninvited guest. "Upon the mage's death, his life force and intellect are held in some inanimate object until he is able to use another spell to free himself. For example, one which displaces the mage's mind into a different person's physical form, essentially taking over the victim's body."

"Curse it all. You would have to guess the truth," the body of Bostitch said. The voice was the same deep rumble, but the words were in Solarrin's usual smug tones. "Still, a nice bit of work, don't you agree?"

"What has become of Bostitch?" Cat asked, horrified. "The real Bostitch?"

"Does it matter? I, Solarrin, have returned to you." He spread his big hands grandly, as if expecting them to fall at his feet. "Do not the high and mighty elves have such magics? They must not, or you wouldn't be so jealous. I took this poor, stupid wretch and made him whole! Now he serves me better than ever! Look on me! The strength of a minotaur coupled with my own incomparable magics. I am a god!"

"You're a monster!" Cat cried. "How could you?"

"It matters not what you think of me, crossling. We are no longer in the castle, and hence no longer under your command." He turned to Arien. "I have come for the books that are rightfully mine. Then I shall take my leave of you and take my place as Archmage."

"Talus Yor is Archmage," Cat said.

"For now. My only regret is that the choicest of books remained with that disgusting husk I left behind." He seemed to consider something, then smiled at Cat. She shuddered at the sight of his many teeth. "You know, crossling, I would pay highly for the recovery of that book."

"No," said Arien, putting his hand on Cat's arm before she could respond. "Selbon is awake. He will have the entire castle on guard and protected. You will not send Cat into that place again, whatever the price."

"Selbon is a used-up old man," Solarrin sneered. "He overcame me once, but I allowed it. My death was all merely part of my plan. How else could I get rid of that loathsome form that imprisoned me?" He flexed his arms and laughed richly.

"And to think," said Arien coolly, "we used to say that you couldn't possibly be as bad as you seemed. Now I see that you're much worse. You disgrace the art of magic."

"Do I?" Solarrin said, still laughing. "It was the art of magic that made this possible! I am a living testimony to all of the power that a true wizard could achieve! You will not find me cowering in a musty library, wasting my talents!"

"You—" Cat started forward, but Arien held her back.

"Let him be," he said.

"Is that a decision born of wisdom, or fear?" Solarrin swept Arien with a look of withering scorn.

Cat felt his grip on her arm tighten until it was almost painful. "I believe you said something about books?" Arien asked coldly. "Take them. I have no wish to keep them. They are as dark as your soul, and equally rotted."

"I will return for them after I have claimed the castle as my own. The one I truly desire is not among them."

"You, in Castle Selbon? That would be worse than Selbon himself!" Cat said angrily.

"Do not show your temper to me, girl. I could slay you with a touch." He bared his teeth at her again. "Not, of course, that I would do anything so quick or merciful. I like your spirit, and I would like it best broken."

Cat fell silent but continued glaring. Her fists were clenched so hard that her knuckles ached.

"Just remember this," Solarrin added as he turned to leave, "Bostitch was willing to give his life for me. So I took him up on the offer."

He swept grandly from the room, slamming the door behind him hard enough to wedge it firmly in its frame. Cat let out her anger in a low growl. Arien released her arm and ran his hands through his already rumpled hair.

"Such a bleak turn of events," he said. "Bostitch, that worthy creature, is lost to us."

"Is there nothing we can do? Is he dead?"

"He may as well be. Solarrin's spell would have turned him out of his own body and trapped him in whatever item formerly held Solarrin's essence. Not being a powerful wizard, Bostitch would be helpless, unable to communicate or free himself."

"Oh, blast Solarrin and all his evil!" Cat swore. "Why did we let him join us?"

"Do not blame yourself, Cat. This would have happened regardless of us. I am certain Solarrin had this plan in mind when he first took Bostitch as a companion."

She sighed and nodded. "I suppose you're right. What can we do?"

"Alas, for Bostitch, nothing save mourning." He sighed sadly. "You must accustom yourself to loss, Cat. Your elven blood will give you a long life, and during its span you may see many of your friends die."

"Is that what happened to you, Arien? Someone died?" She swallowed and asked what she already knew to be the truth. "A lady?"

He closed his eyes and took a breath, about to speak, but before he could, a bellowing from the street interrupted him.

"Halloo! Cat! Arien! Is anyone there?"

"Alphonse!" Cat threw her hands in the air. "What now?" She went to the window.

Arien laughed bitterly. "Perhaps I am not meant to tell you after all. Perhaps the gods send these distractions to let me preserve our friendship."

Cat flung open the shutters and leaned out. "Alphonse, what the—gods above!" She had been ready to scold him, but her voice deserted her. She nearly fell out the window. Only Arien's quick catch, his hands at her waist, kept her from tumbling out.

Alphonse stood in the middle of the street, waving excitedly. A red-bearded man stood beside him, leaning on a crutch.

"Rayke!" Cat cried, and Arien very nearly dropped her out the window in his surprise.

*   *   *

"It was too close," Rayke said. "I thought I was done for. Then Selbon saw the rest of you getting away, and he let out a howl that near froze my blood. He yelled for the orcs to follow you. Unlucky me, I was in the way. They knocked me over and their feet nearly did what their weapons hadn't been able to. Even Selbon must have figured me for dead, because he went with them."

"Oh, Rayke! How terrible!" Sybil snuggled closer to him.

He put an arm around her, lifting his mug with the other. "I gathered my wits and ran for it, reaching the eye we'd come in through. Good thing we'd left the rope tied there! My arms were sliced to pieces and I swear it felt like my guts were leaking down my legs. It was only blood, but I'd seen enough of those pictures in that blasted book of yours--" he nodded at Alphonse, who grinned, "--to give me a good scare."

Alphonse gave a low awed whistle. He was listening with the tilted-head air he assumed when he was trying to think of a song. His fingers drummed rhythmically.

"I got down the rope, half-fell is more like it, and found the horses. Most of it's a fog. I remember reaching the woods. Somehow, I ended up at Tabash, though how I crossed the river I'll never know. They patched and stitched, and finally decided to take me to the Temple of Steel because I was obviously a fighting man. Alphonse found me there, and you know the rest."

*   *   *

Nighttime in the city. She loved it. The warmly lit windows and colorful lamps, the velvet shadows, the fragrant air. Music drifted from taverns all over town. Thief's paradise.

It was the times like this that she missed her father the most. The night was their time, father and daughter, thieves in the shadows. She could picture him beside her, grinning at her with his crooked smile.

She walked to clear her head, which ached from Arien's nearly-revealed secrets, Solarrin's black deeds, and Rayke's tale of adventure.

"Good evening, pretty miss," hailed a high, somehow brittle voice.

Cat glanced in that direction and saw a stooped figure wrapped in a black cloak, pushing a cart. There was no one else nearby, so she motioned to herself curiously.

"Yes, child. I am speaking to you," the figure said. "Come here, dear."

Cat edged closer, suspecting a trick. She and her father had lured the unwary into a robbery enough times to make her watchful, but her instincts did not suggest danger. There was a quality to the stranger's voice, an accent . . .

The figure stepped forward into a circle of lamplight, and Cat gasped as light fell on the large eyes and pointed ears of a true-blooded elf.

She was easily the oldest person Cat had ever seen, ancient even by elven standards. She must have once been beautiful, amazingly so, for an echo of it remained in her face. A thick braid, white shot with pure silver, fell to the hem of her gown. Her eyes were a light, clear blue, and they peered at Cat with no evidence of senility or hostility.

"Good evening, *Nantis*," Cat replied, instinctively using the proper form of address for a respected elder.

"Well, a young lady with your manners about you, aren't you? Come a little closer. I don't bite. Yes, a pretty enough young lady. I approve. Elfkin or not, I do approve. You'll remember that, won't you?"

"I'll remember. But . . . I don't understand. Who are you? What do you want?"

"What is your name?" the woman asked, ignoring her questions.

"Cat."

"Oh, now, that is not much of a name," the woman teased, smiling.

"Cathlin Tahmira Sabledrake," Cat admitted, her full name, which of all her friends only Alphonse knew.

"Much better." The woman hobbled closer, the wheels of her cart squeaking on the cobblestones. "Forgive me for not introducing myself. You'll know who I am soon enough. I wondered if this day would ever come."

"Excuse me, *Nantis*, but I really don't know what you're talking about."

"Oh, I know, child. You will, though. In time. I've been waiting for someone like you. True, you're not quite what I expected, but I think you'll do admirably."

"You do? But I don't even know you."

"I've been watching you. I only wish I could do more. I happen to have some books here. Perhaps one of them might interest you. Would you care to look?" She pulled back the cloth covering her cart, and Cat saw that it was piled with books.

Cat shook her head in puzzlement. "Are you a merchant?"

"Try this one," she said. There was an odd, persuasive command to her voice. She handed Cat a slim book with a dark blue leather cover. A silver design was pressed into the cover, two rearing unicorns holding a five-pointed star between them.

Cat flipped the pages, noting that the book was mostly filled with a neat, even script, written in the elven tongue. She turned to the front page and read the first sentence.

My name is Arien, and today, which would have been my wedding day, I take quill in hand to record these terrible events that will haunt me for the rest of my life.

The summery Thanian night was suddenly cold. "How much?" Cat asked.

*   *   *

The written form is both the blessing and the curse of the sentient races. What a man hears, he may disbelieve. That which is written, locked in ink for all time, is harder to doubt.

The Book of Yor

The book sat on the table. Cat orbited it like an uneasy moon.

"I didn't steal it," she said quietly. "It was given to me. She wouldn't even let me pay."

Perhaps she hadn't stolen the book itself, but by reading it she would be stealing Arien's past, his privacy. He would tell her his secrets when the time was right. He had promised, and she knew he would keep his word.

It was none of her business. Arien would tell her when he was ready.

But did it have something to do with the curse he'd told her about? He'd braved the dangers of the castle in hopes that Selbon's book would tell him how to undo it.

Her elliptical orbit reached its nearest point and she picked up the book. She would lock it up safely and take it to Arien first thing in the morning.

Certain that she was all together in her mind and in agreement with herself, Cat opened the book and began to read.

*　　*　　*

My name is Arien, and today, which would have been my wedding day, I take quill in hand to record these terrible events that will haunt me for the rest of my life.

I have always prided myself on my memory, which made my lessons come easily throughout my schooling, but today I curse it, for the image of my love's tortured face will not leave my mind.

But, no. If I am to write this, and it seems that I must if ever I want peace from my own thoughts, then I shall start sensibly at the beginning.

I have little memory of my true parents, for they died when I was but an infant. My father was Lord Mirida of Taefallon in the kingdom of the Emerin. My mother was a fair and gentle woman born of a wealthy house. The manner of their deaths was unknown to me, though there are rumors that my father took his own life. Now, in my reluctant wisdom, I fear I know their fates.

Orphaned, I was taken in by a childless couple of a neighboring House, Lord and Lady Karadan. The Lord was an advisor to the Elvenking, and we were often at the high court. Ah, the beauty of the palace and the merriment that accompanied each formal occasion!

I must grieve for that as well. My whole life, lost to me.

Again, I lose sight of this. If I write it down, perhaps it will leave my mind for a time.

I was raised as the son of House Karadan, educated in the arts, language, magic, and the courtly graces. It was the wish of my foster parents that I might someday follow Lord Karadan in serving the kingdom. This wish did not sit ill with me, for I was entranced with the court and, like my friends, had no desire to see what lay beyond the elvenwood.

In my fortieth year, as was custom, a marriage was arranged for me with the daughter of Count Elyvorrin, the ruler of a nearby province. It was a good match, a political match. Love was neither expected nor necessary. Both of us were fortunate to be not displeasing to the other's sight, and of a similar age and upbringing.

Yet, during the years of proper courtship, I found myself thinking of her at odd moments, reflecting happily on her fair beauty, the music of her voice. My love for Alinora grew like the pale light of dawn, slowly, but unfolding in a promise of gloriousness.

Even now, as I write and the tears that I will not shed sting at my eyes, I remember her. Like a jewel her image turns and sparkles in the shadowed recesses of my mind. Like a jewel she was, with hair of diamond luster, eyes of deepest emerald, and skin of smooth pearl. I would have given her my heart, had she asked.

I even fancied that she cared for me as well, a rare and blessed thing in arranged matches. We would talk for hours, she debating political matters with a fire unusual in most young women, who cared only for their gowns and dances. I taught her to play Towers one long and rainy week, and soon found myself quite outmatched. How bright her eyes as she studied the board, how quick and decisive the moves of her pieces!

Some may have considered her spirit unladylike, but to me it was refreshing. In earlier years, I had been oft sought by fluttering maidens who considered me handsome, but the blandness of their conversation swiftly bored me. With Alinora, I found one who shared my interests.

Time flows so differently in the wood. The ten years we courted, a fraction of our elven lives, passed like a flash of lightning. We danced at the balls, attended the plays and concerts, and took long walks in the forest with fewer chaperons as the date of our wedding drew near. In all this time, I had not dared speak of the depth of my feelings, and she had shown no more than proper behavior and the occasional fond look that warmed my heart. Many times the words trembled on my lips. I yearned to sweep her into my arms and proclaim my heart's love.

I recall the night it began, a night clear as crystal. I was spending the Summer Festival Season with Alinora and her family. To escape the prying eyes of her siblings, we had taken to walking in the woods at night. Streamers of moonlight danced in the mist and wreathed the trees in cool silver. The stars pierced the sky in dazzling brilliance. Alinora and I walked alone on silent paths. The gentle breeze, our soft steps, and the sweet call of a night bird were all that broke the stillness.

We had a secret place where we met. We were not the first to discover it, nor would we be the last, but for then it was ours. The trees gave way to a smooth clearing. In the center was a fountain, a marble masterpiece of magical creatures circling a great crystal tree. Water fell from the branches in a fine spray, fairy music in the velvet night.

In unspoken decision, we sat upon a graceful marble bench carved in the design of a unicorn. Our hands clasped without our awareness, as they so often did these days. It seems now and even seemed then that the forest listened for our first words that night. Alinora raised her eyes to me, and they were as deep and clear as a spring-fed pool hidden in the shadow of the woods. I held my breath at her beauty. She laid her slim hand over mine and spoke.

"Arien," she said, and hesitated. "Arien, I love you."

How can I describe the sensation that filled me at the sound of those simple words? I could not speak. I was filled with a warm rainbow of emotion. It was as well that I could not speak, for no words would have done. The moonlight painted the mist silver as I took her in my arms. We were all that mattered, all that existed.

We made love there in the clearing, beneath the stars. Livana from her chariot may have watched over us, to assure us a last time of joy before the madness began. All I knew then was the touch of Alinora's hands, like silk, caressing, her sweet breath gasping my name as I lost myself in the wondrous fall of her hair. Had we but died in that timeless instant, that we would have been together in eternal joy.

Alas for what came to pass.

What follows, I cannot explain.

After, as we lay side by side, exchanging soft kisses, I sensed hostile eyes upon us. I leapt to my feet, scanning the woods. Alinora, graceful as a willow, sprang up beside me. How lovely she was, hair and gown in disarray, yet there was a fear in her eyes, an unexplained fear that matched my own.

The barest instant before the sound came, we turned in that direction, as if expecting it. It tore through the night, wholly unlike the crash of thunder or the rumble of an earthquake. It was a roar, but the roar of no beast known to us. The quiet breeze that had escorted us swelled into a raging gale, whipping a storm of leaves around us as we stood clinging together. The boughs creaked in protest. Clouds, black and hideous, boiled across the sky from the west. Our very breath was stolen by the ferocious wind, that seemed unsatisfied merely to blow, but switched direction viciously, the force of it constantly keeping us unsteady.

I glimpsed a shape in the brush, but when I whirled, I saw nothing save the waving branches. Alinora cried out and I whirled again, this time catching sight of something hunched and strange among the trees.

Lightning broke overhead, a dazzling blue-white flash, accompanied by a tremendous peal of thunder that made us cringe like children. A flood of icy rain poured down, pelting us with water and hail. Mindless, like hunted deer who know the wolves are closing in, we fled. I could hear the howls of creatures pursuing us. In the bright flashes of lightning, I clearly saw a hideous form drawing near.

Our leisurely stroll had carried us a distance from the home of Alinora's parents. Our fleeing feet carried us back more swiftly than I would have believed. A square of golden light marked a window, offering promises of safety, warmth, normality. It was almost within our grasp when Alinora stumbled and as I moved to catch her, we both fell to the ground. A dark shape leapt from the trees and landed with uncanny agility on the path beside us.

Even now, my mind refuses to accept what I know I saw.

The creature was dark, covered with coarse fur. Its eyes seemed to glow a hellish red. It had claws of a wicked curve, and it reeked of the slaughterhouse. It opened its mouth wider than I would have believed possible, revealing jagged teeth, and roared at us. It was without a doubt the same sound we had heard earlier.

I made my way to my feet again, somehow, my body moving though my mind was frozen with terror. Alinora crouched on the path like a rabbit, screaming soundlessly. I dragged her with me as I ran toward the door. It was a matter of yards, but seemed like miles. With every step, I was certain the beast would reach us. I expected to feel claws rip across my back. Alinora stumbled again, but this time, finding strength in some untapped well, I managed to carry her. We burst into the house. I dropped her and slammed the door, throwing the bolt.

Her parents emerged from the sitting room, puzzled and alarmed. Count Elyvorrin held a book in one hand and a sword in the other. As Alinora flung herself sobbing into her mother's arms, drenched and disheveled, he took a step toward me as if he was prepared to run me through, suspecting me of harming his dear daughter. Most beloved of all his children was Alinora, and although she knew it, she did not allow it to spoil her.

"Outside," Alinora gasped between her sobs, pointing frantically at the door. Her father strode to it and reached for the handle.

I braced my arms across the door and beseeched him to leave it shut. He looked at me in the careful way one looks at a person who might be mad.

I started to tell him what we had seen, but stopped. I barely believed it myself. The count was not a man prone to flights of fancy. Instead, I stammered out an explanation of a sudden storm.

It was a momentous event in my life, the first ever of the many lies this thing had brought on, yet it passed with quiet ease. That only adds to my dismay. If truth is so difficult, why not seek solace in falsehood that comes so simply to the lips?

Still eyeing me in that cautious manner, the count motioned me aside and threw open the door.

There was no storm. Not the faintest wisp of a cloud, not a stray raindrop or hailstone to be seen.

As I warmed myself by the fire, I pondered the events. Had we possibly fallen asleep, dreamed this horror? Had we fallen in the fountain, as the countess suggested, to account for out wet clothes?

One look at Alinora's pale, frightened face assured me that we had not been dreaming. Even if we had, how could we have shared the same nightmare? That left two choices, neither of them appealing. Madness, or truth. Either we had both gone mad, or these things had happened.

I slept badly, tormented by dreams of that foul beast. Yet, in the dreams, I never reached safety. It always brought me down and savaged me on the doorstep.

In the morning I was confronted by Alinora. She demanded that we find some proof, some answer to this mystery. She was completely lovely in her determination. It was an air uncommon to elven maidens, and I found it most appealing. I would not let myself disappoint her. Therefore, we set out to the clearing.

The warmth of the day melted away our terrors of the night before. Our walk soon became a pleasant stroll through the fragrant wood. We soon reached our clearing, and, seeing no terrible monsters awaiting us, soon began to gather fruit for a picnic. Birds twittered merrily at us. Alinora sang as she picked berries.

Her song turned without warning into a cry of shock. She bent to pick up something from the ground, half-turned to me, and collapsed in the grass. I raced to her side, calling to her.

She opened her eyes and stared up at me, her mouth silently repeating the word "no." I knelt and took from her hand a scarf, pale green. She had worn it last night as a pretty ornament, but what I now held was a tattered, shredded scrap of silk.

The rips looked like claw marks.

I do not recall how long I sat in the grass beside my love, holding her, rocking her gently, like a badly frightened child. She looked up at me helplessly.

"What happened last night was real," she said quietly.

"Yes," I replied. "It was."

We spent the rest of the day searching the woods for further signs of our enemies, but to no avail. As the sun sank in the west, a great blazing copper coin, we had to return to the house. As the shadows grew, we each became aware of a growing unease, a feeling of presence. The beasts were not gone, I sensed. Only waiting. Tomorrow I was to return to my own home. I felt a deep dread at leaving her.

I slept fitfully that night, as if I were, in some way, expecting what happened. It was just past midnight when Alinora's screams shattered the sleeping stillness. I was out of bed almost the instant her scream began, and had reached the hall by the time the first gave way to the next. I raced to her rooms and seized the door handle. Locked! I threw my shoulder against the door repeatedly, spurred on by her cries of horror and the crashing of glass. The door flew open and I fell to the floor. Alinora lay between the bed and the window, crying. She was unharmed, though her screams had been filled with agony. The mirror and window were unbroken, though I had heard glass shattering.

"The beasts, the beasts!" Alinora gasped. "They were here. They jumped in through the window and seized me from my bed, flinging me about like a child's doll!"

I held her and comforted her as best I could, though I was greatly frightened by her tale. The beasts were stalking my beloved Alinora. I could not wonder at their intent. In the depths of my heart, I knew what they wanted. I did not know how to stop them. My helplessness enraged me.

And more disturbing, no others in the household had heard a thing. We could not speak of what we had seen, else they would have wondered at our sanity. More, they would have wondered at my presence in her room so late at night.

The next morning, as the servants loaded the last of my bags onto the coach, she took my hand and led me around the house. Her parents smiled indulgently, perhaps assuming we wished a last-minute embrace.

Alinora showed me the marks beside her bedroom window. The four long furrows were carved deep in the very stone that made up the wall. Claw marks. She told me that no one else seemed able to see them. She had asked her sisters, and both thought her to be playing some elaborate game.

There were no words between us; there did not need to be. I held her close, buried my face in her hair, kissed her. Waving goodbye to her as the coach drove away was among the most difficult tasks ever to befall me.

A few nights later, as I lay safe in my own bed, I was assaulted by a vivid nightmare.

In it, I was running down a long, smooth, apparently endless corridor. The walls were rounded, made of a bluish-black material unlike any stone or metal I knew. I could see a glimmer of light ahead, pale gold as the first light of day, yet no matter how fast I ran, it stayed out of reach. Something shared the corridor, pursuing me. Something huge, white, and bloated, radiating a sickly heat.

For hours, it seemed, the dream went on, with whatever foul and loathsome thing it was gaining slowly on me. I ran and ran, my own feet moving slower and slower.

Abruptly, the passage ended beneath my feet and spilled me into a garden of incredible beauty. A tidy white fence separated this perfect place from the tangled wilds beyond. The bright flowers nodded cheerfully. In the center of the garden was a tree, laden with blossoms. A swing of woven flowered vines hung from it. On the swing, gliding back and forth, was my fair Alinora, in a gown of pure white. Roses adorned her hair. A golden aura of light surrounded her. She smiled and beckoned to me.

I started to go to her when the monstrous thing that had been chasing me shot out of the corridor and struck the white fence. It burst like a bladder of water, but the red-streaked white liquid that splattered from it was not water at all.

The foul bloody substance splashed Alinora. She screamed hideously, her fair skin blistering and smoking as the liquid dissolved her flesh. Her perfect emerald eyes stared accusingly at me out of a face that had melted.

I jerked awake, the bedclothes untucked and rumpled in my lap, a scream caught in my throat.

The nightmare repeated, sometimes twice in a night. A week passed. I was exhausted, yet afraid to sleep. I could not eat, I would not sleep. My clothes sagged on my thin fame. The servants talked about me in soft tones.

When dear Lady Karadan, who was as a mother to me, asked what was troubling me, I could only stare at her with blank, horrified eyes. I took to spending the days on the wide balcony, staring north across the forest toward Elyvorrin, as if the trees might magically part before my eyes to reveal my beloved. A loud crash when once an unlucky servant dropped a goblet nearly sent me over the rail in surprise.

Looking back, I believe I might have been truly mad. Mad with fear and unnameable horror.

At last my wait was rewarded by the sight of Alinora. She did not arrive in a coach, with a retinue, as was proper. Rather did I see a horse gallop across the bridge, a horse bloody and flecked with foam, bearing a rider whose diamond hair gleamed in the sun. I ran to meet her.

As I reached her, Alinora all but fell off the horse into my arms. Her clothing was torn, her pale limbs covered with scratches. The horse, trembling and wide-eyed, was clawed almost to death. I looked about for a servant to send for a healer, but we were alone. The air was still.

I carried Alinora to the house. Her head rested on my shoulder as she told me in a broken voice of the horror she had endured. The shadow beasts had invaded her room every night, growing bolder, pulling her hair and scratching her as they tossed her about. She was soon too frightened to sleep.

She had decided to seek me out, that we might combat this menace together. Alone, she set out. She had come most of the way when the beasts had appeared, loping along beside her with ease no matter how fast she rode. The beasts laughed, she recalled. Laughed and tore at her and the horse with long, sharp claws. The horse, though terrified, galloped onward. When they had come within sight of the house, the beasts had vanished.

My lovely Alinora was shaking, her face pale and haggard as she related all this to me. The weary purple smudges beneath her eyes matched my own. I carried her upstairs to a guest room and rang for a servant to prepare a bath. No one responded. The house was silent.

A feeling of wrongness grew and threatened to overwhelm me. I gave Alinora the key and bade her rest while I went to seek Lord Karadan.

I searched the house. I could find no one. Not the Lord or his Lady, not the servants, not a living soul. More than the emptiness of the house, something was amiss. Though it tugged at the fringes of my awareness as I made my fruitless search, I could not name it exactly.

Standing in Lady Karadan's favorite parlor, idly running my fingers over the table, it suddenly came to me. I snatched my hand from the table and looked in shock at the grey dust coating my fingertips. The room was inches deep in dust, the air thick and stale. The flowers on the mantle, just gathered that morning, were withered and dead. Only my tracks disturbed the dust and cobwebs. Cobwebs. No spider would have dared show its spindly self in Lady Karadan's home, yet the webs clung to the corners and bottoms of the furniture.

As I stood, dazed, in this room of lost and dead times, I was startled by a loud thump from upstairs, followed by a brief scream, quickly stilled. I ran for the stairs. Alinora! I had been such a fool to leave her alone!

A step splintered beneath my foot, wrenching my ankle. I stumbled on, heedless of the pain. The door to the guest room was still closed, a large web strung under the handle. The tapestries in the hall were threadbare and faded. I reached for the door, a futile effort as it was still locked. I heard nothing save my own ragged breaths. I knocked loudly, calling to Alinora. Only silence answered.

A small, grating, whispering sound disturbed the silence. Slowly, not wanting to, I looked down. A brass key, green with age, slid from under the door with no visible means of movement. Once clear of the door, it lay motionless on the mold-covered carpet at my feet. I bent and seized it, pushing it into the lock. It jammed. I struggled with it, sensing a deliberate resistance. Finally it clicked and the door shuddered open on squealing hinges.

The room was empty, ripe with age and decay. The only thing out of place was a tipped chair. Moving mindlessly in my terror, I righted it. Beneath it, a bright patch in the dust caught my eye. I bent to investigate.

It was then that a cry tore free from my throat, a cry I would not have believed myself possible of voicing. It was deep and roaring, full of rage and terror. The cry of a man discovering a wolf hunched snarling over a blood-spattered cradle.

Curled in the dust was a lock of diamond hair. Bright as the sun, soft as the clouds. Bloodied at the roots, as if it had been ripped from the scalp.

The door swung shut behind me with a rusty creak. I heard the key, which I had foolishly left in the lock, rattle and turn. Determined to confront my unseen adversary, I grabbed up the chair to batter down the door. And then I saw that the window was gone. Not broken, not shuttered, simply gone. Where it had been was instead the opening to a tunnel, a curved corridor of some strange bluish-black substance. An endless passage.

I had no choice but to enter the chill darkness. Far, so very far in the distance, was a pale glow. I forced myself to run, though my ankle shrieked. I ran in complete silence, not even my footfalls or breath making a sound.

Some impulse made me look back. Instead of the room I had left, I encountered an expected horror. Thundering silently behind me was the white, bloated thing of my nightmares. I forced myself to run faster and faster yet, but I may as well have been standing still. The heat and stench of the thing filled the corridor. It closed on me with terrifying speed. My ankle bent and I fell.

I fell, missing the floor of the tunnel and landing heavily on the grass. Remembering the garden of my nightmare and the awful events that followed, I bolted to my feet. And saw not the garden at all.

It was our clearing, of course. I should have known it would be. The fair clearing where the fountain shimmered under the moon, where Alinora had given herself to me so sweetly. Yet it, too had changed.

In that instant, I yearned for death, since to know such horror was beyond comprehension.

The fountain had changed. The marble was the pasty hue of dead flesh, the creatures once full of grace now hideous mockeries. The moon above was a leering, yellow skull. The velvety grass was now coarse and brown. The trees themselves were twisted in agony. Alinora was here.

Alinora! Her hair was pulled up and knotted over a branch, her feet dangling. Her clothing hung about her in tatters. A heavy chain joined her wrists.

Surrounding her were the beasts. I could not count them, for they shifted and changed, each more horrid than the last. I heard something behind me, and, remembering my dream, spun. It was not the pale shapeless monster of my nightmares but another of the beasts, crouched in the smooth mouth of the tunnel.

With a gobbling laugh, it sprang at me. I tried to step aside, but my ankle betrayed me again. The furred, disgustingly hot body of the beast slammed into me and we fell. It grabbed my shoulders in its claws and lifted me off the ground, turning me to display to the others. Its strength was terrible.

I struggled, kicked it. It only laughed. A second beast appeared beside it and they held me between them, claws digging into my wrists and ankles. The implication was clear. They could tear me to pieces with ease. My struggles would be futile. Nevertheless, I fought. I struggled and twisted, earning only mocking hoots for my efforts. I ceased my struggles entirely when Alinora opened her eyes.

The sight of her, so filled with pain, drained the strength from my limbs. I could do nothing but watch as the shadows closed around her.

The next moments were the longest of my life, and mercifully the only part of this madness that is blurred. Perhaps because it was too horrible. Too horrible for my mind to accept.

I saw the beasts moving, the flashes of claws. I saw fair skin part like silk and red blood flow like wine. Her screams were the moonsilver cries of wolves. The claws rose and fell, rose and fell, until the beasts stepped back and I was raised high by my captors that I might view their work.

Alinora! I cannot recall that final picture as a whole. Her hands, so light and playful, so gentle, the skin stripped from them like gloves. Her lovely legs, shredded and glinting with bone. Her flesh torn. An ocean of blood soaking the grass. Yet, somehow, she still lived. Even with all they had done to her, she was still beautiful.

Her eyes found mine, and though she could not speak, she communicated to me her love. I will always love you, her eyes said.

Thus, she died.

My heart died with her. I lay numb in the grasp of the beasts, awaiting my turn, awaiting the sharp claws. They laughed again, and hurled me to the ground. One of them leaned over me, misshapen mouth opening. I threw back my head, hoping for it to be swift. The beast's breath, blood and decay, washed over me.

"Never forget this night," it said, its voice the rattle of bones in a tomb.

When at last I opened my eyes again, I was resting in my own bed. The linens were crisp and clean. The room smelled fresh. I ached from head to foot, body, mind, and soul. I was among the living. Lady Karadan, who had been as a mother to me, touched my face. I tried to speak. No sound would come.

With infinite care, she gave me water. It was cool, delicious, healing. I found my voice and asked of Alinora. She bowed her head.

"She is gone, my son. She died three nights ago, in her sleep."

"No, she was here," I insisted. "Three nights? It cannot be. It was just last night . . ."

"Shh, shh. Rest, Arien. This delirium has held you for many days. You are not yet healed. We will mourn for her later, when you are well."

The lies continued. I could tell no one what had happened. None would believe me. They considered me mad, and told of strange wanderings I had done in my fevered illness, strange wanderings I could not in truth wholly deny, for my recollections of that time seemed neither dream nor real. How was I to know what had, in fact, been?

I can still see her in the eyes of my mind, laying amid the roses of mourning. How lifelike she seemed, as if but sleeping, as if at any moment she might breathe, and stir.

Some whispered that I had murdered her myself, and then tried to take my own life in remorse. Lord Karadan was asked to remain away from court for ten years' time, to give us time to grieve, so said the Elvenking, but no similar thing was said to Count Elyvorrin. It was plain we, or rather, I, was unwelcome. Blamed but never accused, punished yet never judged. An exile of the spirit, if not in name.

So it was, unable to bear the sly looks, the whispers, the sadness and unease that Lord and Lady Karadan tried to hide, that I left the house in which I had been raised. I hoped only that they, once freed of the burden that I had become, would be once again taken back into the Elvenking's court, and not made more to suffer for their kindness in taking to their bosom an orphaned child.

I left my homeland, the green elvenwood that had been the whole world to me. I could not bring myself to actively seek death, so I decided to go to a place where death was not such a stranger, and it might someday seek me. I came to the human lands, to this city of Thanis.

I must, if I am being totally truthful in this journal, also admit to that brief but shameful period of excessive indulgence in drink. In an effort to forget, to blot the memories from my mind, I fell far from noble grace. Yet even that did not serve me. That wretched man, that bleary and pathetic drunkard that I became, could not hide from the truth.

Despite my grief and pain, I could not let myself live in that manner. Thankfully, I was able to bring myself out of that hopeless place. Never again, I vow, will I permit myself to become so.

I have obtained work at this great Library. Here, I plan to lose myself among the tomes.

In a place of such history and legend, none will know me. It would take a century to read all the books contained within these walls. I shall read. In knowledge, may I find solace and forgetfulness. In having recorded this, may my mind grant me peace.

Seventh Day of Fourmonth, in the Five Hundred and Eleventh year of Thanis (late evening.)

I thought I would never take up this journal again. Indeed, I had though it lost. That would have been best, for I have no wish to dwell on what is herein contained.

Nevertheless, having found it, I must complete it. I shall record these new events that bear recording, and then I shall cast this book from my life forever.

Six years it has been since I last wrote in this book. Now, certain things have come to pass that may complete the tragic tale. At least I know now that I am not mad, some small consolation, that.

The reality that I had accepted as truth seemed as insubstantial as the world of dreams, yet undeniably solid in ability to cause grief. Now, I must accept the reality of those events in the Emerin, not as the meanderings of madness, but as tangible facts. Facts with a cause.

It began this morning, with a soft knock at the door to my little office.

I opened the door and saw before me an elf so incredibly aged that for a moment I could not determine if my visitor was male or female. Our race ages slowly indeed, and this person must have lived years in the thousands.

"Good morning. I am Talian Maevarra, daughter of the House of Mirida," she said. Her voice was high and brittle.

My surprise at hearing the name of my birth House must have been apparent. Her pale eyes twinkled brightly at me with no sign of senility. Her hair, braided, fell nearly to the floor. It was a deep silver, not unlike my own, though streaked with pure white. Never had I seen a being so ancient.

"An honor, Nantis," I stammered. "I am Arien, also of House Mirida. What a strange coincidence! The Library is not yet open, but perhaps there is something I can help you with?"

"You already have," she said. "This meeting is no coincidence, young Arien. I come to see you. I am not at the Library to gain knowledge. Rather, to give it."

She slipped past me and perched on the stool at my desk like an improbably aged bird. Her black cloak was drawn close around her, and I thought of ravens. Ill fortune. I suddenly very much did not want to hear what she had come to tell me, yet politeness demanded that I respect an Elder.

"Forgive me," I said. "You claim to be of my House. How can this be? I do not know you, do I?"

"No, no. Though I know who you are. Adopted son of Karadan, recently fled to Thanis in the wake of your betrothed's death at the hands of nightmare creatures."

I sank to the edge of my desk. My legs were strengthless. She had mentioned the beasts, when I had never breathed a word of them to a soul! The expression on my face must have been quite comic, for she laughed cheerfully.

"Well now, that has snared your attention, has it not? Perhaps you'll listen to an old woman. Poor lad. How awful it must have been. Worry no longer. I understand. I am perhaps the only living being that does."

I stared at her, struck dumb.

"The things you saw were real," she went on. "And never think they were not. Disbelief is a dangerous thing. This is a long tale, by the way, and if you were to offer an old lady a cup of tea so her throat doesn't dry out, I am certain it would be appreciated."

Gathering the shattered remains of my manners, I quickly set about preparing tea, apologizing.

"Quite all right. This is a strange day for you, and I must say it will get stranger yet. You will regret opening the door to me once you've heard what I have to say. You will be angry, and grief-stricken. I am sorry for that. Still, I must tell you. I cannot avoid that responsibility. If only I had found you sooner . . . " Her voice was filled with sorrow.

She had uncannily gone right to the heart of it. I did not want to hear her tale, yet I knew that I must.

"Long ago and far from here," she began, "It sounds like a children's tale, but that is when and where it all started. At any rate, there was once the greatest of elven cities. It was called Govannisan, and it was beautiful beyond legends. Graceful spires, exquisite gardens. It was said that the streets were gold and the doorknobs gems, though that may have been exaggeration. Only elves lived in that fair city, for when I say this was long ago, I mean quite a long time, many generations of our kind. Humans, who would grow into this world's dominant people, were only just discovering the secrets of fire and tool making. Even the gods were young then.

"The city was ruled by a Council of the noble families. House Mirida was among them. There was another house that rivaled Mirida, House Tokalsis. The details are long-since lost in the mists of time, but what happened is that House Tokalsis, angered by some insult or injury, set out to put upon their rivals a mighty blood-curse. Among the Tokalsis family were many of the greatest Archmages ever known.

"The Miridans heard of this plan somehow and set out to stop it. They interrupted the ceremony, but too late. They disrupted the casting, and the spell misfired. No one knows exactly what happened, but all present, Tokalsians and Miridans alike, were found in the casting chamber, torn to shreds."

She paused and looked at me sadly. "You've gone a bit pale, my lad. Perhaps you can guess where this tale is leading?"

I could. I did not want to, but I knew. I nodded and motioned for her to continue.

"Those beloved of the Miridans began to die, seemingly in their sleep. The Miridans raved of nightmares come to life, of beasts from beyond the walls of madness. Many took their own lives in grief."

I recalled then my father, who rumor said had died by his own hand following the death of his dear wife. Had my own mother shared Alinora's fate?

Talian continued. "At last forced to believe that it was the Tokalsian curse, the Patriarch set out to confront the other house and learn the truth. When the Tokalsian Magelord laughed at the Patriarch and refused to reveal the means to end the curse, the Patriarch, mad with grief, slew him, and bloody war ensued.

"For generations, House Mirida suffered. Those few who survived the war tried to keep their House and honor alive, as their wives, husbands, sweethearts, died. The once-proud House slid slowly into despair.

"Govannisan was then in its prime. The city had grown and flourished, the other Houses rising as Mirida fell. Then, for reasons unknown, disaster struck. Perhaps it was an invading tyrant, or draconian greed, but a flight of dragons descended on the city and destroyed it with fire. Dragons were both more common and more powerful in those days. Immensely more so. Instead of monsters, they were recognized as a civilized race of beings, much as the humans and dwarves are today. And being civilized, they were capable of war. The city perished in their flames. Including, dare I tell you, the High Library of Govannisan, which was older than time and half the size of this city. All records were destroyed. Whole Houses were exterminated in the blink of an eye. The numbers will never be known. All I know is that at least one young woman survived."

"You?" I asked, caught up in her tale though I had no wish to hear it.

She struck me on the knee with her teaspoon. "I am not that old, impudent puppy! This was yet a thousand years before my birth."

I apologized again.

"Young people these days have no manners," she muttered. "Now, where was I?"

"The woman who escaped the city," I prompted.

"Ah, yes. She escaped the city's destruction, bearing in her womb the last of the Miridan line. She knew the curse would end if the child died, but she could not bring herself to kill him. When he was old enough to understand, she told all to him. She had heard the tales and legends, the stories of the olden days, and passed them on to her son.

"The boy grew into a man, always remembering his mother's words. He vowed that he would love no one, so that he would never lose them to this terrible thing. And he kept to that vow as well as he could. It may be that he kept it all his life, for the curse never touched him. Being as he was a young and healthy man, and not ill-favored in appearance, it occurred that a young woman became heavy with his child. He did not love her, but he was honorable, and so he married her. They lived long in moderate happiness, neither loving nor hating each other. The woman bore him a daughter and a son. As his mother had done, he told them all that he knew of the curse. They did not believe him."

At this point, my visitor sighed heavily and blinked back tears.

"The daughter fell dearly in love with a young man from a neighboring province, and the curse claimed him before her very eyes. Then, though it was too late, she believed. The son did not, calling his sister and father a pair of fools. He left to seek his fortune, and after many years earned himself a lordship in a faraway kingdom. He arranged a marriage to a wealthy but unattractive widow. They made a son, who fell in love with a lovely young woman, married her, and had a son before the curse claimed her. Devastated at the loss of his wife, he died by his own hand. Their infant son was taken in by another House, and that child was you, Arien."

I sat, stunned. Nothing in her tale rang false to me. Deep in my heart and in whatever memory ancestors pass on, I knew it to be the truth.

"This curse killed Alinora," I said, barely recognizing my own voice, "because I loved her?"

"And she loved you. It is that, the bright-burning star of true love that summons the beasts. So I believe, at any rate. Not the love of parent to child, nor of companions. Nor even simple desire, might I add."

"Who are you?" I had to know.

"I am your grandfather's older sister. As far as I know, I am your only living kin. I, too, once witnessed this evil curse. I alone understand."

Cursed. My darling Alinora, an innocent life devoured for the crime of love.

"Stop it," Talian said, brandishing her teaspoon warningly as she seemed to read my very thoughts. "How can it be your fault when you did not know? If it is the fault of anyone, 'tis mine for not finding you sooner. I never knew what had become of my brother. It was not until my wandering paths took me to the Emerin, that I leaned his fate. His, your father's, and yours. Blame me, for not warning you in time. Blame your grandfather, for not believing and not passing the knowledge along. But blame not yourself."

"What can I do?" I asked hopelessly.

"The only certain way to avoid it is to take your life," she said with ruthless honesty. "Our once-proud line ends with you, Arien."

"I will never have children," I said. "Alinora is dead. I shall never forget her. She was everything to me, and she is gone. I shall never love again."

She laughed, but there was sorrow in it. "Time soothes grief, my lad. Be it as short as a few decades, or as long as a century, you might feel love again. Your Alinora will become a memory."

"No. She will never fade. I will love her until the end of time."

"I have done what you now set out to do. The loneliness . . . it is dreadful. No matter how many friends, no matter how dear they were to me, always was I apart from them. Always I kept a tight rein on my feelings. They called me cold. Is this what you intend?"

"If it must be."

"The cost shall be great. The pain shall be greater. It is terrible to live without love."

"That is something I am doomed to do anyway. There is no love without Alinora."

"You have made your choice, then?"

"I have." I condemned myself to a life of loneliness with those simple words.

"I wish you well, son of my brother's son."

"Is there no way to undo it?" I asked, knowing the dread truth in my heart.

"None that has been found in thousands of years."

"If there is a way, I will find it," I said. "This may not be the High Library of Govannisan, but it is a start. I will read every book in this place if I must."

Alinora. I shall not forget. The loss of her is the taste of bitter tears.

Talian. I wonder if her final remark was meant to reassure me, or to worry me? "I will be watching over you." What meant she?

The Library awaits me.

*   *   *

Arien had just added the tea to the water when a soft knock sounded. He frowned. It was very late, too late for most callers to be up and about.

He set down the teapot and went to the door. He thumbed aside a little panel and looked through a small hole. To his surprise, he saw Cat standing in the hall. Quickly, he opened the door.

She looked up at him. The blank shock in her eyes frightened him. She was shaking. Her mouth opened. Closed. Opened again. A small sound, the start of a word, came out. Closed. Her throat moved as she swallowed.

"Cat, what is it?" he said, growing more alarmed.

He took her by the shoulders and steered her into the room. She shook under his hands. She was gripping something with a panicky tightness. He closed the door behind her, after peering down the hall. No intruders, no apparent cause for her to be in such a state. To his eye, she was uninjured. What, then, could have so affected her?

"I'm so sorry," she managed to say. "Oh, Arien, I truly am."

"Cat?" He snapped his fingers in front of her face, peered deeply into her wide eyes.

"I knew I shouldn't have read it," she said. "But once I started, I couldn't stop. Here . . ."

She held the object out to him, shuddering so that it fell from her hands. The book landed between them like a confession of guilt.

"Oh, Livana," he whispered. He knelt and skimmed his fingers over the cover. Though he needed no further proof, he opened it at random and recognized his own neat script. His sorrow in the garden of the Lord's Retreat had been a mere echo of what he now felt. He closed his eyes and bowed his head.

"I'm so sorry," Cat said. The sound of her voice pierced Arien's grief and reminded him of her presence. He suddenly realized what a shock it must have been for her. She could not have known the depths of his past's darkness.

Again exerting the strength of will he had built up over the years, he forced his own turmoil back and stood. Her need was the greater one. He started to lead Cat to the sofa, recalled how uncomfortable it was, and sat her down on the foot of the bed. She sat, huddled like a frightened child.

He poured two cups of tea, checked to see that she was not watching him, and added a tiny draught of sleeping powder to the one he handed her.

"Drink it," he said gently.

She took a sip and shivered. When she looked at him, the blank look was gone.

"Her hands, Arien, gods, her hands," she said. Her own hands, the center of her profession, were clenched around the cup. The tea sloshed, threatening to spill.

He made her drink the tea, and talked soothingly to her, saying nothing of import. Finally, her cup was empty, and her trembling eased.

"Where did you get that book?" he asked gently.

"I didn't take it from you," she said. "I would never steal from you. The woman gave it to me. The one who visited you. Your grandfather's sister."

"Talian?" He heard the incredulity in his voice.

Cat nodded. "I'm sure of it. She was just as you'd written her, older than anyone I've ever seen, with long white hair. She said she'd been watching me."

"Did she say why?" he asked, although he knew. He had not seen Talian since her long-ago visit, but had sometimes felt that she was nearby, watching him as she'd promised, watching to see if he was able to keep his vow.

"She said she might have the answers to some of my questions. Did she! I shouldn't have read it, but I couldn't stop myself." She blinked sleepily, the powder beginning to have an effect.

"I intended to tell you," he said sorrowfully. "Yet it seemed we were interrupted at every chance."

"Are you angry with me?" Mournful, childlike, timid of his wrath. He could not bear to see her so, and it melted what little ice of anger had formed in him.

"No." He moved to sit beside her, fearing that she would cringe from him now that she knew the truth, but she leaned against him readily enough. Too readily, and his own body responded far too willingly to her nearness. She pressed her head against his chest, stifling a yawn as the potent powder worked its magic.

"Do you believe it? Or think me mad?"

"I believe it. How could I not? Your lady, your quest . . ." her voice trailed off drowsily.

"Your peril," he murmured, but she was asleep.

He carefully leaned her back on the bed. She sighed and curled up. It was a sensual motion, a motion that made him yearn to take her in his arms and hold her close throughout the night. For a moment, he stood watching her sleep. He touched her soft cheek, her glossy hair.

"Do not love me, Cat," he pleaded. "Do not. I cannot lose you as I lost her."

*   *   *

Magic, in truth, is nothing more than a great game of power, skill, and blind luck.

The Book of Yor.

"This, you say, is the alchemist's home?' Arien laughed. "I find myself unsurprised. It looks just as I imagined it might."

"I just hope it's safe. Every time I come here, I'm sure the place will fall in on me." Cat opened the gate, and the top hinge gave way. "See what I mean?"

The yard was overgrown, almost swallowing the tiny brick house. If not for the green-yellow smoke puffing from the bent chimney, it would have seemed abandoned, for good reason. The shingled roof was badly balding, and somehow seemed uneven, giving an observer the impression that at some point the entire thing had shot up in the sky, reversed itself, and landed askew.

"It seems to violate nearly every principle of Talus Yor's *Guidelines for Wizards and Alchemists*," Arien said dubiously. "Are you certain this alchemist—Doc, was it?—is capable?"

Cat shrugged. "He's a friend of the Nightsiders. We sell him things that he can't buy in the marketplace. Speckled mushrooms, lotus oil, and the like. In return, he pays well in elixirs. I've never used any myself, but my friend Calidar swears by them."

As they picked their way through the wild yard, they began to hear noises from within. Hissing, bubbling, and the occasional muttered curse. Strange smells mingled in the air.

Cat knocked, and the curses stopped. They waited. She knocked again. The door popped suddenly open, and there was Doc.

Arien's first thought was that the name suited him. A nimbus of white hair floated around his bright-eyed, wrinkled face. A pair of spectacles perched just at the tip of his nose, forgotten and unused as he peered at them over the rims. His apron was stained and splotched with colors the rainbow never intended. His hands were scarred and burnt, and one of his fingers was missing the first two joints. An unlit pipe was clenched in his teeth, and he switched it from one side of his mouth to the other as he talked.

"Oh, well, what's this? Visitors? Wait just a moment. Elf and elfkin? Together? Unusual, in fact, downright boggling!" His rapid speech was punctuated by clacks as the pipe jumped around. It was a miracle he didn't bite off his tongue.

"Good day, sir--" was as far as Arien got before Doc was off again.

"Wait just a moment here," he said again, and proceeded to do just the opposite, jutting the pipe at Cat. "Is my delivery here already? Confound it, I told them I didn't want it until two days from now. It has to be fresh, you know. Ogre brains spoil so fast. Takes so many of them to fill a jar, too. Huge creatures, truly enormous, brains the size of a hen's egg. Well, don't just stand there, bring it in."

"I'm not making a delivery," she said when he paused to suck in a breath. "We're here about the elixirs. The ones I brought last week?"

"Well, why didn't you say so?" Doc muttered. He let them in and closed the door. "Good news, actually. About the ogre brains, I mean. Of course now they'll be late. Early or late. Nothing is ever on time."

The walls of the front room were lined with shelves of bottled and other unusual items. A ragged curtain concealed the back room, which was the source of the hissing and bubbling. Cat glanced uneasily that way, then turned to Doc. "Well?"

"Tea?"

"No, thank you," they both said hastily. No telling what odd herbs might find their way into Doc's teapot.

"Lovely weather this time of year, aye?"

"Quite," Arien said, giving Cat a questioning look.

She grinned. "I've been through this before." To Doc, she added, "And we're in fine health. Yourself?"

"Passable, passable. Good, that's gotten polite small talk out of the way." Doc clapped his hands briskly. "Now to business. You brought me thrice half a dozen elixirs. Most are fairly straightforward. Strength enhancements, healing, invisibility, and the like. These three, though, were of great interest. Great, great interest!" He held them up.

"Invisibility!" Cat reached eagerly for the vial Doc indicated.

"That's the last thing Thanis needs!" Arien said sternly, catching her hand.

"What you've got here," Doc went on, apparently oblivious to their exchange, "is a rare elixir of transformation. Be careful with it. The unwary drinker will become the animal closest in habit to his personality!"

"Transformation," repeated Arien, awed. "A powerful thing indeed!"

Doc picked up the next vial, which contained a swirling rose-silver fluid. "Death-slumber," he announced.

"A poison?" Cat asked, raising an eyebrow.

"Not so, only a sleep so deep it might as well be death. The stuff children's tales are made of. Enchanted princess awaiting the kiss of the handsome prince, that sort of thing. Except a kiss won't counteract it. Takes a different elixir altogether to do that. I have the antidote in stock, if you'd care to buy it. A bargain, only eight hundred marks!"

"What is the last one?" Arien asked.

Doc's fingers fidgeted. "If you're interested in selling any of these, I can give you the best bargain in the Northlands!"

"What is it, that you're so keen to buy it?" Cat peered suspiciously at the gold-flecked elixir.

"This," Doc said, caressing the glass vial, "is the pinnacle of the alchemical profession! The dream of my alchemical brethren worldwide! Few are able to craft it, and the recipe itself is so secret as to be nearly impossible to learn!"

"You mean, it turns things into gold?" Cat went wide-eyed.

"Oh, well, all right, mayhap not the pinnacle, but near the peak! It is an elixir of resurrection!"

"Resurrection?" breathed Arien. "I thought that was but a legend!"

"You mean, it creates undead?" Cat wrinkled her nose. "We had Solarrin for that, had we wanted it, and I cannot imagine who would!"

"No, no, elfkin! This restores the dead to life! Well, the recently dead. After a few days, when the soul has fled and the flesh gone stiff, it's of no use. Don't ask me why. Maybe they can't come back after they've gone stiff." Doc puffed and started coughing as great black clouds billowed up.

*   *   *

Cat stopped just inside the park gate, admiring Arien from a distance. He wore soft grey velvet trousers and a white shirt, open at the collar. His hair spilled over his shoulders like a waterfall of silver. His hair, his eyes, his silken voice . . . these were just the sort of thoughts she wasn't supposed to have.

Her first impulse following the revelations in his journal had been to flee, flee far and fast. That urge had lasted only a brief moment, overpowered by her promise and her friendship. She knew now that he did not love her, could not love her.

At least, she thought and smiled at her own foolishness, it wasn't because she was elfkin. The awareness, the truth, had made things easier. No longer did she wonder if he cared for her, no longer did she wonder what secrets haunted him.

She did wonder other things, despite her resolve, things she wasn't supposed to consider. As she looked on him now, a serene portrait against the willows that trailed their leafy branches in the pool where the crested swans swam, she wondered what it would be like to go quietly over to him and take his face between her palms, and kiss him.

She shook away that tempting thought and crossed the park, passing a minstrel who strummed a harp and smiled at a group of fawning young maids. The park was a peaceful haven just off the bustle of Merchant's Row, a haven from the crowds.

She settled down near him. Today was the day. For many days now, he had come to spend a few quiet hours in a mage's trance, using the scroll from Selbon's library to summon a spirit familiar. Today, if he was successful, it should arrive.

Arien did not open his eyes as she sat down, but she knew he was aware of her. She filled a cup with sweet juice and handed it to him. He nodded his thanks.

She started to say something, but he motioned for silence.

"Wait," he breathed. "It is time."

His eyes were still shut in concentration. "*Fel'alalna fan'gilea*," he said softly. The words were filled with a subtle power. His graceful artist's hands formed themselves into a painful-looking gesture that Cat's clever hands could not duplicate.

The air seemed to tingle around him. Cat's skin prickled. It was hard to breathe.

Something rustled in a nearby hedge. Arien raised his voice, repeating the words, almost singing. He made a beckoning motion.

Cat gasped as a small head poked out of the bush. It was wedge-shaped, a deep shiny black in color. Brilliant green eyes fixed on Arien, whose eyes were still shut. The head was followed by a long, curved neck. It inched cautiously forward. Free of the hedge, it unfurled black wings that glistened with opaline colors in the sunlight.

The little dragon seemed to gain confidence and moved up to Arien. It butted its head against his hand, stroking it. He opened his eyes and looked down. It looked up. Green eyes met silver. The mage was transfixed by wonder as he touched the small head. It cooed and blinked contentedly.

"A drake," Arien said. "Never did I expect this!"

He picked the drake up, examining it, smiling in complete joy. "Yes, of course," he said to it. "Oh? I imagine you are. Fear not, little one. We have food for you."

It twined its tail around his arm and looked at Cat, cocking its head curiously. Then, although its pearly-fanged mouth did not move, she heard a voice. A voice in her head, soft and musical. *Who is she?*

This is Cat, my friend, Arien replied, but nor did his lips move.

Can you hear me? she thought. *In my mind?*

Of course. But she isn't a cat, the drake said, perplexed.

Cat heard Arien's mental laugh. *Cat is her name, it is how she is known. But why, I wonder, can the two of you communicate? It must be that you, Cat, were here for so much of the summoning. In a way, he is a familiar to you as well.*

I want a name, the drake declared decisively, not at all concerned with the peculiarities of magics or summonings. *Are you going to give me one?*

Wouldn't you rather choose your own name? Arien asked.

May I? I want a good name, an impressive name. I am a drake, after all. I am quick, and clever, with strong wings and breath of fire.

Like a dragon, Cat thought admiringly.

Only better, the drake corrected. *I don't eat as much. Not *quite* as much.*

This is more than I had hoped for, Arien thought, rubbing his thumb along the glossy ridge of the drake's back. *A black drake . . . a sable drake! Small wonder you and he understand one another!*

I have chosen my name, the drake said, raising his head and puffing out his chest proudly. *I will be named Darkfire Dragonwing Sharptooth Quickflight Weasel's-Bane Clevermind Windshadow. That will do for now, but I might add more.*

That is quite a name, Arien sent, amused. *However, we will need a shorter name to call you by, in the event of danger.*

What do you mean?

If someone was trying to hurt you, Cat replied, *and we wanted to warn you, by the time we finished saying your name, it might be too late. My whole name is Cathlin Tahmira Sabledrake, but I just go by Cat.*

I suppose just Darkfire will do for a short name. He sounded as if he was pouting.

Darkfire is an excellent name, Arien thought, stroking the curved neck. *It suits you perfectly.* He glanced sidelong at Cat. "Cathlin Tahmira," he murmured aloud. "Also a fine and excellent name."

And you are Arien, and she is Cat. Is she your mate?

Cat blushed. To her surprise, Arien also looked flustered.

No. We are not . . . mates. She is my dear friend.

A shame. Darkfire shifted his wings in what Cat supposed was a draconian shrug. *She is pretty for your kind, but her neck is too short.*

Embarrassed but curious, Cat had to ask. *My neck is too short?*

Too short for proper mating. Darkfire sent a brief image into her mind, an image of two drakes, their necks wrapped lovingly around each other. The vision was accompanied by a rush of warm passion that made Cat gasp. The drake peered at her quizzically, then at Arien. *Though it may suffice for your kind, since neither of you have the right sort of necks. How do you manage it?*

That is quite enough, Arien thought quickly, seeming equally affected and unwilling or unable to meet Cat's eyes. *We are not here to discuss mating habits or comparative necks!*

I am very hungry, Darkfire sent, ending the disturbing images and adding an empty, growling, churning sensation. Though Cat had just eaten, she felt starved, ravenous.

He offered some sliced meat and cheese to the drake, who, despite his claim of not eating *quite* as much as a dragon, seemed determined to give it a good try. When he had devoured everything in sight, he gave a contented sigh and curled up in Arien's lap to sleep.

Arien looked down at the drake and smiled indulgently. "What a wonder this is," he murmured, gently touching a folded wing. "I had resigned myself to being ever alone, but now I know that this bond with little Darkfire will ever be my comfort."

*   *   *

The orc cowered before them but it dared not attempt to flee. It paled as they pointed silently toward the altar. It shuffled through the litter of bones that those rude invaders had left on the floor of the crypt. With a pitiful, wordless whimper, the orc climbed onto the altar and laid back, staring hopelessly at the dark, dank ceiling.

Archmage Selbon, who had forgotten how long it had been since they had thought of themself in other than the third person, leaned over the orc and fastened its wrists to the manacles set into the stone.

Their silver arm moved with sureness, but the other arm was weak, shaky. Bits of dried skin flaked off and fell on the orc's upturned, frightened face.

They had almost waited too long. The energies that sustained them were rapidly depleting. It was past the time for a new infusion of life force. In their anger over the attack on their home, they had almost forgotten to rejuvenate themself.

They automatically held out their silver hand, expecting Gisela to pass them the heavy gold amulet they needed to transfer the orc's life force to their own fading body, but Gisela was not there. Nor would she ever be again. One of the callous barbarians who had intruded upon their home had killed her.

It had been bad enough when she'd initially died, so long ago, but at least they'd been able to bring her back as a semblance of her former self. No, she had been better after her death. As a *lichma'rhun*, a member of the Undead, she would never think of taking her own life as she had done before. Fickle female! To think, they had offered her the finest of gifts, her own father's head. Had she not seen it as proof of their love for her?

Muttering to themself, they limped around the altar and picked up the amulet. It began to glow at their touch, illuminating the tiny creature that scurried around inside the gem.

They placed the amulet on the orc's chest as it tried to cringe away from them, tried to shrink into the stone. Its obedience was too strong. For generations, the orcs had been raised and trained to do their bidding. Even the foreign orc, the female they'd taken prisoner so many years ago, had quickly learned that survival in their service was better than a brutal death.

The trouble with orcs was that the energies were so unsatisfying. So thin and bitter. A human would be better, or perhaps another dwarf. They'd had a dwarf once. Oh, the hearty fare of that sturdy race! They'd gone two full years without needing another transference.

The amulet's glow began to brighten and dim, in time with the orc's frantic heart. The creature inside ceased its scuttling and crouched. Selbon put their hand over the crystal, feeling the heat, the energy. It was feeble, but it would have to do.

An elf would be best of all. There had been an elf once. The crossling child had asked about it. For some reason, they'd been getting forgetful lately and could no longer recall exactly where the elf was. They could have asked the orcs, but they doubted they could get a sensible answer. First, they would recover their strength, and then they would go looking for this elf.

The creature started to swell as it ate the orc's life and excreted it into Selbon. A crude analogy, they thought, but apt.

Behind them, the crypt door slammed open. Pain shot through them as they lost control of the spell. The orc screamed hideously, writhed, and died. The amulet shattered in a flare of light.

Their enchanted eye fixed upon the figure in the doorway.

"Now we shall settle this once and for all," the minotaur declared.

*   *   *

What are you doing? Darkfire looked over from his den on top of the tallest bookshelf, where he kept and guarded his "hoard" as fiercely as any full-sized dragon.

Arien set down a heavy tome with a sigh. "Trying to decide which spell to study next."

He could answer the drake's query mentally, but talking aloud seemed more normal. Normal to him, at any rate. He suspected that others, observing him speaking with apparent lack of response, would think him quite odd.

How about one to magically make food? Darkfire suggested helpfully. His long, thin tongue flicked out hungrily.

"Do you ever think of anything but your stomach?" Arien asked fondly.

Do you ever think of anything but your spells? the drake retorted.

"All right, all right. You have a point. What would you like to do tonight?"

Go out to the confectionery for some rum jollies, and then to the park to chase swans.

"Chasing swans is the only exercise you ever get. You've only been here for four days, and you are already starting to get ungainly around the midsection."

I like to chase swans. In fact, I want to add it to my name. I shall be Darkfire Dragon-wing Sharptooth Quickflight Weasel's-Bane Clevermind Windshadow Swanchaser. He paused and craned his neck to examine his belly. *What do you mean, ungainly? Are you hinting that you might be thinking of taking away my candies?*

"You are out of candies, and I cannot buy you any more tonight. In case your snoring kept you from hearing the bells, it is now far too late to visit the confectionery. They have been closed for hours."

*We could go see Cat. *She* always has a bit of candy for me,* he sent reproachfully. *Why doesn't she live here with us?*

"And where would she sleep?" Arien waved a hand at the crowded room. The new shelves, packed with Selbon's books, took up what little free space there had been. "I barely have room for myself."

Darkfire dove from his perch and glided to the bed. He landed on the pillow, flipped his wings back smartly, and cocked his head.

How about here? he suggested, winking first one eye and then the other.

Arien tossed a fur over him. "You are getting to be as bad as Sybil. I told you before, Cat and I are not mates."

Why not? You could be.

"No, we could not. You know that. I've told you my story, my life. Alinora was my mate. It may not have been made official, but in my heart it was true. Indeed, it still is, and shall ever be."

Darkfire crawled out from under the fur and started grooming. *She's dead,* he pointed out.

Arien sat on the edge of the bed. "Yes, she is dead," he said softly.

So why not find a new one? You're not a dragon. You don't have to be alone forever. Elves can have more than one mate. Not at the same time, though. He chewed on his foot, spreading the talons to clean between them. Grooming was his third favorite pastime, right after eating and napping.

"I could not . . . take a mate . . . without love, and I cannot let myself love again. It is too great a risk. I still love Alinora. I always shall. No one could replace her."

But she is dead, he repeated. *You can't change that.*

"No. It is too late," he said wistfully. "Too late by a century."

Darkfire twisted his neck around and nibbled on his wing. *Wouldn't she--* he started, but Arien was not listening.

He stared at the bookshelves, a sudden realization dawning. The implications of it were staggering, overwhelming.

It was too big to put into words. He got up like a man hypnotized. In a near trance, he went to the shelves. Darkfire sent inquiringly, but withdrew hastily from the turmoil whirling through his mind.

He took down the ancient roll of parchment carefully, feeling the edges crumble. The ribbon around it was faded with age. He untied it gently and unrolled the scroll far enough to read the title and the brief summary after it.

It, like many of the scrolls he'd recovered from Selbon's library, had been given only the briefest of glances to assure himself that they were of interest. In the frantic flight from the castle and the busy days following, he hadn't given them more thought except to dig out the scroll of familiar summoning. He'd barely looked at this one, sure that it would have no practical uses.

"It could work," he said numbly. "Dear gods, it could truly work! The elixir . . . but how to go about it? The house would have been well-guarded . . . a need for secrecy, for stealth . . ." he laughed aloud. "I shall need the services of a thief!"

He flung his cape about his shoulders, forgetting that it was late, forgetting everything but the single thought that held him in an iron grip.

Arien? Alarmed, Darkfire swooped after him, just making it through the door before it closed.

*   *   *

The knock was enough to startle Cat from an uneasy sleep.

She got up and crossed the room silently, a knife in hand in case her late visitor wasn't friendly. Though, of course, it had been her experience that the unfriendly visitors usually didn't bother knocking. She suspected it might be one of her fellow Nightsiders, come to see why she had grown so neglectful of her profession of late.

She lived on the top floor of a Fifth Ring townhouse, two small rooms and a bathing alcove, and its own external stair, letting her come and go as she pleased without disturbing the family that lived in the rooms below. By the faint light that came through the shutters, she was easily able to make her way around the furniture.

"Who's there?" she asked.

"Cat, I must speak with you." It was Arien's voice, but he sounded so odd that immediate suspicion filled her. "Please. It is of the utmost urgency."

Darkfire? she thought questioningly.

Cat, can we come in? He's acting strange. Maybe you can help. I don't know what's wrong.

She put down the knife and opened the door. Arien came in, eyes wide and farseeing. "Cat, I have an idea," he said before the door was even closed behind him. "It will be dangerous, I don't know if we can even manage it, but it should work. Oh, Livana, if it works . . . " It was the closest to babbling he had ever come.

Cat lit the lamp and turned worriedly to him. "Arien, are you all right? Are you hurt?"

He started to say something, then stopped, staring at her. She looked down at herself, saw the silken nightdress that had once belonged to her mother, and wished the floor would open to swallow her.

Arien was abruptly shocked out of his daze. The idea that had seized him and driven him through the dark and dangerous midnight streets of Thanis melted from his mind like a snowflake on a warm windowpane.

He wanted to sweep her into his arms, this beautiful girl with her hair still tousled from sleep, her lithe body revealed by the clinging gown. He longed to carry her back to her bed, the blankets still warm from her body, and awaken the passion he knew she possessed. She would be exquisite. He knew that as surely as he knew his own name.

"Cat . . ." he breathed.

"Excuse me! I have to put something on." She spun, grabbed her sensible black woolen robe and struggled with it, the sleeves conspiring to twist and evade her arms. She felt more of a fool every second. Finally the robe was on and she tied it firmly.

When she turned back, face burning, she was relieved to see that Arien had looked away, and passed his hand across his eyes as if waking from a dream.

Darkfire perched on the mantle, amid a collection of cunningly-made wood carvings. He peered at them with interest.

What are these? he sent curiously.

"This one is my father," Cat said, smiling as she touched each in turn. "Here's Alphonse, Sybil, Greyquin and Bear . . ." she grew somber. "Jessa."

By the time she finished showing them to Darkfire, and the drake had exacted a promise that she would soon immortalize him in a carving, and then demonstrated to him how she used the slab of wood set with a dozen complex locks to practice her lockpicking skills, Arien had regained his composure.

Cat gestured to her chair. "Sit, Arien, please, and tell me what's the matter. You looked . . . stricken!"

His purpose returned to him in a flash and he looked at her with bright eyes. "Yes. Cat, the most incredible thing . . . I am sorry to wake you, but it would not wait. I need your help." He chuckle ruefully. "Your thiefly help."

"My thiefly help? Whatever for?"

"Because I've never stolen a body before."

She laughed incredulously. "And you think—*I*—have? Steal a body? As in, a corpse? Why? Who?"

"I could bring her back. Alinora could live again! The elixir, Cat! The elixir could revive her!"

"Arien," she said slowly, "She died a hundred years ago. She's naught but bones by now. The elixir isn't that powerful. Doc said—"

He nodded, waving away her objections. "Yes, yes. But there is a scroll from Selbon's collection, one I had noticed it in passing and filed it away merely as a curiosity, thinking I would have no use for it. The scroll holds a spell titled *Locadio's Temporal Doorway*."

She knew little of magic, but . . . "Arien, you can't mean . . ."

He nodded. "I intend to go back in time, to the Emerin of a century past."

*   *   *

If I could go back and change one thing about my past, I would not be the man I am today, and it is because I am the man I am today that I might want to change that one thing about my past.

The Book of Yor.

"All right," Cat said, "Let's go through it again. You want to open a doorway through time. We go through, steal Alinora's body, and use the elixir to bring her back to life."

"Yes. There is one problem, however."

"One? I see at least a dozen, never mind the one about how to steal the body in the first place." She ran her hands through her hair. "What problem do you see?"

"The portal does not last long. Therefore, we will need to open it near the Elyvorrin estate. That requires a visit to the Emerin in our own time."

"Oh. My life wouldn't be worth a bent mark in the Emerin. And you're exiled!"

"Not precisely," he admitted. "I left before the Council could formally make such a declaration, to spare the Karadans the shame of it. Still, my return would likely be unwelcome."

"Let's forget about that for now. We'll go in secrecy and disguise if we must. But what I wonder, Arien, is this. Did they have a funeral for her?"

"Yes, of course. She was a count's daughter, after all. A fine and grand ceremony, I would imagine. I did not attend, I couldn't have born to even if I'd not been suspected in her death."

She nodded. "So I'll need to know everything you can tell me about the tomb. From what Doc said, we shan't have much time to spare. Don't elven funerals last for days?"

"Yes," he said, mentally berating himself for not thinking of it. "Yes, of course, she would have lain in state for some time before the actual wrapping in rosecloth bindings and the processional to the tomb."

"We can find a way around that, if need be," she said. "But, Arien, most of all, suppose we're successful? Suppose we succeed, and bring her back to life? Won't the curse only strike again?"

The blood drained from his face. He closed his eyes and let his head fall forward.

"Oh, no," he said miserably. "Always it comes back to that."

She touched his arm. "You can't put her, and yourself, through that again!"

"I cannot do it. I cannot bring her back to doom her to the same fate. What am I to do? To have the possibility within my very grasp, yet forever blocked by this infernal curse! It would work, Cat!" He clasped her hands beseechingly. "Wouldn't it?"

"I don't know, Arien. I'm no sorceress. But we must think of all the possibilities."

"The curse, the curse, the triple-blasted curse! What am I to do?" He hung his head. "There is no hope for me, then. Every time it seems life, rather than this shallow existence, is within my reach, the curse snatches it from me! Better to die than to live without hope, to live hollow and empty."

"No, Arien, don't speak that way! There is a way, I know there is!"

"Cat, my fiery one," he sighed sadly. "So young, so full of hope and fighting spirit! Would that I had your courage, your determination!"

"You do," she said. "I am with you, Arien. Your quest isn't ended."

"No, it is not, it shall not be until this curse is lifted, even if I must travel to the ends of the earth in search of an answer. Better to die in the attempt to undo it than to throw my life away."

"That's more like it! Never give up, never!"

He touched her cheek. "So you would be my *aether,* to give me strength? There is no one I would rather have beside me on such a journey, but I cannot allow it. Going without you may endanger me, but staying near me endangers you far more."

Cat covered his hand with her own, pressed his smooth palm to her face. "I'll take the chance."

"Too many chances, dear Cat. Too many chances. I could not bear to lose you."

"You won't," she promised, and before wisdom could prevail, she brought her lips to his.

He did not pull away. Rather, he returned her kiss with a desperate longing. His hand slid from her cheek to her ear, gently tracing its shape. Enticing sensations whirled through her. She forgot all shyness, all modesty, wanted nothing more than to be in his arms, to be his completely.

She reached to caress the line of his ear, and for a moment he trembled beneath her touch. And then he did pull away, catching her wrist, his breath quick, his normally fair face flushed.

"No, Cat, we mustn't," he gasped. "We risk too much. Ah, gods, I am going mad! You . . . she . . . all of us doomed if we permit this thing to . . . no! I must go now. We are both muchly overwrought. The dawn will bring us again to our senses. Farewell!"

He seized up Darkfire, jostling the drake from a sound sleep, and all but flew out her door.

*   *   *

Cat paused just inside the door of the Empty Mug and took a deep breath. "Home!"

Sometimes she needed to smell smoke and leather, hear the rattle of dice and the occasional argument. It was her only remaining connection with her father. She could easily picture him sitting at one of the back tables, a fan of cards in his hand and a pile of coins in front of him, and a knife in his boot in case the game turned bad.

"Welladay, look who's finally come a'visiting!" One-Eye grabbed her around the waist and swung her feet off the floor before she could stop him. "Cat Sabledrake, as I live and breathe!"

He more resembled an aged swordsman than a thief, though in his sixty-plus years, Cat knew he had done much of both. A twisted scar ran across his forehead, down through the place where his right eye had once been, and down his cheek to his chin.

"We thought you'd forgotten all about us, what with the new company you're keeping," Stryker teased, giving her a wink. One-Eye's son was tall and broad-shouldered. Though she'd never paid much attention before, Cat now realized that perhaps Sybil hadn't been far wrong in her assessment of his handsomeness.

"Good evening, gentlemen," Cat said when she'd at last gotten her feet back on the ground.

"Where have you been, kitten?" One-Eye held her at arm's length, looked her over critically, and shook her with rough affection. "You still look all right. Your father would skin me alive if I let anything happen to you. So, tell us about this elflord."

"About time our Cat found a fellow," Stryker said.

"It's nothing like that," she protested, blushing fiercely at the memory of the previous night's kiss. Never in her life had she felt that way, never even imagined that she could.

"Now, now," One-Eye relented. "We're just having a bit of fun with you, kitten. Your da would be doing the same, you know. But, come now, I've heard talk of treasure!"

She pulled a silken cord from around her neck. Strung on it was a small pouch of deep blue velvet. She opened the pouch and spilled the midnight sapphire into her hand, and relished their exclamations of approval.

"Now, that's a pretty little stone," Styker remarked. "Valuable, too! The castle of Archmage Selbon?"

One-Eye took a shiny gold coin from his pouch and set it on the table. A privacy coin, Cat knew, enchanted to prevent anyone else in the room from eavesdropping. Thus, she could sit safely within a roomful of thieves, for the Empty Mug was one of the places where Nightsiders gathered, and tell her tale of adventure.

When she came to the part about Selbon, One-Eye grew very quiet. His one bright eye focused on her intensely. She'd never had him look at her so sharply. At the end of her tale, he sat back and signaled for another mug of ale.

"So the old mage is still alive?" He scowled. "I remember him. Blast his black heart. I ran afoul of him when I first came to the Northlands. That was how I lost my eye. Did I ever tell you that story?"

"I thought you lost it to a Tradersport coinwench, the one who knifed you because you couldn't pay," Stryker said.

"You told me it happened in a fight with Montennor dwarves in a gambling house," Cat said.

"Oh, that's right," One-Eye agreed, nodding at both of them. "Hard to remember. Still, glad you got home safely. Your father would be proud, kitten. Many's the time he talked about going up to that castle himself, to find out what happened to his old friends and unearth some of that treasure."

"I do have some other information for you," Cat said. "Have you heard aught of Lords Marl and Taron?"

"Taron again?" Stryker chuckled. "Isn't he in enough trouble?"

"That family isn't ever out of trouble," One-Eye said. "Remind me to tell you about his daughter sometime. Now there's a wench who'd be a good Nightsider! Not many women are."

"Oh, really?" Cat asked loftily.

He chuckled. "Exceptions prove the rule. Now tell me about the lords before I die of old age."

She recounted the conversation she'd overheard in the garden. One-Eye scowled. "It could be nothing," he mused darkly, "but, then again . . . I'll look into it."

"There is one more thing," Cat said reluctantly, and told them about her run-in with Tanneivan.

"That pompous goat's dropping!" One-Eye swore. "I should have known he'd come back around! Ah, if only your da had run him through when he had the chance!"

"He knew my father?"

"They'd a duel once, back not long after your folks were married. Come to think of it, 'twas right when your da announced he was going to be a father! In fact—bloody fire! why didn't I think of it before—he went out of sight for a time right when your mother vanished!"

Cat's eyes bulged. "You don't think he—?"

"Yes, I do," One-Eye said grimly. "I'd bet my last mark he had something to do with it. Curse me for a fool! The ones that took your mother—"

"What? You know who did it?"

One-Eye cringed, caught out. "Now, Cat . . ."

"Then you must know where my father went! Two years, I've been going out of my head with worry, and you knew all along?"

"I can't tell you, kitten. I shouldn't have even said this much. Your da, he made me swear. They say there's no honor among thieves, but that's not so. I swore on my sword."

"He didn't want you running off after him, Cat," Stryker said uncomfortably. "He'd not want to see you hurt."

"Then he shouldn't have made me what I am!" she flared. "Half my life I spend in dark alleys, never knowing if this is going to be the time my luck runs out. I've drawn steel more times than I can count. I've scrambled over walls in the dark with dogs on my heels. I've been cut, clubbed, stabbed, bitten, enspelled, and turned to stone! If he didn't want me hurt, why did he raise me to be what I am?"

"Enough!" One-Eye's sharp tone cut through her tirade. "Your father knew what he was doing. If he can, he'll be back. If not, he won't. You couldn't make a difference. You may be good, Cat, but you're not your father."

She flinched. It was the strongest reprimand she'd ever received from him. "One-Eye, I'm sorry."

"That's better," One-Eye said. He relaxed and reached for his mug. "Now then, we'll drink to your father, and you can tell us how you came to befriend an elf. Is this the missing part of your story about Rolle?"

"It is," she admitted, and began telling One-Eye and Stryker how she had happened to save the life of an elven wizard. She chose her words carefully, trying not to betray her true feelings, but through it all One-Eye smiled as if he already knew more than she knew herself.

*   *   *

Arien woke completely disoriented.

Usually an early riser, he was accustomed to the morning stillness. Instead, the markets were closing and the taverns were opening, and the streets were filled with people going between one and the other.

He remembered coming home in the predawn light, his mind had been awhirl with plans and possibilities, and over all else was the sweet but painful memory of Cat's kiss.

How close had he come to spending the night in her bed? She would have welcomed him, and in each others' arms they would have found such pleasure—

"Put it out of your mind, man!" he counseled himself scathingly, but still remembered her light, innocent touch along the rim of his ear, she having no way of knowing how it had set him aflame.

He flung himself out of bed, cast a quick spell to fill his washbasin with icy water, and plunged his head into it. The cold slapped all passionate thoughts swiftly from his head.

"Better," he murmured. He raised his head, and for a moment wondered if he had addled his brains more than he meant to, for there seemed to be two drakes perched on his windowsill.

Two drakes? He scrubbed his face with a cloth, then looked again. Yes, there were two. One was unmistakably Darkfire, but the other was a petite reddish-gold female. She and Darkfire chirped at each other and touched wings.

Who is your friend? he thought to Darkfire.

She has a name, the drake sent, sounding impressed. *Her person calls her Ilgilean*

Powerstone? he sent confusedly. *She is someone's familiar?*

Darkfire warbled at the red, who chirped back politely. She cocked her head at Arien, extended her shimmering wings, and did a credible imitation of a curtsey.

She says her person is called Talus.

Not Talus Yor, the Archmage?

Another quick draconish exchange. *That's her person. She says he is the best wizard in the city. I told her you were, but she just laughs.*

As well she should, Arien thought. *Talus Yor has been studying magic longer than I have been alive. Tell her that I bid her good evening.*

The red dipped her head, looking pleased.

She says the same. Now that you're awake, are you going to feed us?

"We wouldn't want to be rude to your guest," he said aloud, and after a quick rummage came up with enough tidbits to soothe the ravenous maws of two drakes.

As they nibbled and cooed at each other, it made him smile for Darkfire's budding romance, but that had the unwanted effect of reminding him of his own.

He closed his eyes, ashamed that he had let himself give in to his impulses. He had no right to be kissing Cat, no right to put her in such mortal danger. Ah, but she was impossible to resist! Not only for her compellingly unusual beauty, but for her clever wits, her loyal heart, her intriguing duality. Elf and human, innocent thief.

His actions became even less forgivable when examined in the light of the possibility of Alinora's return. The gods were giving him a second chance, if he could but find a way.

Alinora could live again. In his heart that meant that she was alive, and if she was alive, he could not continue being untrue to her.

He was so close, so maddeningly close! Yet, at the same time, he was exactly where he had started. The curse was like a giant boulder, blocking his way. There had to be a way around it.

He had just settled down to his own breakfast—or was it supper since the sun had already vanished beyond the mountains?—when a possibility stuck him like a bolt of lightning.

Darkfire!

What? The drake flapped his wings and nearly fell out the window, startled by the abrupt call.

Ilgilean is Talus Yor's familiar. Talus Yor is the greatest human mage ever to have lived. He is known and respected even among the elves. Ask her if she could talk to him and arrange a meeting. If anyone would know a way to break the curse, it is he!

You want me to arrange a meeting with the Archmage, just like that?

Yes!

Darkfire rolled his eyes, then chirped and cooed at Ilgilean. After a few exchanges, the red drake nuzzled Darkfire's ear and flew off.

She says she'll come back at midnight with his answer, Darkfire reported.

That does not leave us much time. Come, we must find Cat.

*   *   *

Cat paused, pretending to examine the wares displayed in the cabinetmaker's window. Up ahead, a portly man staggered to a halt under a lamppost and took another swig from a bottle. His heavy pouch bumped and swayed below his ample belly.

She directed her attention instead to the man walking behind the wealthy inebriant. He was tall and lean, the sword at his side a functional piece of steel. He kept a watchful eye on the other man and the dark street.

The wealthy man, probably a merchant, reeled down the street. Cat paused, weighing the risk the guard presented against the merchant's bulging purse and jewelry.

She followed, carefully, quietly. Her slight, non-threatening appearance was an asset, but so were speed and silence. By the time the merchant weaved around the corner, she was only a few steps from the guard. She clung to the shadows, clung to the silence.

Music and laughter from the building covered any sound she might make. She gripped her dagger, the hilt poised to strike. One blow to the head was often enough to drop a man.

She started to raise the dagger, and the guard moved suddenly. She tensed to flee, then saw that the merchant was sprawled in a puddle, laughing like a madman. The contents of the bottle dribbled onto the cobblestones. The guard smothered a disdainful snort and moved to help him up.

It was the perfect opportunity. As the guard was bent over, Cat slipped up behind him and hit him on the head. He grunted and fell on the merchant, who laughed harder.

"Who's the drunk one now?" he hooted, poking the guard. He looked up and saw Cat. "Oh, hullo, missy. My friend here has--" he hiccuped "--imboobled . . . imbibbied . . . had too much wine." He started to laugh again, then spared her the trouble of clouting him unconscious by passing out on his own.

She robbed them quickly. The merchant's pouch was crammed with silver and gold. He had another pouch tucked inside his sleeve. It contained some small gems. She stripped off his jewelry and moved to the guard. She had just cut his purse strings, noting that the purse was much lighter, when a shadow blocked the dim light.

She looked up sharply, ready to run, the pouch in one hand and the dagger in the other. A slim figure stood over her, staring down at her in shock. From his shoulder, a small dark shape peered forward.

Here she is, Darkfire announced cheerfully.

*   *   *

"What were you thinking? What were you doing?" He walked swiftly, forcing her to hurry to keep up. "Were Selbon's treasures not enough for you?"

"Arien—"

"I could not believe my eyes! What had those men done to earn them sore heads and empty purses?"

"Arien, I'm a thief!" she said as loudly as she dared. "You knew that. I rob people in the dark. What do you think I was doing that night I saved your life? Not many honest young women go for midnight strolls on the rooftops of Thanis."

"You were hunting Rolle and his ruffians, not looking to commit robberies."

"You say that as if I'm some special member of the city guard, in the service of the Highlord with a mission to rid the streets of crime!" She laughed aloud at the absurdity of that notion. "I was doing a favor for One-Eye, out of loyalty I owed him. As a thief, as a member of his guild. And you, you yourself, only last night asked me to use my skills on your behalf!"

"For a good cause, to help rather than hurt! To undo a century-old tragedy, not . . . that!" He gestured back toward the street where the merchant and his guard remained.

"It's only a bump on the head," Cat argued. "They've money and to spare."

"So do you."

"Well . . ." she began, then shook her head. "You're right, it isn't the money. It's because I enjoy the challenge. I'm good at it, Arien."

He stopped and looked at her. She expected his eyes to be as cold as she'd ever seen them, but instead they were dark and troubled. "You don't have to be a thief anymore," he said softly.

"It's not what I do. It's what I am. It's what my father taught me to be. You could decide right now to never cast another spell in your life, but you'd still be a mage. It's your talent, it's in you, you can't change it any more than you can change the patterns of the stars. My talent is different, but it's every bit as true."

"It but saddens me, it seems so unnecessary now. That the woman I—" He broke off, his words like a splash of cold water over both of them.

Cat stared at him, but he would not meet her eyes and swiftly turned from her. He began walking again, very fast. His cloak flared behind him.

"The woman you what?" she whispered. "Oh, Arien . . ."

He was beyond earshot, or pretended to be. As he reached the corner, he looked back. She was still rooted to the spot, but forced her legs to move.

Something must have brought him into the night seeking her, and she had to know what it was.

Yet, at the same time, she knew in her heart that whatever his purpose was, it involved Alinora and his quest.

Would this puzzling knot ever be unraveled? And what would be revealed at the center of it? Happiness? Or doom?

*   *   *

There are only two great mysteries: what the past really holds, and what goes on behind a woman's eyes.

The Book of Yor.

Talus Yor listened to the entire tale, punctuating it with nods, hisses of indrawn breath, and the occasional oath.

It did not surprise Arien that the legendary mage . . . one hundred and eighty years old by all accounts . . . only appeared to be in his mid-thirties. Human mages had need of spells that elves did not, spells to retard aging. Otherwise, a human could never live long enough to fulfill a sorcerer's potential.

He was also not surprised by the mage's casual manner. Humans as a race tended to be blunt or even rude. So, while it might seem odd to some for the Archmage of all Thanis and the Northlands to tip back his chair and prop his boots on his desk, Arien practically expected it.

What did surprise him, however, was his twinge of jealousy at the appreciative way the Archmage regarded Cat. The fact that Cat was oblivious to her own charms made her that much more appealing.

The Archmage of Thanis was an attractive man, with warm hazel eyes, dark hair touched with silver at the temples, and a neat moustache. A gold dragon-shaped pendant rested on his chest and a large opal signet ring glinted on his right hand. The opal glimmered with its own faint radiance, a powerstone, and a potent one at that.

Arien had expected to wait a month, at least, but they had been invited to Yor's tower a scant three days after Darkfire's meeting with Ilgilean.

The tower was impressive, fitting as the home of the land's most powerful mage. The tower gate was guarded by twin marble golems shaped like dragons. The servants were man-shaped forms of sparkling white mist. The interior gleamed with rare woods, marble, velvet, gold. Hints of exotic spices and the vague, unplaceable scent of magic itself tinged the air.

Cat had been quiet since they arrived, stunned into silence by being invited into the one place in Thanis that every Nightsider dreamed of robbing. She gazed at everything with delighted awe. Arien could tell that she was brimming with questions, but she kept them to herself.

Darkfire and Ilgilean were cuddled up on a cushion, crooning to each other and touching noses. Yor had indulged them with a full tray of rolled meat slices and chocolate-dipped berries.

"That is quite a story," Yor said when Arien finished. "It's got all the makings of a good ballad."

"Alas, every bit of it is true. Would that it was only a tale."

"So, now you're looking for a way to break this curse." Yor looked significantly from Cat to Arien. "Before it happens again?"

Cat blushed and shook her head quickly, then bowed it and would not look at either of them. Yor raised a quizzical eyebrow at Arien.

He thinks you and Cat-- Darkfire sent.

I know. Everyone seems to think so. Even you. "Allow me to continue," he said aloud. "We have recently, in our travels, come across the means to bring Alinora back to life. I would have attempted it already, had my friend Cat not pointed out that the curse remains unbroken. We might restore her, only to have the curse tear her from me yet again."

This time, Yor's quizzical look was directed at Cat, but she appeared completely occupied with her boot laces.

"Well," Talus Yor said slowly, "I have a few ideas. The name of the city was Govannisan, correct?"

"That is where it began, or so my grandfather's sister told me."

"Then that is where we'll begin." He shot a last puzzled glance at the quiet Cat, and got up.

They followed him into a small garden nook, on a balcony high in the tower. The view of the city was stunning. In the distance, black clouds were stacked high. Bright flashes and muffled rumbles told of the approaching storm. They came each year at this time to Thanis, a series of brutal thunderstorms that lasted a few weeks and then gave way to autumn and winter.

A climbing rose had far outdone itself, covering the walls with thorns and late blooms. Petals scurried on the wind, blowing around their feet. The drakes chased them, pouncing and snapping.

In the middle of the wedge-shaped nook was a perfectly round marble basin set into the ground. Its surface was untouched by stray leaf or petal, its water seeming almost to glow.

Cat was drawn to the rail at once, entranced by the view. From here, she could see over the wall into the Highlord's Palace, another place that every Thanian thief had dreamed of breaching.

Arien went immediately to the pool. "A scrying basin?" He could not, and did not even try to, disguise the degree to which he was impressed.

"The very same." Talus Yor knelt by the side of the pool and skimmed his fingers across the still surface. Ripples circled out, each taking on a different hue as they did so, making a rainbow expanding from the center. Amber light began to shine deep within.

Arien knelt on the other side. Cat stood behind him. As the amber light in the pool darkened to rich gold, she leaned over him for a better view and rested her hands on his shoulders. The drakes perched on the pool's rim, peering into the depths and chittering excitedly to one another.

How could he have thought the pool was a shallow basin? It was as deep as the sky, bottomless. Far within, the golden light pulsed like a magical heart.

"Govannisan," Talus Yor intoned. "The elven city. Just before the death of the Tokalsian Lord, at the start of the war between House Tokalsis and House Mirida. One of Miridan blood asks to see." He glanced at Arien. "Touch the water."

"How is this possible?" he asked. "I know something of divination, and this is most unusual."

"I have a few tricks up my sleeve," Yor said, smiling. "Just touch the water."

Silver ripples spread out from his fingers. As he watched, his reflection vanished and the pool shimmered with pale radiance.

A scene formed in the water, like nothing Arien had ever seen or even dared imagine. He saw graceful spires, towers of spiraling rainbow crystal, gossamer-thin bridges. The trees that grew amid the towers were taller than any he knew. The flowers were unfamiliar but beautiful.

His heart sang with the fairness of the city. It was a glimpse of paradise, the true elven homeland. His heart also sang with grief, for it was lost to them forever. The cities of the Emerin, though considered unearthly by most who viewed them, were only a pale echo of this marvelous place.

The scene was not a frozen picture, he saw, but a window. The leafy white boughs swayed, and elves moved along the shining paths.

Arien caught his breath at the sight of them. How far his race had fallen! These elves were eerily beautiful, ethereal, taller and more graceful than any elf he knew. They wore garments seemingly woven of mist and light. Their eyes were deep and filled with peace, wisdom, an awing timelessness.

He fancied he could hear them, these fair and ancient elves. Their voices were like spring rain, like the music of the stars. Cat gasped, and he knew then that he was not imagining things. They *could* hear them. They could even smell the light perfume of the flowers and the freshness of the breeze.

The scene closed in on a tall, spiraling tower. A design, a crest, was over the arched doors. The doors grew larger and larger in the pool, until it seemed they would crash. Then the scene seemed to pass through the doors, and they were looking at a vast and airy hall. A group of elves stood in the middle of the hall.

None of them shared the look of serenity that the elves outside wore. Here, hands were set to weapons, fingers curled in gestures of attack magics.

Two men were at the center of the group. One was very tall, and though thousands of years and dozens of generations had passed, his features were a near-mirror of Arien's own. He was pale and wracked with despair, struggling for control of his emotions.

A silver circlet gleamed on his brow, in the shape of two unicorns flanking a star. It was the same symbol on the cover of Arien's diary, the design he remembered from his own father's shield. The man he now saw was his own ancestor, ages ago.

The other man was black-haired and haughty. Several other elves in the room bore a resemblance to him. The rest displayed the symbol of the House proudly on livery or shields. Arien realized that this was the point at which the war began. It was the confrontation between the Patriarch of House Mirida and the Tokalsian Lord.

"What have you done?" the Patriarch was saying. They spoke in a dialect of elven, which had changed enough in the intervening years for Arien to have a bit of difficulty following it. "This must somehow be your doing. What evil madness have you wrought upon my house?"

"Rather, ask what evil your sons wrought," the Tokalsian Lord said imperiously. "Who disrupted the casting? Who caused the deaths? Surely you knew what might happen when you sent them on that mission."

"You blame my sons? Who was casting an evil curse in the first place? Who looked in the *Book of Shadowed Paths?*"

The Lord laughed cruelly. "The curse we intended was far worse. I blame your sons for ruining that, I blame them for the deaths of my kinfolk and friends, but I must thank them as well for their ineptness. They weren't fully successful at stopping the spell. The curse was only ruined in part."

"End it," the Patriarch said. It was more a command than a plea. He appeared grim and stern, every inch a noble lord, though his eyes were haunted and bleak.

"End it? I admit that it would be a simple thing. Oh, so very simple." The Lord laughed. "Any of my bloodline could do so. Yet why should I? Why should I spare you after all you have done?"

The Patriarch's jaw tightened. It was clear that the words were painful to say. "I have but one son and one daughter left to me. Spare them this evil."

"Oh, yes," said the Lord, his voice rich with false sympathy. "Your dear Lady passed on not long ago, did she not? I am most terribly sorry. How the loss of her must gnaw at you. What a terrible emptiness there must be. How do you go on living?"

The Patriarch had been unarmed, but with a swift movement, there was a sword in his hand. It seemed to have appeared from thin air. He may have been older, and distraught, but he was quick enough to have the point beneath the Lord's chin before any of the others could react.

"End it," he said calmly.

The Lord's eyes widened in alarm, but his voice was even. "I will not," he said. "None of our bloodline ever shall. I have seen to that. You and your line are damned for all eternity. Kill me if you will. It will accomplish nothing."

"It will accomplish your death and my vengeance," the Patriarch said. "Which means more to you? Damning my House, or living?"

"You are weak, Mirida. You would not kill me in cold blood." He laughed.

The sword plunged through his throat.

The Tokalsians stood in shock, staring at their Lord. The Patriarch withdrew the blade in a clean movement. "It is done," he said softly.

The Lord took a faltering step back, touched the mortal wound, and looked at the blood on his fingers with disbelief.

"We will never end it," he gurgled, the words thick, his last upon this world. He fell.

The Patriarch turned to face the kinsmen of his fallen foe. He raised his sword. A dozen bowstrings twanged in unison. All but one arrow missed by the narrowest of margins. The last one struck the Patriarch in the chest. He winced but did not fall.

The men of House Tokalsis fell upon him.

Arien pulled his hands away, unable to see any more. The last image, that of the desperate but determined look on the face of the Patriarch as the others closed in, would remain with him for the rest of his life. As his fingertips left the water, the scene faded until they saw nothing more than their reflections.

Arien's breath was ragged in his throat. The city, the elves, had seemed so fair and wondrous. Yet they spilled blood with as much skill and joy as the lowest human mercenary. His own ancestor had murdered a man in his own home. He had struck in the name of revenge, and many lives had been lost as a result. He was shaken to find that he stemmed from such a vicious line.

As if she sensed his shock, which she probably did, Cat gently squeezed his shoulders.

"Lord Tokalsis as much as said there was a way to break it, and that it was simple. Now all we have to do is find out what it is," Talus Yor said.

"Maybe if we went back a little further, to right after the curse happened," Cat suggested. "He said he'd made sure it couldn't be broken, so he must have known how to do it."

"Excellent idea," Yor said, favoring her with a brilliant smile. He touched the water and motioned for Arien to do the same.

At first, his hands shook so violently that the water churned. He forced himself to be calm, reminded himself that it had all happened long ago. He was seeing the past, not the future, so there was nothing he could do to prevent or change it.

The pool rippled again and a new scene appeared. They saw a round room with a very high ceiling. The floor was green marble inlaid with a silver and white pentacle, but the room was littered with bodies. Some wore tattered grey robes, others were in armor and the blue and silver of House Mirida. All were dead, savaged. A thick white candle sputtered and went out in a puddle of blood.

Two men stood in the doorway, staring in horror at the carnage. One of them was the Tokalsian Lord, his face tight with anger. The man with him was short and rather stocky for an elf, his dark hair turning grey. He wore white robes trimmed with green, though the hem was spotted with blood from dragging on the floor.

"What could have done this?" the Lord asked, eyes riveted on a young blond elf whose torso was ripped wide open. His armor had protected him no more than a corselet of parchment would have done.

"The spell failed," the other elf said. "It must have. That is the only thing that could account for this. The shadow beasts, the spectral assassins they meant to summon, only they could have done this. I sense them, I smell them."

"These are Miridans!" The Lord kicked the blond elf. "They attacked the mages! This is their doing!"

"I fear it is so," the stocky man said.

He crossed to the center of the room, stepping over and around the bodies. The raw, hideous sights did not seem to overly affect him, though he made an effort to keep his robes free of the floor.

A twisted bag of meat in soaked robes stared up at him with one sightless eye. Gingerly, with the toe of his shoe, he flipped part of the torn cloth over what was left of the face.

"What are you doing?" the Lord demanded. He knelt, heedless of the blood that instantly soaked through his clothes, and tenderly touched the body of a young woman. A sister, perhaps, or a daughter. Her eyes were closed, and she could have been sleeping if not for the unnatural position of her neck and arms.

"I am trying to find out exactly what effect the spell had. It was far enough along to summon the assassins--"

"Assassins!" cried the Lord. "Butchers!"

"I must know if they are still free of the spirit world, and if so, who they hunt."

The Lord fell silent, gazing around the room with renewed horror. "Still free? The shadow beasts might yet walk among us? My house . . . my children!"

The stocky elf closed his eyes and chanted softly. His hands moved in a dance of magic. A look of surprise crossed his face. "Yes, free. They hunt, in their hunger. They hunt those beloved of the Miridans."

"What do you mean?"

"Not those of the Miridan bloodline. Instead of seeking out and destroying the members of the family, they will hunt their dear ones in nightmares and kill them."

"They'll be ruined," the Lord said, an unpleasant gleam growing in his ice-blue eyes. "At best, they will destroy themselves in grief. They will be unable to present a threat to us. The entire house will fade and diminish, and vanish!" He clapped the other elf on the arm. "Brilliant! Far better than killing them outright. Let them suffer!"

The stocky elf looked doubtful. "I do not know, Galevan. It punishes the innocent as well as our enemies. What if one who is undeserving falls victim to this? What if your darling Marella fell in love with a Miridan?"

The Lord was outraged. "She would do no such thing! My daughter knows her place! I would not permit it!"

The elf shook his head. "I think we should break it. Despite your assurances, it could come to affect our own. Do you not remember Aunt Roella and Lasadur Mirida?"

"We have no Aunt Roella," he said coldly. "She betrayed the family."

"It could happen again. There are tales of it. Children of rival Houses falling in love. It is a popular romantic theme. Have you not read the ballads?"

"We will not break it! The Miridans deserve every anguished moment." He glared at the fallen bodies. "Besides, do you even know how to end it?"

He nodded. "Any of us could break it with the words of power and undoing."

The Lord studied him grimly. "Who knows these words?"

He looked sadly around the room, seeming to actually see it for the first time. "Now, no one but I. They are written in Lorevan's grimoire, but Lorevan will never have need of it again." He sighed, an expression of loss and hopelessness crossing his rounded face.

"Why in the name of all the gods did you even bother to write it down?" snapped the Lord.

"Some day, our Houses might resolve their differences. If, by some strange means, we become allies, our descendants may prove better men than we," he explained.

"You are a visionary fool," the Lord said. He crossed behind the stocky elf. "This was meant to be a weapon, an utter destruction of their line. We did not attempt this on a whim, or as a warning. It is absolutely inconceivable that our kinfolk would ever ally with the Miridans. Not now, not in a thousand years, not at the end of time!"

The stocky elf shook his head and gestured to the strewn bodies. "Perhaps we should reconsider, Galevan. This blood feud is a useless waste of lives. Look at this!"

"You are too soft, cousin." With that, the Tokalsian Lord drew a knife and drove it hilt-deep into the stocky elf's back. "I am sorry," he said as the other man fell.

The scene vanished as once again Arien tore his fingers from the water. "I never would have believed the Elder Elves could be so harsh," he said shakily.

"At least we know there is a way to break it," Talus Yor said. "The only problem is, we don't know exactly what."

"Continue the scene if you can," Arien said, regaining control. "The Lord would assuredly look for this grimoire. Mayhap we can at least have a glimpse!"

"Yes!" Cat said excitedly. "He wouldn't want to leave it lying around for someone to discover later. He'd hide it, or—"

"Or destroy it," Arien said grimly. "Either way, we must know."

Talus Yor bent back over the pool. "Continue," he said.

The Tokalsian Lord strode purposefully out of the room. "Soon someone will look in," he muttered to himself. "They will think the Miridans killed him as well. Now, for Lorevan's book."

The beautifully furnished halls and rooms he passed through no longer seemed so fair, tainted by blood and betrayal. The Lord quickly made his way to a small set of rooms that obviously belonged to a wizard. On the ornate desk was a book, next to a stoppered pot of ink and a quill. Arcane symbols were inlaid in gold on the cover.

He opened the book, flipping past pages of spells. Finally he found what he sought.

"There," said Talus Yor. "Stop."

"Livana," Arien whispered. "Can this really be it?"

If ever we or our kin should earnestly wish to undo this thing:
Lhasorra, dahn fellina bur radan
(Assassins, come and hear me)
The assassins will come. Freely summoned they must be, for if they sense unwillingness, they will destroy the caster and all nearby. Hence, we cannot be forced to undo this thing, or charmed by means of spell. It must be by free will.
Rhuna elsannita fanneros mak enita
(By blood I call and command your power)
The assassins will resist. They are a foul sort.
All that they can, they will do to frighten the caster or weaken resolve. If the caster falters, they will attack.
Annifea alestor, rhuna verenis
(I release your bonding, by blood I banish)
Here the caster must allow the assassins to taste of his blood, for in the blood is the power. In the way that spells are, it shall also be draining of the energies. There can be no use of other power, from a stone or a circle, unless it is a circle of our own blood kin.
Sornanis rhuna, rhuna fanneros
(Mine is the blood, by blood I command)
Rassitis droala rhuna elor shahlarri
(Those once my foes by blood I forgive)
Dharsis elen bur tolnias esseton
(You must hear, you must obey)
Verenisa, annifea
(I release you, I banish you)

"That is all?" Arien whispered. "They were right. It is so simple a spell!"

Talus Yor gestured, and a sparkling white form appeared. "Fetch me a sheet of parchment and the eagle quill," he said. The form seemed to bow and hurried off. "Don't consider it done yet," he cautioned Arien.

"Why not? Here, at last, is the formula to end the curse." He heard the excitement in his voice, realized he was nearly weeping in his joy. After so many years, the end was in sight! The curse would be done! Once the spell was—

"Who's going to cast it?" Yor asked.

Arien dropped his head into his hands, his joy snuffed like a candle flame.

What's wrong? Darkfire sent, at the same moment as Cat asked, "What's wrong?"

"The quest is far from over," Talus Yor answered when Arien could not speak.

"Why?" Cat persisted. "Here's the answer, right here. All Arien has to do is cast the spell."

"No." Arien raised his head and looked at her, inwardly cursing himself for being such a fool. "I cannot cast this spell. Only one of that House can, and they were destroyed in Govannisan thousands of years ago."

*   *   *

The tower shook with the force of a thunderclap. Cat went to the rail and leaned out, the wind whipping her hair. She craned her neck and peered at the spire rising from the top of the Tower. A bolt of lightning speared down, striking the spire and erupting in a shower of sparks. Brilliant lights danced around the Tower.

"How does it do that?" she cried, unafraid.

Can we go inside? Darkfire sent. Arien felt his surge of terror. The two drakes were huddled together like children, cringing whenever the thunder crashed.

"Perhaps we should retire indoors," he said, while Talus Yor said, "Let's go in."

The enchanted quill was nearly finished copying the words reflected in the surface of the pool. It scratched the last line and Yor picked it up.

"Magic, obviously," he explained to Cat with a grin. "Since this is the highest point in the city, it attracts the lightning. I had to do something to prevent my home from being damaged."

Cat leaned out even farther, laughing delightedly as the show of lights burst around her again. Thunder crashed, shaking the stones beneath their feet.

Arien and Talus Yor gathered the terror-stricken drakes and carried them inside. Cat paused, the wind ruffling her hair, wild and brave in the face of the storm's raw power.

Her beauty again caught Arien by surprise, riveting him as surely as a bolt of lightning would have done. She waited until the last possible moment, watching the blue-white splinters arc across the dark sky, then leapt indoors just as the rain began pelting down. A few stray raindrops glinted like diamonds in her hair.

"How I delight in the fall storms!" she said merrily.

"They are impressive, but they make a mess of the city." Talus Yor stroked the shivering Ilgilean, comforting her.

Darkfire crawled to Arien's shoulder and burrowed his head under the mage's long hair. *It's not the storm that bothers me,* he explained. *It's the noise.*

Talus Yor suggested that they stay a while, until the leading edge of the storm passed. He insisted that they were not interrupting any important research, and offered to serve dinner. That, of course, got both drakes chirping eagerly, so they could not refuse. Arien was aware of the great honor.

It turned out to be a surprisingly relaxed meal. He found that Yor shared many of his ideas and opinions. They fell naturally into a discussion of magic, while the drakes curled together in a makeshift nest under the table and gave frightened cries when thunder broke overhead.

Cat listened with more interest than Arien would have expected, and he wondered if it had something to do with the flattering attention that Yor paid her. Or, he began to wonder, did she have some talent for sorcery? Some humans could learn magic. Why not her? Surely her elven blood would give her some grasp of it. But no, if it were so, then why would elfkin infants be put to death for their lack of talent?

The talk eventually turned to the scenes they had viewed in the scrying pool.

Arien had already memorized the words to break the curse, for all the good it did. It seemed that every time he got close to his goal, some impossibility popped up and cast his hopes into ruin. He held in his very hands the means to undo the curse, he had a way to re-store Alinora, and yet he was still helpless. He would not let himself bring her back just to lose her again.

His thoughts turned like a jewel in his mind, and came upon an unexpected facet. If it took one of House Tokalsis to break the curse, he could conceivably use the scroll to go back and find a member of that bloodline. Perhaps bring him forward, show him what the future held. There was no need for the curse in this time. Both Houses had fallen, the city no long-er existed. The rivalry had perished long ago.

But if he used the scroll to find a Tokalsian, he could not go back and recover Alinora. How could he live with himself, knowing he had the chance to bring her back and gave it up? How could he bring her back to have the beasts come for her again? It was a dilemma, the worst he had ever faced. He could end the curse, but give up all hope of being reunited with Alinora. Or he could bring her back and still be tormented by the curse.

"How do we know they all died?" Cat asked. He looked up.

She was sitting on a large cushion, her legs folded in a curious but evidently comfortable position. She danced a coin along the backs of her hands as she spoke, glancing from Yor to Arien.

"I beg your pardon?" Arien had lost track of the conversation.

"She has a point," Yor said, smiling at Cat again, his gaze lingering.

Apparently unaware of Yor's interest, Cat looked seriously at Arien. The coin, bright gold, flickered between her fingers. She used each hand with equal ease. Her dexterity would give her a great advantage in spellcasting, he thought, if she ever chose to give up her criminal ways, if she did have the talent of a mage.

"At least one of your family survived," she said. "How do we know that none of them did? Mayhap there are Tokalsians alive even now—" she waved at the window "—with no idea that it ever happened. You knew nothing of it. Maybe they wouldn't either."

"Once the curse was cast, the cursing family would not need to pass on that knowledge," Yor said.

"They would not even want to," Arien picked up the chain of thought. "It was a shame-ful and horrible deed, dishonorable, malicious. All they would tell their children was that the Miridans were enemies. The tales and legends might mention a curse, but there would be no proof. Any records would have been lost with the city."

"So, all we have to do is find out what happened to the Tokalsians," Cat said brightly.

"How? As Arien said, all the records would have been lost." Yor shook his head. "It's hopeless."

"Wait," Arien said, an idea beginning to grow in his mind. He found a piece of parch-ment and made a quick list and a sketch. "We do have something to start with, and the per-fect place to begin."

"What do you mean?" Cat asked, springing up and coming over to him.

"The Great Library of Thanis, of course. And this." He showed her the paper, where he had listed each name the Tokalsian Lord had mentioned, and drawn the crest that had ap-peared on their doors and livery. The crest was an upthrust sword entwined with a flowered garland, between two black stars on a field of squares, which Arien remembered were green and white.

"In elven families," he said, "it is common to name children for ancestors. As for the crest, symbols remain when names are forgotten."

"My clever mage!" Cat said, tracing it with her fingertip and smiling brilliantly. "We'll find them, I know it. If they live, we shall find them!"

*   *   *

The cell was five paces to a side. He had measured it countless times in the past twenty years.

Twenty-one years, three months, and nine days, to be precise. He'd counted them.

The thick door was made up of six boards held together by three iron bands and twelve rust-clotted bolts. There were four bars in the square window in the middle of the door, which no amount of pulling and cursing could loosen.

He had tried everything he could think of to escape, and all had proved fruitless. The door was too heavy to budge, though he had battered himself senseless repeatedly. The iron bands would not pry loose, and the bolts would not turn, though he had bloodied his fingers trying to grip them and even lost two teeth when, in desperation, he had tried to turn the bolts that way.

Digging a tunnel was pointless. The floor was solid stone under the layers of straw and filth. The lock resisted him even after twenty years of practice.

What could he expect, trying to open it with no better tools than twisted straw and chicken bones, and the handle of a spoon he had hidden and carefully filed down by scraping it against the floor. That misbegotten sneak-thief Sabledrake could have opened it with a wink.

If only his magic worked here! That would be a different story!

If his magic worked, the escape possibilities would prove nearly endless. The floor or walls could ripple and open beneath the force of his earth magics, or the door could burn, or the lock could shatter. His talent and skill had at one time been worthy of consideration for the rank of Archmage, needing only a bit more lore, a touch more practice, before he took the Challenge.

But, no. He was stuck in this dank, stinking cell without sufficient magic to light a candle.

He could feel it, the lack of *aether*. The absence of power from which to draw the energies. It was not unlike being atop a high mountain, where the air was thin and the blood seemed loud in his ears.

He yearned for the mountains. The snow-capped peaks of Northern Lenais, where the redwoods combed the sky and the faerie lights lit the sky at twilight.

It had been a mistake to leave, to seek his fortune among the humans. Their world, and especially their filthy dungeons, were no place for an elf of House Antokal.

Not that his kinsfolk would recognize him. Not now, with his hair grown long and matted, his teeth broken or rotting away, his hand a shriveled lump.

He wondered, not for the first time, what had become of his fine clothes, although after all this time he had come to tolerate the coarse feel of the shabby orc-wove cloth against his skin.

He had gotten used to the heavy brown bread and the vegetables with white fur growing on them. He no longer minded the watery stew with meat that might be goat but he suspected was rat.

And the very idea that he, Donnell Antokal, who had once lived on rich wine and the finest cuts of meat, silk and velvet, music, dances, finery, luxury . . . that he had grown accustomed to this horrid fare, these ghastly conditions, was the worst outrage of all!

The food was delivered twice a day, or at least he assumed they were days. He used to make a scratch on the wall once a day, but it had grown too depressing. If he was to be here for the rest of his long elven life, he would run out of wall space.

His meals were not even delivered by guards, which might allow him a chance of escape. Instead, there was a slot in the wall through which his meals were shoved by someone or something unseen, never speaking a word. There was a narrow chute in the corner, for his waste. Water constantly dripped from the ceiling above it, so if he wanted a drink, he had to stand near the chute and catch the water in his cup.

His cup. Oh, yes. That was good. That was clever. His very own cup. Look upon these vast riches! He had a baggy tunic, a spoon with a sharp end, a chipped wooden cup, a matching bowl, and all the straw he wanted. A veritable wealth of treasure!

The first time he had awoken and found a bale of straw in the corner, he had been confused. Now, he understood. They drugged his food when the cell got too rank, and threw in a new bale. It was his task to dump the old stuff down the chute, or else live like a complete pig. His unseen captors did not seem to care. He had never been able to catch them. They always came when he was asleep. Although they drugged the food, he dared not stop eating. He had to keep up what strength he could.

He kept telling himself that if it became too much to bear, he would drive the sharp end of the spoon through his neck, though he shivered at the knowledge that his corpse would become one of Selbon's legion of undead. But one thing and one thing only kept him alive, gave him the will to endure. That he might someday be free, free to find Tahm Sabledrake and make him suffer.

It should have been Tahm locked in the dungeons. It should have been Tahm eating rotten turnips and growing old in this stinking pit.

Never mind that Tahm could probably escape. Never mind that if Tahm had been with them, they might have gotten out of the castle alive.

It was a vast, grotesque piece of injustice that Tahm should be safe and happy, while he, Donnell, was a crippled wreck of a prisoner. He vowed again, as he had vowed every day for more than twenty years, to get even with Tahm Sabledrake.

Worst of all, even his nightly dreams were of the smug bastard. Tahm, who had dared to seek wife of an elfmaid. He sometimes dreamt of the maid herself, who was fair enough to be a noble's daughter, yet common enough to respond to the overtures of a lowly thief.

How could she? When an elflord sat at the very same table? Spurn him, handsome Donnell, who could have had his pick of the ladies of Lenais? And to spurn him in favor of a scruffy human a full head shorter than she was! Had the woman been mad?

He told himself that she was beneath his interest, but the words were thin bandages to his wounded pride. He had wanted her, wanted her strongly, and she had not even considered him.

He crouched in the cleanest corner of the cell, chin resting on the ruin of his right hand. His arms and legs were covered with sores old and new, and bites from the vermin that infested his prison. His eyes, still large and slanted, still a deep elven green, were full of a bright, fevered madness.

Something strange began to happen outside his cell. A funny orange smear touched the curved stones across the hall, touched and began to grow. Donnell blinked. Light? Firelight? A torch, a candle, a lantern. His elven eyesight, always keen, had become even sharper in the dark. But just that faint smear of light made his eyes water and sting. He cupped his left hand over his face, but could not look away.

Could it be, that for the first time in twenty years, he was to be visited? Was it Selbon himself, whose secrets Donnell had sought as the final tribute to his magery, shambling down the corridors with a candle gripped in one withered hand?

He scrabbled backwards, bracing himself in the corner, and realized that the keening whimper he heard issued from his own lips.

Something was moving in the hall. He had heard the occasional rat go by, and for the first few years there had been distant screams and cries of other prisoners. Donnell had never screamed. He was not weak. He had never called for his mother, or the gods. He was strong.

The sound approaching was much bigger than a rat, and since when did rats carry fire? A sun suddenly blazed in the window, the sun crashing to earth, brighter than any fire since the dawn of time. The door staggered open on squealing hinges and the sun poured in.

Donnell finally screamed. He fell to the side, blinded, pawing at his eyes to block out that horrible, burning light. His eyes were boiling in his head. The light speared through his fingers, right to his brain. He howled.

At once the light dimmed. Donnell sprawled on the floor, straw poking his face. He groveled. The door was open, but escape was the furthest thing from his mind. Something came towards him. Something large. He moaned.

He heard a deep rumble. Far down in the murk of his memory, he recognized it as language. The words gradually shaped themselves out of the rumble. Words of the human language, which had spread to become the main tongue of the Northlands and neighboring kingdoms. The humans had no patience for the flowing complexity to the true speech of the elvenfolk.

Human though they were, they were words, and they eventually made sense to him.

"How long have you been here, you miserable excuse for an elf?"

He did not know how long it had been since he'd spoken. At first, he had yelled and cursed. After a while, he had even pleaded. Even that had ended long ago.

How long had it been? He could not remember. His cracked lips tried to form an answer. All that emerged from his throat was a strangled moan.

"There must be a reason why you would be held in this dungeon, devoid of magic. Are you a wizard?" The voice was cold, demanding, not the least bit sympathetic.

"Donnell," he said, alarmed at how weak his voice was. "That is my name."

"I did not ask your name," the other person said sharply. He nudged Donnell with a hooflike foot.

It was a monster, Donnell realized with alarm and sorrow. A fanged, hoofed, whip-tailed monster had come to rend his body and consume his famined flesh. What else could it be?

"I am mageborn," he gasped. "My skill . . . superior. My talent . . . the strongest. I would have become Archmage."

The hoof nudged him harder. It was almost a kick. "Do not flatter yourself, wretch. If you wish to leave this foul place, you will do exactly as I say. Is that clear?"

Donnell writhed on the floor, trying to escape the merciless prodding. "Yes! Yes! I understand!"

Large, rough hands seized him and flopped him over. A bottle was held to his lips. "Drink this," commanded the monstrous voice.

He could smell it. Sharp, yet smooth. Brandy? After so long, a drink of brandy.

He gulped it eagerly, not caring if it was poisoned. Perhaps it would be better for him if it was. It roared through his veins. He imagined himself glowing as the brandy restored life to him. He shuddered. The wonderful warmth passed over him. Suddenly, uncontrollably, he vomited all over his visitor.

"Great Haarkon! I should leave you here to rot!"

Donnell whimpered. He did not want to be left here in the dark. He tried to beg, but all he could do was weep helplessly.

"Still, I may have a use for you. If there is a mind left between those ridiculous pointed ears, that is." The monster picked him up easily, as if he weighed no more than a bundle of sticks.

He lay in the arms of this mysterious stranger, unable to resist even if he had wanted to. He was rocked and swayed, his protesting stomach rolling in protest.

He felt himself carried into the hall, and then a wonderful thing occurred.

Like water returning to the desert, the magic flowed into his parched body.

He gasped. They took it for granted, mages. They did not truly appreciate the cool, soothing wash of magic. He had learned his lesson. Oh, had he ever. He reveled in the magic. It was like breathing the rainbow. His spells, all his arcane knowledge, pushed to the front of his mind.

"*Salahin Roas*," he whispered.

For the first time in far too long, he felt the comfortable draining that came of a spell well-cast, and he healed himself. His limbs tingled as the old bites and scrapes cleared of infection. His burning eyes soothed and ceased pouring tears down his face.

It was too late to help his wasted hand, but the rest of him felt whole and well. He laughed and sobbed and sobbed and laughed, patting himself with his good hand to remind himself that he was alive.

He was carried up some stairs, down some halls, into a place that smelled comfortably of smoke. He kept his eyes closed as light tried to seep in. They did not hurt nearly so bad, but were still sensitive. He was set down on a wonderfully soft chair. Gingerly, he opened his eyes.

He was in a sitting room, with a wide stone fireplace and bearskin rug. The chair he was sitting in was real velvet, a little faded on the armrests and a little musty-smelling, but as soft as a cloud. The flowers on the mantle and the table beside him were long dead, but their sweet fragrance still echoed in the room.

A shadow blocked the firelight as the figure stood in front of him. It was a big shadow, because it was a big figure. Tall, broad, and muscular. The head was strange, wider than normal, with long horns.

His fears resurfaced briefly, but then subsided as he realized he was looking at a minotaur. A minotaur in long maroon robes. He wondered if he was really still in his cell, raving to the walls.

"Let us have one thing straight right from the beginning," the minotaur said. His haughty, educated tone contrasted greatly with Donnell's image of minotaurs as barbarians. "You may be a wizard, and you might be skilled. But I am by far your superior. I am Solarrin, Archmage of the Universe." The name was not so much said as announced, making Donnell feel as if he should recognize it. He squirmed guiltily.

The minotaur mage rolled his large brown eyes. "Why must I be plagued with a world of idiots?" he asked the room. He looked sternly at the elf. "Well, then, just remember that I am Solarrin. Selbon beat you. He did not fare so well with me!"

Donnell grinned obligingly. He nodded like a fool. Whatever the nice minotaur said. As long as he didn't have to go back to the dungeons. Thoughts of escape dwindled to the back of his mind. He did not seem to be in any danger and would not have been able to do anything about it if he was, so he grinned and nodded obligingly and foolishly

"I have a proposition for you, elf," Solarrin said. "And you had best be prepared to accept it. You have nothing in the world save your pitiful life and your magic. Work for me, and keep them both, plus substantial rewards. Or return to your cozy cell, where your magic is nothing, and what life you have left is worthless."

"What do you want me to do first?" Donnell stammered, leaning forward eagerly.

Solarrin chuckled. "Good. Very good. I think we are going to get along admirably."

*   *   *

A long journey begins with a goodbye.

The Book of Yor.

The reaction of the elf at the doors took them both completely by surprise.

Arien was like a man possessed as he hurried through the rain-drenched streets toward the Great Library. The sun had set, but the lamplighters had not yet made their rounds, so the only light was the blinding but swift stuff that accompanied the ferocious thunder.

Arien nodded to the doorman as he entered the lobby. He headed for the stairs, toward the third-floor section on elven history.

Cat followed, shaking her rain-damp curls. While she was thus engaged, the elven doorman stepped forward and cuffed her smartly across the face.

The slap was loud in the quiet lobby, falling neatly between roars of thunder.

Cat's head snapped back, but she wasted no time. She spun and dropped into a fighting crouch, realized she wasn't wearing her sword even as she reached for it, and drew a knife.

The doorman moved toward her, fist raised. She backed up. Arien turned, and the look on his face was so comic she could have laughed if she hadn't been so angry.

"Go on, away with you," the doorman said, lip curled in disgust. "Back into the gutters where you belong, wretched vermin."

"What?" Arien said, shocked.

"Not you, Librarian," he said, never taking his eyes off Cat. "This creature followed you. I'll take care of it."

"I demand an explanation of this." Arien turned his cold, cold eyes on the doorman, who quailed under that icy gaze.

"Sir, no animals are allowed in the Library," he said defensively. "This one must have come in to get out of the rain."

"Animal!" Cat said. A few late visitors and other Librarians glanced toward the disturbance. "Do animals use knives? I'm very good with this one. Shall I show you?"

"If animals are not allowed, why did you permit my drake to enter?" Arien asked. His anger was like steel beneath his velvet voice. Darkfire peeked out from Arien's hair and chirped accusingly.

The doorman's brow wrinkled in confusion and distaste. "Familiars are one thing. This . . ." he pointed at Cat. "This is an affront to all that this Library represents!"

"And what is that? Ignorance?" Cat snapped.

"Culture and civilization!" the doorman shot back triumphantly.

"Culture and civilization both human and elven," Arien said smoothly. "Not to mention a dozen or more other races."

"That is not a member of any race. It is a foul, unnatural mixture!"

"Shannia teaches us mercy and forgiveness," Arien pointed out. "Valannin teaches us to learn from our own experience. It is a pity you are so ignorant, my friend."

The red-faced elf darkened toward purple, his throat bulging as he struggled to find the right words to express his outrage. Two other Librarians, both human, hurried up to him.

"Junior Librarian Mirida, what is going on here?" one of them demanded.

"He . . . he brought that . . . *thing* in here!" the doorman jabbed an accusing finger toward Cat, who bared her teeth like the feral beast he thought her to be.

The human looked at her curiously. "Yes, so? Is it against the rules?"

"Even if it were, which it is not," Arien said, "Rules made in ignorance and blindness have no place in this house of learning. I shall speak to the Lord High Librarian about it if you'd like."

He took Cat's arm and led her up the stairs. Behind them, he could hear the furious voice of the doorman shouting that he would lose his position for this insult. He went quickly down the hall to his tiny office and closed the door behind them.

"Burn and blast them all!" Cat slammed her knife back in the sheath. "Stupid, arrogant elves!" She kicked a chair and hurt her foot.

"Oh, Cat, this world has been cruel to you," he said softly. "Alas that I cannot take it away. Indeed, I fear I add to it."

"Arien, they're going to turn you out!" she said, distraught. "It's all my fault!".

"Lord High Librarian Haleric is a man of wisdom and learning. Halvoriel is known to be temperamental. I am certain I can salvage my position here, if I choose. Do not blame yourself, my dear. Perhaps it is time for me to consider leaving the Library. After, of course, it has served its purpose. Wait here, and I will send for those books."

He opened the door again and called for Apprentice Pellander.

*   *   *

"I'm starting to get dizzy," Cat said as she scanned another page of elven crests.

"Do not rush so," Arien suggested. "I have waited a hundred years. Better to wait a bit longer for success than to miss the clue and fail."

She sighed and rubbed her eyes. Page after page of carefully-drawn and inked coats-of-arms had left her dazed and dizzy.

"Here it is," Arien said calmly.

"What?" She nearly jumped out of her chair. "Which one?"

He tapped a design. Green and white squares, black stars, sword wrapped with vines and flowers. She leaned over his shoulder to read the small writing beneath it.

House Antokal, Northern Lenais.

"The name . . ." she said.

"Antokal . . . Tokalsis. It is close, and it makes sense. This must be the family we seek" He copied the inscription onto the paper with the sketch.

"Lenais . . . I remember seeing it on the map in the Selbon's library. It lies to the west, past Hachland."

Arien sighed. "Then it seems I must go to Hachland and beyond."

"Not alone," she said.

Not alone, echoed Darkfire.

"It is a long and doubtless perilous road--" he began.

"I have to go, Arien," Cat said, quite serious. "One way or another, this affects both of us."

He looked at her for a long time. She wasn't sure of what she saw in his eyes.

*   *   *

Cat always hated visiting Sybil at the temple.

It was a beautiful set of buildings with lots of arched and white marble columns, surrounded by lush gardens. There was nothing outwardly frightening or threatening about the place. The priests and other staff of the temple were all young, attractive, and friendly.

Too friendly for Cat's comfort, and therein was the problem.

She hurried through the halls, past the elaborate tapestries and graphic statues depicting

Talopea in a variety of acts which seemed not only uncomfortable but downright impossible.

Cat kept her eyes on the floor and wished for wax to stop her ears as she passed the spacious chambers where the faithful loudly celebrated the glory of their goddess.

Sybil's rooms overlooked the central courtyard. The rooms all lacked doors, hung instead with elaborate beaded curtains. Cat rapped softly on the wall and peeked through the curtain, ready to retreat at the first sight of anything shocking.

Sybil appeared, clad in a surprisingly modest yellow frock, and of all things, an apron. "Cat! What a surprise!"

"Hello, Sybil. Am I interrupting anything?"

"No, just Mischa's lunch. Come in, come in."

"Who's Mischa?" Cat asked, wondering if Sybil had decided to keep a pet.

Sybil's face lit up in a radiant smile. "That's right, you two have never met! Well, I'll just have to introduce you. Mischa, sweetheart! Mischa, say hello to your Auntie Cat."

A chubby, dark-haired little boy looked up from the table. Jam and honey were smeared across his pink cheeks and rounded little chin. A bit of bread was pasted to his forehead.

Cat dropped onto on a bench, gaping at the child. He goggled comically back at her and laughed, showing tiny teeth. His eyes were the same cheerful hazel as Sybil's.

"You've got a baby," Cat said when her mouth would work again.

"And isn't he Momma's little darling?" Sybil crooned, wiping his face. He pursed his lips and twisted away.

"Nu, nu," he said. "Nu wass. Mama, nu wass!"

"He doesn't like to have his face washed," Sybil translated, chuckling indulgently.

"Where did you get a baby?" Cat could not believe her eyes. She never would have suspected . . . Sybil of all people . . . !

Sybil tossed her head and laughed. Mischa broke off his complaints and mimicked her.

"Dear Cat, I know you're not *that* innocent. Auntie Cat is being silly," she said to the baby in a confiding tone.

"No, I . . ." Cat tried, flustered, "I never knew you had a baby. When?"

"You were off in Arrowood with Jessa when he was born. I thought I told you . . ."

"You've never mentioned it," Cat said firmly. "I would remember. How come I haven't seen him before?"

"Most of the time, he stays in the temple nursery with the other children. Today, I was feeling particularly motherly, so I brought him down to my rooms for a while."

"But Sybil, you're not even married!"

"What does that have to do with it?" She picked up the child and planted a loud, wet kiss on his sticky face. "Isn't he handsome? The women will adore you when you've grown, won't they, Mischa? Do you want to hold him?"

"No." Cat hastily stood and backed away. "I don't know how."

"Oh, Cat. He's just a baby, not an egg. He won't break."

Mischa stretched out his chubby pink arms. "Go Mama," he announced.

"There, see, he wants you to hold him," Sybil said.

"No he doesn't. He said Mama."

"Oh," she waved dismissingly, "he calls all women that."

"But you're his mother."

"The children belong to the whole temple," she shrugged. "They're the price we pay for Talopea's gifts. We all share the pleasure, so we all share the responsibility."

Unable to argue with Sybil's logic, Cat reluctantly reached for Mischa. He was a sturdy little boy, warm and wiggly. She rarely felt clumsy, but holding the small, fragile child, she felt incredibly awkward, all thumbs and left feet.

"Perfect," Sybil said. "You hold Mischa while I clean up, then we can talk. Why don't you take him into the other room? Some of his toys are there."

Cat set him down near the sofa and watched him as he tried to stack a cloth ball on top of a wooden block. He looked nothing at all like Sybil, except for the merry hazel eyes.

"Sybil?" she called, not wanting to ask but compelled. "Who's his father?"

"I don't know," Sybil replied casually. "Does it matter?"

Cat choked, thinking of her own father. "It might matter to Mischa someday."

"I doubt it. My parents have brought me nothing but grief." Sybil untied her apron, tossed it over a chair, and sat. "What brings you to visit? I thought you were afraid of the temple."

"I've come to say goodbye. I have to go away for a time."

"Away? When? Where? Why? Cat, this is terribly sudden." Her eyes narrowed suspiciously. "You're not running off with Arien to get married, are you?"

"No!" Cat cried, then got control of herself. "It's a quest, something he needs to do, and needs my help."

Sybil frowned. "Do you think that's wise? I've been worried about him ever since we had dinner at the Lord's Retreat. He acted so very peculiar!"

"I . . ." she started to deny it, but halted. The burden was too great. She needed to tell someone. None of the Nightsiders would understand, and she certainly couldn't go to Alphonse with a problem like this.

Slowly, haltingly, carefully, she told Sybil about the ancient elves, their feud, and their curse. She did not mention Arien's plan to save Alinora, knowing that Sybil would think her a fool for helping him in such an endeavor.

She could not meet Sybil's eyes while she spoke, so she watched little Mischa instead. He was sitting in the middle of the room, his eyes drooping closed for longer and longer blinks. He yawned hugely and slowly tipped over, fast asleep.

"Oh, Cat," Sybil said when she was finished. "You always wanted a life of adventure, but this is unthinkable! Couldn't you find another man? Why, there are several in this very building—"

"I don't want them," she said, startling herself with her outspokenness.

"Why is it that out of all of the men in the city, the one you want is cursed? You couldn't find someone safe. No, not Cat Sabledrake. You've got to risk your life." Sybil patted her arm. "Oh, how could you resist those silver eyes? He doubtless kisses well, too, I'll wager. The thoughtful, scholarly ones often do, once you break through their reserve."

She blushed. Sybil pounced immediately.

"Ah-ha! So he's kissed you, has he?"

"Once. Only once," she admitted.

"And did you like it, Cat?" she persisted.

"It was just one kiss, Sybil. It doesn't mean anything."

"Oh yes it does. To a girl like you, your first kiss means everything. Did it make you tingle all over and ache for more?"

"Sybil!" she protested, but her protest was a confession.

"What did I tell you, Cat? See what Talopea can do? Just have a little faith. You'll find a way to beat this curse. I know it."

*   *   *

The rain fell upon the just and unjust.

It fell high in the Bannerian Mountains and flowed down as streams, gathering and gaining strength, roaring down gullies dry since the previous autumn. Unwary animals were caught by the floods and swept away, coming to rest against the stone doors of the dwarven tunnels. The rain fell in the lowlands of the river valley, swelling the already full river to new heights. Some boats broke their moorings and were lost.

It soaked the holiest temples and the lowliest hovels. It pounded the roofs and turned the cobblestones into tiny islands. It fell upon the Highlord's Palace, where the Highlord's arrogant son ordered a servant beaten for breaking his favorite mirror. It leaked through Doc's backward roof and caused a batch of simmering elixirs to change in some small and subtle way.

Alphonse, Greyquin, and Cat heard the rain as they sat around a small table, and all three of them found it dismal. The rest of the patrons of the Golden Lion seemed to share their opinion. The inn was quiet. Conversations were muted. The only performer present was a mournful harpist singing of unrequited love.

"What a gloomy night." Alphonse fingered the sword-shaped pendant resting on his chest. It was a new ornament for him, the sacred symbol of the warrior-god. He was now officially an Initiate to the Brotherhood of Steel, having finally found the acceptance he'd been searching for since leaving his father's clan so long ago.

"I can't believe you're leaving," Greyquin repeated. "This is no kind of weather to send a dog out in." As if to prove his point, Bear barked softly from under the table.

"I think we should go along," Alphonse said to the gnome. "Two riding alone. Dangerous."

"Besides, we can't let them win all the glory and wealth," Greyquin replied.

"This is not a quest for glory and wealth," Cat explained. "This is Arien's quest, remember?"

"He wants more books? Hasn't he got enough?" Alphonse waved his mug. "Ale!"

"We'll be back before you know it," she said.

"What of Lord Marl? You told us he was going take over the city." Greyquin poked his spoon at Alphonse in imitation of a spear. "Run him through, that'll end his plotting."

Alphonse took the spoon and slapped the gnome's knuckles with it. "Don't point a weapon unless you know how to use it."

"Somebody should do something," mused Greyquin, nursing his sore knuckles. "Why not us? We could save the city."

"When Thanis has to rely on misfits like us, it's a dark day for the Northlands," said Alphonse. "They've Duncan Farleigh, and Talus Yor. What could the likes of us do that the likes of them couldn't, faster and better?"

"No sense of humor, orcs have no sense of humor," he muttered. "I still think it's a good idea."

"Either way, I agree with Alphonse," Cat said. "Let the Highlord and the Archmage worry about Lord Marl. We've troubles enough of our own."

*   *   *

Cat stepped aboard the *Dorolea* with thinly-disguised dread.

She had never felt at ease near large amounts of water. Her father blamed himself, for he had once taken her to a swimming hole when she was small and the current had carried her away. Tahm had rescued her unharmed, but the fear remained constantly with her. Whenever he told her of the vast sea to the south, her nerves drew tight as harp strings.

The *Dorolea* was a river barge, not a seagoing vessel. Both shores of the Maikha were visible through the misty rain. They would not be out of sight of land, but Cat remained very aware of how vulnerable they would be with but a thin shell of wood between them and the river.

Arien was forced to haggle briefly with the captain, but secured them a private cabin, space for their horses, and a promise that the crew would mind their manners. The eyes of the sailors were bright and greedy as Cat walked by. She was glad she wore her sword prominently at her side.

Their cabin proved adequate and clean. It was in most respects like a normal room, except for the view of the river and the constant sense of rising and falling movement.

Darkfire flew to the wide window and looked out. *How exciting!* he sent happily.

Cat sat at the desk and gripped the edge. Her stomach seemed to be rocking in time with the boat and she wondered if she was going to be sick.

"Are you all right, my dear? You look pale." Arien closed the door and came to her.

"I've never been on a boat," she said.

Concern crossed his face. "You can swim, can't you?"

"If I have to," she said, slowly and doubtfully. "but I don't like it. What if the boat sinks?"

He rubbed her shoulders. "If it does, I shall insist that the captain returns our money."

His hands felt incredibly good. They seemed to seek out the tense spots by magic. She let herself begin to relax under his touch.

"You are shaking," he said. "I did not know that river travel frightened you so. But then, of course, it is only sensible, cats don't care for water."

How long is the journey? Darkfire asked.

"Slightly more than a week," Arien said. "If we rode to Rappikan, the best road would take us more than twice that."

With a bump and a jerk, the boat started moving. Cat gasped and grabbed the desk again.

"All is well, Cat," he said soothingly. "You will become accustomed to it. Soon, it will not seem so strange to you."

"My entire life has become strange. I thought to find my parents and perhaps a bit of adventure, and now I'm on my way to Hachland."

His hands moved up the back of her neck and stroked her hair. "During my years in the Library, I read all the great ballads, all the tales of heroic deeds and magical quests. Never did I picture myself living such a tale, journeying to faraway lands. I find it strangely exciting."

So do I. I can hardly wait to try Hachlanian food!

"Darkfire is right, even if he is guided by his gluttonous urges. We ought to try to enjoy this." His fingers moved slowly through her hair. She tipped her head back and closed her eyes. "Feeling better?"

She nodded. "Thank you. I think I can bear it now. Let me see."

He stepped back. Rain hissed on the river and pattered on the roof, drowning out the voices of the crew. Steeling herself, Cat went to the window. The riverbanks and farmlands were sliding by. The river itself was dark green. They were surrounded by water. It was below them as the river, above them as the clouds, and all around them as the rain. They were alone in a curtain of water.

"It's not too bad," she said. "I can see the land." She closed the shutters and latched them. "But we don't want the rain to come in."

"Shall we unpack? We have to live here for the next week, so we may as well make it cozy." He examined the bookshelves. "Clever. The shelves are angled, and these bars fit here, keeping the books from falling out if the boat rocks."

"Um . . ." Cat toyed with the velvet pouch around her neck, feeling the hard facets of the sapphire. She cast about for a good way to bring up the topic, but finally just had to come right out and ask. "Where are we sleeping?"

He turned and surveyed the small cabin again. "Ah. There are hammock hooks between these beams. We could obtain a hammock from the captain. However . . . I wonder at the wisdom of that."

"What do you mean?"

He hesitated. After seeming to search for the words, he said, "It might be safer if we do not ask for a hammock. River men are not known for their honesty, and they might be less troublesome to you if they assume we are . . . traveling together."

"Oh." She blushed and looked down. Her pulse quickened.

Well, you can't sleep on the floor, the drake sent. *You'd roll all over the place. There's a perfectly good bed, big enough for all of us.* He flew to it and curled up.

"I assure you, Cat, I am suggesting nothing untoward," Arien said, sounding as awkward as she felt. He looked at her, then looked quickly away, having trouble meeting her eyes. "We may as well both be comfortable, and it would be safer."

She could not think of a single thing to say, so she just nodded and started unpacking. Finally, the cabin was arranged to their satisfaction.

"Shall we go above and look around?" Arien suggested.

"It's still raining," she said.

"Observe." He touched her forehead. "*Elnia.*" He repeated the word and gesture on himself.

"What did you do?" She did not feel any different. If he had cast a spell on her, she had no idea what it was supposed to do.

"I will show you. Come on." He led her to the deck.

As they emerged, the crewmen glanced at them curiously. They were a rough sort, the type Cat had seen before on the infrequent occasions her work took her to the lowest Rings. Many had colorful designs inked into their skin. They were all wearing oiled cloaks of a peculiar design, with slits in the sides for their arms and a shorter overcape to protect them.

The rain was pouring heavily. Cat expected to get drenched at once, but to her surprise, she remained completely dry. She held out a hand. No drops struck her outstretched palm. She looked in wonder at Arien. A fine, hazy mist of water droplets surrounded him, but he was untouched by the rain.

"Magic," he said in answer to her questioning expression. "Do you recall the spell I cast to shield myself from arrows? This is similar, though it is designed to counter raindrops."

The crewmen muttered to each other as they passed. Arien held her arm, meeting their furtive looks with a cool gaze.

"River rats," Cat snorted, remembering something the captain had said during his lecture on the dangers of the river. "I'm more worried about the sailors."

"Fear not, my dear," Arien replied. "If it is in my power to defend you, I shall."

She looked sideways at him and grinned. "Thank you, m'lord, but if you don't mind, I'll be sure to keep my sword nearby."

"Do you doubt my ability to protect you?" he teased.

"Not as long as you can swim," she gasped, clinging to his arm as the boat dipped sharply.

"Fear not. You shall not drown. This I promise you. The shipboard food may do you in, but the river itself shall not claim you."

Even in the fog and rain, the river valley was an impressive sight. The Bannerian Mountains loomed high on either side, their tops lost in the heavy clouds. A few twisted trees clung precariously to the mountainsides, leaning out over the river.

"It is lovely, in a way," Arien said. "I imagine it is far more fair when the sun dances along the river and the sky is clear." He turned and looked back, then turned Cat so that she could see Thanis slipping away behind them. The Tower of the Archmage rose above everything else. It was hard to believe they had been there, looking down over the city.

Cat leaned against Arien, watching her home dwindle in the mist of the valley. He put an arm around her. The motion of the boat rocked them together.

"Goodbye, Thanis," she said softly.

"We shall return," Arien added.

*   *   *

The dusk was the darkest she had ever seen. During their journey to Castle Selbon, they had always made camp before full dark and gotten a fire going. In the city, a streetlamp or someone's window was always lit. But when darkness fell in the clouded river valley, it was very dark. Dark, and quiet. There were no sounds except the lapping of waves on the hull and the creaking of the decks. She couldn't even hear the calls of animals of night birds.

They were given a single candle for their cabin. Cat took it below while Arien remained to find out some information about the river from the captain.

She changed quickly, choosing thick hose and a loose shirt instead of a nightgown, certainly not wishing a repeat of what had happened last time . . . well, wishing it with all her heart but not daring . . . and slipped into bed just as she heard Arien approaching the door.

Darkfire crawled across the pillows and curled up next to her head. He did not purr, but his deep, even breathing was almost as good.

Arien came in. Cat pulled the covers up to her neck. She'd been sleepy, but now she was wide awake, alert, and nervous.

"You two look comfortable," Arien said. He closed the door, turned the lock, and wedged the bar through the handle. "Now we're all shut in for the night."

"That reminds me of an old ghost story," she said. "It was supposed to be the shortest one ever."

"The shortest ghost?" he asked teasingly.

"The shortest story. A man took a room in a haunted inn. He locked the door and the window, and got in bed. He leaned over, and just as he blew out the lamp, a voice whispered, 'now we're all shut in for the night'."

"I though the shortest tale was the one about the man and the candle."

"Wasn't that it?" she asked.

"No," he said. "A man woke in a dark room wishing for a light, and a lit candle was placed in his hand."

"I've never heard that one. Greyquin and I used to trade stories around the campfire. He told me the one about the inn, but of course he said it happened to him. Six months later, I heard the same thing from a traveling bard out in Arrowood."

He skimmed his hands across the door. "*Firadalar*", he intoned, then explained. "My magic will alert me, even awaken me, if a hostile presence enters the room. If this spell was commonly used, it might force you to give up stealing altogether." He smiled. "I ought to teach it to everyone in Thanis."

"Then I'd just have to learn magic to counteract it."

"Not from me, you would not." He blew out the candle and stretched out beside her, a careful distance away. Cat was torn between fright and hope, knowing that if he reached for her, she would not resist, could not resist.

Now we're all shut in for the night.

"Darkfire!" Their mingled laughter broke the tension, and moments later the sound of the rain lulled them all to sleep.

*   *   *

Pearly light filtered through the slats of the shutters. Arien awoke slowly, with the sense that something was different. There was a warmth against his side, a soft weight on his chest. It was too large to be Darkfire.

He opened his eyes and saw Cat snuggled close against him, her head resting on his chest. One hand was loosely fisted under her chin. Her other arm was draped over him.

In sleep, her features were relaxed. She looked so young, so innocent. Her long lashes were dark against her golden skin. Her glossy hair spilled over his shoulder. He could see the slight point on the tip of her ear, the fragile line of her jaw. When she was awake, it was so easy to see only the fiery, determined side of her. Now, as she slept so trustingly next to him, he was reminded of how vulnerable she was. And how beautiful.

Her nearness stirred a response that he could not control. He was just a man, not a saint. How could he fail to react to the presence of such a desirable woman? It had been a very long time since he had felt such passion. A long time. A century, in truth. There had been that one priceless night with Alinora, and that only.

In the intervening years, he had read many books on the subject, but he had never made use of that knowledge. He had remained buried in the Library, hidden behind his self-styled mask of solitude. Despite what he had said to Sybil at the Lord's Retreat, he was no artist in the ways of love. Such acts, he had always felt, were meaningless unless shared by two people who cared deeply for each other. After losing Alinora, he had never let anyone come that close, until Cat entered his life.

It was wrong. He knew that. Every fiber of his soul cried out that he was taking a deadly chance. He should have put a stop to this attraction weeks ago, but by the time he'd been made aware of it, it was too late. He should have gone away, never seeing her again, never putting her at risk, but he was not strong enough. Just as he had not been strong enough to end his own life so many years before. He could not bear the loneliness anymore.

A lock of Cat's hair had fallen across her face. He reached down and brushed the stray curl away, letting his fingers linger on her smooth skin. She was so warm, so soft. He wanted to awaken her with his kisses.

His right arm, trapped beneath Cat, began to tingle. He needed to free it before the pins-and-needles sensation became unbearable, but he was loathe to disturb her. He shifted, trying to ease his arm out from under her, while also bringing his face closer to hers.

Cat stirred. Her brilliant, deep eyes opened and looked directly into his. She gasped, eyes wide, and jerked away from him as if she'd been burned. With a yelp, she tumbled out of bed, dragging all the blankets with her.

Help—! came Darkfire's startled waking thought as he was caught up in the tangle.

Cat hit the floor with a solid thump that made Arien wince. He got up and hurried around the bed. He tried not to laugh aloud at the sight of Cat, completely enshrouded except one leg and part of an arm. Of Darkfire, all he could see was a frantically waving tail.

He knelt and uncovered them. Cat looked up at him, tousled and disheveled, her hair crackling and standing on end as the wool blankets were pulled away.

"Good morning," he said.

*   *   *

Coincidence is the word a man uses when he does not want to believe that someone is up to something.

The Book of Yor.

"Choose," growled the lead beast. Its thick black tongue flicked eagerly over its fangs. "One for you, one for us. Make your choice."

Two other beasts stepped forward, diverse yet oddly similar in their hideousness.

One carried Alinora, head lolling, her diamond hair trailing almost to the ground. She was dressed in frothy white lace. The other yanked Cat roughly out of the shadows. She glared defiantly at it, struggled to free her arm from the manacle of its claws.

"Two fine, sweet morsels. Which do you want?" The leader moved to Alinora, took a limp hand in its shaggy paw. "So fair and fragile, this one."

"Let go of her!" He could not think of a single spell. He could not concentrate. Where was his knife? Where was Darkfire?

Rotting laughter gurgled in the beast's throat. It dropped Alinora's hand and skimmed its claws over the curve of her bosom. Her eyes opened. She gave a small, weak scream and fainted again.

"Alinora!" Arien cried.

"This one looks tasty, too," the beast said, turning to examine Cat.

She twisted in the grip of her captor and snapped a kick at the lead beast. It batted her foot away and seized her jaw, forcing her to look at it.

"Feisty little thing, aren't you?"

"Give me my sword and I'll prove it," she shot back. The beast squeezed her jaw. She hissed in pain but did not cry out.

"We hunger," it said to Arien. "One must feed us. One *will* feed us. You will choose."

"No! I cannot!"

"Then both will die," chuckled the beast, flicking its tongue again.

"Let them go," he pleaded. "Both of them."

An evil, mocking semblance of a smile curled across its face. "Impossible. Only one. Choose, and be forever bound by it!"

Alinora lay unconscious, so innocent and helpless. How could he doom her again? She did not even know why this was happening. She did not understand. It was most unfair. All she had done was to love him. That was her only crime. She was so precious, so perfect, a link with everything he'd ever wanted and lost. She had not known about any of this. She did not deserve to suffer again.

Cat returned his gaze evenly. She understood. She had known the risks, and loved him nonetheless. He realized now, now that it was too late, how much he had been fooling himself. Her feelings for him, and his for her, did truly go far beyond mere attraction. She loved him, and he was only beginning to know what a rare and wonderful thing that was. A woman like Cat came along only once, even in an elven lifetime.

You're going to choose her, her eyes seemed to say. *I've known that from the beginning.*

I do love you, he thought, knowing that it was true.

"Choose now!" roared the beast.

"Do not make me do this," he begged.

The beasts moved closer, refusing to answer him. How could he give up either? Each answered a different need in him. He could not do this, could not, could not . . .

"Alinora," he said heavily, the word wrung from him painfully.

Cat bowed her head in acceptance. The defiant tension, the unwillingness to yield to the beasts without a fight, drained from her.

The beasts flung the elfmaid toward Arien. He caught her in his arms. He had forgotten how light and delicate she was, how dear to hold.

The lead beast pulled Cat's head back by the hair. Its wicked claws sliced the air menacingly in front of her face. She did not flinch away, showed no fear. Her eyes gazed serenely to the stars.

A ripe, awful smell assaulted Arien. Alinora's body grew heavy and loose. Horrified, he looked down and saw that he held her rotting corpse. Spidery strands of hair clung to her scalp. Sightless worms birthed themselves from her mossy flesh. Her skin withered and peeled away before his very eyes.

"No!" Even as he cried out his denial and let the corpse fall from his arms, the beast ripped its claws across Cat's exposed throat.

Her back arched. Her mouth opened in a silent scream.

"No! Cat, no!" He was somehow at her side, reaching helplessly toward her as she clasped her hands to her ruined throat, trying to hold in the scarlet river of life that poured between her fingers.

Arien, wake up!

His eyes flew open. His heart slammed wildly.

You were having a nightmare. Darkfire shuddered. *A bad one.*

Moonlight streamed through the shutters. Cat was curled up beside him, sleeping peacefully. He took a deep breath, then another. He was clammy, shaking.

What time is it? he thought.

Past midnight. Are you all right?

The dream was slipping mercifully from his memory. He let it go gladly. He did not want to remember. He rose carefully, causing Cat to stir and murmur softly in her sleep, and went to the window. The dark river was sliding past, streaked silver by moonlight. High in the hills, a wolf raised its voice. He buried his face in his hands until the last vestiges of the nightmare were gone.

*   *   *

"Arien, look!" Cat said. Her eyes held the wondrous expression of a child seeing fairies dancing among the lilies. He looked to see what inspired such innocent delight, and saw a sword.

It was a saber, of the style used by the Southern Plainsfolk, light and small enough to be wielded with ease from the saddle. Yet it was clearly dwarf-crafted, for the nomadic Plainsfolk could not produce such clean steel. The blade was inlaid with designs in mystic truesilver and the pommel was set with a large blue gem.

"It's the most beautiful sword I've ever seen," she breathed.

"It is enchanted," Arien said. "Do you see the mark on the sign above the door? This is the shop of a sorcerer."

"A magic sword!" Her eyes gleamed even brighter. "What do you think it does?"

He laughed. "There is only one way to find out. Let us go in. Perhaps they have powerstones, or other items to interest us and tempt our purses."

Thanis was the heart of the Northlands, but the marketplace and shops of Hachland's capitol city of Rappikan were impressive by any standards. Merchants came here from all over the Northlands, from the Southern Plains, from the northern coastal forests of Lenais, and even from the fabled lands across the sea. It was a bright, vivid, dazzling place, full of life and laughter.

Cat went eagerly into the shop, and stopped short. Arien, following closely behind her, nearly collided with her and looked to see what had so caught her attention.

Elfkin!

The man behind the counter, wearing proudly the badge of a wizard upon his shoulder, was elfkin! His golden-bronze hair was braided back from the temples, fully exposing his slightly pointed ears. His eyes were the deep soulful brown of a doe's.

"Greetings, little kinswoman!" he said, coming forward to take Cat's hands and bow over them. "I am Derevin Spellcrafter, and bid you welcome to my humble shop!"

"You're . . . you're like me!" Cat gasped in complete absence of all good manners. "Part human!"

"But of course . . . ah, you must be a stranger here! I should have known, for I would most fiercely berate myself had I seen and forgotten those lovely blue eyes! By your skin, I see that your ancestry is of the Southern Plains, yes?"

"My father was born to the Plainsfolk," she said, nodding. "But I've never seen another of my kind before! I thought . . . "

"Why, pretty one, there are many of us here in Rappikan!"

"The elves, they don't drown you at birth?"

He recoiled, appalled. "Drown us at birth? Is that what they do in the east, in the Emerin? I hasten to assure you, the elvenfolk of Lenais are not such barbarians!"

Arien started to protest out of instinctive allegiance to his homeland, then fell silent. He had come to a similar conclusion regarding his people, but never had he imagined that Lenais, which was even an older kingdom, be less severe. He had expected Lenaisian traditions to be even more rigidly hidebound than those of the Emerin.

Those thoughts, though, paled in comparison to the jealousy clenching his heart as he saw how the elfkin man smiled at Cat, how he took her arm when she asked about the sword in the window and led her to examine it, how close he leaned to her during his explanation of the enchantments upon it, close enough that their ears nearly brushed.

Darkfire, dozing on his shoulder after having stuffed himself on various delicacies, gave a sudden twitch, as if disturbed by the turmoil in Arien's mind. He petted the drake gently, then inwardly scolded himself.

What right had he to feel possessive of Cat? Should he not be happy that she might find a place where she could belong, free of scorn? Should he not be happy that she might meet men who would shower her with compliments and open interest?

But, oh, as he watched her eyes dance while she turned the saber one way and another, marveling in the lightness of the blade, and looked upon Derevin with such delight and awe that she had once afforded him, it caused the very bottom to drop out of his soul.

He turned away, endeavoring to convince himself that he wanted only what was best for Cat, sickened by his own hypocrisy that he should begrudge her the interest of attractive men when they were on a quest to restore his own Alinora to his side.

Behind him, Cat and Derevin began bargaining for the sword. Caught up in his own agonizing thoughts, Arien had completely missed the description of its enchantments, but evidently it pleased Cat enough so that she agreed to what he felt was an extraordinary price.

He studied some of the other wares, now also having occasion to be envious of Derevin's skill. Here was proof positive that elfkin could learn magic, and excel at it.

A shimmer of silver caught his eye. It was his turn to be stricken with wonder. He went to the table and ran his fingers across the cloth. It was smooth as silk, light as air, yet when he held it by the edge and tried to tear, not so much as a thread would break.

"Silversilk," he murmured, awed.

Cat came happily to his side, her purse doubtless much lighter but the new sword gleaming at her waist. "What have you found, Arien?"

"Silversilk," he repeated, shaking his head admiringly. "Even the dwarves envy this. It can turn an arrow, stop a blade, as well as steel armor. Should it be damaged, it will in time re-weave itself to be good as new."

"Truly?" Cat caressed the fabric. "How many times I've yearned for something like this! Metal is too heavy, too loud, too inflexible for what I need, but this would be perfect! Would that I had brought more money!"

"You have the midnight sapphire," he pointed out, touching the velvet pouch she wore on a cord around her neck.

She clutched it swiftly. "Not for all the enchantments in the world!" Then she blushed and averted her eyes, and whispered something that he was perhaps not meant to hear, but his ears were keen. "You gave it me."

Selfish relief, followed by chiding guilt, washed over him. He turned to Derevin. "The Silversilk, we'll take it. How much?"

*   *   *

"Here's your road north," Bredwyr said as Cat and Arien rode up to join him. "A pity you're not continuing west. We've enjoyed your company."

"Likewise," Arien replied, gripping the trader's arm in a friendly gesture. "Again, our thanks for allowing us to travel with you."

"A pleasure. The small ones will miss you, that they will."

Cat dismounted to say her farewells to Bredwyr's wife and children. It was the oddest family, excepting her own, that she'd ever known. Bredwyr was elven, but far different from the Emerinian elves. Like most of the Lenaisians, he worshipped Denethel the Hunter, and respected the woods and all that dwelt therein. His wife Tulia was human, a plump and cheerful lady of unending generosity. They had four elfkin children, ranging in age from thirteen-year-old Lindwyr to baby Malia.

The road from Rappikan north had been a safe and easy one, and in the forest-border town of Lashinan, Cat and Arien had made the acquaintance of Bredwyr, who was heading north with goods to trade for the cloud-soft furs made by the Lenaisian elves.

Cat had never felt so at home. Here, it was no crime, no evil, to be elfkin. Here, humans and elves married, and it was not so unusual at all. Her parents could have passed unnoticed among these folk; her da's southern looks might have been the most unusual thing about them.

She accepted a parting gift of a blue silk hair ribbon from little Rhedyn, and gave the girl a woodcarving she'd made of a fawn, then rejoined Arien and they waved as the line of ponies started down the western fork.

Arien looked north. "Ahead of us lies Ralistar, where the Antokal family is said to live. We've done well, dear Cat, well indeed, and come further than I ever imagined."

"And with more ease than I dared hope!" she added.

At that moment, off in the depths of the wood, a wolf howled, and they both shivered with a sudden chill.

*   *   *

"I've never seen such snow!" Cat cried, bursting into the tent and showering it everywhere.

"It snows in Thanis," Arien said, brushing it off his bedroll. "You must have seen it before this."

"It's not the same at all." She shook more snow out of her hair. Her cheeks were red from the cold and her eyes danced with excitement. In her fur-trimmed garments, she looked like some sprite or woodland pixie. "The wagons and horses churn it into a muddy mire. This is different. Everything is white and sparkling."

"*Lace in the winter and lace in the spring: one the kind that is made of ice, one the kind that the flowers bring*," he quoted. "Elwyndas, of course. Did your father never take you out of the city, into the mountains or Arrowood, in the winter?"

"No." She laughed. "He was born on the Southern Plains, where it never gets cold, and thus he always dreaded the winter. He used to dream of building a tunnel between our home and the Empty Mug, so that he needn't even set foot out of doors until spring!"

"Then I imagine he never showed you how to make a snowball."

"Snowball? Mean you that ice spell I've seen you cast?"

"This is different. Come on, I will show you." He led her out of the tent.

He had to admit, it was pretty up here. The forest was primarily made up of tall evergreens, dripping icicles from their dark needles. Heavy clouds, promising more snow, whirled across the sky. It was quiet, the breathless stillness that only comes with winter.

You're both as mad as rats in a bag, was Darkfire's comment as they headed out. The drake had taken a few mincing steps in the strange, cold stuff, and decided that enough was enough. *Go play; I'll keep an eye on the food. I'm going to add Snow-hater to my name. Darkfire Dragonwing—*

"If you eat all of our supplies," Arien called, "I will bury you so far under the snow that you must wait for the spring thaw."

Their Silversilk, purchased without a qualm despite the cost, and easily sewn together by use of a simple spell into close-fitting garments, had an unexpected benefit. Though light and thin, it nevertheless kept the worst of the cold at bay. With the addition of their warm outer furs, they were quite comfortable.

Cat looked around happily. Her breath plumed out. "It's so pretty," she said. "Tell me about snowballs. What do we do?"

Arien bent down and gathered some snow in his gloved hands. "First, you take a handful of snow, like so. Then you pack it together into a ball."

"Like so?" she asked, imitating his actions.

"Perfect. Then, all you do is this." He threw the snowball in her face.

Whatever she said was muffled, which was just as well, since he suspected it would have been something unladylike. Her snowball dropped from her hands as she pawed the snow from her face and shook it from her hair.

"*Firalel,*" he whispered, casting a quick spell upon himself. He knew it was unfair, but an evening of darts at a Rappikan inn had convinced him how uncanny was her aim.

She looked at him, eyes wide, sputtering. "You—you," she said.

"You *are* going to say something unladylike." He scooped up another handful of snow. "I feared that you might. Perhaps I shall have to strike you again."

"Oh, no, you won't!" She darted behind the tent.

He ducked around the other side. She was already gathering another snowball for herself. He threw his and hit her in the leg. She squealed and hurled one at him. It skimmed by, missing by inches. She looked surprised. The she looked amazed and outraged.

"You're cheating! Arien Mirida, of all people!"

"We must each use whatever advantages the gods favored us with," he replied.

"You're not going to win this," she said, determinedly packing more snow.

"I plan to." He stood still, smiling, confident in his magic though he knew there was always a very slight chance his spell would be unable to turn it aside.

She missed again, and he realized that, had she not, he would have taken the snowball full in the face. Leisurely, he started making another for himself.

Sometimes he forgot how quick Cat was. She kicked a spray of snow at him and ran across the clearing. She was headed for the trees.

He went after her, but she was *fast*. He could not overtake her. Fortunately, he did not need to. He had his wits. What she might not suspect was that her tracks gave her away. She could run, but she could not hide from him.

Tossing the snowball from hand to hand, he moved quietly along her trail. The forest was silent except for the low, ominous creak of boughs bending under their weight of ice. He followed the tracks between the trees, until they suddenly ended. It was as if she had vanished into thin air.

He looked around. There were no trees close enough for her to have jumped or climbed. Yet the tracks came to this spot and ended.

He heard a stealthy sound behind him. She leaped on him just as he started to turn, giving him a shove. He fell full-length in the snow. His snowball flew from his hand and shattered against a tree.

At once he understood. He had underestimated how quickly she learned. She had stopped, backed up in her own tracks, and waited behind a bush, effectively hiding from him until the right moment to pounce.

He rolled onto his back. Cat stood over him, hands on her hips, laughing.

"If I can't throw it at you, I'll bury you in it," she said merrily.

"Point well made. I am far more snow-covered than you." He sat up and dug snow out of his collar.

"So, you admit I win?"

"It does look that way, does it not?"

"That's right." She offered a hand. "Here, you'll catch cold."

He seized her hand, swept her feet out from under her, and pulled her down. Snow flew everywhere as they struggled. He rolled onto her and dumped an armload of snow across her face. She shrieked, and stuffed some down the back of his neck. It was his turn to cry out.

He captured her hands and pinned them over her head. "I can see there is only one thing to do," he panted.

"Surrender?" she gasped, shaking snow off her face.

"No, this," he said, and kissed her.

She stiffened in surprise, then melted. Her body moved with innocent passion beneath his, and his desire became as a flame within him.

"You win," she breathed when he finally lifted his head.

He looked down at her. In the still, frozen forest, the only color was the incredible sapphire of her eyes. He could see his reflection and the towering trees above them.

The forbidden words were at the threshold of his lips. Why not say them? He knew their truth.

Or was it the speaking of the words that gave the curse its power? He had loved Alinora long before she confessed the same to him, and it was on that night the nightmare was begun.

Just as he now loved Cat, a love unspoken but shining as a star within his shadowed heart. Each night, he dreaded yet expected to hear the howling begin, and each night it did not. He wondered, even dared to hope if her human blood might somehow render her immune to a curse cast in a time when humans were all but unknown, that the beasts might not recognize or touch her. But he could not permit himself the deadly luxury of that belief, lest it prove to be false!

Fragments of his dream came back to him, the beasts, a choice that was no choice at all. Would he lose them both in seeking the one he perhaps should leave to her rest?

Such thoughts were unthinkable, and cooled his ardor as quickly as the icy air cooled his breath.

*   *   *

They reined in their horses and looked for a long time at the town of Ralistar.

"I've never heard of elves living in caves before!" Cat finally said, doubtfully. "Might we have taken a wrong turn?"

Caverns dotted the steep sides of the narrow valley, their openings connected by smooth spans of stone. A river, now frozen into a wondrous expanse of ice, glittered along the valley floor. The mountaintops were shrouded in clouds, and snow lay over the scene, softening it. It was a view worthy of a painting or tapestry, but not at all what either of them expected to see.

"Bredwyr said these folk live muchly by mining," Arien remembered. "Opals are found here, and the precious truesilver." He threw back his hood and stripped off his gloves, then extended his hands. "Yes, I can feel it, the *aether* is stronger here, more potent. Behold the bridges, how they've been shaped from the living rock. This is a place of strong magic."

"I . . . I do feel it," Cat murmured. "Like a tingling within my skin."

He turned to her, delighted. "You do? You feel the *aether*? I thought you had the potential, and now I know it to be true!"

"The potential for magic? I do?"

"Perhaps that might tempt you to give up your thiefly pastime," he teased.

She winked at him. "On the contrary, I imagine there must be a lot of spells that would come in handy!"

He sighed exaggeratedly. "Is there no mending your ways?"

Are you two going to stand there jabbering all night, or can we find an inn before my scales freeze off? Darkfire sent grumpily from within his special fur-lined satchel.

"Very well, very well." Arien led the way down the steep trail, and hailed a man. "Pardon, good sir, where might I find an inn?"

"No inns here, kinsman. Have you family in town?"

"No," Arien said. Nor did he choose this moment to mention his quest. He wanted to learn something of the Antokals before he approached them. Already, given the power of the area, he would surmise that they were powerful mages, perhaps even Archmages.

"It is customary, then, that visitors share the lodgings of the Loremaster, Careldon. His cavern is yonder. I will show you there, if you wish."

"Thank you, friend!" Arien squeezed Cat's hand. "A Loremaster! That is more than I'd hoped!"

"Loremaster!" the elf called as they approached the modest opening of a cave. "I bring guests!"

A figure appeared in the entrance, a tall and graceful mature elfwoman whose foxpelt-colored hair fell in a single thick braid to the hem of her gown. Her smile seemed to light the entire valley.

"That's your Loremaster?" Cat asked, a bit taken aback.

"No, no," laughed their guide. "That is his wife, Shandrala. She'll talk the ears off you, but you'll find no kinder heart in all of Lenais."

*   *   *

By the time Cat and Arien had tied their horses in the stable-cave and divested themselves of their outer furs, they knew that Careldon and Shandrala were four hundred and seventy-five years apart in age, but she had known since she was but a girl that she would marry none other. They had no children, but they did have a sleek white cat named Blossom who had recently produced a litter of kittens. They had plenty of room and enjoyed tremendously when visitors came by. They were especially delighted this time because they hardly ever got visitors so late in the year and thought it would be spring before they had company again.

Shandrala all but flew about the entire time she chattered, helping them off with their cloaks and packs, and then led them into the living area of the cavern.

It was certainly far from primitive, putting to rest the last of Arien's worries of orc-caves and the like. The floor was stone, but it had been shaped smooth and covered with rugs. In one corner was a breathtaking limestone formation that glimmered with a rainbow of colors as the firelight played over it. The effect was tranquil, almost hypnotic. Most interesting of all, one entire wall was given over to bookshelves.

The Loremaster Careldon wasn't as talkative as his wife, although that may have been because she scarce let him get a word in as she introduced them. His blond hair was streaked with grey and worn in several long braids tied with different colors of leather. He moved with youthful energy despite his frail appearance and advanced age. Arien guessed that his wife had much to do with it. Their affection toward each other was at once endearing and embarrassing.

"Well, what can we offer you to drink?" Shandrala asked enthusiastically. "I was just preparing dinner, so we will be eating soon. By Denethel's horn, I'm glad I made extra! We keep a little bit of everything, since you never know who might be coming by. Careldon's favorite is the snowberry wine; I do recommend it. We're having roast featherfeet tonight. Are there any spices either of you cannot eat?"

"Not that we have discovered," Arien said. "And everything sounds wonderful."

Someone mentioned dinner? Darkfire sent, crawling out of his carry pouch.

"Oh, how charming! Look, Careldon, he has a drake! What a fine, glossy fellow. You must take very good care of him."

Tell her you starve me for days at a time.

Behave yourself, Arien sent back. "This is Darkfire."

"You are welcome to our home, to stay as long as you like," Careldon replied, finally getting a chance to speak. "There are hot springs below for bathing, if you'd fancy."

Soon, Cat and Arien were feeling better than they had in days. Hot baths and a change of clothes made a world of difference after so long on the road.

Dinner was a festive occasion, marked by wine and laughter. Darkfire adored Shandrala so much that Arien began to worry that his familiar's loyalty might shift.

After the meal, of which they had all eaten far too much, Shandrala shooed them away to let her clean up.

"Please, let me help," Cat said.

"Oh, mercy, no. You're a guest." Shandrala deftly slipped a stack of plates from Cat's hands and carried them to the kitchen.

Cat followed her. "There must be something I can do," she persisted.

"It is hardly necessary. I know you've come to talk with Careldon. Everyone does. That is part of what I love about him. Being the Loremaster's wife is never dull. People come from miles around with questions. Sometimes it isn't even history they're looking for. Sometimes it's but advice."

"You seem very happy," Cat said enviously.

"I am indeed. Here, if you positively insist, you can help." Shandrala dunked the dishes into a steaming pot and handed Cat a clean rag. She glanced around, then added conspiratorially, "and before you ask, he's not too old for me at all. I keep him young. Sometimes it's all I can do to keep up with him." Seeing Cat blush, she giggled. "Oh, my, I'm sorry. Did I embarrass you?"

"No, that's all right. I'm used to it. I have a friend, Sybil, who's Talopean."

Shandrala rolled her eyes. "Them! I've heard of them. Forgive me for saying so, but they seem to have a most unusual outlook."

"I know," Cat said. Shandrala was so easy to talk to that she found herself unburdening something that had troubled her for a long while. "My other friend, Jessa, used to have the worst arguments with Sybil. Sybil always told me I should . . . well . . . and Jessa swore that I shouldn't, that it was a horrible, awful thing. I never knew who to believe."

"And what think you now?"

"I don't know," Cat sighed. "I don't know what to think. It can't be all the same thing, can it?"

Shandrala paused and tossed her long russet braid over her shoulder. She looked at Cat seriously with her velvety brown eyes. "Oh, dear. You and Arien are not . . . ?"

Cat shook her head. Amazingly, she did not feel as embarrassed as she normally did in these situations. She merely felt shy and a little confused. "No. We're not. He's in love with someone else, and in truth I really don't know what to make of how I feel. Of how he makes me feel . . ."

"Poor child," Shandrala said, leading Cat to the table. "Your mother never spoke to you about these matters?"

"No," she said sadly. "She's been gone since I was just a little girl. I barely remember her, and she certainly never had the chance to advise me. Sybil's tried to tell me about it, but . . ."

Shandrala flapped her hands alarmedly. "Oh, Cat, don't listen to a Talopean. They believe in pleasure, yes, but that is all they believe in. They omit the most vital aspect of all."

"What's that?"

"Love. Caring. What happens between a man and a woman is supposed to be a very special thing. When a woman is with a man she cares about, it is the most wonderful and beautiful thing in the world."

"In a way, I wish you hadn't told me that," Cat said sadly. "Because I'll never find out."

"What do you mean?" Shandrala asked.

"What do you do when the person you want doesn't want you? At least, I don't think he does. Sometimes, when he's kissed me, it seems like he might, but how do I know?"

Shandrala hugged her. "If he kisses you, he must feel something."

"When we're done with our quest, I'll never see him again," she said softly. "I couldn't. It would hurt too much."

"If there is one thing I've learned as the Loremaster's wife, it is that life is filled with difficult choices. You'll make the right one, Cat. I know you will."

Cat touched the sapphire in the pouch around her neck. "I have to," she murmured. "My life depends on it."

*　　*　　*

As Careldon finished a long and hilarious story about a foolhardy elf and thin ice, Shandrala and Cat came in and joined them. Arien then turned the conversation to the reason for their visit.

"Are you familiar with the Antokal family?" Arien asked.

"Oh, yes. I grew up with Lorevan Antokal."

Arien blinked at him. So did Cat. Could it be so simple? That name, Lorevan, was the very name of the Tokalsian Mage himself, handed down through the generations.

"Theirs is an old family, correct?" he asked.

"It is indeed." Careldon sipped his brandy. "In the Book of Lines, it goes back to the crowning of the first Lenaisian Elvenking. Mirida, Mirida, hmm. Your family's name is in the book as well, I do believe."

"I should very much like to see it." He tried, and failed, to conceal the desperate eagerness in his voice. As always, books provided the answer!

"Well, shall we look?" Careldon rose and took a thick tome from a glass case, then returned to his chair. Shandrala sat on the floor beside her husband, resting her head on his knee. He absently stroked her long hair as he turned the pages. They presented a picture of happiness and contentment.

Arien felt a swift pang of envy. How he yearned for such a life. A cozy home, a simple life of books and brandy, with a lovely wife to make it all worthwhile. He tried to imagine himself in such a setting, but not entirely to his surprise, he could not clearly picture the woman at his side. Was she blond or dark? Elegant or spirited? Alinora or Cat?

He glanced at Cat. She was watching Shandrala wistfully.

"Aha. Mirida." Careldon's brows drew together. "There are not many names. The last ones shown here are a Talian and Lanarien Mirida."

"My great-aunt and grandfather," he said, with a sense of growing excitement. "Talian herself told me that her brother left his home to settle in the Emerin! But I had not realized they came from Lenais!"

"You've fallen generations behind in your record-keeping, my love," Shandrala chided affectionately. "You really must amend it."

"Yes, yes, I know. I'll start right now. Fetch me my pen, would you, darling?"

She got him a quill and ink. Questioning Arien for all he knew about his family, he filled in the rest of the Mirida line. It was an honor to see his own name written in such a treasured book. He hoped that his parents, wherever their spirits might have flown, were pleased.

"Would you show me the Antokal line?" Arien asked.

Careldon looked at him curiously. "What is your interest in Lorevan's family? This is the second time you've mentioned it."

Arien sighed. "It is difficult to explain. One of my earliest ancestors, Rhiannon," he tapped the name at the top of the page, "escaped the destruction of the lost city of Govannisan. It is my belief that the Antokals are descended from that time as well."

"Oh, yes," Careldon agreed. He turned back to the front of the book. "There is a direct line from this man, Elhewen Antokal, who changed his name from Tokalsis when he was knighted by Aradahel the First."

The confirmation of his research and suspicion both chilled him and made him blaze with hope. They were the same, the same family and bloodline. He leaned over and scanned the page. There were far more entries, he noted bitterly. His own line was a tenuous thread, and he was the last strand.

"This one, Lorevan. This is your friend?" He touched the last name.

"Was. He died twenty years ago, in terrible times. The winter of '18, I believe. The trolls and ice wolves attacked together. Lorevan fell defending his land. His sacrifice gave his wife and her brothers a chance to escape."

"For shame, Careldon," Shandrala said, tapping the book. "You have forgotten Felorna. Add her at once."

"Did they have children?" Arien asked hopefully.

"Lorevan and Felorna? No. They had only been married for five years."

Arien felt ill. Hope and despair passed over him in turns. He put a trembling hand to his brow as Careldon and Shandrala argued good-naturedly.

"Forgetting my own cousin. Why, I wonder if you've even recorded my name by yours."

"I'm a busy man," he replied. "I'll record you next, my heart. This I vow. Hmm, I must add Danicia before Felorna."

"Oh, yes. His first wife. Whatever happened to her?"

"She married that Hirilorn fellow, the King's Chancellor."

"Lorevan was married twice?" Arien sat up, hope stirring again.

Careldon nodded. "Danicia was his first wife. She never should have married an Antokal. She thought she could change Lorevan's roguish ways, and her disappointment was bitter."

"She did try," said Shandrala. "She tried for decades."

"True, true. And she did give him a son. We cannot blame her for how he turned out."

"A son that you have not yet recorded either," she scolded.

"Where is the son?" Arien asked, cautioning himself against an excess of hope.

"I haven't any idea," Careldon admitted. "He left Lenais years ago. He should have returned to claim Lorevan's lands, but he never has. Knowing Donnell, he was likely killed in a duel long ago. Arrogant young hothead."

"Donnell," Arien said slowly. The name was familiar, yet he could place it.

"Was he a wizard?" Cat asked suddenly.

Arien remembered where he had heard that name. From Cat. From Cat's story about her parents.

"Yes, he was," Careldon said. "One of the most promising young mages I'd ever seen, but too ambitious. Too impatient."

"That's the name of the elfmage that traveled with my father," Cat said, turning to Arien, her eyes wide. "I told you of him!"

"We must find him," Arien said.

"But how? That was twenty years ago. Father never saw them again." She gasped. "*He must be the elf in the dungeons, the one Selbon spoke of!*"

"Why are you two so set on finding Donnell?" Careldon asked.

"Yes, why? What is all this?" Shandrala added.

Arien looked at Cat. She nodded. "Go on, you may as well tell them."

"I will try to explain," he said heavily. "We need very much to find someone who descends from the Tokalsians. There is a curse on my family placed by theirs, long ago in Govannisan. Only one of that bloodline can undo it."

Careldon raised his eyebrows. "There are vague legends of a curse from long ago."

"The curse is real," Arien said. He closed his eyes briefly and swallowed. "I have seen it. To end it, we need Donnell's aid."

"But, Arien! Return to the castle? What about Selbon?" Cat asked.

"Selbon may be dead, if Solarrin was as powerful as he believed himself to be," Arien said grimly.

"Solarrin! We have to ask him for help?" She threw up her hands. "All he'll want are our souls."

"Cat, we must try," he said, looking seriously at her. "You know that as well as I. It is our only hope."

"What do we do if Donnell is dead?"

Arien got parchment, quill, and ink from his pack. He turned to Careldon. "It seems we need your aid further. Would you look in the book for others of that direct bloodline?" At Careldon hesitation, he added, "Please, Loremaster. Lives, mine and Cat's not least among them, are at risk."

"Oh, we must help them, my love!" Shandrala implored.

"I will do what I can," he said, bending to the book again.

"We are eternally in your debt," Arien said.

"Do not place yourself in debt until I have aided you," Careldon cautioned. "Now then. Lorevan had a brother and a sister. Dairnin was killed by an ice wolf when he was little more than a boy, and Tiriona died in childbirth. Her son, Doratir, died in the Archmage's Challenge." He paused. "Hmm. This is not going to be as simple task as I'd thought."

"I had feared as much," Arien sighed. He listed the names anyway, making a neat mark beside them all to show that they were no more of this world.

After poring over the book and muttering to himself, Careldon finally shook his head. "Excepting Donnell, I fear that all are lost to us."

"Oh, no!" Shandrala cried, her pretty face a mask of anguish though she'd only but met them.

Arien closed his eyes. All was surely lost. He would never regain Alinora. As for Cat, what would become of her?

Careldon stared thoughtfully at the fire. "I wonder . . . "

"What is it, my love?" Shandrala asked.

"Lorevan did have a daughter," he said.

"That is little more than gossip," Shandrala said accusingly. "It is unkind to even mention it. You always tell me to pay no mind to idle talk."

"It is not mere gossip. Lorevan was my friend. He confided in me. When Danicia ended their marriage, it was not only that she had tired of attempting to change him. She knew of the other women, but when she found out about the girl, it was the final blow."

"Are you saying that Lorevan had an illegitimate child?" Arien asked.

Careldon nodded. "Lorevan kept several mistresses. One bore him a daughter."

"Where is she? Does she yet live?" He pulled his parchment back in front of him.

"Well, that is the problem. No one knows. She left Lenais thirty years ago. It was a shame. She was a lovely young woman and a talented mage as well."

"What was her name?" Arien dipped his quill.

He paused, searching his memory. "Miralina," he announced.

"That's odd," Cat said. "My mother's name is Miralina."

Arien froze. A large drop of ink splattered across the parchment, blotting out his list of names. Slowly, not certain he believed his ears, he turned his head to look at Cat. She met his gaze, puzzled.

"What's wrong?" she asked.

"I'd been thinking you looked familiar," Careldon said. "You've got her eyes."

Cat's eyes suddenly widened and her mouth fell open as she realized what she'd said. Arien leaned down and took her hands.

"We've done it. We've found the answer," he said, amazed.

"No, we haven't," she wailed. "Arien, my mother is gone! She's been gone for years! I don't know where she is or even if she's alive!"

"You silly girl!" He pulled her to her feet and swung her around. "It is you, Cat! You're the one we've sought, and you have been right here all along!"

"Me?" she gasped.

"You!" He embraced her, laughing. "We've been looking for you!"

*   *   *

If we were living a tale, wouldn't you like to get your hands on the man who wrote it?

The Book of Yor.

He had never seen her more beautiful. The moonlight cast her slim shadow on the ground, shimmered on the Silversilk she wore beneath a fur-trimmed tunic.

There was no elven etherealness about her. She looked wild and fierce. Her human blood burned like a fire within her, making her the brightest thing under the watching moon.

Arien stood at the edge of the ring of trees. The natural clearing, with the sheared-off stump at its center, was the perfect site for the casting of a spell. She'd wanted him to remain at their campsite, not wanting him to witness what would become of her if she failed, but he could not let her face them alone.

Cat stood atop the stump, the wind stirring her hair. In her hands, she held the paper with the incantation he'd copied from the scrying pool of Talus Yor. "If something goes wrong—" she began, her voice shaking slightly.

"Do not even think it!" he said vehemently.

"Yet if it does!" she persisted. "Find my parents, if they live. My mother might succeed where I could not, and my da, well, he probably *has* stolen a body before!"

"I will," he promised, though it was a promise he knew he could not keep. If Cat perished in this attempt, he would find no forgiveness, and only some rough atonement in his own death.

"Now," she said simply, then tilted the paper to the moonlight and started to read aloud the words.

Arien tensed, recalling that the spell was first to summon the shadow beasts, that they might then be cast out. By blood, Cat's own blood, which she would need to spill to drive them into the nothingness from whence they'd risen. For that, she was prepared, her knife and saber at her waist.

The night continued unchanged.

She frowned, and read on, and still there was no sense of presence, no sense of magic. No sign of beasts, shadow or otherwise.

Finally, she lowered the paper and looked at him, distraught. "It isn't working, Arien! Nothing happens! Am I misreading it?"

He shook his head. "You've said the words correctly. I do not know why . . . there were no other conditions in the grimoire!"

"Is it because I'm elfkin?" She touched her ear. "My magic not strong enough?"

"It shouldn't be that!"

She sat on the stump and slumped disconsolantly forward, head in her hands. "I've failed you, Arien. I've failed."

He sighed, feeling the familiar crushing weight of his despair. Doomed, he thought, doomed for all time. To have come so close, and be undone at the last moment . . .

Cat's head came up suddenly. "Arien! I haven't failed!" She jumped to her feet, eyes alight. "There is no curse!"

"No curse? What are you saying? That I have been merely mad? If so, then Talian and Talus Yor share my madness, for the proof was in her story and his scrying!"

"No, not that!" She laughed aloud, bright and merry. "Don't you see, Arien? It's already broken! Broken, a hundred years ago!"

"What?" The breath was driven from him by an unseen force.

"In the past, Arien! I will . . . I did . . . whichever! . . . break it in the past! Though I've not done it yet, it has already been done! Now, tonight, there is no curse!"

"No, it cannot be!" He staggered, a hand to his temple.

She ran to him, clutched his shoulders, gave him a brisk little shake. "Arien! I know this to be true! When we visit the Emerin of a century gone, *then* I will read the words, cast the spell. Do you see?" She laughed again and shook harder. "Or does your strict elven mind balk at such a notion?"

"It does, of course it does, any sane mind would!" he cried. "If what you say is so, then I have not been under a curse for the past century! I have . . ." he reeled and leaned against her else he would have fallen bonelessly to the earth ". . . I have lived in solitude and fear for a hundred years with no need?"

*   *   *

"We must find shelter!"

"What?" He could barely hear Cat over the wind, though she was only a few paces away.

Heads down, the horses plodded through the blizzard. He and Cat were huddled between them, but not even the animals' large bodies could block the weather's rage. If not for his spell of shielding, they would have been battered by hail and freezing sleet.

She says we have to get out of the storm, Darkfire sent petulantly. *I've said so myself. Why do you talk aloud when you can't even hear each other?*

He's right, he thought.

Shouldn't we be there by now? Cat asked.

"Aha!" He spotted the bulk of a building looming out of the blinding snow. They had reached the town, and just in time.

Find us an inn, Darkfire ordered. *A warm one with hot food!*

I agree, Cat thought. *A few more minutes in this storm, though, and I won't care if we have to sleep in a barrel.*

The town of Nail Rapids was in the middle of its Wintersfest celebrations, and the jovial Hachlanians weren't about to let something so trifling as a blizzard interfere with their festivities. The streets were decorated with winter flowers and evergreen boughs, most of which were stripped bare by the fierce winds.

A happy drunken man directed them to the Shady Tree Inn, where they found that only one room remained available. Rather than battle the weather again, they took it gratefully.

"I've had my fill of snow, I think," Cat said, falling into a chair.

The room had its own small fireplace, and a full box of wood, so Arien quickly started a fire. Darkfire crawled from his carry sack, gave them silently reproachful looks, and got so close to the flames that sparks landed on his scales.

The wind howled in the shutters, but from below the sounds of music and merrymaking drifted through the floorboards.

"When we've warmed ourselves," Arien asked, spreading his cloak over a table to dry, "shall we join the festivities below?"

Cat nodded. "Though I'd pay a pretty mark to be back in Ralistar, up to my neck in a hot spring. I feel I'll never be warm again."

"The innkeep told me there are bathing chambers, and hot water aplenty."

She shot to her feet. "Which way?"

By the time she returned, Darkfire was alone in the room, curled on the hearth a bit further back from the fire now, and gorging himself on a pouch of candied berries.

"Where did you get those?" she accused.

I found them in your backpack, he sent smugly.

"You little sneak! I've only been giving you a few at a time!"

*I was *so* hungry,* he sent mournfully, accompanying it with gnawing pangs of starvation.

"You're going to get sick, and have no more candies for the trip," she scolded.

"What are you two arguing about?" Arien asked from the doorway.

He had obviously also indulged in a bath, for his hair gleamed and he was freshly clad in trousers of black, a cream-colored silken shirt, and a vest which had been a gift from Shandrala, dark grey sewn with silver thread.

She's upset because I stole something, Darkfire sent. *And her a thief! The nerve!*

"What did you steal?" Arien asked the drake sternly. Darkfire gave him a look of innocence and said nothing.

"He took the candied berries I've been saving for him," Cat explained.

He turned his stern glare on her, but she could see the twinkle in his eyes. "Look what an influence you are!"

"You're right," she said, pretending chagrin. "Why, now I wish I hadn't stolen the candies in the first place."

Darkfire choked. *These are stolen?*

She laughed. "I'm teasing. I bought them." She waited until he took another bite, then added, "But I stole the coin I bought them with."

She's heartless! the drake protested.

Arien shook his head, smiling. "I shall not intervene. You, Cat, are too lovely to stay cross at for long." He gave her a long, appraising look.

She, too, wore a gift from the generous Shandrala, a midnight-blue skirt sewn with hundreds of tiny silver stars, and a silvery blouse with a black bodice laced in silver cord. Her hair had grown quite long on their journey, and she'd tied it back with the blue ribbon that Rhedyn had given her. It quite exposed her ears, and she was beginning to realize that doing so was fairly daring.

"Too, too lovely," Arien murmured. He offered her his arm. "Shall we to the festival?"

"Yes. Now that Darkfire has a treat, we needn't bring him anything," she said brightly.

Wait, Cat—

They hurried down the stairs, laughing together. As they entered the common room, they were nearly trampled by a line of dancers. Someone bellowed, "Welcome, strangers!" and gave them each a goblet of wine.

"Friendly folk," Arien said, a bit taken aback. "Happy Wintersfest, my dear Cat." He tapped his goblet against hers and sipped from it. "I apologize for not having a gift for you."

"I'll settle for a dance," she said boldly.

"I would be delighted."

When the song ended, the dancers called for another tune. "Show us an elven dance!" someone called to Arien.

"Yes, show me!" A buxom red-haired woman pushed forward. "Dance with me!"

He smiled. "I am honored, but I have promised the next dance to my current partner."

The woman looked crestfallen, but another man quickly offered to partner her.

"You did not," Cat giggled, amused to catch Arien in a lie.

"I did," he replied smoothly. "I simply had not said it aloud." He approached the musicians and gave them the tune, humming until they were able to play it. He then took Cat's hand and led her to the center of the floor.

They danced a graceful dance popular in Thanis. Her natural agility made up for the fact that she was only passingly familiar with the steps. The other revelers soon joined in, with varying degrees of skill but a good deal of enthusiasm.

When it was over, they escaped to the back of the room where a matronly woman urged them to eat. With loaded plates, they found a corner table that was halfway quiet.

Cat nibbled on the spiced goose. It was rich and tasty. "As good as the Lord's Retreat," she announced.

For the first time in her life, Cat found herself liking the way the eyes of the men followed her. She didn't know what had caused this change in mood, whether it was the heady black-berry wine or just a sense of freedom and relief knowing that the curse was undone—Arien remained doubtful—but she was determined to enjoy it.

"They would not permit you to eat with your fingers at the Lord's Retreat," Arien said.

"Try to eat fowl any other way. It can't be done. You miss too much of it." She licked her lips and sighed.

He was strangely quiet, looking at her in a way that made her pulse quicken. Instead of looking away, this time she returned his gaze directly. He was the one that finally lowered his eyes, seeming uncertain.

"It really is true, Arien," she said quietly. "You'll see."

"Let us not think of it tonight. This is a time for celebrating. Let us do so. Would you dance with me again?"

She let him lead her to the floor, where they joined a complex couples dance. The pattern separated them and carried them around the circle, dancing with other partners. Nobody drew back because she was elfkin. Nobody seemed repulsed. Quite the opposite. An attractive young man seized the opportunity to whisper in her ear as he spun her.

"I have never seen such beauty. Won't you come up to my room with me? "

Her reaction was swift and sharp. She elbowed him in the throat and stepped on his foot. The man gagged and stumbled back, bumping into another couple.

"You could have but said no," he choked.

"I'm sorry," she gasped. "I'm not from around here!"

"I'll pay my attentions to local girls from now on! Much safer." He backed away, eyeing her cautiously.

Ashamed, she quickly left the floor and found her glass. When the dance ended, Arien came over to her.

"There you are," he said. "I suddenly found myself without a partner."

"Oh, Arien, am I a fool?" she asked.

"Of course not. Pattern dances are hard to remember. There is no shame in leaving the floor if you become lost."

"That isn't what I meant. A man . . . asked me something, and I hit him."

Arien's eyebrows went up. "You hit a man? Why? What did he say?"

"He invited me to his room," she said, unable to meet his eyes and knowing that he was trying to hide a smile. "In the alleys of Thanis, that's a threat and not a question."

"Cat, Cat, Cat. What a life you have led. You simply must learn better manners. At most court occasions, it is considered impolite for the dancers to strike one another."

A minstrel began a memory song, reciting a list that grew ever longer. It also grew louder as participants laughed at their own mistakes. When all but the minstrel had been eliminat-ed, Arien suddenly took up the song. He flawlessly recited every item, to the applause of the crowd.

After another few dances, the revelers began to drift away, seeking a good night's rest before the morrow's festivities began anew.

Cat and Arien went upstairs, bearing treats wrapped in a handkerchief for Darkfire. The drake was asleep on the hearth next to the empty berry pouch, his stomach distended, oblivi-ous to their return. Snow ticked against the shutters.

Arien blew out the candles and sat in front of the fireplace. "Few things are nicer than re-laxing by the fire while winter walks outside."

Greatly daring, Cat sat beside his chair and rested her head on his knee as she had seen Shandrala do. As Careldon had done, he began stroking her hair. She closed her eyes.

"What will you do when all this is over?" she asked. "Will you still be a Librarian, or will you go back to the elvenwood and claim your title?"

"You make it seem so grand, as if I were heir to some royal name." He sighed. "It has been a hundred years since I was last in the Emerin. I do not know if I would even be welcome. Or if I would find it to my liking. I have more friends in Thanis than I ever did as a youth."

"I'll miss you," she murmured, thinking he wouldn't hear, but of course he did.

"I will still be in Thanis. Why would you miss me?"

"Because I'm leaving," she said softly. "I have to go find my father. I have to know what happened to him. And . . . "

"What is it?" His hand rested on her head.

"It would hurt too much to stay," she said in a rush.

He said nothing for a long time. When the silence became too much to bear, she lifted her head. He was looking at her with sorrow.

"Why are you so willing to risk your life to reunite me with another?" he asked gently.

She looked away quickly so he would not see the tears in her eyes.

"I never even asked you to break the curse. I merely assumed that you would, even at your peril. You've asked for nothing in return. Cat, why? Please, if you say that it is enough to see me happy, I will shake you."

"Not only for that reason," she whispered. "I wanted adventure, Arien. I wanted to travel. Look what you offered! A chance to go places I'd only heard of, to even travel through time!" She got up and went to the window, feeling a cool draft on her face. It was coldest around her tear-damp eyes. "And . . . it was a chance to be with you."

"You hoped that I might come to care for you?"

She nodded, unable to speak.

"Oh, Cat, this has been madness for me! The curse . . . I did not want to endanger you! Had something happened to you, I would have been destroyed. Those times I held you, kissed you . . . I should not have, yet I could not resist."

"I'm glad you didn't," she whispered.

"In these few short months, a mere moment in the span of my life, you have become dear to me beyond words. I do care for you, Cat."

She sighed. "How I wish I could have been your lady, even for just one night."

She heard him rise and move to stand behind her. She kept her head down. Tears stung her eyes. She hadn't wanted to say it, but the words had slipped out before she could stop them.

He gently grasped her shoulders and turned her around. "Are you certain? Certain you want this, certain of your safety?" He tipped her face up, making her look at him. She nodded mutely, losing herself in the silvery depths of his eyes. "I desire you, Cat. I have since nearly the first night we met. One night, I think we can spare, if that is truly your wish."

"Yes, Arien. Yes," she said, barely able to speak.

She kissed him, and as he did so he lifted her into his arms. He carried her to the bed and set her gently down, then lay beside her. He propped himself up on an elbow and gazed down at her tenderly. Hesitant, wanting to please him but unsure, she reached for the laces of her bodice. He caught her hand and pressed it to his lips.

"Slowly, my dear. We have the entire night."

"I've never--" she said, but he stopped her with a kiss.

"I know," he murmured against her mouth.

His kisses quieted the last of her doubts. For a long, dreamlike while, he did no more than kiss her and hold her. His fingers found and traced the rim of her ear, and this time she understood what it meant, how it made her feel. How it made him feel, when she did the same in return, and heard his breath quicken.

Slowly, as the fire burned low, he awakened feelings she had never suspected, a pure, clean passion that filled her like a silver light.

She was shyly curious, eager to learn what pleased him. "Here," he guided. "Like this. And like this."

"And this?"

"Oh, yes, like that!"

Jessa had been wrong. There was no pain, no fear. And Sybil had been wrong. It was more than just the pleasant contact of bodies.

She had never known it could be so wonderful, so powerful, as at last they moved together and became one. Soon all she could do was cling to him, weeping tears of joy for what was, and of sorrow for what would never be.

*   *   *

Life is simple. Death is simple. Living is the difficult part.

The Book of Yor.

The snow in Thanis was much as Cat had described it. The air was damp, not brisk, and did little to invigorate him as he walked along one of the high roads. The drifts were piled on the sides of the road, stained with mud and soot and unmentionable rubbish that the citizens dumped from their windows. In a few places, the snow was clean, and he passed groups of children bundled against the cold, sliding down on planks.

The clouds were very low, so low that the top of Talus Yor's tower was obscured. They were as heavy and dark as Arien's spirits.

In a matter of weeks, he would be standing once more beneath the boughs of the Emerin. His exile, self-imposed though it was, would be broken. He would be home.

Home, and he dared not contact his few friends or Lord and Lady Karadan, who had been as parents to him. Home in secret, cloaked in deception, a thief of the past, a grave-robber, rendering false the decades of mourning the Elyvorrin family had done for their beloved daughter.

Yes, in a matter of weeks, he would be looking once more on Alinora's lovely face, hearing the soft music of her voice, touching the pale silk of her skin.

He remembered the sly whispered rumors that had followed her death. The household physicians could not explain her death, and even speculated that she had been poisoned. Arien himself, who had been known to be suffering odd fits of madness at the time, was not above suspicion. Lord and Lady Karadan had attempted to shield him from the unkind tales, but they could not fully protect him. Was it not in part to escape those accusations that he had first fled the Emerin?

Perhaps he had been guilty after all. Not the youth, who had been shattered by Alinora's death, but the Arien of now, who hoped for her return. Thus was Cat's plan, clever but fiendish, giving substance to those long-ago rumors.

Cat. To think of her was to mingle love and pain. How enthralling she was, how intoxicating in her passion. One night, that which he had promised her, had not been enough. A thousand nights, a lifetime of nights, would not be enough.

He believed now. She was right, she spoke true, the curse had been undone. He was free to love, and love he did. Yet the unquiet specter of Alinora hung over him, pleading for life. To leave her in her tomb would be tantamount to murder.

Cat, he knew, deserved far better. Far better than a man who would enlist her aid to restore his former beloved, and then take his leave of her. His past and his future, both were entwined, and the center of that entwining was Alinora.

They should dwell in the timeless twilight of the elvenwood. They had been betrothed. That was their promised future. She was his first and truest love. Why else had he gone through all of this? He had to bring her back. She belonged by his side.

He gazed eastward, toward the Emerin. Explaining her return would be difficult but not impossible. Her parents would be so relieved and delighted to once more have their daughter with them that they would forgive anything.

He would of course bring her to Thanis first, to give her time to learn of all that had transpired in the past century. And then, when they were once more as close as they had been before cruel misfortune tore them apart, they would go home.

Yes. Home. His life restored, as it was meant to be. Absolved of suspicion in her death, for behold! had he not brought about her return? Was that not worth any price?

Even the price of losing Cat?

*   *   *

Nightfall in the Emerin.

The great poet Elwyndas Maevannen had once written a ballad about it which had gone on to become a classic of elven literature.

The sky was a deep twilight purple overhead, shading to rose and gold in the west. Fluffy clouds caught the colors of sunset. The silver chariot of Livana rode low in the east, nearly full. The brightest stars pierced the sky, bright and fair as diamonds.

The trees were bare of leaves, but were adorned with lacy patterns of ice. Winter flowers turned the ground white, in anticipation of the snow that would soon cover them. The air was cold and crisp.

Arien stood beneath the trees, oblivious to the cold. He was home. After a century, he had again set foot in this forest. The Emerin had changed little in the intervening years. He, however, had changed considerably. He was an outsider now. He could feel it. The trees did not close around him in welcome.

That would pass, he was sure. When he had righted the wrongs that led to his exile, once more would the Emerin take back its lost son.

The horses and Cat waited behind him by the river. The boat they had hired had dropped them off here, far from any docks or towns. They could not risk encountering any elves. Cat would be at best driven out, at worst killed. As for himself, he had no idea what reaction his return might cause.

A few day's ride would take them to the lands of Lord Karadan. Not far from there would be the manor used each festival season by Count Elyvorrin and his family.

Scant days separated him from the end of his quest. Give or take a century, that was.

He held tight to his satchel. It was the same one he'd had since that fateful night when Cat had dropped from a rooftop to save his life. At the time, he thought the spell books in the satchel were the most important things in the world. He knew the items it now held, four elixirs and a scroll, were the truly vital ones.

He waited until the fires of the western sky had darkened. The stars grew bolder, brighter. He had forgotten how beautiful the Emerin was. He breathed deep of the cold night air.

You're afraid to go on, aren't you? Darkfire quietly interrupted his thoughts. The drake was still hiding in his fur-lined sack, though the winter here was much less harsh than that of Hachland and Lenais.

What do you mean? he sent.

We're so close. I'd expect you to ride without stopping to be done with it. Yet you're wasting time. What do you fear more? Failing? Or succeeding?

Of course I am afraid to fail. But why in Livana's name would you think I am afraid to succeed?

Because then Cat will leave us, the drake sent sadly. *I'll miss her. Won't you?*

More than I can say. He looked at Cat. She smiled, but edgily. The Emerin welcomed her even less than himself, and she could clearly sense it. "Shall we ride?" he asked.

"Lead the way."

When they finally made camp, both were quiet, The end of the quest grew ever closer. Even Darkfire was silent. They retired to the tent. Arien was unrolling his blanket when their eyes met. That was all it took. Wordlessly, they reached for each other.

She was too beautiful, too exciting to spend her life alone. There would come a day when another man shared her life. Arien bitterly envied that man, and at the same time cursed himself because he knew it could be him.

*   *   *

In the world that should have been, he should have been inside the manor, with his fair Alinora at his side, celebrating the wedding of her brother. He would never have been crouching in the bushes, watching through a window.

Count Elyvorrin had changed little in the past century. Never a warm man, he seemed only to have grown colder. His wife seemed as charming as ever, but her smiles were touched with sorrow even after all the years.

Alinora's younger brother had matured into a fine, handsome man. The youngest of the Elyvorrin sisters, only a babe in arms in Arien's memory, was now a lovely maiden.

He recognized many elves as they moved about the room. His childhood playmates had become adults. Some of them even had children of their own. Could that be Delian? Delian, with a lady on his arm and a sturdy boy following him? Was that Leranna, once shy, now a ravishing beauty? Or Chrylar, Chrylar who had struggled so with his lessons, wearing the badge of a master wizard? The changes . . . so difficult to accept.

Arien caught his breath as another familiar figure passed the window. It was Lady Karadan, clad in deep maroon. Her hair was pulled back in an elaborate twisted knot.

"They have changed so," he whispered to Cat, who watched the elegant elves with an expression of mixed fear and admiration.

"Well, it has been a century," she replied. "Even for elves, some things had to change."

"That woman is Lady Karadan, who was as a mother to me," he said. He bowed his head sadly. "She is clad in the color of mourning, and she wears her hair in the widow's knot. Lord Karadan, the only father I ever really knew, is dead."

She touched his arm. "Oh, I'm sorry."

"I was not here for her in her time of need. I should have been. My life was here. Now it is lost to me forever."

"Not forever," Cat said, blowing on her hands to warm them. "That's why we're here."

The newlyweds, amid much applause, approached the magnificent cake. Alinora's brother had made a good match. The young lady at his side was lovely, and beaming with the special joy that only a bride possessed.

Arien sighed. He and Alinora would have been married with equal splendor. Perhaps they would have had children. His life, his happiness, had been stolen.

He did have another chance. It was not too late. With Alinora by his side once more, he would find the happiness that cruel fate had denied him.

"Let us delay this no longer," he said. "The time has come."

*   *   *

The woods beyond the manor were quiet. The night was cold enough to discourage even the most foolhardy from going out for a walk. Only such fools as they, driven by their quest.

Arien unrolled the scroll and read it over silently. The spell called for a great deal of energy. He had his powerstone, his *ilgilean*, and prayed it would suffice.

"I'm ready," Cat said.

He took a deep breath and began reading. The words flowed easily from his lips. Keeping the time and date of their destination firmly in mind, he spoke the final incantation.

The spell drained him, leaving him aching with weariness. The air in front of him rippled like the air above a fire. Before his very eyes, an oval hole appeared in thin air, framed by misty glowing hues of all the rainbow.

The trees on the other side of that window were in full leaf, and flowers bloomed along the path. Fog swirled in the opening, where the winter air of this time met the summer night breeze of the past. He could hear night birds trilling sweetly.

"Incredible," Cat breathed.

"A passage through time," Arien said. He could not help but smile. Cat's eyes were bright with excitement. She at least could enjoy the adventure of the moment, and forget the sorrow the outcome would bring to her.

At least it will be warm, Darkfire sent crossly.

"There is no turning back," he said solemnly. "Once we step through, our course is chosen."

She nodded and stepped lightly into the past. Arien followed. The balmy sweetness of the Emerinian summer night washed over him like a rebirth.

I much prefer the summer, Darkfire said, crawling out of the sack, shaking his wings, and taking his customary place on Arien's shoulder. *No drake has ever crossed time before. I shall add Timeskimmer to my name. Darkfire Dragonwing Sharptooth Quickflight--*

The drake broke off, alarmed, as Arien fell to his knees. "Dizzy," he gasped as Cat rushed to his side. "The spell has weakened me more than I thought."

"We'll wait until you're rested," Cat said.

"No, no, we cannot." He clutched urgently at her. "You must begin your spell!"

A distant howl split the night, carried on the rising wind. The cry of the shadow beast. A sound that had haunted Arien's nightmares for a century.

"The beasts!" Cat cried. "They've come for—"

"For you, Cat! They sense that I love you."

She almost laughed. "How I've longed to hear you say those words, Arien, but this is hardly the place or time!" She stroked his cheek, kissed his lips. "Know that I love you too, whatever happens."

Something's coming! Darkfire warned.

Arien struggled to rise, but the world seemed to be spinning around him. Working his magic had never left him in such a state. It had to be something more that left him this way.

The leaves whirred busily in the wind. Cat sprang up, alert, watchful, her hand to the hilt of her sword. "They're here."

A low-slung, hunched form leaped from the undergrowth, its hideousness clearly revealed yet at the same time mercifully concealed by the mystic moonlight.

"Lhasorra dahn fellina bur radan," Cat called in a clear voice. She raised her arms and made a beckoning gesture.

The beast recoiled, baring its fangs in a snarl of loathing and fear. It tilted its muzzle to the sky and howled so that their very bones shivered.

Arien could do nothing but watch, as helpless as he'd been as witness to Alinora's death, as more howls answered the beast, more shadows appeared amid the trees.

Cat waited. The wind grew stronger. Her cloak flapped. Her hair whipped back. She stepped away from Arien though he tried to hold her back, his fingers slipping nervelessly from her sleeve. She sprang lithely onto a flat stone and raised her arms.

"Who calls us?" came a dark, deadly voice.

"I am Cathlin Tahmira Sabledrake, descended from House Tokalsis," she replied. "*Rhuna elsannita fanneros mak enita.*" She gasped in sudden pain as the spell began to drain her energy. He had tried to prepare her for the sensation, but she had not fully understood the price of magic.

The beasts leaped and capered. Cat paled at the sight of them but did not try to flee. They lurched in an intricate circle around her, laughing.

"You will not control us. We will destroy you!" the lead beast roared as it lunged at Cat. Claws and steel flashed as her sword flew by magic to her ready hand and she parried the beast's strike.

All of the beasts writhed and howled, echoing the pained cry of their leader. Two pieces of its claws fell severed to the ground.

"Annifea alestor . . . " She faltered as the pain of casting grew.

Beasts came at her from behind, from the sides, from above. She was surrounded by a bristling ring of fur and claws. The beasts howled again, this time with a note of triumph and hunger.

"Stand away from her!" Arien called, forcing himself to rise.

The lead beast looked at him. "You again! Your love died screaming, as this one shall!"

"Annifea alestor, rhuna verenis!" Cat raised her sword and sliced open her palm. The blood of the Tokalsis line welled forth. It was dimmed by passing generations and mingled with humanity, but still powerful. The beasts drew back, hissing and growling.

"Sornanis rhuna, rhuna fanneros!" She swung her arm in an arc. Their fur smoked where droplets of her blood splashed them. A beast slashed her leg, ripping even through the Silversilk. She fell to one knee on the stone.

"Rassitis droala rhuna elor shahlarri!"

Their howls nearly drowned out her voice.

"Dharsis elen bur . . . "

The beasts swarmed at her, overwhelming her, bearing her down. One drowning, bloody hand rose above the bristling pile of fur and claws.

"Dharsis elen bur tolnias esseton," she said weakly. *"Verenisa, annifea."*

Such a piercing keen arose from the throats of the beasts that the moon itself shivered, as if it would shatter. Beasts writhed and fell, then sank into the earth. Curls of sulphurous smoke and blackened patches of earth marked where they had been.

Arien felt a strange lightening, the lifting of a burden he hadn't known he carried. It was done. It was over. The curse was removed.

The wind had diminished to a steady breeze. The moonlight was clear. Too clear, clear enough to reveal Cat, who lay where she had fallen.

"Cat?" he said hesitantly. He dragged himself to her.

She did not respond. She did not move. The stone and the earth beneath were black with her shed blood. Her eyes were closed, her face peaceful and beautiful.

"Oh, Cat. No. Please, no." He gathered her into his arms.

Her head rolled limply against his shoulder. He could not find a lifebeat, could not feel the stir of her breath.

Praying to Livana as he never had before, he whispered the words of healing. *"Salahin Roas."* He poured his energy into the spell, ready to give his own life force to spare her.

The magic did not want to flow into her. Her spirit had all but fled.

He held her tightly, head bowed. "Cat, Cat, come back to me," he pleaded. "Do not leave me. Do not die."

She breathed then, a ragged gasp. He sobbed aloud in relief and cast the spell again. Beneath his hands, the wounds drew together. The flow of blood ceased.

Sapphire eyes looked up at him. "Arien. Did I . . ."

"It is over," he said. "They are gone forever."

She smiled, raising one trembling hand to twine her fingers in his hair. "Told you so."

At that moment, he desired her more than ever. This madness had all begun when he had made love to Alinora in a wooded glade. It would seem so right to end it by making love to Cat. Here, now.

He could not resist. He lowered his head and kissed her. She pressed against him, returning his kiss with a passion made stronger by her brush with death. He started to lower her to the ground.

Her hiss of pain as her injured leg reached the earth brought him to his senses.

He drew back and looked down at her. He could see the stars reflected in her eyes, the love and longing shining within them. Shame filled him. He was not worthy of her.

"Cat, dear Cat, if this was a tale such as the bards might tell, now would be the time for us. Alas that it is not."

"It's Alinora," she said. "Letting her stay dead would be like killing her a second time. I know, Arien. I know"

To see the future, to know one's own fate, these are not things to be wished even upon an enemy.

The Book of Yor.

"The house is just ahead," Cat reported, creeping up on them so stealthily that not even Darkfire heard her until she was at Arien's side. Except for a slight limp, and a lingering pallor, she showed no sign of her recent ordeal. "Where would they be keeping her?"

"Lying in state in the grand hall. The same room in which we witnessed her brother's wedding, though surely not adorned so gaily. There will be roses, the flower of death, red for mourning and white for her youth and innocence." He stumbled and fell. Cat may have recovered, but he felt his energies steadily draining away.

"Arien! What is the matter? Shouldn't you have regained your strength by now?"

"It is not that," he said shakily. "Rather, I think, it is that I am alive in two places at once. My younger self lies in his delirium some distance away, and here am I."

"We must get you out of here!"

"Not yet," he said. "First . . . Alinora."

She nodded and moved wraithlike to the side of the house. All was dark and quiet within. Arien followed, pausing to rest himself against the wall.

Cat had taken a thin piece of metal and slid it between the windowpanes, and was patiently jiggling it against the latch. Arien despaired of her ever managing, but the latch lifted and she pulled one side of the window open.

She boosted herself lightly through, then leaned out. "You're in no state to do this. Give me the elixirs, I'll go alone."

"No. I must go." He let her help him, indeed, let her nearly haul him through the window, for his limbs did not want to function properly. He sank to the cool marble tiles, breathing deep the scent of roses.

"Over there." Cat edged toward an alcove, where a single candle burned.

She drew up and raised a warning hand. "She's not alone," she hissed.

In truth, she was not, but as Arien peered around the corner, he could at first see nothing but the dais which held the slender rosecloth-wrapped body. Petals adorned her, a single red bloom rested upon the curve of her bosom. She was completely concealed, not so much as a strand of hair or glimpse of skin revealed, yet he knew her.

Beside her was seated a man, his brow pressed to the dais beside the body, his hand resting upon one wrapped shoulder. He moved not, save for slow, even breaths. By his pale golden hair and the signet upon his finger, Arien knew him.

"Her father, Count Elyvorrin," he whispered to Cat. "Of all his children, he doted most upon Alinora. A stern and severe man, reserved even in joy. I can well understand that he should show his grief only by this lonely vigil."

Cat drew her dagger. "I can render him senseless—"

"No!"

"Arien, we cannot do this under his very nose!"

"Let me enspell him to sleep," he suggested. "He'll not then awaken until morning."

"You're too weak!"

"If you strike him, he may awaken and catch us here. Permit me to try." He stepped forward. "*Dhalas Noran.*" The energy flowed from him, sending the count into a deeper sleep.

Arien himself would have collapsed as well, had Cat not moved quickly to support him. She led him to a chair and bid Darkfire watch over him, then opened his satchel.

He tried to protest, tried to argue, but could not find the strength. It was all he could do to lift his head and watch as Cat ever-so-carefully moved the count's hand away and began to undo the wrappings which shrouded Alinora's face.

Show me, Arien thought to Darkfire. *Show me through Cat's eyes.*

He closed his own eyes and opened his mind to Darkfire's, then found himself looking down on Alinora as a last band of rosecloth was peeled away. For the first time in a century, he looked upon the face of his beloved, and knew that memory had been false in recalling the true splendor of her beauty.

In death, she was even more pale, her skin a translucent pearl. Diamond-bright hair framed her delicate features, her shapely white ears. Her palest pink lips were parted, as if at any moment she might speak. Her golden lashes lay softly upon her fair cheeks, keeping from him the yearned-for sight of her leaf-green eyes.

Cat stood for a long moment, staring down. *So beautiful,* she thought, and through Darkfire Arien heard. *Small wonder he still loves her so.*

She uncorked the priceless elixir of life and tipped it to Alinora's lips. The world held its breath, and Arien along with it.

Alinora's throat moved, swallowing the elixir. She stirred, her eyelids fluttered. She gazed unseeingly up at Cat and frowned faintly.

"Who are you?" she sighed.

"A friend," Cat replied, sadness thick in her voice.

Arien stood, his weakness unimportant. He seemed almost to float to the dais, and with his own sight now looked upon his beloved. Her eyes shifted to meet his, and her frown became a hesitant smile.

"Arien? Is it you?"

"It is." He wonderingly touched her cheek.

She uttered a ghost of a giggle. "You look so *old!*" Then, as she tried to move, her feathery brows knit in puzzlement. "My arms . . ."

"Arien, we haven't time," Cat said urgently.

He glanced at her, but could never remember what she looked like in that instant. Alinora's bright star had eclipsed Cat's dark one.

"Rest but a while more, my love," he told Alinora. "Soon I will be with you again."

Cat held another elixir to the elfmaid's mouth, but this time Alinora's eyes fell clearly on her. "What . . . what *are* you?" She drew away as well she could, for even in her sheltered life she would have heard the rumors and frightening tales.

"Mayhap you'd better." Cat swiftly passed the elixir to Arien and retreated, out of Alinora's sight.

He nodded. "Drink this, my fair one, and rest."

She accepted it, wrinkled her nose. "It tastes . . ." and exhaled in a sigh as her eyes once more drifted closed.

"It worked," Cat said.

"How can I ever repay you, Cat?" Arien stroked the fine silk of Alinora's hair. "You've given me back my life! Your plan, so simple, so perfect!"

"You yourself told me that the elves knew little of alchemy, especially in this time. They'll have no way of knowing she isn't dead."

"And yet, to consign her to her tomb, while she yet lives! How can we do such?"

"We must, Arien. There is no other way. She'll sleep, sleep timelessly, until we return for her."

"To cover this fair face again with rosecloth . . ." he bent and kissed Alinora's cool lips, then drew a deep breath. "Yet it must be. It must be."

"I'll do it, if you'd rather," Cat offered.

He shook his head somberly. "Had I been her husband, such would have been my unhappy task. I will do so now, as a promise that they will be again undone."

His hands trembled, but he slowly replaced the bindings. When he could no longer see her, it was easier to finish, and soon all was as it had been. Count Elyvorrin slept on, unaware that his cherished daughter did the same.

"It seems so cruel to leave him to mourn her," Arien mused. "Never were he and I close, but now, joined in our loss, I know him well." He tenderly replaced the count's hand on Alinora's shoulder. "Forgive me, my lord."

*   *   *

"I cannot go on, Cat," Arien said, his voice little more than breath shaped into words. "Even had I the strength to stand, I cannot open the portal. I must rest, must sleep!" He held out his hands, palms down, and observed how they shook. "To cast any further spell would put us all at risk!"

He speaks true, Cat. Look how pale he is, how shadowed his eyes, Darkfire sent privately to her.

Cat noted that even the drake looked unwell, his scales faded and dull. "All right, but we must at least get away from this house. If we're found here, Arien—" the rest went unheard as he lost consciousness.

Darkfire chuffed a small wisp of smoke and went limp, his little body draped over Arien's chest.

"Arien!" Cat said, loudly as she dared. "Oh, no!"

An elfkin, on her own in the Emerin? She liked a challenge, but this was a bit much! And it wasn't just herself she had to take care of. Arien and Darkfire needed her.

"What madness and stupidity you inspire me to, my love," she murmured, touching his brow. "When our friends hear to what lengths I've gone to help you leave me for another, I'll never hear the end of their scolding."

She was not able to lift him. But, as she heard to her horror elven voices drawing near, she dragged him swift as she could behind a tapestry and concealed him.

Candle flame etched a thin line under one of the doors into the grand hall. Cat peeked out, and saw Darkfire, who had fallen from Arien as she moved him. He was sprawled in the middle of the floor, black against white marble, impossible to miss.

She ran. Her soft-soled boots were silent, but even as she scooped up the fallen drake, she heard steps just outside the door.

Confound these elves, who so loved wide, airy spaces! With no other choice, she pulled a small glass vial from her belt and yanked out the cork with her teeth. As the latch clicked and the door began to open, the line of light widening into a bar, she poured the elixir into her mouth.

It tasted of rainwater and woodsmoke, and a sensation like a night breeze tingled her skin.

Two elves stood in the doorway.

"I should not be doing this, Arien," one of them said.

Arien!

She needn't fear her breathing or pounding heart would give her away, for it seemed both had stopped. He looked so young! Though still, she knew, at least thrice her age, he was barely more than a youth as the elves reckoned things.

"I must see her, Celin, I must," this Arien of the past pleaded. "My lady Karadan thinks me too ill yet to attend the funeral, but oh! I cannot let her go to her tomb without one last farewell!"

Celin, the other elf, was even younger, still a child. Cat realized with a start that his was the wedding they'd witnessed, some hundred years hence, before opening the portal and stepping through.

They did not see her. The elixir rendered her invisible, so that their eyes passed over her though she stood right in front of them. Even Darkfire, cradled to her chest, went unseen.

Arien, the young Arien, passed within arm's reach of her and stopped mere inches from the tapestry where his older self lay hidden. What would he do if he chanced to look? But small risk of that, Cat saw, for his sight was fixed upon the rosecloth-wrapped body.

"My father!" Celin gasped, the candle he held wavering so that a dollop of wax splattered upon Cat's boot. She edged away lest he stumble into her. "If he wakens, and finds us here—!"

"A moment only," the young Arien begged. "Let me but look upon her one last time!" Without waiting for an answer, he moved dreamlike to the dais and began turning back the wrappings, which his older self had only moments ago replaced.

"Poor sister, bright beauty," Celin murmured. "How you will be missed!"

As Alinora was once more revealed, the young Arien uttered a harsh, agonized cry. He gathered her body into his arms and wept. Her father's hand fell away but the spell did not break, so the older man slept on undisturbed.

Tears welled in Cat's own eyes, witnessing his anguish. She ached to go to him, to tell him that Alinora but lay under an enchantment and would someday be restored, that the beasts which had taken her from him had been driven back into the shadows from whence they'd come. Anything to bring him some comfort.

She could not! Just as she had not permitted Arien to ease the count's grief, so could she not ease his. He must go on believing her to be dead, else it might undo all that they had done, undo everything. He would not grow into the Arien she knew, and the events of a century might be altered.

"Arien!" Celin said, setting aside the candle and trying to gently wrest Alinora from his grasp. "She is gone, friend. Let her be at peace."

"Gone," he echoed painfully. "Gone." He laid her body down and smoothed the mussed tresses. "I cannot believe it to be true. How lifelike she looks, Celin! As if she but sleeps, and might at any moment breathe, or stir!"

What a terrible thing, to stand silent and leave him to suffer, not only now but for the next entire century! Yet it had to be, if any of this was to be!

The young Arien turned away from Alinora and buried his face in his hands. "I cannot cover her, Celin! Ah! The sickness! I feel as if I might—"

As he fell, unconscious, his hand caught the tapestry and pulled it down.

Celin froze in shock at the sight that he now beheld. His gaze switched rapidly from one to the other, the youth and the man. His eyes grew ever wider, his mouth opened in what would have been a scream to rouse the household and indeed the entire estate.

"Celin," Cat whispered, right in his ear.

He exhaled in a terrified gust and whirled, seeking and not finding the source of the voice.

"There is sorcery at work here," Cat continued, wishing she'd just smote him on the head the instant he'd seen. "Question it not, speak of it not."

"Livana?" he asked tremulously.

Cat grimaced. She did not want to impersonate a goddess, and could only imagine the furor that would arise in the cosmos if a lowly elfkin presumed to speak in the name of the elven lady of magic and moonlight. Still, she had precious little choice.

"I give you a sign." Her fingers fished dexterously into one of her belt pouches, and withdrew a shining coin, aglow with magical light. Arien's spell, so much more convenient than troubling with torches or flint and steel.

She flicked the glowing coin high overhead. As it left her hand, it left also the effect of the elixir, spinning and filling the room with pale radiance. It arched over her and came down. She leapt to catch it. Her hand closed around it and the light was engulfed once more by invisibility.

"I will speak of it to no one," Celin swore, eyes wide. "But . . . pray, tell me, what does it mean?"

"It means only this, Celin. Hope."

As he mulled over what she'd said, she silently asked Livana's forgiveness, and then really did smite him on the head.

*   *   *

Darkfire made a gargley keening sound, which Cat took to be a pained groan, as the drake's jewellike eyes reluctantly opened. He peered up at her, then swiveled his long neck to take in the room.

Bodies everywhere, he sent foggily. *Looks like the last act of an Elwyndas tragedy.*

"Yes, but none of them are dead," she said lightly. "Gather your wits, Darkfire, because we must go before someone else comes wandering in, and I'll need your help. We have to put this room to rights. You gather the flowers—" she gestured to the spill of roses that Young Arien had swept from the dais as he fell "—and I'll try my hand at the tapestry."

Darkfire bobbed his head agreeably, then got a better look at the newcomer elves. His expression remarkably mirrored Celin's.

"I know," Cat said. "This has turned out to be much more complicated than I planned. Still, we've no other choice."

Working swiftly, they restored the room to how it had looked before they came in, with the exception of the two younger elves. Cat didn't want to risk moving either of them, for fear she might accidentally rouse one and be right back where she started, so she left them where they lay.

Her Arien . . . rather, the elder Arien, she couldn't really very well call him hers because he never truly had been . . . she was able to get an arm and shoulder under long enough to carefully dump him out the window onto the velvety grass surrounding the Elyvorrin manor.

"That'll have to do," Cat said when the tapestry hung as straight as she could make it and Darkfire had picked up all the scattered blooms and petals he could find. "Let's go."

She closed the window behind him and used a Montennor lodestone to jiggle the latch into falling again. An old trick of her da's, though sometimes earning of ridicule from her fellow Nightsiders. Why bother to re-lock the lock? they'd sneer. She considered it a matter more of politeness than anything else.

Arien mumbled something as she tried to lift him again. She got him more or less to his feet and stumbled along, supporting his weight so that they lurched like a pair of drunken soldiers. As she'd suspected, the further they got from the house and his younger self, the more he came around. Until at last, as they reached a secluded hollow, he managed to stand on his own and rub wearily at his temples.

"Cat?" he asked faintly.

"Here. I'm here." She held his arm to steady him.

"Where? I cannot see you!"

"Oh! The invisibility!" She chuckled, then had a worrisome thought. "I wonder how long it lasts! How do you feel?"

"As if I'd been put in a barrel and rolled down Spiral Street from the First Ring clear to the river docks," he replied.

"Yes, that's about how you look," she said with a smile. "Arien, it's done. Our work here is done. We can return now to our own time."

"And Alinora?"

"She sleeps. She waits. Just a short while more, Arien, I promise."

"A short while for us, a century for her. I pray her dreams be sweet!" He unrolled the scroll and began the incantation that would open a portal to their own era.

*   *   *

Once again, Cat withdrew her lockpicks. This time, she did it in the winter's chill, knee-deep in the soft snow that blanketed the graveyard. All around her were skeletal trees, their boughs clad in glittering ice.

Before her was the door to the Elyvorrin tomb, twice her height, with a keyhole so big she could almost have reached her very hand within to turn the tumblers. She blew on her fingers to warm them and went to work.

This time, she ran little risk of being interrupted. In the wake of Celin's wedding, the entire household had gone to the court of the Elvenking. She and Arien had watched them depart, fine white horses, sleighs, a stream of merry elves in their best furs and finery. Chief among them had been the newlyweds, who both wore garlands of winter flowers. Minstrels joined the procession, their music light and joyous.

Arien stood beside her, his satchel, where Darkfire had hastily retreated and refused to budge until they were once again someplace warm, slung over his shoulder, and a lush fur wrap in his hands.

"Are you sure you don't want to awaken her here?" Cat asked again.

He nodded. "She shall need time to acquaint herself with all that has happened. I would not wish to plunge her suddenly into the midst of her family, not so soon. As we haven't the proper traveling clothes for her, nor is she so hardy as to endure such a lengthy voyage, it will be kinder for her to let her sleep until we have come to Thanis. There, I shall awaken her."

Cat did her best to hide her relief. She hadn't been looking forward to spending a weeks-long journey in the company of both of them, not when it would surely pierce her heart like an arrow every time their eyes fell upon each other. Nor could she leave them and strike out alone, for without Arien as a guide to the paths of the Emerin, she would swiftly become lost, or blunder into other elves.

She unlocked the tomb and opened the door, scraping a wedge and a drift into the snow. Within, all was dark and even colder than the winter's day. Glowing coin held high, she stepped into the house of the elven dead, her nose tickling with the scent of dried roses.

"Here," Arien said solemnly, resting his hand atop a casket of white aspen inlaid with traceries of silver. He lifted the lid. "Here she lies. No more shall these wrappings give her the semblance of death."

He unwound the rosecloth. Cat suffered a terrible moment when she feared the elixir hadn't worked, that the face revealed would be as withered and ghastly as the *lichma'rhun* of Selbon's crypt. But her fears were groundless, for Alinora's face came into view as fair as ever.

Beneath the wrappings, Alinora was clad in a simple gown of purest linen, the hem and cuffs embroidered with alternating red and white roses, her slim waist girdled with a rose-red sash. Around her neck was a golden chain, and a pendant with the crest of her household picked out in bright diamonds.

Arien tenderly lifted her from the casket. He crossed the threshold of the tomb and emerged into the frosty light, a belated groom with his bride in his arms.

Cat lingered in the darkness, staring down into the casket that now was as empty as her heart itself seemed. For love and friendship, she had given him the one thing he held most dear, and in so doing lost her own love.

She reached in and crumbled a rose petal slowly between her fingers. The dust sifted down onto the heap of discarded wrappings. "Love him well, Alinora," she whispered. "Give him the happiness he's been so long denied."

With that, she replaced the lid and left the tomb, drawing the heavy door closed behind her.

Only in tales does anyone live happily ever after.

The Book of Yor.

Brother Alphonse disarmed the boy with a single motion and threw him down. The other youths, gathered around and shivering in the chill morning air, winced in sympathetic pain as their classmate crashed to the canvas mat.

"That's why you never stand with your feet like that. This is a fighter's stance," he growled, demonstrating. "Better balance, more leverage and room to swing."

A sturdy little pony pulled an equally sturdy little wagon through the gates and the orckin looked up, then grinned.

The nearest students groaned. When Brother Alphonse grinned, it usually meant that someone was going to be taught a lesson. A particularly painful lesson. This time, though, they were spared.

"Pair up and square off," Alphonse ordered. "Hachlanian hand combat. If I see any of you standing wrong, someone will be on the way to the healers with a broken nose." With a final threatening glare, he stomped across the courtyard to the wagon.

"Ho, Cat!"

"Ho, Alphonse!" She was wearing warm traveling clothes, high boots, and a jaunty cap with a blue feather. Her dark curls tumbled to her shoulders. He'd never seen her looking prettier, though there was a shadow of sadness in her deep eyes that was new and unfamiliar.

He swept her up in his burly arms and swung her around. "What did you do to your hair?"

"Nothing. I just haven't cut it all winter. What did you do to yours?"

"Aw, all the brethren wear it this way their first year." He set her down and rubbed self-consciously at his scalp.

"Is that why they always wear helmets?" she teased.

"Are you making fun of me, little girl?" He loomed over her, drawing his eyebrows together in a menacing scowl.

"What if I am?" She stood her ground, jutting her chin at him defiantly. "I can still outrun you, big fellow."

He lunged at her with a mock snarl. She dodged neatly and faked a kick. He blocked it with one arm and seized her boot.

"Now, stop it. I don't want to make an example of you in front of my class."

"You just mean you don't want them to see you lose to a woman." She twisted out of his grip.

"For that, maybe I ought to make an example of you," Alphonse said. He saw some other priests looking her over, and glowered at them. He draped an arm over her slim shoulders and steered her protectively to an alcove away from the main courtyard. "Wasn't sure when I'd see you again. How was Hachland?"

She tucked the fur collar of her cloak tighter against her neck and looked at the sky. "It's an interesting land. The marketplaces, the merchants . . . a good thief could live quite well there. Even better was Lenais, where my mother was from. Small wonder she never seemed ashamed of my da or me. Elfkin are common there, common and accepted."

"Did you find what you were looking for?" he asked.

"Yes," she said after a lengthy pause. "Well, yes and no."

"Why so sad, then? No treasures?"

"None that can be counted, spent, or hoarded. Alphonse, I've come to say goodbye. I'm leaving again. Leaving Thanis. For good."

A low growl rumbled through his chest. "Who's been giving you trouble? Not the Nightsiders, is it? Tell Alphonse, and he'll take care of it." He smacked his fist solidly into his palm.

"It's nothing like that." She sighed, then shook her head briskly as if to shake away unhappy thoughts, and smiled so that her beautiful eyes shone like jewels. "I think I know where to find my da! One-Eye heard from a Tradersport thief that the Duke of Gamelin recently granted a land holding to a Lord Sabledrake." She laughed. "Can you imagine, my da as a nobleman? I'm going to Gamelin, to find out for myself."

"There's more to it than that," Alphonse said shrewdly. "I know you too well, little girl. What about Arien?" He swallowed thickly. "I rather had the notion that you . . . well, fell for him."

She nodded and looked away, until he put one big finger under her chin and made her meet his gaze.

"He's in love with someone else," she admitted. "The quest we were on was to reunite them. Alinora . . . she's the most beautiful woman I've ever seen. Everything the elves admire is alive in her. It's no wonder that Arien's been in love with her for a hundred years. She's tall, willowy, fair, highborn . . . everything."

"What was keeping them apart?" he asked, letting his hands fall to his sides and hoping she wouldn't see the way they wanted to clench into fists, or close around some scrawny elven neck. Cat was hurting, and as always his first instinct was to find the cause and beat the stuffing out of it. He fought down those impulses and forced himself to listen as she began haltingly to speak.

As Cat spoke, unraveling a tale of curses and death and resurrection, his anger grew but was coupled with a nearly overpowering sense of awe. In his father's clan, life had been very short and often ended suddenly.   Orcs lived for the moment, never thinking ahead farther than a day or so, never wasting the present to dwell on the past. His human blood had made him different from the rest of the clan, but even he could barely grasp the concept of elven time. Arien had sustained a lost love for a century, carrying a weight of grief heavier than dwarf-iron. No brief love could rival that, not even Cat's.

"We brought her back to Thanis," Cat continued. "Sleeping, like an enchanted princess. Arien wanted to have everything perfect for her. He even moved out of that tiny boardinghouse and bought a place here in town. The Marshall House, do you know it?"

"On the third ring, the one that used to belong to the Highlord's wife's family."

She nodded. "When he woke her from her sleep, he wanted her to meet me. I don't know what he was thinking. We snuck through the Emerin like thieves, hiding from elves because of how they might react to me, yet he insisted on introducing me to Alinora as if expecting her to thank me for helping save her."

"She scream?"

"And then began to cry, and then fainted." Cat kicked a stone and watched it skitter across the courtyard. "She cannot stand the sight of me, and it destroys Arien. Just one more reason for me to take my leave."

"Doesn't he know how you feel? Doesn't he care?"

"Of course he knows. And he cares for me too, but no one could ever replace Alinora in his heart. If you saw her, you'd understand."

"There's more to a person than looks," he grumbled, then forced a laugh. "Leastways, I hope there is, or with my face, I'm doomed. But, for someone as smart as that point-ears is, he's a fool."

"Arien is not a fool!" she flared.

"And you keep defending him?" He patted her shoulder. "Little girl, anyone who would choose someone else over you doesn't keep all his arrows in the same quiver. I ought to give him a good pounding, that's what."

"Alphonse! I knew the risks, I knew what would happen. Getting mad at Arien shan't help."

"Well, it'll make me feel better," he muttered.

"It would make me feel worse. Let it go, Alphonse." She laughed softly. "Besides, he's already got Darkfire angry at him. It seems that Alinora doesn't much care for drakes. She screamed nearly as loud as she did when she saw me!"

He stretched, feeling his tunic strain across his back and chest. He looked around the courtyard that had become the first real home he'd known since leaving the rugged hills where his father's clan lived. He'd found acceptance here, made friends, earned respect that was undimmed by his orckin blood. He was happy here. He knew that he could be happy here for a long time.

"I'm going to go to Tradersport with you," he declared.

"You're what?" she asked, staring at him incredulously.

"You heard me. The road is dangerous for one person alone."

"I don't need a nanny, Alphonse. I'm trained with a sword, remember?"

"Two is safer than one for traveling. Besides, your father owes me a drink. I beat him at arm-wrestling once. The loser was supposed to buy. He didn't have any money at the time."

"You're going to ride all the way to Tradersport for a drink?"

"Well, a good drink. Sounds like he ought to be able to afford the best, being a lord and all."

"You're impossible," she said, throwing her hands in the air. She waved at the wagon. "I have one, count it, one wagon. It's barely big enough for me."

"I've got a tent, and my horse Bugstomper. With that pony, you'll be moving so slow I could hobble on my knees and still keep up."

"Alphonse—"

"No arguments, Cat. I go with you or I follow along behind. Your choice."

*   *   *

You're really going to let her go, Darkfire sent accusingly.
What choice do I have? I cannot make her stay. I have no claim on her.
You could have had one.

Arien did not answer. He stood on the wall, the wind rippling his hair and cloak, watching the wagon and the warhorse cross the bridge.

Will we ever see her again?
I do not know. Perhaps, someday . . .

"Arien, what are you doing up there?" Alinora's voice drifted up to him. He turned and looked down.

The wall on which he stood was the edge of the Third Ring, and formed the back border of the garden behind his new house. It was a modest manor, which had once belonged to the king's marshall back in the days when there had been kings in Thanis. She who had once been Highlady of Thanis had been born within these walls. The house had a feeling of history that appealed to Arien, while being young enough to seem new.

The previous owners had obviously spent a lot of time tending the garden. Different kinds of flowers shared the same beds. Willows swept their long branches along the ground. They formed a fitting backdrop for the beautiful elfmaid clutching a heavy woolen cloak around her slender body.

"Admiring our view," he replied.

"You will fall," she protested, alarmed.

He glanced over his shoulder. The wagon was on the road now, out of the city, heading south, growing smaller. His sharp eyes glimpsed a slim figure on the seat, clad in blue and grey. The sun glinted off the shield of the massive warrior riding alongside.

You never thought you'd be jealous of Alphonse, did you?

I am not jealous.

"Please come down from there. You are frightening me."

The Queen is calling, Darkfire sent sarcastically.

Stop it. She is my beloved, oh familiar mine, and I will not have you antagonizing her. You must learn to accept that.

She doesn't call you a lizard. Lizard! I am a drake. Not a lizard, and not a runt wyvern! Cat never called me that. Cat liked me.

"A moment, rose of my heart," he said to Alinora, taking a last look at the distant wagon. Was it just a trick of the light, the wishful thinking of his wistful eyes, or did Cat turn back and raise one hand in a wave?

"Shalis," he murmured, and stepped off the wall. Unbidden, the memory of Cat falling from the stone skull came to mind. How he had caught her, held her to him. That, he thought, was the moment his feelings had crossed that invisible point between friendship and love.

Alinora gasped in dismay and ran toward him as he floated to the ground, gently as a leaf. There was no excitement or wonder in her gaze, only alarm and worry.

As he took her hands to reassure Alinora of his health, even as he led her into the house that they would share, though their rooms would out of propriety remain separate until she had grown accustomed to her new life, Darkfire's question haunted him.

Would they ever see Cat again?

*   *   *

Solarrin the Great, Archmage of the Universe, leaned back and drank deeply from a golden goblet, swilling the wine so that it ran down his face and splashed onto his robes.

The leather chair with its brass fittings had dwarfed Selbon, and would once have made Solarrin himself look like a child. A fat, crippled, ugly child.

Now, the chair was his favorite because it was the only one in the study that could support his huge body. Even so, it creaked in protest as he shifted his wide shoulders.

Once, he could not drink spirits. The smooth liquid fire of Selbon's private cellars would have gone another age untasted if he had stayed as he once was. The merest sip would have burned his throat, sent him into spasms of coughing that would have wracked his tortured frame. If he pressed on, he would have fallen quickly into a drunken stupor, possibly choking on his own vomit as he writhed and gagged.

Not now, however. Now, he could drink the entire cask without becoming more than pleasantly warm. Now, he could eat instead of surviving on that foul-tasting elixir.

Could he eat? Like the mightiest warrior in the grandest hall! Meat that dripped with juices and tore between his teeth like the flesh of an enemy! Whole loaves of bread, soaked in butter and honey! Not for him were the platters of thinly sliced beef in strange sauces, or the fruits carved into decorative shapes. He left such whimsy to Donnell.

He threw back his head and laughed, the thunder of his mirth rolling across the table. His horns dug deep scratches in the back of the chair.

Donnell, who was smarter than he looked and therefore not to be trusted, laughed with him. The elf bore little resemblance to the filthy wretch Solarrin had pulled from the dungeon. Donnell cleaned up well, though why he affected that idiotic moustache was beyond

Solarrin completely. Perhaps he was proud of his accomplishment, since most elves were beardless and as smooth-skinned as a woman.

It irritated Solarrin. Someday, he knew, it would become too much to bear, and he would rip it from the elf's lip.

His guest also chuckled, albeit uncomfortably. His gaze kept shifting to Donnell, as if he believed the elf to be in command.

Solarrin bit off his laughter and slammed a fist on the table, making the dishes dance and clatter. "What are you laughing at?" he roared at Donnell.

The thin elf twitched in surprise, swallowing his laughter. The guest gulped, not so much as a giggle emerging from a throat gone tight with fear.

Donnell raised both hands, the natural one and the enchanted silver one that replaced the one he'd lost years ago. Selbon's workroom had contained more interesting magical and alchemical advancements than just the black *Soulshade* powder, and Donnell wasn't too stuffed with snobbish elven pride to be above a little experimenting.

"My mistake," Donnell said in the slick, oiled tones that Solarrin hated so much. "I thought someone said something funny."

Solarrin brought his brows together, which he knew contorted his whole face into something more monstrous and fierce than normal. "When I say something funny, *then* I will expect you to laugh. If you laugh when I do, for no other reason than that, you may find that I was laughing at the thought of your slow disembowelment."

Donnell paled and his eyes widened slightly, but otherwise he appeared unaffected. "Of course, masterful one."

He did not sound sincere enough. Solarrin decided to press the point home. "I advise you to never let the memory of the dungeon slip far from your mind. Enjoy this fine fare while you can, but always remember this: all that you have, you have because I allow it. If you provoke me, I shall twist that new hand from your arm and cast you into the dungeon, where the rats will feed on your flowing blood."

The elf was trembling now. Good. The guest was sitting as if paralyzed, his hand bearing a goblet frozen midway between table and mouth. Even better. Let him learn that Solarrin was not someone to be trifled with.

"And do not think that death will be the end of your torment," he said in a low tone that positively throbbed with menace.

His old body had never been able to give forth such sound. Weak lungs had required him to interrupt flowing evil speeches to gasp for breath. Treacherous, wobbly legs had made him grab for support instead of standing sinister and firm. A weak heart had jittered wildly whenever he cast a spell.

Ah, but look at him now! He wondered why he hadn't done this years ago. If not Bostitch, someone else. The world was full of brawny, yet foolish, swordsmen. He could live forever. He would live forever.

Donnell bowed his head, broken, betrayed by his fear. So, the skinny fool still dreaded the dungeon? Excellent. Selbon may have been an overconfident dolt, but he had done some things right.

"I hear, Archmage," the elf whispered.

The guest stared at Solarrin, obviously consumed with terror and doubtless regretting his ignorant bravery in coming to the castle. Solarrin decided to let him suffer a while longer.

*   *   *

"Mmm. Rayke, that's wonderful," Sybil purred. "More, please."

With a pleased, proud smile, he served her another piece of apple cobbler. She took a bite and closed her eyes in delight.

"I never knew you could cook," she murmured, licking cream from her full lips. "I thought you just wanted to own an inn so you could drink like a sailor all day and attract other mercenary lowlife like yourself.".

"Well, aye, that's part of it," he admitted. "But if I can cook this well, won't I also attract beautiful love-priestesses like yourself? By the way, have I shown you what I've done with my room?"

"Why, no. I don't think you have," she lied, batting her eyes.

An hour later, when he was lying across the bed convinced he would never move again, Sybil bounced out of bed and went to the window. Heedless of her nakedness, she flung wide the shutters. The cold air swept across Rayke's skin and gave him the strength to move. He dragged the blankets over himself.

"What are you doing?" he cried.

"Wondering where Cat is by now," she said, not seeming to mind the snowflakes that swirled through the open window and landed on her rosy skin. "I'm going to miss her."

"Miss teasing her, you mean."

"That, too. She did turn *so* red. Not anymore, though. Not nearly as much. I knew Arien would be good for her. I'd wager he was very good. Very, very good."

"You don't think that those two . . ." he began skeptically.

"I don't think so. I know so. Cat told me herself. Well, she wouldn't say so out loud, but I could tell. I knew it would happen, though. Talopea can't resist a challenge."

"Close the blasted shutters, would you?"

"Cold?" she inquired sweetly.

"Freezing."

She closed and latched the shutters. "I'll warm you up."

"Good luck, lady. I'm exhausted."

Her lips curved in a slow, sensual smile. "That's what *you* think. I'm a priestess of Talopea, remember? Let me show you . . ."

*   *   *

Cat couldn't suppress the familiar tingle of excitement as she crossed the border of her known world and entered a land of unknown adventures.

She'd been through the Scattered Hills, east to the Emerin, and west deep into Hachland and north to Lenais. Now she was headed south, into new lands to explore. Tradersport, city of the tall-masted ships. Tradersport by the sea. Fear mingled with her excitement. What would she do, she wondered, when she was faced with the sight of the vast ocean?

Tradersport, where her father lived. She believed in her heart that what One-Eye had heard was true. Windclyffe Manor was her destination, where Lord Sabledrake lived by the grace and reward of the duke.

Lord Sabledrake and his wife, One-Eye had said. Was it Miralina? Would she meet that lady and look into eyes as blue as her own? What had happened to them? Why had they failed to find their daughter? Would Cat find acceptance and family, or two strangers?

She missed Arien more with each mile that rolled away behind her. She missed Darkfire's sending, and the gentle echo of Arien's thoughts. She missed the drake's comic antics. She missed the way Arien looked at her, the way he touched her. She felt alone without them, alone in a way she'd never felt before.

A jarring, discordant sound broke her thoughts.

"Ooooh, hear the song of the red-bearded man, how bloody and torn from the castle he ran, followed by monsters of all different kinds—"

Cat winced. Birds scattered in scolding masses. Alphonse, lost in the joy of his orc music, kept torturing his lute and belting out his ballad of Rayke's escape. The driver of a passing wagon searched for something to throw while his children covered their ears and gaped in disbelief at the massive armored rider.

She no longer felt alone, no matter how much she might have suddenly wished to be.

*   *   *

Solarrin cracked the bone in his powerful jaws and slurped the marrow out. His guest watched in polite horror. Donnell, still wisely subdued, drained his glass.

"Clear the table," Solarrin commanded.

The skeletal servants moved forward and gathered up the dishes. Solarrin waited until they had gone, then waited a while longer.

The guest fidgeted and grew increasingly nervous as the sand slipped from the hourglass. Solarrin was pleased. It was good that this man feared him. Fear was a more useful tool than even the wheel or the lever.

"I have considered your proposal," he intoned, making sure his words were slow and even.

"And what do you think?" the man asked. Solarrin noted that his voice shook, though the man struggled to appear calm.

"Elves," he murmured thoughtfully, rolling the word around his mouth and watching his guest for a reaction. "I have no objections to allowing the elves to work for us."

He was not disappointed. The man started to say something indignant, thought the better of it, and fell silent. Donnell recovered sufficiently to curl a lip in appreciation of his master's wit.

"The elves would not exactly be working for us—" the man began hesitantly, unwilling to meet his host's stern gaze.

Solarrin thumped his goblet on the table. The heavy gold crumpled in his fist. "I cannot believe you have the nerve to come here suggesting that I serve as an underling to those scatter-minded pointy-eared dolts! I am Solarrin, Archmage of the Universe!" The last words were a barely-contained roar. "I will not be an elvish pawn, as you so obviously are!"

Aha. He had touched a sore spot. The man reacted as if burned.

"I am no pawn!" he snapped. "The plan is mine. I seek only their support, as I seek yours." He suddenly whitened, no doubt expecting to die.

Solarrin laughed again. This time, Donnell waited for a permissive nod before joining in.

"So, the dog has teeth," he chuckled. "It pleases me to see that you have some spirit." He stopped laughing abruptly and fixed the man with a glare. "Not, of course, that I could not break your spirit with a gesture and leave you a mindless shell."

The man's throat moved as he swallowed. Solarrin thought about driving one strong finger though the man's neck. He envisioned the way the blood would spurt, how the soft flesh would give way. He made sure to let his face show what he was thinking. His sharp teeth ground together.

The man was sweating freely now.

Solarrin decided that he hated his guest. The man reminded him too much of his former self. The fat, slovenly pig! His thinning, greasy hair barely covered his round head, and a waterfall of chins cascaded over his flabby chest. He was a disgusting mass of humanity. Disgusting.

Still, his plan was amusing. A distraction, to pass the time until he had decided what he wanted to do with his newfound power. It would also be a way to rid himself temporarily of Donnell. He flashed a wide smile at the man, which failed to calm him due to the number of teeth it revealed.

"You seek my support. You have won it." He raised his glass. "I drink to the taking of Thanis, and to you, Lord Marl."

*   *   *

The End

About the Author

Christine Morgan has spent a lot of time in fantasy worlds since she discovered role-playing games in 1981. She has playtested several GRUPS supplements, is a frequent GM and seminar speaker at conventions, and her work has appeared in Pyramid Magazine.

She currently lives in Seattle with her husband Tim, who is also a long time gamer and manager of Gary's Games. Their daughter, Rebecca Jaenyth, was named for characters from role-playing game, to prove to what degree this hobby dominates their lives.

In addition to holding down a full-time job as a residential counselor, Christine also has a thriving Internet following in the fanfiction arena (pay a visit to her website at http://www.eskimo.com/~vecna or e-mail vecna@eskimo.com).

Christine's other interests include British comedy, Disney animation, thunderous classical music, reading, and experimenting with cheesecake recipes.